Chris Wilson

is the highly acclaimed author of five previous novels, including *Fou*, *Blueglass* and *Mischief*, which was shortlisted for the Whitbread Prize in 1991. Until 1988 he had an academic career, completing a doctorate on humour at the London School of Economics, researching at The London Hospital and, for ten years, lecturing in Communications at Goldsmiths' College.

Also by Chris Wilson

CHRIS WILSON

The Wurd

Flamingo
An Imprint of HarperCollinsPublishers

Flamingo
An Imprint of HarperCollins*Publishers*
77-85 Fulham Palace Road,
Hammersmith, London W6 8JB

Published by Flamingo 1996
1 3 5 7 9 8 6 4 2

First published in Great Britain by
Flamingo an Imprint of HarperCollins*Publishers* 1995

Author photograph by Jonathan Minster

ISBN 0 00 654688 9

Set in Linotron Plantin Light

Printed and bound in Great Britain by
Caledonian International
Book Manufacturing Ltd, Glasgow

FOR JEAN KENNEDY

The years shall run like rabbits,
For in my arms I hold
The Flower of the Ages,
And the first love of the world.

W. H. Auden

close to a Mediterranean coast
thirty-five thousand years ago

> | The pebbels of hope

It wur Boy Lips who tort me Hope, after the kwakes, befor the Ice, wiv seffern pebbels, an a gushing stream of talk. But I thort he wur babbling wurdsik. An I wur slow for take it in, for dowts strayed frisky into mind, blaa, blaa, like bleating gotes.

Lips said he'd swap me sum Hope for sandstone rabbut I'd carved. It wur well smooved frendly, for shape of a buck wiv fore curved legs, a smile an a wink.

Els, he cud lift sum shames from my shulders, Lips says, if I give him my turtul shell.

'Not so fast,' says I. 'Where this *Hope*? An what this *Swap*?'

Neva heard tell of them befor. Neva knew the need. Becaws I'd bin away – tugged apart from peepil fore hots, fore chills, living wiv sum ruff booboons, befor I cleaved tender for a woom-man. I made her for myself. By hand.

I tell her later. Yu got for wait for her. A stubborn woom-man. She only cum when she's good an reddy.

Any ways, I'd only juss cum back amongst peepil, who took me for a fool, till I lurned all the sense fowk thort out while I wur away. Sins peepil gon ahed of me, in their minds, wiv wurds an cunning, leaving me stumbling far behind, neva waiting for my return. Neva mind. That's a diffurnt story.

So Lips starts telling me what a swap is. As yu purbly know yur self all reddy, it's giving sumwun sumthing – wiv a mind for getting better back.

'That's cleva,' I says. 'Whateva will fowk think up nex?'

'An Hope's the best a man can eva find,' Lips says, 'being kinder than a muvver for her newborn booby, warmer than sun, more nurrishing than pork.'

'How it taste, then?' I ask. 'Is it joosy, chewy?'

'It sweet as hunny, an juss as clingy sticky,' says Boy Lips, an kwick as a lizzurd flicks tung, for snaffle fly. 'An wunce yu've savurred Hope, flavurr neva leaves yu. But lazes on, back of the throwt. So yu bring it up when yu need it most, wheneva yu're lonesum, cast-down, cut-up, or gooz-bumped by cold.'

Enuf said. I wur decided then for scoff on sum Hope, soon as I mite. Becaws I cud all ways carve anuvva rabbut, or any animul I chose, as long as it wurn't larger in life than stones.

An this rabbut carve-up, which Lips liked, wurn't finished any ways. Becaws it got no ears, sticky parts, nose or a tail. But I didn't tell that for Boy. If he cudn't see it for himself, he wudn't need those missing bits. Any ways, smooving that stone only took me fife days. Becaws stone an I wur cum firm frends. So I knew how for rub it up the rite ways, hard an fast. So it cum juss how I ask it. In-my-mind told in-my-hands.

'Here's carving.' I lay it hevvy in his tacky chile's palms. 'When yu've given me yur Hope, I'll tell yu stone's name. So yu can call on its strenf. An maybe make sum rabbut kills. But yu better speak respeckfull for it. Becaws spirit of buk rabbut is terble prowd, all thow he's fond for larf.'

'Well,' says Boy Lips, 'I'll do for yu as yu've dun for me, an give yu back what yu give me . . . Are yu reddy? Here's stones an wurds. Hope cums like this . . .'

Then he's thrown down seffern pebbels. Black on the yella sand.

'There!' he says.

'What?' says I.

Becaws I wur expecking diffurnt, or rarva more. Sumthing for put in my mouf, an chew on. Els sumthing gawdy for wear on my hed, that'd make woom-men look twice. Or a feeling in mind that cums better than spusms between the legs, wiv a prutty wun, eager, clingy by moonlite.

So I muss have got sum Hope wivin me, all reddy. An yet I didn't know it. Not by name.

It starts bad. But it gets better. Wait a while. Give hope a chance.

First, he points for those pebbels on the sand. Seffern in a line.

'Those yur trubbles,' Lips tells.

'That many?' I ask.

'Touch them,' he says, 'wun by wun, till yu reach their very end.'

Well, I'm not a man for fingur trubble befor it cums. But I've sworn the swap all reddy. An I don't want Boy for see I'm scared.

2

When I've touched all seffern, kwick as I mite, for they're scorchy hot for my fingur tips, I've reached the end of the line.

'See!' says Lips. 'It wurn't so terble, after all. Yu got many trubbles. But there is a start an a finish for them.'

'Now!' says he. '*These* the pleshurs in yur life.' An he points for pebbels again.

They're the very same stones, by chance.

'That few?' I ask. 'All of them small? An all of them dark?'

'Wud yu like them for be endless?' asks smirky Boy.

'I wud.' I agrees it kwick as I cud. 'If it's up for me.'

'Then I can place them so . . . There!' says he. An he's fingurred them tricksy, snug for a circil, faster than my eyes can tell. Sudden, them stones are all moved about. They're sitting in a round.

'Like fowks gathered by a fire,' I larfs.

'Trew enuf,' says he. 'Now, touch yur joys, piece by piece, an tell me when they're at an end.'

But howeva many I'd felt, there wur anuvva for cum, wiv anuvva beyond. Then wun more, nex for that. So on. Endlost.

'How yu dun that?' I ask. A hot smile's split my face. I know my first swap bin a lukky, strong wun.

'Medsin!' he says. 'Magik.' Then his gaze gon downcast, sorry. Sadly, they're tears cum into his eyes, spilling trickly down his gowfer cheeks.

'Boy, what's wrong?' I ask his sobs, an hug him fast.

'That's all I can show yu . . .' He spreds his boy's empty palms, an snuffles lowd. 'I give yu all we agreed.'

'Cudn't we swap wunce more?' I ask. Sins I'm kwick for clutch new things. So swapping wur all reddy cum a habit wiv me.

'Cud do . . .' His brow wrinkles. 'Maybe. Mite . . .' He's gon pawsy like a sulky chile.

'What wud yu like, Boy?' I cowx him sweet.

'Yu cud give me yur turtul shell,' he ansurs kwick. 'Then I cud show yu how for *suppose*.'

I don't like for snare them yung. I got my pride. But it wur his suggesting, after all. It wur an offer I cudn't refuse. I'd cort plenty turtuls in my time, but I neva tasted stuff befor that wur near so rich, nor heddy as this. An I thort whateva he got for give wud cum more use for me than him.

'Is it good as Hope?' I ask, juss for be sure.

'It's effen stronger. Hope rests on it,' Lips says.

'Then here's my turtul shell. Now, give me yur Suppose!' says
I.

He looks about for make sure there's no nearby ears for hear.
'Those pebbels . . .' he purrs throwty. 'They're plenty uvva things
besides.'

'What?'

'Wud yu like for die?' Lips asks.

'I wud not.' I confess it, blinking kwick. 'If it's up for me.'

'Then, those pebbels can be the fresh mornings of yur life,' he
says. 'Juss see them in that dawning lite.'

He watched me a while, smiling kind, then he left me prodding
my new dawns, my fingurs circilling endless.

Cum dusk, my arms wur weary an my fingurs sore. I'd stopped
counting, an thort sum, an while I wur plenty pleased wiv my new
long life, numbaless joys an such, an saw the strenfs of circils an
sefferns, still . . . wriggles of wurry wur cum wurming in my mind.

First I find Boy. Then I spill my wurrys. They cum spurting
out.

'Lips,' I says. 'Yu talk good. Yur magik's strong . . . I neva says
yu've tricked me. Yu're wellcum for keep my carving, an turtul
shell. But those seffern pebbels yu gave me in return . . . I've
noticed sumthing purtickler about them.'

'Yes?' he smiles up sly.

'They're only . . . *pebbels*, when all's said an dun, when yu look
at them close.'

'Yes,' Boy agrees. 'Hope's like that . . . It cums an goes.' He
shrugs helpless. 'But I'll tell yu sumthing els for nothings . . .'

'Go on, then,' I says.

'If yu hurry back for them, yu'll find they've turned into sumthing els.'

'Happen yu know what?' I ask, hoping for very best.

He sucks sum, then gobs out yellagreen flems. 'Those pebbels
. . . They're them woom-men who lay down wiv yu. Them deer
yu kill. The times fowk respeck yu. All things yu still got for lurn.
All the ways yu make peepil larf.'

I chuckle at this, patting Boy's hurr. He mite be slite an yung
in his body, but he wur awfull strong an cleva in his old thort.

Then a cold thort slivvers thruw me, like a maggut in a rotty

4

fish. So I'm turned, running back way I cum. Back for my pebbels, fast as I can. Becaws I'd left them there, ungarded on the sand. An sumwun mite steal up an snaffle them, while me back wur turned. Taking all my days, lays, larfs an pleshurs for themselves.

An I neva blamed Boy, trew for my wurd, after I saw he'd tricked me good. Becaws he tort me plenty, when all's said.

I'd cum for wurds befor him, but he knew better than me how for string them along. He went reddy wiv those ways of them, like I saw eye-to-eye wiv stones. He had a cleva mouf. Like I got cleva hands.

So it wur, I wept my greef for him. When Lips lost his last skwabble – which was wiv the Ice – an went all blew an chilly still.

Then effen Lips cudn't disagree – that he wur ded. Becaws he neva got the breff, for haggle any more. So wurds had met their match at last.

So, be warned an heed my morul. If yu eva cum by them seffern lukky pebbels of Hope, neva swap them. Best hug them for yur chest.

| Lame an Blind

I ain't juss any old skinfull. Mine's the oldest gob on Urf. An I wur there when wurds first cum, bursting out a buzzing swarm, from the blowt belly of a black-brissled ded pig, near that salt marsh, befor the kwakes.

This makes me older than talk, more telling than storys, an a yawn yunger than these wind-whittled rocks, an a prowder man wud brag of it. Neva me.

My names wur plenty. Bin called Gob, Mows, Maggut, Rabbut, Lame in my times. An I juss shed a name, when I outgrew it, like a lizzurd sluffs old skins. So fowks can call me the wurst they got. Wurds can't hurt me any more. Juss water up a duk's arse.

I suffurd Luv, the Ice, the Famine, the Pox, the Flud. I've dun wurs than most. So sum ruff fella's glare, or glint of teef, neva fritens me, effen thow I'm lame, an got soff gums, an can't bite back.

Still, I got a norty mind, besides a nasty mouf. So I won't suffur any wun cast their shadow on my chill bones, by cumming between us, me an my sun.

I'm fond of sucking eggs, joosy frewts, soff offals. So if sum kind sowl got any scoffs hid about them for shares, warm in the pits of his arms, moist in their cheeks, or whereva, my gob all ways remembers them sweet. An whispers their name for Hystery.

I'm far seeing, an too knowing for my cumfort. But misty eyed an forgetful, an there are seffern first things I've neva known, an recent times gon clowdy. Wurms have chewed holes in me trewfs. Or maybe the berrybrew dun it. It gives yu staggers, puts hard things in yur way, spins yur hed around, so the cash of murmury gets strewn.

My kin wur the first fowks for truj this bellyskin of Urf, hovering like flys on the rump of an ox, prickling her hide. Old Urf is pocked

6

an wrinkled now. For she's grown weary an suffurd much. She an I, both.

I seen Time herself grow old. I seen fore generashuns snuffed. This is a stubborn old buzzurd, who's perched there skwawking as his childrin's childrins died. But I neva chose for live so long. I juss survived me. Becaws those shrinks neva shrunk me, that yella-pox neva blistered me, I flowted thruw the Flud, slept thruw the kwakes, shivered thruw the Ice, an no savage jaws eva took me for parts. Yes, a strong spirit stood gard of his meats.

Now I'm a levver powch of cold creaking bones, an me mouf has stolen the power of me legs, so me legs won't go, while me mouf won't stop.

'Walk,' I howls, an slaps them ruff. Do they move? Do they fuk. These legs of mine neva lissen now. Me nees won't bend me. Me futs can't stand me. Me brittil bones can't bear me. An a man slumps sorry so. Wiv his legs turned deff for his demands. So I slivvers along arse-ended, scraping me bludding buttuks, clawing wiv me horny nails, snaking furrows in the dust. It's a backwuds progress of sorts, for death.

I'm bent, broke an nearly gon. A dry shrunken gord. Age has wevvered me skin for wrinkled levver, an wivvered the flesh from me skull. The hide of my face wears a crusty tortus scowl – all scales, grissel, dark suspishuns an sunken holes. I can drop my hed into the hollows of my shulders. A gift of age. I don't see anything I don't wish for. Besides, I've lurned for look the uvva way. An I sleeps winter thruw.

My bones an flesh are almost kwit, but my hart won't yet submit. My voice grunts an rasps. Things rattle loos in me mouf when I speaks. An spatter out blud speckled. But neva my teef. As I keep them safe, strung on a fong, round the cords of my scrawny neck. These! Between the mows skulls. Clack, clack. All mine. They used for sit snug in me gums in days when Gob got bite. I save them for when I'm gon ded, Beyond, so I can chew in the Uvva Place. While my spirit wonders, wheva for return. There's always a big bellyfull Beyond. So those ded tell us – when they can rows them-selves for speak. Lame deer an pig limp the pastures of me hopes, wiv blind gooz, sleeping duks an lazy eggs laying all around. Urf bliss us all. Evry wun.

*   *   *

7

Too winters an wun summer Blind an I bin tite together, root an branch, hog an grunt, bee an sting, itch an scratch.

There's sicks things about Blind for know from the start:

- there's nun so blind as she that will not see.
- besides she's got harf her tung bit away.
- there's a terble secret about her missing bits.
- she ain't harf so bad as her fowl tung makes her sound.
- she may not be much, but she's the only living thing I got. So bad-mouf her an yu'll ansur for me.
- there's a mistry that joins us. She for I. I for she.

We're luvvers of sorts, Blind an me. But dry, unspilling. Sins my desire can't embrace her. Not between the legs. An my jooses cum thin now, trickling slow. Any ways it wudn't be proper.

But we sleeps the nites rapt together. I snuggles those hot nubbles of her spine, hugging her flat paps an downy slack fatbelly. An this is sum cumfort, an an old fowk's pact, as too sleep warmer than wun, effen thow they barely rub. An pursins are nothing if they neva reach out. For grasp wun anuvva.

But laying so close, our grunts grasp, an sleeps entwine, an I have spyd Blind loitering in shadows, at the ejs of my dreams. She steals from them, of caws. For murmury's first, nex desires, then sum sites are gon missing from my hed, so nex nite I creep into her dreams, for have back what's mine. There are startling touches, ardent clutches, frenzid luvvings, shamelost urges, moving feelings, thick strong smells. But Blind's dreams are black as jet stone, an there's nothing for be seen, becaws evrywun's siteless in a blind woom-man's dreams. An yet I can hear, in that blow an bluster of her thorts, she has sum inklings of the Wurst.

But Blind an I are bound by knots of need, an more. Together we make a pursin. The blind wun walks. The lame wun sees. Between us we got it all – eyes an storys, legs an bite, hop an hindsite, prides an regrets.

'Desire hunts harts,' I says.

'Envy stalks,' warns Blind.

'It's the urly wurm,' I agree, 'that catches the carryon.'

★   ★   ★

Blind feeds me now, sharing her teef wiv me, bite an grind, joos an meats, mulch an spittle, chewing ruff, skwirting the pulp down the brown gape of me mouf.

'Best part of dik-dik is his liver,' says I.

'Trew,' says Blind. 'An don't dik-dik know it. He screams when yu tug it from him.'

'His life is close an dear for him. It make me weep for eat him.'

'Ummm!' Blind agrees, 'Aaah!', an as we tear dik-dik's steaming liver apart, salty water skwirts from us, eyes an moufs, trickling down our chins. An it's not juss from the burning jooses, nyva, scalding us lips an tungs. We are all sorry, now. Becaws there's wun less dik-dik in the wurld. An yu can only eat him wunce.

'Eva taste Tree-Pig?' I asks.

'No . . .' says Blind. Her jaw slackens, chewing slows, as greed twitches the yella jelly of her siteless eyes. 'How does it eat?'

'It pleshurs the mouf, but barely bothers the teef.'

'Tell, then!'

'A Tree-Pig is surprise chile of gawdy drake an warthog sow.' I tell it all. 'His hed an shulders are bald an pink, but his nether end is fevvered blew an green. He's very shy an rare. They're so few becaws they're so few. They can neva find a mate. An so they neva breed. Only wail lonely when the moon is up . . .'

Yes, I busy myself in telling trewfs – storys about then, storys about time sins, storys about food, tales of how-cum an becaws, the follys of us familys, adventures born of cupplings, cleva snarings, brave slayings, the antics of spirits, the storys of storys, an offen sumwun will paws for lissen.

My bones are stuffed wiv yore, not marrow. There's a dark, distant passed only I can reach back for. The passed skwirts out of me, like pus from a bursting boil. This ancient Gob is a gaping, weeping wound that neva heals. So don't mind me if I dribble. It's only spit an Hystery.

At the start fowk got no wurds. But wind wur always bursting from us. Becaws langwij kicked wivin our bellys, wriggling like a chile unborn, pressing for cum out.

For be sure, we skwealed an jibbered. Like the booboons above in them trees, we had warning shrieks for savage things, an guggles for fondles, besides hoots for frewts.

Fowks wud croak in frite, when they saw a slinking cat. As the moufy booboons screamed 'Hachacha, eek, eek, hachahacha.' An such. They screech on. An on. As tact is lost on them. So heed me advice. Neva dwell under booboons, in the shadow of they excitings, beneef their chatter an splatters of droppings. Beware. Booboons spit. They bite yur ears, an give yu fleas.

Also, fowks signed wiv their hands – no, yes, do-yu-smell-a-hunny-hole-in-the-belly-of-that-tree-?, there, up, down, behind, but-go-now-kwick-or-I-will-slap-yur-ears!'

An, after they'd made a big killing, there wur a deal of snuffling, grunting, coffing an burping, as warmblud trickled down them cheeks.

But sumthing wur missing from the feast. As the firelite flared an flickered, a sudden silence fell. Shadows danced the ground, circilling around us. We sensed an absence. Darkness lay between us. It wur more than we cud say.

Many long conversings passed unspoke like this – befor wurds crossed our minds for talk.

Knowlij then wur fresh an scarce. Now there's plenty trewf – enuf for all who paws for think. Sins fowks got evrything they need – cuppling, seasons, smearsmells, necklaces, cookry, cloves, gossip, plenty passed an much still cumming, brew, burials, dogs, hats an medsins, besides more wurds than wants, an plenty I forget. But these wur neva given for us. No, fowks carved them from hard confusings wiv the cutting ejs of our flinty minds.

I saw it, an lived for tell the tale, an that tale is a mistry, hidden in a story, born of an adventure wrapped in yarn, concerning yu-and-I-and-we, the few an only fowks who stalk on the bellyskin of Urf.

It is the story of how we fowks found our minds. An minds wur fast, cunning, skittery prey. As the hunter turned out for be the prey. So we wur stalking our very own shadows, tracking the spaws of our thorts, harking the eckow of our wurds. Then, for catch ourselves, we had for get cleva.

>>> | First pursin

I bask on the high ground, rooted as a prickle bush, snake-sly, lizzurd-still, looking down on fowks, as when the sun burns high, I rise above the ground, flowt up the slope of vally, as Blind humps me in her arms, an kin are shrunk for scuttling termits, as I watches their bent manners, cluking at their twistit ways, still chuckling, thow nothing changes.

'Carry?' I asks. Sumthing wivin me weedles, an around it shivers a shame, now I'm shrunk for no more than an old woom-man's burden.

An Blind stoops for slide her plump warm arms beneef my cold wivvered thys. I hug her taut neck as she strains for stand. Soon she's all grunting an muttering, becaws thow I'm an empty rattle-bag of brittil bones, I'm clutching my powch of hevvy stones, the slope is steep, an Blind's split tows spit blud, stubbing rocks.

I peek round watchy an skweaky as a skwirrul, minding our step, watching frail futs slivver, skweezing the sinews of her shulders, guiding her wide of a bolder or dip.

When we've tottered for our high place, I spred a dik-dik hide, fur up, on the granit scarp. I thank the gasping Blind for her arms, neva forgetting she legs it too.

'We walked well today. Yu wiv yur legs, an me wiv me eyes. We neva fell. Barely cut our futs. An only stumbled wunce.'

'How does she . . . look . . . Urf?' Blind's bent, panting, twig fingurs on callussed nees. 'Are there plenty good cullurs for be felt? Strong shapes for yur eyes for touch upon?'

But Blind's eyes are long sealed for lite. She hasn't the sites in mind for knows or says. So it is I muss invent.

'That blew of sky is chilling winter water. The grey of clowds is lonely as waking alone at dawn. The white of stones is clean as wulf scavenged bones.'

'Brrr.' She shivers. 'Is nothing a frend?'

'The grasses wave. Yella blossoms smile. Trees lean our way, their branches beckon us.'

'Good.' An she smiles an cluks.

'And what do yu . . . smell?'

'The gust of Urf's breff. Pine resin. Lemin grass. Bone ash. Fresh rabbut cack. An I hear wind's whispers, an a litter of piglits, snufflerooting in the woods.'

'Good.' I nods.

'Do yu remember Rabbut?' Blind sprawls down, leans my way, face screwed, tensed for tell.

The old storys are the best. She forgets I first told the tale for her. No matter. The sun is high. The ground is hard but warm for us. We have a sweet melon between us, crisp but soffer than my gums. I'll need her, grasp an favour, for carry me down.

'Rabbut danced on embers,' I remember. 'He bickered wiv spiny frewts. He howled at the stones. He cumplained himself against seffern moons.'

But I neva says that Rabbut of seffern storys wur me.

'That wurn't *him*,' she says.

'No?' I asks, curiuss for hear tell of who I wur.

'*That* wur his spirit. It pushed him for it.' Blind nods forlorn.

'Why?'

'I neva ask, so I neva lurn . . . It wur sum spat in a skinbag, a family skwabble between a mind an body, or a sowl an its man.'

'Well . . .' I agree. 'There's too sides for evry bussom. An too buttuks for evry bum.'

'That's not the harf of it,' she agrees. 'A duk is kware enuf in its way, but there's nothing so odd as a man.'

Talking of the Rabbut I wur, I've waited long enuf. There are things that muss be said. Between us. Befor it is too late.

I look on Blind. My parched eyes gon watery. There's a clawing beneef my ribs. I can't see peepil as they are no more. Round their ejs I see a shadowy rot, feeding on their helf. In their chatter I hear eckowd the rattle of their death.

'Yu feel that?' I wince.

'What?' Blind asks.

'Juss a twinj' – I sigh – 'of the tie between us. Did yu feel nothing tremble close by yur hart?'

'Not me,' she says. 'What shud I feel for yu?'

'Lissen,' I urge Blind. 'Pity this scabby old buzzurd.' I slap my levver thys. 'It is the evening of his fall. Soon he'll flutter down, wivvered, dry an ded, a shed leef, carryon for crows, paste in wriggle wurms, mulch for gorse.'

'Trew. Yu go ded soon,' she agrees, too reddy, 'an I'll dig yu under by the olive bush.' The small regret in her voice sounds mild an dry. She spills no wetwurds of greef.

'I will leave yu all I have.' I promiss fife things.

'Yur toof necklace? An yur sleeping-skins?'

'Those,' I says. 'Also my stones, my tung an Hystery . . . there are storys that muss be heard, remembered an retold. Or our suffurings an lurnings wur cum for nothings.'

'Keep yur storys,' says she. 'I've heard them enuf. Yu got a tung like a bobbing coot. It all ways flapping jerky, crazy away from us. It wags on about sum man who gets turned into a warthog, or sum woom-man giving birf for a gote.'

'Happened,' I says. 'I saw it. Long ago. Any way, it's Hystery says so, neva me.'

'Or yu babbling about sumwun who looses their wurds in the dark, so they neva speak for seffern years . . . Or drops their sowl down a hole. Or an owl bit off their dick, an swallowed their desire. Els they got eaten by cats while stalking the moon.'

'Trew enuf,' I agree. 'An it needs be said. So we can lurn by it. An neva make them mistakes.'

'But yu neva tell me what I ask . . .'

'Yes.' I nod. This woom-man neva take 'don't-know' or 'won't-say' for an ansur.

'I got the storys yu want.' I tap my scalp wiv my nukkels. Sounds like a dry Ocka nut. Lowd enuf for her for hear the empty promiss of my hed.

I got for tell her about her lost eyes. Got for say about her bit-up tung. I muss tell her where her muvver went. An who her farther wur.

'Now the day has cum' – I nod, I gulp – 'to coff it all. How it was.'

'Yu will?'

'About fowk, about yu, about us. Befor I'm gon. Today is the day I give yu the passed. Yurs an ours. Then yu becum Hystery – the blind bag itself. Together wiv my powch of stones.'

I can't leave it till after I'm gon. If she won't lissen for me face for face, lowd as life, she won't lissen for me shadowed whispers, ded.

Blind's all I have. Her hed's the only place I got, for cash my storys safe. I muss push them thruw her ears, wun by wun. Like a gowfer hords his secret nuts down the creviss of some wood.

It don't matter, that her eyes don't see. It's better, all told. The passed is blind itself. Deff too. Also lame. Hystery is all behind us now. There's nothing new for see or add. An being as she's blind, she cannot twist or cullur it. Besides, it concerns us. She an I. Far an odd.

'Yu muss lissen for it, how it cums,' I says. 'There's an order for the passed. First things cum first. Then the muddel. So yu won't cum till late. Yu muss hear me out.'

'Tell it, then.' Blind nods. 'I'll hear yur storys. But be sure yu knap them breef.'

'Lissen,' I warn, tapping my hevvy hed, 'this is no task for the lazy. Hystery ain't a lite load. It carrys back a long way, an won't be told in less than a day. I need yur ears all the way for dusk. For tell yu evry thing I know . . .'

I draw breff for the long tellings. The wind has slowed. Silences gather round us, settling in the shadows for hear.

'Where for start?' I ask the still air. 'Blud wur spilled. Mistakes got made. There wur findings, killings, terble trubbles, poxes, medsins, cupplings . . . I tamed the first dog. An I wur the first man for make a woom-man by hand. But befor that I'd found seffern, on an Ocka bush, when I wur picking frewts.'

'Seffern what?'

'Juss Seffern. The numba herself,' I says. 'She's got a cleva spirit, that wun. Gets about. Peeps out offen where yu least expeck.'

'Start at the start,' says Blind, clawing our melon open, fishblud red, black pipped, crunchy.

'Well . . .' I says. 'Perps I start wiv my birf. But be warned . . .'

'Yes?'

'It ain't prutty. Back in Hystery. An it's cold, wivout cloves. An it's harsh wivout moruls. Startling too, wivout any sense. Things ain't all ways what they seem. So don't believe all yu're told. Nyva expeck for sit easy. An neva forget for look over yur shulder. Becaws sumthing terble mite be slinking up behind. Stelfy clawed. Split-mouf hungry.'

'Reddy, then.' Blind yawns, patting our dik-dik hide. 'For the yawning, white-toofed horrur of Hystery.'

So, here I cum. First breff.

'Whaaaaaa?' I howl, then I says it again, so I'm noticed an known, soon as I'm cum.

'Gobby for start.' Blind cackles. 'As yu mean for go on.'

'It's my birf day.' I shake my weary hed. 'Can't a littil man get himself born wivout a woom-man's interfering . . .'

Yes, so I'm cum at last, skwealing into Hystery. But not wivout the usual trubble an scuffle of birfing, wiv wun party shy an the uvva insisting, which hurt me more than her. As I wur cum a raw, sore surprise for myself, while my muvver got hurt expeckings.

But I'm cum at the exack trew time for myself – given all I muss witness, in the proper order of things, the hurts an joys for be heaped upon me, the countless knowings for be lojd in me hed, an the cord of living given for me, now stretched whisker fine. So if I'd cum later I'd have less for tell. An if I'd cum urlier I'd all reddy be gon. As I've tired my arms an out-stayed my legs, so my spirit has a mind for wander out, swivelling my gaze, jellusly eyeing the yunger flesh that clings round fresher bones.

Yes, I scream when I first cum.

'Strong boobys let their cumming be heard. An sound their feel-ings too,' Blind tells.

'Becaws yu see yu are born a pursin,' I agree. 'Yu howl at the pain of life, catching glimmers of what lys ahed. An yu're skweezed out face first, seeing the wurst befor yu're cum. But yu feel the path closing behind yu, pressing on yur legs. So yu know there is no going back, inside.'

'No,' Blind nods. 'A booby don't know enuf for wriggle out of life.'

When I first cum, the wurld is frobbing fresh. Mists hang hevvy, so most is blurred, an there's scarce sense for be seen, but the din of it all is deffning, over the gentle cooing of my muvver, an the stench of it spills ripe, over the sweet scent of tits.

It's scalding hot an aching cold. There's spilt milk. Yu're sat in shit, awash in vomut. There's a deal for cry over, an no end of sulking an suckling for be dun. There's always sum fresh stench, getting up my nose. My skin feels evry touch. My mouf is neva still, my ears neva close, an my eyes blink endless surprise. Nipils loom large. Breasts cum an go. Faces peer close, gusting sour breff. Shadowy, clowded shapes take their place. It's blinding brite. An the dark of it is thick as gore. The wurld is strong an new for me, as it is for my kin. Things are still being made, haggling over their shapes. So I understand no better than the rest of my fowks. We wur all childrins then. An the littil that wur known cudn't be spoke.

Carf is the muvver of me. My spirit sort her out for me. He crept up as a stranger for her. In the nite an entered her as she slept.

'Neva,' says Blind.

'But, yes. We did it diffurnt then,' I remind her. 'Farthers cum late for Hystery.'

Yes, rite up her nose, as she sniffed, my spirit slivvered inside her, easy as gizzum, soff as a whisper of wind. Me sowl hungered for grow an be born in flesh. An her belly hollowed a nest for me, where she grew me out of her own blud. An thruw spring into summer, as the grasses sprang uprite, then bowed their heds hevvy wiv seed, I swelled inside her. All thow she neva knew what she wur fattening for until after I wur cum.

But when I wriggle out, she looks me over curiuss, from scalp for tow, an took for me from the start, forgiving that me cumming made her scream an wail. Thow I'm bluddy, wrinkled, helpless an small, she gesses I'll swell a fuller thing in time. At least I'm better out than in.

Yes, I'm cum a fond site for her eyes. She holds onto me, tugging me for her chest, where I snaffle the honeyed sap of her breasts. All for myself. So I'm a blissed chile, becaws me spirit chose me muvver well. For which I thank it. Sly old buzzurd.

'Ain't yu missed parts out?' Blind asks.

'What?'

'Did nothings happen befor yu wur born?' she says.

'Trew . . .' I suck on it. 'There wur things that did cum befor. But they're gon hazy in my hed.'

Becaws befor fowks there wur only confusings. Time wur in a tangle – the future wrapped up in things passed. All wur twined an twisted as a matted ball of wind-blown tumble-grass. Urf wur dim, hazy wiv fog. There wur no starts nor ends in site. Ground an sky wur mixed up together, as above an below hadn't wresseled apart. An the waters bogged the land. Far wur close as near. Hot an cold clasped each uvva, burning icy. Here grasped there. This clung for that. High wur pulled down low, while beneef rose up above itself. In reached out. Nothing had its name yet. The start wur joined for the end, as a snake biting its tail. There wur no break or join. Not that a human eye cud tell. Becaws fowks wurn't cum yet. So littil is known, yet more is told, an that is lys, so that's all I will tell of it. Be warned.

'That slays time kwick,' Blind says. 'An cuts it clean, hacking the fat away from the lean. I remember it all. Ain't there more that cum befor yu than that?'

'Yes. Lissen on,' I warn. 'There's plenty more for tell. That's no more than wun pink, tid tow of it . . .'

'Who's the first pursin?' Blind interrupts.

'Yes. There wur too of her. I'm juss cumming for them.'

>>>> | Earsay

I know enuf of the start of us, as ancient gossip an earsay told me.
An after she wur gon Beyond, my muvver took for talking for me,
thruw my dreams, an told me how it wur.

My family wur in the thorny thicket of it. Me muvver's-muvver
started much. She wur wun harf of first pursin, an it wur she who
first found cuppling. That wur her lasting gift for us. If she hadn't
cum by it, anuvva wud have made up sumthing samey, but purbly
using diffurnt parts, or putting the same parts diffurnt, sumways,
so maybe not so good. Still, thank her plenty. She did the best she
cud, wiv what she got.

First pursin wur too sappling girls, born of the Muvva of Mistrys.
It's told. She wur Wun. An The-Uvva wur her sister.
    They get pushed out from Urf's birf hole, where all first things
cum, skwealy, slippery.
    They are small, scrawny, puny, skweaking, sticky-fingurred
things. Ignorant an curiuss, all moufs, ribs an hungers. They have
no wurds. But cram their moufs wiv berrys insted, an talk only
trickles of purpil joos, winding down their pulsing cheeks.
    Where they cum from they neva knew, becaws they juss wake
wun dawn, together in the swishing grass. Fore eyes are opened,
an blink surprised, for find themselves alive. Sisters look about an
whimper, wincing at the waken wurld. Then they eye each uvva
an smile.
    Urf crowds too close around, an presses them too close an ruff
– ripe, rich, crazed an lowd. So they cling together for cumfort, an
wun neva strays from the gaze of the uvva. When a sister falls, the
uvva tumbles too. Then they're sobbing together, tossing the hurt
between them, like a scorching baked yam, thrown between too
hands, so each can palm off her pain.

They share evrything between them – joys, roots, thirsts, suspishuns an berrys. So when wun itches, the uvva scratches her same spot. Then they both coff together, an splutter, as wun has juss swallowed a fly.

They've no need of talk. They understand. Their eyes see the same, they frob wun pulse, they lap the same stream, piss wun water, gulp the same breeze, shiver the same chill, bask under wun sun, sharing all. Their bellys rumbul a single hunger. An they belch the same satisfyings.

There's no I. Only a we of too.

When they nest at nite under a scatter of hay, they ly tangled together, in a hot huddle, their skins stuk by swet, carelost which breast is whose, which thy goes where, or whose hart throbs in what chest. Both moufs breef for the uvva. An there is only a small wit between them, wivout a tid of nous for sepert them. Becaws there's no join or split, but juss wun flesh, limbs twined, wrapped up in itself, snuffling an twitching. An a single sleep flows wivin them. An each is the uvva's dream. Till they spring awake, startled by the crackle of dry grass snapping beneef sum sly slinking futs. Then they whimper together. An hear the ansurring skweal or snort as fast drubbing hoofs or trotters turn bolting in terrur.

They gather frewts, seeds an roots. An chew slugs, wurms an bugs. Suck eggs. Crunch on snails. An hunt mows, rabbut an frog, scrunching bones, spitting out fur, swallowing dollops of warm wet flesh – ravenuss for life.

They eat small things an flee from larger.

They fear size. But evry beast grows bigger, looming close for scare them. Plenty have claws. An most boast teef.

Sisters skirt the shriek-panting howlers. Deer scatter as they pad past. Startled pigs surprise them, bursting out from the bushes, brushing past, brissling, skwealy.

The sisters neva see their like. So they know they walk alone, too-fut, uprite in life.

They perch at the ejs, on the frinjs of places, between dawn an dusk, parting a path thruw tall grasses, following meandering rivers, skirting the open plains, lying in the shade of trees at the merging of woods.

The wurld is fierce an harsh on their yung being. The days are too brite, the nites too dark. Sun blazes too hot. Sister Moon hides Her face, or glimmers cold.

The forest is too deep an dense, the plains too flat an open. The trees grow too high, the ground always lay low at they futs.

But Urf neva wellcums their tread. The rocks slice open their futs, stones make them stumble, mud sucks at their ankils, the river drinks their legs. As for the air, it can't bear them. When they rest on it, it lets them down, tugging them into a terble tumble.

Kindness is scarce. Trust isn't cum yet. The sun scalds them, the urf trips them, the waters swallow them, the wind keeps changing its mind. Gnats bite them. Hornets sting. Food hides. Wulfs slink behind them.

One sky bluds red, the nex glowers black. Rivers overflow their banks, or shrivel parched for muddy trickles. The urf cracks open, or bogs down for marsh. The wind lashes their faces, then scurrys away, leaving them airless for a scalding sun. Water goes cold an hard, or cascades down from the sky. Flashes of white fire leap the air. Grey bolders crash, rumbulling in the sky. The sisters cower, fearing the rocks will plunge down an crush them.

Their favorit food is speckled eggs. But duks steal them. The burds sit on the eggs for hide them from sister-site. But by the time they uncover the burd-cunning, all the eggs are shattered or flown.

Fog falls. They walk on. But when the mists rise, the hills are grown an darkened. The woods are fled behind them. An the river is all flowed away.

A wurm slivvers under a stone. But when they lift the rock, a snake coils out hissing. Wun scabbed towd plops into the water, then leaps up as a shimmering fish.

A mows scurrys across the sand. Nex there is a flurry of hurrs an fluffs, an it rises, dripping bluds, as an eagil from the ground.

In those first fresh days the beasts are fiteing for their shapes, an keep stealing each uvva's forms, furs an fevvers.

Rocks cascade down the face of a hill. Too warthogs cross their path snorting. Rain spills. A flyblown carcass of an ox lays befor them. The sun blazes overhed. The wurld smells of elderflowers. Too sisters sneeze. A coot larfs far away.

But they neva see the cawses of it, sins their heds are empty of reasuns, a clutter of dark confusings.

Each day they move on, towards a place they belong. Their futs seek it, ahed of their minds, treading hopefull, towards the ej of sumthing, sumwhere.

Each dawn they wake again from their dream. But they do not know which is the trew time – asleep or awake – or which shows the trew site of things – dreams or life.

An thow sky an land can neva be trusted, an beasts are fierce, still they find goodness – in the scent of blossoms, sweet cashes of hunny, the clasp of a sister, cool water on a parched throwt, bitter-sweet syrup of berrys, the storm after blistering sun, the sun after rain, dawn after dark, relief after fear, caves an peaks, here an there, this an that. Besides, they have each uvva.

An evrywhere they go spirits dance about them, skipping in their steps, hid from the sun, casting their shadows, dreaming their dreams, startling them awake when a strange thing stirs nearby. An they glimpse their garding spirits – prancing alongside on glint-ing water, or smiling up curiuss for see them from the rippelled face of a lake.

Anuvva mistry stalks them, becaws if the wurld an its parts ain't shrinking, then they themselves are swelling. But they don't know of growing yet. They thort the beasts choose their size. An a small thing is a shy thing that shrinks from being seen, while a large thing is fierce, swelling for give frite.

Each summer the grasses spring lower against their thys. The bushes that wunce brushed shulders reach no higher than waists. The trees sink into the ground, till the sisters can reach up for the lower branches. Frogs had bin larger than their hands, but are grown shrunken. Now sisters can cup them skwirming in their palms.

Despite this waxing an waning, they feel much the same in them-selves.

Until their jutting hips get wrapped up plump, an their ribs sink beneef their skin, as the rind of flesh thickens. Their breasts have swelled sheeny, juddering as they walk. An they fingur each uvva curiuss, feel their fullness, shiver an giggle. An they blud together when the moon is full. But wivout wound or reasun.

Muvver Moon has reached down for them, but they cannot stretch for touch Her back. At nite they sit gazing up, skweaking, nodding. The sense of it is missing. They're grown woom-men but neva know it yet.

They mite have spent a lifetime so, searching for stuffs they cannot imagine, reaching for things beyond grasp.

Insted, the first man cums upon them.

'How does first man look?' Blind asks. 'Is he a handsum wun?'

'He looks terble ruff,' I tell. 'A prutty site he ain't. He looks fearful odd from afar. Then wurs as he cums close. Neva mind his smell.'

Woom-men shiver, gooz-bumped, gape-gobbed, eyeing first man, neva gessing what ruff beast he is – chaser or chased, solitary or frendly, browser or biter, sweet or fowl for the tung, tuff or tender, a creature of nite or day, a sniffer or see-er, cleva or dull. She gesses it mite be the male of its kind, sum beast of the trees, cum down for urf. But woom-man cums wivout a passed for warn her, or telling manners for nuj her knowings.

Those gon have made legends of their lives. They talk of their time as Hystery. They neva lissen, not after they're ded, becaws they know it all, their spirits tell. Yet they made sum kware mistakes. An repeat them shameless, evry vain retelling. An I prefur they neva cum shout thruw my dreams, but go an chatter elswhere.

But pity those poor sisters, wandering lost an nakid, ignorant of their sorry mate an fate.

'Yu see woom-men's trubble?' I ask Blind.

'She don't know what for make of man yet.'

'Yes.' I nod. 'Becaws man an woom-man ain't reached out for grasp wun anuvva. They still got for cum for grips.'

Woom-man an man cum. Together

I neva bin a greedy man who hords things for himself. If yu want yu can have my moruls. Ate I got, all told. An they cum less use for me as I get old. So take as many as yu like –

Neva fukfuk wiv kin. No good eva cum of that. Yu purbly go invisible. Sins time gets tangled an caws unravels. The passed cums undun. A dawter cannot be her muvver, nor a son his farther be. If yu go back where yu got yur birf, yu becum The Invisible, returning for the unborn, in a puff of mist, an musty whiff.

That wur the way wiv No-Wun, who did a thing unspoken. Then he wandered forlorn amongst us, an wur nowhere for be seen, only a lingering fusty smell.

Thank the beast.
When yu kill it. Or its spirit will suckle a gruj. An its kind will hide from fowks, an neva submit for be slayn again. As it is wiv Tree-Crab, or Water-Rabbut.

Share that meat. If yu stretch it, there's more.
There's littil enuf left for eat in this wurld. So nun muss grab more than they share.

But neva eat peepil.
Fowks ain't food. Sept yu mite eat yur kin. Sum small parts. But not from hunger. An neva befor they're gon. For show respeck, an keep them wiv yu. Then bury the rest well, facing the rising sun. Neva forgetting for bind their futs. Spirits muss cum an go as they please. But it's best that corpses neva walk.

* * *

Mind yur mouf. Don't stare.
Wurld's so large an empty, we huddle close for cumfort. We are
gathered too near an tite. So most muss stay unseen, unsaid.

If yu got sum cumplaint against anuvva, neva speak it for their
face. Turn yur back for the gathering, wander away from the fire.
Mutter yur spite for the darkness. An trust for be overheard. See
the shadows dance back from the flames, as Anger slinks away in
shame.

Nun are better than uvvas.
But sumtimes wurs. There's littil enuf respeck in the wurld. Ances-
tor left it for us, for share. We muss give an take. We are all hewn
from the wun flesh. So nothing muss tear us apart. Envy stalks us
daily. We mussn't be gnawed by the jaws of it.

*Sniffem good – under arms an muddel. Then count their nipils. An see
what's what between the legs.*
Juss for be sure, becaws there are strange wuns about. Ape-men,
Slouchers an Grunters, Nuckel-scrapers, Nearly-peepil, Almost-
beasts, Rock-Peepil, River-Fowk. Sum cud pass themselves off as
pursins, easy in the gloom. So take care for watch them well befor
yu bid them sit as fireside frends, or lay wiv yu awhile. Look if
they stan uprite, stoop, or drag their nuckels thruw the dust. Watch
for fangs when they smile. See if there's a trew hurrline for their
scalp – or juss receding hurr for their face. Look out for tell-tale
fur, or a purpil glow for the buttuks. Be warned away by a stumpy
tail. Neva forget for count their nipils. Take care if the numba's
not too.

Pity the human spirit
It got no safer hide than wrapped up tite in a pursin's skin, an so
cums trapped in a lifetime of thirst, hunger an fear, until it makes
its escape. But still it'll cum again. So suffur littil childrins. Their
spirits are ancestors returned.

Now, when I hear a chile babble, my first fresh times cum back
for me. An I smile at the booby, whose spirit is an old wun cum
amongst us again.

This is howitis boobys speaks our urliest wurds.

'Aama, maa, da, di.' The chile gurgles. Becaws thow his flesh cums new, his old sowl remembers from befor, an muss have known me well as a yunger, walking man.

'Slug, is it trewfly yu?' I deman of the chile, shaking him hard, till I hear the far rattle of an ansur, deep wivin.

'Lizzurd? Loon? Look! It's me . . . Gob!'

An booby's gaze twists round for scowl on me, an glissens a wise lite, as an old spirit glares out behind fresh glister eyes.

Then he screams out. 'Aaah. Ohooh. Whaa?'

And, neva knowing, he starts howling well an wise. But in an urly tung, saying 'cupplewe darkly', or 'breakit neckbones', or 'itchycumscratchit', 'suckitansee', 'snuffit ratburd' or sumsuch wise telling, whose feeling an time is long passed an lost, stranded in sum ancient occashun.

But booby neva know what he's saying. It's the sowl in him that says it all . . .

'Yu going for keep them apart foreva?' Blind demands.

'Who?' I ask.

'Man an woom-man,' she says. 'Becaws they got for get together, if Hystery's for get a move on. An yu an I for cum.'

'Trew . . .' I agree. 'But it ain't no easy thing for make the seckses mix.'

Woom-man don't see man's a pursin for start, as he's cum an ugly frite, a stab of shock for her flinching eyes, a poke of pain in her belly, a thrust of disgust in her mind, an a gasp choked back in her throwt.

Woom-man's pain cud've bin ended there an then. Only man turned out obstinit, an wud not leave her be.

Both sisters drop flat for Urf, blinking thruw the grass, they see the beast slouch bandy-legged towards them. It stumbles out an uprite thing. Neva mind its hunch. The sun behind its dark wild hurr shines its tangled ejs for oranj flames.

Swaying from the shade of the oaks, it trujs splay futted thruw the scrub, cumming up the slope for where they ly.

As it spreds larger on their moist eyes, it swells for a horrur in their heds. Their arms gooz pimpils, puckering wiv chill. Their inbreffs cum kwick in pants. Their outbreffs gust wheezy. Tows curl on earth, clawing a firm hold. Fingurs reach out, jab an pinch.

25

Beast stops, peering up towards their hidey place. It scratches the folds of its belly, sniffs the air, then wriggles itself flat, laying an ear for the whispering stalks an rumbulling ground. Woom-men shiver as they watch. This ruff beast muss be stalking them, following the prints of their futs, now pawsing for scent or sound.

It rises clumsy, hands on nees, tosses a tuft of grass in the air an watches the strands drift, paws hesitant an fall. Then, grunting, tugging on its snout, the beast slouches up, downwind.

The sisters' heds pound their pulse. Their faces twitch as they skwirm on the ground.

Wun sister makes a clench of a fist. The uvva makes a show of chewing. Wun touches a hefty stone. They nod, as they slivver apart. They'll surprise it from too sides, an club it broke up for the ground.

Over the waving frinj of grass, the tangle-hurred bobbing hed of man shows first. Then a thick neck. Nex meaty shulders. An a brawd chest, that's surely stuffed wiv plenty offal. But it's the bluddy hart they'll reach for first. Man's hart is tuff but nurrishing. Wiv plenty for chew on.

Its slow dark ox eyes roll in its flat face. He looks down an over them, crouching in the grass. Sisters skwint back into the sun. Its shadow sways forwud for touch a woom-man's shulder, then slides back as she cringes away.

The beast's eyes narrow, its nostrils gon twitchy. Its brow furrowed. An it snuffles, as thow a fly wur trapped up its nose.

The sun blazes over the beast's shulder. Air shimmers off the baking urf. Dancing pollens powder the air. The grass shivers. The cicadas click silent.

Man sees woom-man. Woom-man sees man. Hunter an kwarry eye each uvva. There's that kwiet still that cums juss befor a kill.

Remember, mockry wurn't known then. Wit cums after wurds. Jokes didn't know they wur born. So woom-men wur neva moved for smile or larf. Insted they frown at this sorry tangle of man, crusty in his skin, mimicking their form, like a blowted warty towd borrows its shape, but short-sited, dimly, from a sleek an sheeny frog.

He shuffles from fut for fut, an ill-dreamed thing, twisted an coarsened from a woom-man's form, like a sister's look-back tossed on trubbled water. He stands small parts harmless, but largely hurry an misshapen – a breastless, tufty-cheeked, coarse-boned, sniffling thing.

The hurr of its cheeks makes a lap of its leaking mouf. Perps it pisses thruw its dripping nose. A frontail swings where sisters hold a fold. An the mass of it is brissly. Nyva downy like a pursin, nor furred thick as a beast.

In the dumb slackening gape of its mouf they see small yella teef. Its paws hang blunt, like empty hands. So it is cum wivout claws or fangs. An cannot rip them.

The wits of it are twisted too. Its clevaness is stupid. Thow it tracked them, they saw it cumming. Sniffed it stale too. An as they lay low, cunning an kwiet, its hevvy tread an careless snuffle had frobbed in their trubbled ears.

It wur higher, stouter thing, but too sisters cud surely bring it down for urf together. Then throttle it, gut it an eat it. Later, maybe, they cud make sumthing handy of its bones. An lay warm wiv its skin by nite.

'Hoho,' the beast sounds off. 'Haha.' It's surprised by a pleasing site. An scratches the split of its buttuks. Becaws she an she together are more than he cud wish.

The sisters are startled. They've got a samey call. But this beast voices gruffer. An they are fearful he's so drawn for them, neva gessing how he oddly desires.

Then sisters rise up skwealing, as Wun hurls her stone. The beast sways away, an stone's fled fast past its hed.

'Here paths of Hystery crossed,' I tell Blind. 'It's sure as fleas.' 'If the first woom-men had slayn an eaten him . . .' Blind agrees '. . . the only man in the wurld . . . things wudn't be as they are.'

Or suppose they had juss wandered by, wiv a passionlost glance of indiffurnt eyes, like dik-dik trotting past deer? So it's as well that man wur dogged by desire. An that woom-man had imaginings. Thow much mischif, an terble tangles, wud cum of the mix. Juss give them time.

Too sisters flinch, backing away. They neva met a beast befor that sees for time ahed, gessing the flite of stones.

Still, the food ain't fled yet. Only shuffled back a tid. Sisters brace themselves for fell it.

But beast gesses as much, raising a hefty stone, tossing it as a warning between too brawd hands.

This cums a shock – the fret of being ansurred in kind. No creature eva threw back at them, sept peevish booboons, hurling rotted frewts.

Sisters step backwuds scowling. Beast drops its stone an smiles. The gaze of it grazes their chests, then clings close round their hips.

It nods, sucking lowd. It has spyed a glad site, an too woom-men please its eyes. Being wun more than his hopes.

It stands there gaping, split-moufed, its face crinkled an tufted, tugging a woom-man's startled eyes for its own. There are nipils for its chest. Its teef an hands are larger, but knapped for their own shaping. It slouches coarse an vile. An strangely far familiar. As thow they'd seen sumthing simlar, like as not, sumwhere, long befor.

They turn an flee. Grunting, the beast trujs after them, lagging a stone's throw behind, a scavenger sniffing fowksblud, payshent for satisfacshun. But snuffling, sure enuf.

As stalkings go, this went too far. As chasings go, this wur a long wun. It's said. It lasted seffern days an nites, crossed fore vallys an free hills, swam too rivers, wading wun pond. Much sleep wur lost foreva. Many moufings got heard – jibbers an hoots – an there wur plenty gestures from both sides, as well as more castings of stones.

Man won't go away. Woom-men cannot loose him. It is a wearying time for all concerned. It tells well of man's insistings, an the dim hopes woom-men rows in his mind.

When a sister tosses skwirmy in her sleep, dreaming monstruss things, the uvva stays awake an watchful, an takes the calmer rest.

Man has broken their slumber. Their dreams are no longer wun.

On the dusk of the sicks day, the sisters see the man shake frewts down from an Ocka tree. Woom-men watch it eat, picking the flesh apart from the rind, an spitting out the stones. Cunning moves its mouf. Slyness fingurs both its hands.

When he's dun eating, man gathers up sum of the windfall an

tosses them at the woom-men, strate enuf for hit, but not so hard for hurt.

Maybe understanding enters here, born of a long shared jurny, weariness, togetherness an food.

Sum trust muss have sloped in too. As the woom-men nibble the frewt. Then she swallows it whole.

Nex day the man finds eggs. He leaves too on a mound of moss for them. Wun duk egg an wun gooz egg. Wun sucks the big wun. Wun sister smiles, The-Uvva scowls.

One sumhow knows the beast had laid the larger egg for her.

They've neva met anuvva beast befor that counts their numba, or trubbles for tell them apart.

They let it lay closer when they nest that dusk. Wun stays awake for watch it, as The-Uvva sleeps.

They eye each uvva askance in the gloom, man an Wun, pretending for look uvvaways.

A smile surprises her, but she doesn't know why it creeps upon her face, stretching her mouf wide.

Beast senses a wellcum, belches, grins an slivvers close, wriggling glinteyed, bellydown thruw the dewdamp grass.

Fingurs reach out. First the tips touch. Palms rub, then hands grasp.

They stroke each uvva, beast an woom-man. She feels the harsh hardness of it, an wonders at its bulk.

They sniff each uvva, carefull then curiuss, like they wur sniffing carryon, for see if it wur fresh enuf for eat. It nuzzles at her chest. She strokes its hed. It lays hevvy callussed hands on her soff hips.

Its stench is not a sister's smell. It mingles rot, wet an fear. The swet of it clings sour strong. The breff of it is strong meat. The hurr of it is rank fat.

But from the fowl, anuvva scent rises fresh – fierce, odd an sharp, like pine thruw woodsmoke, like a thrush at dusk, sounding above the skwawking crows. An thow the stench prickles her nostrils, the scent sends shivers wivin.

Sumthing in him is risen snake-sly, watchful, poised for strike. While sumthing in her soffens for him. Her hart kwickens but not from fear. Thow the grasp of the beast is harsh on the outside, it tickels under the skin, then goes fingurring deep. Wivin her, beneef her belly, sum unreachable part is moved. An she feels herself strangely touched.

'They dun it then?' asks Blind.
'They dun it,' I admit.

Wonder tied them hide for hide. Desire stuck them skin on skin. Discovery moved them. So they cum together. Free times, it's told. In urgent, frenzid ignorance, neva pawsing for count, nor effen caring what they did. For the while they wur lost in it, tangled past reasun an sense.

This much wur known for oldest earsay reaching back beyond wurds. But a lot remains untold, unseen.

'How they know what for do . . . wiv themselves?' Blind asks.
'They made it all up,' I say, 'as they went along.'

Yes, it's easy enuf for touch anuvva an feel that sumthing kwivers an moistly stirs.

But for invent cuppling asks more besides. It wants imaginings, urgings, suspishuns an feelings, an calls for more than nifty hands. Juss getting started needs plenty wit.

A stranger's body is a land of mistry, when it reaches out from anuvva secks, an no wun's bin befor. Yu need for find the landmarks, an feel the rutes around. Many are the openings. Few are the ways. Entrys ly hidden from site. Small things matter. Outward parts mislead.

So cuppling wur no easy thing for find. It tells well of my muvver's-muvver's wits. An of the man, too – whateva parts he brort for it.

They'd have watched, bewildered, the fore-leg beasts in rut. But they have bin discuraged for copy that. What wiv the hed-butting, goring, strutting, roaring, chasing, skwawking, snuffing an such.

There wur an approach for find, back or front, an a grasp too, of the parts that matter, an what fits where. Then they had for find the moves for make it go – a rocking an jerking, a for an fro, that's nyva proply in nor out, an doesn't thrust strait for mind. An when too are bound up in it, insted of juss wun, an those too are strangers, an they are man an woom-man, misunderstandings will purbly arise.

30

There'd have bin urgings in the greedy end for a lifetime famine. Yes, there muss have bin frenzy in it. But a fumbling too. An a stiff awkwardness, in this first meeting of unknowing, stranger parts.

When his loins sneeze the fird time, man rolls away, snorting, blinking back at the winking stars. His enthusiasm is breefly gon. Wun crouches alone, shivering, frust aside.

The-Uvva glowers at her, hissing in the gloom. She stirred awake an saw it all. Man has split them apart, tugging them sepert ways.

Deepblud glissens dark on Wun's thys, all thow it isn't her time by the moon. Beast has ripped her tie for the sky. Brort her down for Urf. He's bin made a human being. But she has found no more than man – who snuffles content, scratching an idle, satisfied part. His hooded eyes ain't for her any more. He watches The-Uvva now. He looks for know them apart, his face tugged by a foolish, near-human grin.

At sunrise, the sisters ponder the crazed clasps of nite, an look at wun anuvva, sag-moufed, moon-faced bemused. Man wur sumhow less than they wanted. They sense more wur taken than given. An sumthing feels foreva lost.

Both faces crinkle in their dawn confusings. Each slack lap smiles sore, remembering what's bin dun for it.

But man is gon. He's no where for be seen.

There's juss the flattened grass where they lay wiv him. An a moist yawning tenderness in too woom-men, where he had cum wivin an between.

Now we've found enuf trew an telling wurds for fukfuking, all sorts, evry which way – for say which parts are enjoyed, if it's artful or clumsy, langwid or brisk, joyful or tender, brave or humble, brazen or furtive, kwiet or lowd, uprite or lying, late or urly, forwud or backwud – wiv our tooing, freeing an bunching, jiggers an jaggers, redwing an lapwing, legs up an legs over, fox an duks, dipping an diving, rub-a-dub, find hunny an suckle, huffing, puffing an blowing, purring an hurring, neeling an skwealing, on the slopes an down in the vally. We ain't gripped by cuppling, but we see furva than our noses. We care for call things apart.

But pity this Wun. She didn't have a single wurd for say for it, an cudn't see the sense, neva gessing the wriggler chewing her up wivin, only knowing that her stomak had started skwabbling wiv her food, so she spewed, an neva blud when the moons cum full, an her belly started swelling, all thow she neva felt full, an took for skwabbling wiv her sister, who she now knew apart from herself, sins the man had cum so strange between them. An The-Uvva felt all the same ways too – burdened down, hevvy-legged, swelled up slow.

*-> | Birfs

'There boobys cumming by-an-by?' Blind gesses.

'The first birfs,' I agree. 'Howls, screams, tuggings on the breast. Nites will neva be kwiet for peepil again . . .'

Dark's rising, juss as the sun slides low. The lake shivers, puckered oranj, its rippels gliding yella. The water licks, gurgles an spits, lapping away at the land. Wun strains her back against the mossy rock, raises her nees an splays wide her jerky thys. Sumthing is struggling for cum, from her insides out.

Wun neva knows what it is, this wriggler wivin, like a grub in a frewt, or sqirming wurm in a gall. An she's ravenuss for feed, as the greedy blowt is eating her insides, an she feels the wrive an kick of it beneef the taut bulj of bellyskin.

Waters burst between her legs, an she shrieks, panting an whimpering wiv a terble muvver of all pains, sobbing for it for cum. She strains, heaving for be rid of it. An howls for it for go. But it's shy for cum, taking harf the nite for show a wrinkled, grimaced face. Then more slivvers out behind.

What's cum out is a small raw, bluddy, gizzum-smeary, lamed thing, like a small booboon, skinned. She is startled for see it. She neva knows how that cud cum out of her, there, becaws she'd neva seen nor felt it go in. An the opening is tite, besides she gards it well.

Thow a terble tiredness tugs her down, she's cort the small thing kwick in the misty gloom. Its cry gives it away. It hasn't the wit for crawl from her reach, but lys there wounded, wriggling, shaking its plump arms in an ignorant frenzy, splutterings between her spatter thys.

Small eats on the wun hand are worth a stuffing in the bush. So, Wun knows enuf – for eat it there an then. For give her strenf. Until she hears the sorrur of its scream, which pierces a hart wiv spines, as she sinks her teef into a jerky plump leg.

33

Then she chews the cord, insted, an hugs the dirty slippery thing for her, which soovs it, soon as it chews on her chest.

A kware turn. She'd thort for eat it. Now it's eating her. An yet she lays content enuf. Sumthing's kwarely satisfied, as it chews, tugging swollen nipils, wiv its grasp where for feed, sucking up warm skwirts of her, melted down for joos.

Nex dawn, The-Uvva has a small skwirmer rip its way out of her, but this wun hasn't a sister's shape. Not between the legs – where it got small frontail of man. Woom-men blink bemused, then cluk knowing. Becaws they'd thort back in their heds. Now they remember him. The man who'd passed thruw them wun nite.

Sisters brood on man's cunning. Resentment stings them, now they gess he's had sum part in their swelling. An yet, they take for the small grunting things, gnawing at their breasts.

When The-Uvva sees a speckled lizzurd flit past her futs she pounces for clutch it befor its gon. Food is food. Lizzurd is small parts good – pop-eyes, crunch-hed, fleshy tail an legs. Yu muss grab it when it cums. Most times it only passes wunce. So she seizes lizzurd too handed for tug it apart.

Of caws, this is her mistake. Sins in grabbing herself a lizzurd, she's tossed away a son. The booby's gon tumbling, bouncing howling down the ravine, till rocks break its fall, an it splits open against a jag, an both pieces blud, twitch then shortly fall still.

Having kwickly chewed small food, The-Uvva chokes on a long large sorrur, howling until after dusk, then sniffling thruw the dark, but still hugging too darkening, dripping parts of booby for many days, until the smell of them grows soursweet rotten, so the life of both bits is sure gon out. Soon there's only levver an bones.

So woom-men lurn that newborns are eggy fragil an splattershell delickut – breaking apart if yu drop them, an addling if yu let them grow cold.

Wun wur my muvver's-muvver. She first conceeffed of cuppling, an uvvas wurn't slow for follow.

The man found them again the nex Berry-Moon. He took for cumming offen. He juss wudn't stay away. He cum swaggering down bold at dusk, slinking away into dawning shadows. He found a fonder wellcum wheneva he brort food. But as a diffurnt animul, he lived apart, by a diffurnt water, anuvva place.

'Diffurnt?' Blind asks.

'Like hare an rabbut, duk an gooz, fox an wulf. Simlar sum ways, an diffurnt uvva parts. Man an woom-man didn't know they belonged together. Sept the man has his suspishuns. Becaws sumthing kept him cumming.'

Man cums in sevral sepert skins, from all around. He got the nous for change his place, face, shape an size – offen as he changes his mind. He cums over the scarp, round the lake, or out thruw the woods, smiling an frowning, giving an taking, limping an prancing, lean an stout, tall an short, his hurr grey an black, his skin sandy as a lion, or sow-udder pink.

'But ain't these sevral diffurnt men . . .' Blind gesses.

'I know. Yu know. Woom-man don't. Not juss yet. She think he juss the wun, changing his looks an cullurs like a lizzurd.'

'Burd shit,' Blind supposes out lowd.

Wun time the man cums wiv blud-raw, weeping claw marks on his belly. But at dusk, when he visits nex, his skin has forgotten an forgiven the paw of the cat, an his dull brown eyes are smiling glister blew.

An he don't cum alone wiv himself, but takes for splitting into sevral skinfuls, sumtimes surprising himself, arriving befor he's left, or finding himself there all reddy, befor he's cum. Then there's jibbering an hooting. Man wressels himself, flings stones his way, clowts himself wiv sticks, biting himself till blud runs, as thow he ain't his own frend.

Wun an The-Uvva lay wiv the sevral skins of man. They knew him as the limper an the strider, grunter an snuffler, uprite an hunched. An the sisters cum for know all his shapes apart in the dark. But, still, they neva spoke of it. Not a wurd. Shud have, wud have, but they cudn't yet.

Sumtimes parting gave the man charm. Uvva times, his cumming bent or aged him. But woom-man always knew him, seeing below the surface hide, sniffing that scent in him, sensing he wur always wun an the same, beneef the skin. An man all ways knew woom-man.

Wun liked best that skin of man who brort yellaberrys an buk rabbut, wrapped in the brissly hide of a hog.

She feels full when fed, then kindness clutch her. She lys wiv man, clinging for him. Her fingurs flick his hard, lean haunches, her palms stroke the hollows of his back, an rub the firm of his belly, an she cluks a pleshured surprise.

Then they're cuppling free times.

First he cums from behind, frenzid as a beast. Then he lys on top, eager like a man. Then Wun sits astride, riding his loins, taming him slow.

Till a tingle tricks her tung for whimper, an an odd frob cums inside. She's startled by a sly wet pleshur, mingled wiv an odd kwiver of surprise.

Wivin her hurt are shivers of joy. In the soreness, sweetness lys.

'Cos spusms jiggle her fancy,' Blind advises, rubbing her tired, slack old thys.

Yes, the tang of yellaberrys still clings sharpsweet on her tung. An after many lean days, a belly feels full.

There wur plenty cupplings after that. Then more. Becaws fowks took for it eager, wunce they lurned how it wur dun, an that the doing wur good. Man an woom-man lay down, skwirmed together, then rose apart.

Then more boobys cum from that. Becaws until a woom-man has layn wiv a man her wisdum's stunted small, an her desire's incomplete. An no new sowl can slivver into a woom-man until a man has cum befor, showing the shaded, narrow path for it for take . . .

'A stack of cack,' says Blind, 'an a drizzle of pizzle.'

'What?' I ask.

'These *men's* wurds,' she says.

'I tell it how we saw it,' I say. 'This wur then. Not now. It takes fowks time for lurn the way that boobys cum . . .'

Blind is braying like a hyna, shaking her hed in disbelief, slapping her legs ruff.

36

'Becaws there's nine moons between the cuppling an the birfing. That's far back for remember, if plenty happens between . . .'

But Blind juss bobs her hed, jerky mad like an eager coot, cackling her old woom-man's larfter, harsh as ripping levver.

Yes, there all ways bin plenty skwabbles an spites between man an woom-man, reaching back for first lite. There's sumthing between the seckses that neva kwite fits. So yu still hear the old arguments, effen now, about who spoke first, who told the first ly, concerning fuking, who shud fetch the meat home, who shud cook it, who shud count, an who shud be thanksfull after.

Any way, she begat her an him. An them. An more. Then these begat uvvas, who then begat more. The story bin told too offen befor.

'Who?' asks Blind. 'Many?'

'I can't name names, or give a tally. We didn't have names then. Besides, I ain't born yet. An fowk hadn't cum frends wiv numbas. Still, countless many got born, sprowted, seeded an died away, nameless.'

A booby's a small thing in these fresh days, a nobody, that scarcely matters, sept for itself – if it braves it for live . . .

'But a muvver's luv?' Blind asks.

'There wurn't muvvers then. Not for speak of. An there wur no luv. Not by name.'

'The woom-man who birfed it?'

'She cum attached for the small thing, offen enuf . . . When she remember what it wur, an where she put it.' I nod. 'Wulfs wur all ways fond of a booby too. An hynas sniff the trail of its drippings. But the flys it wur that luvved it best.'

Few boobys stay long. Many sowls flee in terrur, turning back beyond, soon as they're cum, gessing there'd be hard time ahed. Uvvas ail a few days befor parting weak-harted wiv a sorry whimper.

Only strong harts cud bear bite of life, few cud take the knocks, or stand the tumbles. Those tarried an grew. But by the time they are sprowted for a pursin they'd forgotten they wur eva born a booby. It seemed so odd then, an far ago. So grown peepil had few fellow feelings for littil lowd things, cum leaky newborn.

'Yet a booby's cry. It tugs on yur innards . . .' Blind imagines.

'There wur plenty crying. From yung an old. Yu had for plug yur ears, for hold back the flud of hurts.'

An a booby neva helps itself. It give nothing. It neva share. Only takes. An juss lys there, howling out its hidey place, spilling jooses like a split melon, drawing buzzing swarms for its dripsy cracks, bludding when man-handled, wivvering like plucked frewt, when yu leave it for dry in the sun. Or it breaks apart when yu drop it, or gives up its breff under waters, or looses its spirit in a gorse bush, being careless an feeble.

No, a booby is juss a lowd dirty bundle sum woom-men clutch for, joggling on her hip, riding her back, clinging for her hurr. She keeps it close for her chest – for stop it getting snaffled by sum animul as eatings. Still, many get lost or forgotten. Or struk wiv a stone, being needless lowd.

But when it can walk, a chile knows for gard an retrieffe itself, for totter among fowks, bite back, swat its own flys, hold its tung, poke its own pokey stick, an grub around for small food, beetils, roots an frewts. Then it becums a small pursin. An soon lurns its way, as I do.

When I'm cum there's family all reddy, waiting on me. The first solid bite I eva take is the hand of me bruvver Mows, who tastes sour an salty, but dry, becaws me wobbly milk teef cudn't broach the joos of him, thruw the tuff stuff of his skin. An Mows offen gets bit on, as his spirit rowses spites an spats, kindness scorns his bulj-eyed flatface, an charm won't eva be seen wiv him.

Befor I stumble for walk, he makes off wiv me, an teases me, like a trapped gowfer. Its his pleshur for prod me wiv sticks, drop me in a spiny bush, hide me in holes in the ground, leave me dangling from trees by tired tugged arms, or lay me thrashing on the waters – for see if I did flowt. Or maybe not.

He got no strong luv for me, but still he lurns me for swim an be brave, an howl my feelings from the very start.

He doesn't wellcum me born, an neva knows any need of me. He wants the ly of a muvver's lap for himself. Perps he envys my nose – sins I given no wun caws for chew it off. He hopes if I'm lost for site, Carf will forget me. But she offen cums running, ansurring for my screams or sobs. Then she clowts Mows about the ears, or butts his hed wiv hers. Then more fondness is gon missing between a bruvver an myself.

'I suppose he luvved yu in his own purtickler way,' Blind consoles.

'Then why he kept burrying me? In ant hills?' I ask, scratching away for soov the prickle of murmury.

Childrins are spoiled now. Most is known. Too much gets told. An many adventures in life are lost. So there's scarce that's left for chiles for find for themselves.

They get told – 'This is yur mouf. Open it so . . . Food goes there', 'An piss thruw that', or 'Those are yur nose-holes, so use them for smell.'

But when I first cum, there's no wun speaking for tell me so. I cud do no more than copy. An fowks got odd, ignorant ways wiv their bodys. Becaws manners aren't cum yet. An slimes an slujs trickle out of us, all cullurs, from evry opening, an uvvas besides. As our bodys are leaky. An we have more holes about us than we've lurned for keep closed, leaving moist trails whereva we go, smeary as snails.

So I meet my puzzild parts perplexed. My pieces an I are all gathered together, unawares. Each part knows best. But each tells it diffurnt, as my eyes can't hear, an my ears neva see. So the deff are leading the blind, but neva find the scent, or touch upon the taste of it. So I chance upon my bits as many strangers, that have for meet an greet, befor they take for each uvva as frends. So we bump in the dark, tumbling arse over lug, an eyes got poked, tung is bit, legs twisted, arms bent, till I lurn the joins an togetherness, see what is attached for which, an what's for be dun wiv it. So many parts hung about idle, uncertain, befor I found a use of them, or they led me for their wants, but for start I think I'm cum for the wurld missing, incumplete. Faceless. Sins I seen evry body's hed but mine. An thow I can touch me nose, an stuff my mouf, still seeing is believing, an feeling ain't the same. Till I'm lurned by my look-back in the water, or peer close in a bruvver's eyes. Which show me how my eyes peer out away from themselves, beyond their own see. So water it wur that first showed me the ly of my sullen face. Which wur no happy site. As I seldum smiled upon myself frendly, but scowled back sulky. An yet I'd cum oddly attached, knowing I wur wrapped up in myself, an wud surely cum for know myself more, like it or not.

There are many storys about Carf, Mows an me, wiv seffern warps an seffern weavs. The strands criss-cross like a glissening spider's web, an there are many routes around an wivin, so I can travel the first seasons of my life, an visit the places passed, an in the very centre of the web yawns the hole she left empty when she went. For go Beyond. Where the ded are living an the living are ded, an the unborn wait. But this is anuvva tale.

*->> | Pity

'Evrything wur change for us,' I say, 'wun pigday in the Dust-Moon, when the wurd first cums on us.'

Blind's face tugs itself tite, wrinkled as a dried fig, as she gobs suspishuns, over her shulders in froffy brown skwirts of bekelnut spit.

'Wurds pounced on us,' I tells. 'They lay hid in the belly of a ded sow.'

'So yu neva saw them cumming.' Blind knows. There's a siteless woom-man's smurk at the ignorance of eyes when it cums for grasping talk.

'We searched for them in their burrows.' I admit it. 'We peered in ears, gawped in gobs, but cudn't find the beast that made the noise. Still, they struk the ears strong. The din of them eckowd terble lowd in our rattling skulls, till we cum used . . .'

'Like urf-breff cracking the trees?' Blind gesses.

'Like wulf-howlings close in the dark,' I says.

'The clowd-clatter after sky-flames?'

'Like the scream of the ground as she cums ripped apart.'

Maybe I say it stronger than it trewfly wur. Blind muss have it poked hard in for her ears, for feel it, if she's for hear it how it wur.

'What wur it, then? The first wurd?' she asks. 'Pork or duk, I gess.'

'Nyva. But there wur a sour pig-stench for it.'

'Aaagh! or Aaaah!'

'There wur sum of that for it, too,' I agree.

'Cupplewe, or itchit?'

'Nun of those, at all.'

'What, then?'

'It's a lost wurd now. The sense of it wur cutting as flint, piercing as a splinter-bone burin.'

41

'It said this – "Whaa, I ain't ate. Not free days, now. So I'm weary of waiting on this rotted meat for cook. Famish skwirms in my belly like a nest of eels. An the hurt is clattering my skull like tumble rocks. Besides, my swollen tung's gon dry as a cava root . . ."'

'Wait,' Blind cluks. 'Wun wurd? It said all that?'

'It did. Becaws it wur a terble strong wurd. An it borrowed from its purtickler time an place. But it neva cum on its own. Anuvva wurd wur needed first. That wur the kwareness for it. The first wurd wur . . . the second wurd.' I gulp an paws. 'It's a tangle for unravel. Remember I wur a chile then. My murmury of it is no fuller than a kwarter moon, glimpsed thruw moist eyes in a mist.'

'Go on, then . . . booby,' Blind allows.

Juss as a jurny cums in futfalls, the strides between too places, so sense is the space between too things, the vally between too hills, or the hill between too vallys. So there cud not be wun wurd until there wur too. Sins meanings ly between things, not wivin.

There wasn't wun pursin till there wur anuvva for see her diffurnt, standing apart, but belonging wiv. Man wur cum human by his diffurnce for woom-man. Woom-man wur woom-man by not being man.

Juss as we neva had secks till there wur the tangle of too, so we had no wurd till we got dubble that. But for start we neva knew it – being yung, frisky as piglits, heedless dumbskulls bent on gobbling.

'Ha!' Blind spits thicker, darker, furva. Onto my futs.

'Yu're only Blind caws evrywun els sees. If we all had gizzum-gummy eyes like yu, we'd only know yur seffern smells, fife feels or free tempers, we'd call yu diffurnt . . . Flaky, or Surly, insted.'

Her jelly yella glisterlost eyes drift my way. 'This cums no cumfort,' she says. 'For me.'

'I crawled wun summer, shiver wun winter, an totter thruw anuvva summer, befor Talk cums for us. Speech wur born for us too times . . .'

'Well, it cudn't cum wunce, till it cum twice?' Blind says. She gesses good becaws she's lissened hard.

'Those wur the prickles of it,' I agree.

'Who spoke first, then?'

'Crow,' I say.

'Man or woom-man?'

'A man . . . Man found Talk first. After woom-man had spoke it befor.'

'How did he look, this Crow?' asks Blind.

'He had sum of the dark of his namesake burd. Also a crest of hurr, an sparkle eyes suspishus an startled. He offen sqwalked, wiv a sharp twist of his hed. Then he'd look down at his chest gon solem, wondering what he'd dun an why.'

'What cullurs his eyes?'

'Brown as a new tumbled acorn, wiv flecks of willow-leef green.'

'Wur he old?'

'Most of his teef wur wiv him still. He wur a stag at second rut. A warthog, he'd be harf-tusked, full-brissled.'

Blind sucks on this, tasting it for trewf. 'Go on, then . . .' she allows.

'Can't.' I shrug. 'Not yet. There's more that cums befor.'

Most of my kin walk befor me, being longer wiv their legs, so I soon fall behind, when Carf doesn't clutch me, an keep low cumpany wiv Broke who offen stumbles my way, an Wurm who crawls behind. Weak, puny an ignorant, that's how this chile feels himself, an uvvas muss've felt it the same. An needy. There's always sum skwirming wurm of want, gnawing away a hole in us. When we aren't famished, we're shivering, an when we aren't thirsty we're scared. An when we aren't scared by sumthing seen, we fear we know not what. Also we itch plenty. An shed skeins of skin in flaking scabs, an leave a dotted trail of spat-out teef.

An our blotched sore-scratched bodys are neva content, always aching for this an that. Moufs are wurst. Yu cud neva keep them full enuf. An whateva yu feed yur throwt, it's neva stayed content for long, but only yearning eva cum of it, besides cack the uvva end.

Yur spirit's shrunk a small tite thing, curled up shuddery behind yur eyes. It muss be hard for bear the blows. Becaws the days are joined endless together. Sept fearful nites cum between. When we're hunted down by merciless dreams.

Most evrything knows more than us. Water neva has our dowts, but rushes its course wivout weariness or paws. Fire neva knows our fears, but juss scorches a path thruw whateva it meets. An most beasts are faster, crewler, more cunning than fowk.

Howlers swing thruw the branches above us, chattering an mocking. Crawlers hide, being cullured for blend. Burds soar high over our heds. The beasts all ways know befor us when the hot an cold will cum an – molting fur, shedding fevvers – they travel on, leaving us flat-futs beneef, behind, smarting or shivering, whining nakid, bemused.

Fish slip our grasp. Turtuls outswim us. Prey smells us cumming, an runs. Deer have eyes in the back of their heds. Cats creep up when us backs are turned. Flys nip us sly. The buzzurds swoop down on the ded befor us. Lice bite us bad. So we're offen moved by clowt our heds, for soov the itch wiv hurt.

Burds wove nests. Rats dug holes. Booboons climbed trees. Trees grew roots. Crabs made shells. Deer held themselves snug in fitting hides. We had only hard places – patches of ground an a rocky perch. Yes, evrything had fit themselves snug in a place befor us. Fowk alone are homeless. An got nothing but fire, an clammy, cast-off skins. An arms for rub an hug us selves warm.

We're so few, stuck hevvy-futted, dull-witted, on the ground. Only eggs, snails, slugs an bungo grubs know less than us. Easy for catch, but tiresum for taste, discurajing our tungs. So our moufs yearn more an diffurnt, gaping wide, whimpering for rabbut, deer or pig.

'Whaaa!' we howl.

For we've stalked the limping carf a long way, all round the thorny bushes. But as soon as we're crept near enuf for tug it down, it's fled in a clowd of dust an drubbing of hoofs. Effen a free-legged carf cud outrun an outwit us.

It's a sorry time for being human. Only ignorance keeps fowk going. An shamelessness. That an copulation.

See us in yur hed, then. Pity us in yur hart.

We know too littil for cumfort. An we imagine enuf for keeping afraid. The nite hides too much, an suckles dark its teef-chiles.

At dusk we clamber the stony crag, build a fire an huddle around. Becaws the dancing flames hold dogs an cats at bay, warning the gloom an arm's lenf apart.

Below us the lake lys still as a lizzurd, blending for the darkening sky – oranj, red, purpil for black. Urf lays down her hed for sleep. The gusts of her breff cum cool as sighs, whispering thruw the trees. The lid is falling over Urf's burning eye of Sun. The blind eye is opening, but the glint of Moon is dim. Urf don't see herself now. No more can we. There are only the flicking tungs of fire an the amba circil of our sprawl. A skwirming, snuffling heap.

This is our trajdy. We are wun flesh. But our sevral skins hold us sepert, apart. But in fukfuk fowks thrust for hope, wresseling for merge.

My chile-eyes blink on it, an wonder at the sorry, whimpering tussle of cupples, thrusting an heaving, wresseling for cum together, wun. Rabbut wiv Duk, Crow wiv Lark, Skinks wiv Moonsik, Guppy wiv Gooz, Fox wiv Flames. But Broke an Wurm look on bent an lame, rocking, hugging themselves alone.

The men strain, faces screwed in effort, as they jerk away. Hesitant between cum an go. An the wandering woom-man-eyes look hopelost in the face, as she chews upon sum meat, an the man tires of the struggle, falling grunting away. Any fool can see the way's too tite. When man tries for get up woom-man, he'll only push a small part in. But hopes sprowt fresh. He'll shortly try again. Thow nothing deeper nor furva eva cum of that.

At dawn there's the shriek of burds an shock of brite. Yawning, rubbing eyes, we heap of fowk look down on ourselves, straining for remember what we are. We frown an look the lenfs of our bodys, then smile. We are fowks. An still living. Nite has taken or added nothing. Our parts are much as we remember them from befor. We draw our sevral legs apart, for find out who's attached for them an which futs muss walk wiv who.

The water's woken below, rippelled by wind. Fear flees the dawning lite. We see things cumming now. We trip down the stony slopes for the lake, drink, an eye those startled faces, swaying in the lapping water.

All gathered, we're too handfuls, but less than the pips in a spiny frewt. Forgive the misty view on it. I can see no clearer than that chile's urly murmury shows.

There's eats for be scavenged, pokey sticks for be poked, wriving mowses dug up skweaking, crabs cracked open, bulbs unurfed, bugs chewed, locust sucked. Berrys smear in yur fingurs an yu lick the winding trickles of joos. Yu eat what cums for hand, sniffing out the rotten, musty things, favurring the fresh, chewing a way thruw small life an whateva won't bite back.

There are moons for food. Things cum plentiful, then soon go scarce. Eggs cum an go. Then there are sago roots an mussels. Nex is the time of the crabs, befor the acorns an spiny frewts. Then there's plenty bungo grubs. After that, the best are hunny an mussels. Then snails an beans.

I totter about, between woom-men's legs, grubbing an skwealing. But men gon far. I don't know where, lost for site. Then their scent is drifted clean off the air. Sun dips befor yu smell them cumming again. They swagger back, ded stuff hanging off them, dripping – dik-dik, booboons, pig an deer. But now I know the numba of legs for a beast, I see the carcasses cum all reddy torn an chewed.

These aren't the new, kind men, the likes of I, but the old, crewl kind – dumb, grunting, chile-slappers. The smell of them bites like a gnat in yur nostrils. They stroll off moons on end wivout paws for care on what they've left behind. They spirits take them wandering. They're coarse-faced, bandy-legged an restless as howlers. They aren't full fowks yet, unlike woom-men an chiles.

I eye men cumming, wiv hungry fear, as a movable feast. They bring meat. But they are angry, ruff-hewn, clumsy things, an what's cleva about them all ways strikes yur ruff. They swat noisy childrins away. They envy us chiles the careless embraces, happy guggles of woom-men. Becaws chiles got charm. I only got for burp for bring a smile for Carf-eyes. But she all ways looks for more in a man.

I wear no thing, mostly. Only drape my scrawny shulders wiv a pig hide, an grunt, when it cums cold. Becaws we neva think for cut our cover for our shape or size, neva try for better the cunning shape of a faster, wiser beast. If a skin wur good for sum deer for wear befor us, it hangs well enuf on fowk. We only wish we had antlurs, hoofs too or – better – fangs an claws. An we're thankful for share in the old warmf of the beast, still clinging onto its rancid skin.

No part of us needs covering. Eyes seen it all befor. What yu see is what we are. Shame ain't shuffled flush-faced between us yet, hand in hand wiv red-faced bruvver Blame.

I know evry body from the legs up, by the callusses an scars of nees, the grain of thyskin, the bulj of belly, the nipilbrown puckers an swells of breasts. An – furva – by the curl of evry lower lip, the downward glower of evry eye, the dark burrow of evry nostril. This wur my chile's view on it – upwuds from thys for breasts.

Yes, fowk are foreva looming over me, slapping me ears, their tufty pryvuts smiling down blind, grazing me scalp, soff an moist. So at first, I barely saw faces, but know evry body apart, an closely by peering up between their legs, lurning which hurry split went wiv the cuff of which horny hand.

Our feelings wur all ways too strong. Tears blurr our site, pity trips us, kindness stalks us, pity snags us on its spines.

So when a large beast's felled, there's a sickening pain. An effen men snuffle pity.

As the hog rolls snorting, thrashing its legs, froffblud bubbling from its mouf, we clutch hands for ears an cast our welling eyes away. Only a sharp stone gashing thruw hog's windpipe can end that suffuring shared. Then Fox who cut its breff slinks away. An we hear him choke an retch behind us. For give us food, the killer muss forfit his own – effen the small sluj his hungry belly clung to from befor.

As the last twitch parts the hog, we see sumthing more is gon. It lys still an stiff, a lesser thing. Only ded meat is in it now. The sniffle, the skweal, the grunt, the gleam of eye, the pride, the knowings, the swagger, the pigspirit have all flit out.

An as we chew on it solem, pain an loss cling as a taint for the meat. Only hunger kept us eating.

But we feel each uvva wurs. An any hurt becums a sorrur shared.

When Flewk crys, we all suffur its booby noise, an those piercing howls skewer us all. An if Rabbut begins retching, many are kwick for follow. If Carf has frips, all who know her lap are sure for share. When Skinks's face blisters, many followed. An then we all shiver wun feva together.

This is our trubble, the pity we fell into. Our sharing feelings, an most uvva sorry things besides.

Like when Skinks takes Mows's nose off him, out of spite an a haggle, thruw a rude awakening.

Mows spills a stone on Skinks as he sleeps. It wur soff an flaky as stones go, but still harder than a hed, an splits open Skinks's brow. Blud gushes out, as from a hidden well. This wur Mows's mistake, as he's a small thing, littil more than pesty nuisins, while Skinks is full grown, an plenty brutal.

Anger burns in Skinks, so he tugs Mows by the ears for the gape of his jaws an chewed away the nose. Wun kwick bite, then wun long joosy suck. Nex plenty slow, thortfull chews.

Both are raw, bluddy an sore, but Mows hurts more an howls the lowder. Nor wud he stop. Thow they slap him ruff enuf for cokes him kwiet.

Thruw the nite we cum ansur him. Whimper for wail. His suffuring moves us all. Effen Skinks, who did the damage, spits out the chewed up piece of Mows, an palps it back, close as it goes, for the shape of a nose, an is moved for hand it back. But Mows cringes back. He wants to hang on for his ears.

Yes, we all lost sleep an a nose that nite. Pity bit us all.

We know plenty now. We see what hugs which, what slinks behind, which hides in the shadows. Hot keeps cumpany wiv fire. Cold wiv wind an wet. Dusk tugs nite behind as its shadow. Hunger follows food, stalking a day behind. Yu can't get blud wivout stones. Thirst flees water, but snares us unawares when we're strayed into the dusty lands. Sun an moon take turns. We know our outsides well enuf. It's us insides that holds the puzzil an hurts.

We're neva surprised by nite an day. Caws we know dark is the shut-eye of Urf an, being big, she's blinking slow. But rain falls out of the blew. An winter shocks us all for shivers. We look at the fallen leefs in dismay, an scowl at the wivvered grasses. Ice is a chilling betrayal. Winds buffet us. We wonder what we've dun, for bin slapped cold in the face by a frend. We wail together in a circil. But Urf stays frosty, an many moons pass befor she soffens, warming for us again.

We knew then we'd brort anger in Urf, but we can't tell what we'd dun.

'Whaa?' we whimper.

But we juss can't say.

Speech has still for cum skwealing out, from between the ribs of that pig.

*->>> | The wurd

The first wurd eva said wur 'Whaa?aa!'

It wailed sharp an plenty, all bewildered bickerings. An yu cud taste it, gall-bitter for yurself. Best start by rumbulling deep down yur throwt, then bring it up slivvery, rising lowd an shrill, till yu feel it rip yur gob, rattle yur skull-bones, pierce yur ears. Thow it's no happy howl, an so for shriek it good yu best feel it hard, cumplaining lowd while asking strong – why life is crewl. Best have yur murmury howl those crys of a shivering muvverless booby, screaming that ending 'aa' as long as tears salt yu, scalding cheeks.

Sense splutters out misted, hartfelt hazy, mixing many hurt askings, muddling plenty pains – Why are we froze? Why are we famished? Where is safe? Where is happy hid? Why do those lice always chew on me? What am I, any ways? Muss I all ways suffur for me? How are fleas cum under my arms? – an sevral more besides, all mindful whines about nothings for be dun.

We skipped from jibber for joke so kwick, an while I saw it all an lived it, that's the tangled tale for tell, becaws those wurds for its telling are still swelling, budding an frewting. Effen as I says.

There wur ate things we neva knew at first –

- Cawses
- Reasuns
- Urf
- Our arse from our elbas, our hurts from our harts
- Moruls
- Wurds
- Numbas
- Sumthing els. I juss forgot

So we cum dumb for Talk an ignorant for Trewf. An no sooner we spoke our mouffull, an heard an earfull, than evrything gets going crazy, restless an moody, shifty as wind, flowy as waters, fickle an fierce as fire.

Wisdum lay at the roots of it. Langwij wur its trunk. Knowlij wur those trembling branches, an talk the russling leefs.

Yes, it wrapped us up sudden as Spring.

Meanings sprowt all about, thrusting up between our futs. Wurds burst open like ripe frewt, scatterseed. Tendrils of sense snagged us on their spines, then ripped us ruff. That thicket overran an trapped us. Then we saw that we wur snared.

No, perps it cut us cold an crewl as Winter.

Caws it wur torrents over us, heds an ears, as a storm of knowlij raged, an reasun blazed its bolts of litanyng, an sense thundered. Suspishuns streamed down incessant. We wur thunderstruk, deffened an drenched. An indicashuns spilled hard as hail, sharp an striking on our scalps.

Yes, we're dazed by Trewf. It flashes dazzling brite. Storms of it struk fierce. Chill damp trickled into that darkplace between our ears. At first we grasped only small bits – glimmers behind dark clowds, rumbuls an ansurring eckows, sins the size of it wur stunning. Neva mind the noise an wet. Nor the clowts between our ears.

We neva knew what wud happen nex, or what a thing wud be cum nex day, what mover wud shove us, what maker did shape us, what cawser wud change us. As nothing stayed its same from dawn for dusk. But got odder. An more so. Effen us. So evry dawn we woke strangers for ourselves. An evry nite we wur gon kwarer still. An when first lite cum, we look for see what dark dun behind our backs. Then, whereva we looked, there wur more than befor.

We neva saw her fullface – Trewf – but always twisted, shy an shaded. What saved us, becaws we'd be struk ded as rock in shock if we saw the full of Reasun, down that yawning chasm of her nakid lap.

We hardly got a future for start – not beyond our nex meal. But dug pits of passed whereva we went. An the present went so fleeting furtive we barely knew we lived. Only we hurt an hungerd.

We trod Urf lost. We'd move on, for cum for a new place we'd only juss left. Then we didn't know where we wur gon. Forwuds on Urf, or backwuds in life. Back-and-forf wur for blame for this. Our futs wur playing us tricks, misleading our heds.

Countless numbas gather about us in time. But for start, we knew only nothing. Then wun, too an free. Nevaless. Beyond wur more. Then cum enuf. After, lay the misty marsh of many, where yu got sucked over yur ears into kwagmire.

So, of caws, we make urly mistakes.

In that dampdark of our confusions, we didn't effen know we wur peepil, skinfuls of harts an minds. We didn't know nothing – where Urf ended, how she begun, how boobys cum, where those ded dwell, why sky weeps on us. Nyva wun good way of rowsting pig.

Woom-men bin doing it all reddy. Moufing off. But kwiet, sly.

Duk, Carf, Gooz, Flames an Moonsik bin speaking sum for moons. A murmuryn huddle of elokwent backs an kwivering chests. But they kept mum about it, mumbling amongst themselves, as the mists rose from the marsh, whilst the bull-frogs wur croaking, as dusk thickened for nite. So the men cud neva see or hear. Or wonder what. But, hugging me mammi Carf's shulders, I'm touched by the shake of her voice thruw the frob of her skin. Yes, I hear those whispers. An sups their sense like muvver's milk, thick, warm sweet. After yu've taken it in, yu start for burp an murmur.

Yes, ancient sounds.

'Yu know,' says I. Wiv a wink for the blind.

'Know what?' she asks.

'!waʔawaya,' I tell her, testing. 'Mumm!aaya!'

She reddens, turning her siteless eyes on me. '. . . oomawa**!' she admits.

'Wa'baafa* haha,' I console. 'Haafafa*!'

Of caws, I'd gessed it long ago. That woom-men still got those pryvut, moist sounds, woom-man wurds, folded in on themselves. Men can neva grasp.

'Don't tell,' says Blind. 'Woom-men wud neva forgive me.'

'I'm not wun for tell storys. My mouf is closed, as eva,' I say.

The ground is parched, powdering for dust. Life has sunk deep into the dark cracks of urf. Roots an bulbs are wivvered an dry. Nuts are shrivelled bitter in their husks. The game has fled. Deer are nowhere. The duks have flown, skwawking their mocking farewell, as they winged it over our heds. Nothing gon into our moufs for days, sept sum hard nuggets of sago, crunchy beetils an gritty blow-fly eggs, which are poor, dry, sour meals. The shadow of Despair skulks at our heels, casting its gloom on the stragglers, lying dark on the back of Wurm, who slivvers behind.

'Whaaa!' wun moans.

'Whaaa?' anuvva pleads.

'. . . aa . . .' a kwiet wun mumbles.

Then our pleas are eckowd, solid in meat. We stumble on a pig whose grunt is gon. It's fresh ded, mind, as its eyes still bulj its surprise at its going, the buzzurds barely picked at it, an the wurms have hardly wriggled in. So thow pig is gon it ain't long gon, an smells fresh enuf in itself, sept stale, ded airs cum hanging hevvy around, tainting it. It's that stench that only fire cud cure.

So we hunch around the flames, scalding our noses sniffing the smoking carcass, scorching our fingur tips, picking at its crackling skin, ravenuss for its flesh burn grey. Becaws the pink stink of it is poisunuss. An thow yur mouf can take it in, wiv a push, yur stomak is loaf for cling for it.

It's then that Crow has his wurd, an makes it speak out lowd.

A slippery, moaning thing, mucus moist, slivvers out between his twitching lips. The bump of his throwt is gon jerky as a mows beneef a sleeping-hide. He's belched then gulped like a watchfull frog.

We neva see it cum. That wurd. Only going, bursting from a bubbel of spittle. Then it's away – fast as it cum, gon blurry. All we catch is its noise. An like a moskito, it makes itself heard too lowd for its size. We swat the empty air from lazy habit. An are sum small parts glad it neva bit us.

All yu know of it is the sound of it passing. But silence flys back, fast on its tail. An in that kwiet, it sounds on in our ears. Like yu still see the glare of sun when yu close bedazzled eyes.

It's no mere grunt or gurgle. Thow shrill, it's a full-grown, mussly sound – a strong hunter of sense, snaring meaning.

Well, we've neva heard the like befor.

There's sumthing inside the cover of sound. An emptiness, a coiled cavity, like the wurl of a snail shell.

It's a noise shaped for carry. Yet its load's gon missing.

It's empty, hollow from yearning, tormented, howling.

'Ooo-whaaa,' Crow moufs. 'Ooo-whaaa.' Then it's passed again. Still, we hear it in the rippelling wake of silence.

He clowts his gurgling hollowed stomak wiv his palms. Yu can hear the howl of bowels in the sound, then a hungry whimper.

So it is we understand. He's sounded sumthing skwirming in us all – the spusms of us bellys.

'Ooo-whaaaa . . . Ooo-whaaa . . . Ooo-whaaa,' we howls. It cums for us together. We're all at it, clapping the taut drumskins of our bellys. We're wun, agreed. Hunger fills us all, swelling us airy an empty.

Crow tears a rib from the carcass. He sniffs it an moans. The sweetness is cloying, but the sourness is gon. Harm's burnt away.

He nods for us knowing. Then we're all fell on the belly of that well-rowst sow in a skwealing, wresseling pack, like piglits at the udder.

Of caws, soon as the first wurd is spoke, the ly flits behind in its shadow.

'Oo-aa,' Crow says again shortly. But this time he grins an sounds it sly, his tung flickering pink between the blowt of grease-shone lips.

The hollowed yearning has gon out that wurd. It sounds lazy now, full an stuffed.

Then Crow tugs on a tube of bowel, sucking out the steamy sluj of soffened acorns. An pig knows what besides. Crow's scoffed more than his share of pig all reddy. In trewf, he ain't hungry but greedy. Which is a diffurnt story.

An we all feel same as Crow does. Our bellys are blowted. Still we yurn for stuff ourselves more.

That day we all lurned for speak – an ly – together, men an woom-men, yung an old. This made us all knowing, all ekwal, each for the uvva. An we all took for Speech together. Sept for those Mutes, whose silent story neva speaks out of turn.

So the wurd wur out. Crow said it. He'd bin skwawking so long, shrieks an aimless splutters. Least now he'd spoke some sense.

'Hungry!' he said. 'But more. Wiv sum on top of that. Wurs than famished, cos yur belly ain't used for nothings . . .' So we understood him at the time.

We wur agreed. It touched the feelings of all, saw deep wivin us, spoke us insides out.

So we wur glutted by our wurd for start. Enuf said. Too littil ate. It told all that needed saying. So we neva felt the lack of uvvas. We juss stayed close an trew for the wurd we got.

An fowk wur fond for repeats, wheva hungry or not. Then say it again. Then tell it anuvva time. An more.

'Ooo-whaaa,' Wurm says.

'Ooo-whaaa!' Potto agrees.

'Ooo-whaaa?' Fox asks.

This wur as close as we cud get for Talk yet. It wur the first conversashun, offen repeated.

We tasted the wurd, an slid our tungs down its bendy lenf, the way yu fondle a flint in yur palm, or run yur hand along for fingur the strenf of a pokey stick, or stroke anuvva's thy, remembering the sound wurks of it, idly admiring its use, wondering when need wud wake it again.

It wur like a burst of splashing in the lake, this speaking. Wun starts it, seffern copy. Then we tire of it. It's gon stale on us. We stride out of the lake. An the waters fall still.

So we mite have left it there, lurning juss by pigribs, sticking close by hunger, neva summoning anuvva wurd. No wun gessed that the screech of speech wud be a lasting thing. We neva knew that wurd wur juss wun of a swarm.

But Crow juss babbles on. Only too days have passed, but all reddy he says anuvva wurd.

Potto has found a pricklebush, hevvy wiv frewts. The berrys are bitter but dripping joos. They rest easy on a belly, so yu ain't moved for heave them back.

We're gathered in the slender quivring shades of a willow. We pass water round in pig-bladders. We sip. We smile. A pile of prickleberrys is spred amongst us. It's a glut. We chew. We spit out the seeds. We're all stuffed, frewty.

'Ooo-whaaa? Whaa!' Crow snears at the thort. Then chops the air, choking Hunger wiv a blow for its scrawny neck.

A breeze ruffles us like the stroke of a frend. The air is dusty sweet wiv dry grass an resin. There's plenty pleshur in us. A bellyful all round.

'Weeee . . .' Crow screeches. 'Weeee . . .' He giggles his joy. A hot smile splits his face.

His arms spred for hug us. Then he points at each of us in turn. All thow we're swelled well past numbas. The sound is soff but insisting. It teases our ears. It trickles shivers down our spines. The hurrs rise, brissling on our necks. We sense he's spoken strong. We gess he speaks of us – all – together. But wurds are still closed as husks for us. I strain forwud, teef clacking, for crack the shells of sound, for snaffle the sweet nuts of sense.

Then his tung moves on. Wurds ain't finished wiv him yet. His lips part, kwivery. His brow is sliced by struggle. We lean towards him, hands bending round ears, straining for a grasp of it.

Gooz hisses. Flames's glance flickers over Carf's scowl. Moonsik winces. Woom-men shrug for each uvva. It's the wurds, they cud hear. An juss as they feared.

Men started speaking. Woom-men's secret is spilling out. From a man's mouf.

'Weee . . . Weee. . . .' Crow says again. His eyes roll upwuds, his hand clench blew for crushing fists. Ain't offen yu see such strain for a face, unless it's a woom-man, an most times she's birfing sumthing or uvva.

An his wurk wiv wurds has wearied him sore. He sighs an slumps. He's cum a far way, humping a hevvy load, wiv the mussels of his mind. Pride glissens on his watery eyes, as if he's made a big killing. So there's much for us all for feed on.

There's a still wrapped in kwiet. We suck on the lingering taste of sounds.

Then Gooz crushes evry silence.

'We, us,' she mutters peevish. She nods for Crow but her look ain't admiring.

'Us, we,' Duk says weary. The woom-men speak together. They repeat what Crow's said. Then add their own inventing. As if they knew wurds all reddy.

But there wur still plenty still unsaid, yet for be spoke. If we cud snatch the trew sounds of things.

We wur into the dark wood of wurds. This way starts the long naming.

*   *   *

'Yu know Urf got a strong mind for her. Howeva small a thing, she counts its parts. She got her favorit numbas.'

'She likes that *Wun*,' says Blind.

'Yes,' I agree. 'Mouf an brain an dipstick. Evrything's wun in itself, then offen free wivin, besides.'

'Plenty toos,' says Blind. 'Purrings an cupples. Eyes an ears, hands, kidnys, lungs, nipils an nose-holes.'

'Fore for the beast legs. Most times.'

'Fife for the fingurs, counting the fum.'

'Sicks for the inseks.'

'Seffern?'

'The numba of my mistakes,' I remind her.

'Ate?'

'Them spider's legs.'

'Free?' Blind's mind crawls backwuds.

'Plenty frees. Urf likes them good. So she hides them.'

'Tell us, then.'

'Each of us – body, mind an sowl. Our fates – unborn, living, ded. Our ages – chile, grown, wivvered. The start, the muddel, the end. Our trubbles, the Kwake, the Pox, the Ice. My makings – a dog, a woom-man, an carvings.'

'Dawn, day an dusk.'

'Here, there, nowhere.'

'The passed, now, days cumming.'

'Hungry, famished, starved.'

'Full, blowted, stuffed.'

'So!' I nod. 'There's plenty frees. Only look for them. Unurf a few an they cum crawling out together, like a nest of termits . . . There wur a free for langwij too. We get the wurd, then there's the naming, befor we got us storys . . .'

I totter low. I see wiv yung eyes, hear wiv fresh ears, an watch Talk blowt.

It's a ravenuss booby – all mouf. No sooner has it skwealed its birf than it's tugging on evry chest. Becaws it takes evrywun as muvver. We're feared it'll suck us dry, so fierce is its thirst, howling for the name of evrything. An howeva many wurds yu fed it, Speech neva has enuf. When it has chewed its mouffull, it juss gapes silent, becaws it still wants more. An wurds don't cum easy for us in these fresh days. No. It's picky wurk, plucking them, wun by wun, like tart berrys from the thorny bush, tugging the spiny wildness of things into the sense of speech, gathering morsels of meaning for Speech for swallow. Then spew it up our way, lowd an messy.

Befor long there's more wurds amongst us than moufs for speak them. But there neva seems a glut. No, still there wur too few. Sins in this bud of time, fresh things keep cumming born. An many things all reddy wiv us haven't bin said yet. No, yu can't walk effen fife paces wivout stopping in yur tracks for give sum sorry, yearning, mute thing its name. Like a rabbut, wurm, or root, chile, rat, or simlar. So littil hunting gets dun. Offen we go hungry, chewing on wurms or wurds for consolings.

'Whaaa?' cums the cry.

Gathered round the nitetime fire, in a circil, fowk pass stuff between them, straining for the sound for say it rite. Offen, we'd had for snuff it first, for stop its wrigglings, an hold it still beneef our curiuss, kind eyes, struggling for cum for know it better, for clutch for it wiv wurds.

'Gaa?'

'Gaaga?'

'Gagaa?'

Then we pass it around, an nibbel it. For see if its taste wud tell us. But thow it knew what it wur in itself, it wasn't offen saying.

'Uuh!'

'Errr!'

'Eehh-uch!'

Fowk sniff it. Toss it up, for see how it falls. Pound it open wiv stones, an fingur the dripsy pieces.

'Splo.'

'Ooo!ff?'

'Aaa-wgh.'

But evry thing wur too much for say, holding more than we can eva utter, having cullur, hevvyness, smell, a touch more knowing than fingurs. Wiv a fresh life an a rotten death, an inside an outside, a taste, a hardness an soffness, a wetness an a dryness, a cumpleteness an a breaking, a wholeness an a scattering of broken pieces.

Offen, when we'd finish picking a thing, an eyeing it well, it wur cum apart sum, no more than a spred of pink pulp, wiv small spiky bones, smeared over many sticky palms. Then a lizzurd looks much like duk, an a towd smells much like rat, wunce we've finished admiring, an got beneef the skin of it, fur, scales or fevvers.

An still we ain't grasped how for say it. We're weary. Our lips gon num from so much mumbling. Then any name wud do. As long as we agreed sum sound.

When sum name's cum, ruff but sound enuf, fowk nod or snuffle, agreeing it solem.

We wur cum Creators, calling up the pieces of this Urffull.

'Ha?'

'Ho!'

Which only makes for more wurk – mumbling into murmury, after taming it by naming. For stop sum stuff being said then soon forgotten. An sent speechless – lost again for talk, soon as it wur said.

Trew, we made plenty bad calls. Thow we don't find all our wurds in the dark, it wur a mistake tugging so much apart, then naming it in the gloom – our picky fingurs gon tired, our heds frobbing, our gaze lit dimly by the glow of a dying fire.

*—>>>> | Carf luv

Blind whimpers, 'Aaagh', clutching the twitchy crack of her mouf. For she got a pain in her tired broke-up teef, she says.

'That's juss the wandering hurt of life,' I console. 'It'll leave yur gob when it's good an reddy. Then make yu suffur sumwhere els. Here . . .' I toss her a stone. 'Try tapping yur futs wiv that. It'll give yur tows sumthing for feel that'll take yur mind off yur mouf.'

'Aah!' she moans, neva heeding the cumfort of advice.

'We all got our pains,' I says. 'Thank yur lukky gob yu still got sum bite.'

'My life ain't easy . . .' Blind whines, shaking her sorry hed. 'Not wiv gummed-up eyes, an harf my tung bit away.'

'Life's neva bin easy for no body,' I agree. 'But it's the best we got. Wud yu prefur be gon ded?'

'The ded do grumble . . .' she conceeds. 'They cumplain enuf. Then, as soon as they're gon, they howls for cumback.'

'They miss their own warm bodys,' I say. 'They cum attached.'

'It's kwiet Beyond,' Blind tells. 'They forget the frite an famish. They remember the chatter an larfs. That's why they drift back for talk.'

They pester terble. Blind knows the ded better than most. They gather for her becaws she can't run off. Not wivout tumbling into ditches or falling over rocks. They sneak up on her an whisper cool into her ears, wheva she wants for hear or not. That's why she jumps at nothing for be seen, an her face is jerked by winces an twitches for sounds we neva heard. That's the ded for yu. They won't let her sleep calm, but wander into her dreams, cackling rawcuss lowd. Then she shrieks back at them. So it is I'm woke too.

'So content yurself,' I urj. 'Be payshent. At least yu got teef an legs . . . An nex living yur sowl will make up for lost sites, get itself far seeing eyes in a pruttier face.'

Sun's risen near high as she goes. Urf lys spred below me, grass for forest, an beyond the creases of vallys an rippels of hills, tufted by gorse.

It's like the view when I lay my hed on Blind's bellyskin an gaze down her pocked, scabbed thys.

The down of her belly is the windbent tufted grass. The lap hurrs are tangled gorse. The too bald mounds of the far peaks are Blind's gnarled nees.

'It's always green near, but blew beyond,' I say, 'where the land clings for the sky. Howeva far yu walk thow, it cums no closer, but still stretches beyond.'

Blind's hed is bent over, as if she's gazing thruw the rock. Becaws she can't see out, she lissens more for her insides. Denied the surface site of stuff, she reaches for the guts. So she gets under yur skin. She can touch upon feelings yu neva knew yu had.

'Too futs cumming up the crag,' she tells.

'Don't hear them,' say I.

'Smells yung an girly. Climbing strong but sad.'

'Yur son's dawter, Pod.' I see her now.

'Carrying water on her hed . . .' Blind's nostrils twitch. '. . . an tears on her cheeks. There's rabbut an bekelnuts in her hands.'

'Hornet stung me arm . . .' Pod sniffs, clattering the water gord down on the rock. Cool drops leap up for flecks my chest. '. . . Drinks,' she tells, '. . . an eats. For too old moufs . . . Buk rabbut. Haunches an guts. Best eat it kwick. Befor the flys.'

'Mm!' I admire them, the bearer an the gifts. 'Wise chile. Slender an strong. Shiny brown hurr, an dukshell eyes. Stout legs, strong teef. Yur spirit chose its flesh well . . . But why she want those splay futs, an a booboon snout?'

The girl doesn't know, or els won't tell. Skwatted, she's rocking shaded from my site on Blind's far side.

'Hush!' Blind warns. 'Chile is shy.'

'Nothing pryvut about her nose,' I protest. 'It's plain for all for see, in the muddel of her face.'

Blind strokes the girl's hurr an cluks. 'Too more summers, then yu'll cum a woom-man.' Foresite mixes sadness wiv warmf.

'If the cats don't get her, or the shrinks,' say I. 'What wud yu want, Pod? If yu lukky an live for grow?'

'What?' The chile spits, as thow gobbing out a bitter pip.

'Well . . .' I say. 'Yu cud grow prutty, or stay like yu are. Yu cud be barren, or purbly have chiles yur own. Yu cud have a bear's-claw necklace, or wear a bone of bewty thruw yur nose. Yu cud carve yurself in legend, or barely leave a scratch. It's up for yur spirit for choose. The future is yurs. I shan't interfere.'

'If I mite,' the chile says clear an shrill, after a paws for muttered thorts, 'there's things I'd like best of all, that only yu can give . . .'

'Ask,' I indulge. 'An it's yurs.'

'I'd like yur ears, then.' She smiles. 'For remember yu by. For wear on a fong around my neck. An I cud carry yur scrotum as a tiny powch.'

'Ha!' I clap my hands an larf. 'They're yurs all reddy. Only wait till I'm ded.'

But she's up an clambering down the crag.

'Wise chile,' I nod. 'Sharp tung, cleva hed, sour mouf . . .'

Blind's begun chewing on rabbut. I wriggle up an put my gawping mouf close, noddy like a peevish hatchling, skwawking for be fed. All the time I'm watching hard – how many chews she swallows an how much she skwirts down my throwt.

We'd juss begun for talk. An thow we kwick for see each uvva, we wur slower for call ourselves names.

Well, look at anuvva an see too much. Evry skinfull's too much for be said. Most fowks have a living, free limbs an a face untold.

Distance shrinks us in uvva fowk's eyes. All ways has. All ways will. For Far respecks nyva age nor strenf. It favurrs the wise no more than the fool. Juss blurrs them up, all alike. Yu wander close an see the shape a spirit has made for itself. This wun stretches for the air, that wun spreds for grip the ground. See this ungarded back, those burdened shulders, these swell breasts, those tite, mean thys, sum stiff necks, slack bellys, loos-legged gait.

See the bends an curves, swells an dips. Each has its leans an stance, a bandy-legged hobble, a slender grace, a shuffling slouch. See the Hoggish man, Deer woom-man, an Skwirrulling chile.

As they draw near, watch the darkness slide from their face. Yur eyes meet, or glances graze. Suffur the cold lizzurd stare, but smile for calm those skittery, kind doe-eyes.

61

Read their temper. Becaws the face can't hide an shows more than it knows. Brow is moved by a mind behind. Nostrils twitch wiv spirit. Mouf splits for betray its insides.

Now he stands at arm's lenf. The breeze of his scents wafts up yur nose. Yes, yu don't have for sniff the soursweat underarm, or fishy matted bush, for know this wun apart. The beads of swet on his brow are enuf, wivout the uvva sour moists. His breff gusts into yur face. Yu can taste the savurr, an know what he last ate, wivout effen eyeing the gooey trickle from its lips, or knowing it's a roach leg, or fish eye, wejd between them yella, broke-up teef.

That is their very own patturn, sepert an purtickler as evry egg – those freckles, speckles, pits an pocks of fly bites for their shulders. An did yu eva see the like, dangling so, free parts uncertain, or yawning langwid, between a pursin's legs? Uvvas may have simlar, but no wun's got the very same.

Reach out for a hand. See that taper for the fingurs, the crinkled skin of the nukkels, the tufty hurrs, the trove of sluj beneef its nails. See the tiny pores of skin. Peer close. Anuvva wurld is stowed wivin.

Yu cud spend a day gazing up those nostrils. An neva get near the bottom of them, understand their fullness, or know them inside out.

This wur our mistry. A skinfull of pursin's too much for be spoke. So whateva their given name, most evrything stayed untold or got badly said.

Take Hare, but the name don't catch him much. All it tells is a crazy spirit an a split lip. His calling neva paws for say what matters – that he smells spirits passing, or catches mows in his teef in the dark, by lissening sharp for their scurrying claws, or that he perches up trees, an talks for unborn sowls as they drift past on the wind. An there's nothing for his calling for say the seffern cullurs of his hurr.

So we had small trust in peepil's names. As they spoke only breef, an said as much about wurds as ourselves.

Still, we needed call wun for anuvva. So we looked for each uvva, saw what was purtickler, an spoke us apart by that.

There wur hard an fast, fierce names we cud have took – Storm, Bear, Sun, Ice, Mire, Hyna, Fog, Lion. But we neva saw ourselves so sly, bold or strong. When a buzzurd's got more cunning, an a skwirrull's kwicker, an a blow-fly's braver, then fowk look for their faults, an pride hadn't crawled amongst them yet.

Wun-ear had the uvva wun chewed off. But we broke his name for Ear. Which told of his remaining lug, neva hinting at the missing wun. But later we took for calling him Skinks. Sins he got a scaly skin, hasty temper an a lizzurd's lonesum manners.

Gooz hissed plenty. An I'll tell yu what her name all ways forgot for say, that she wur stout wiv too hevvy breasts, but only wun tit. As she'd lost a nipil suckling Flewk. An it neva grew back. While Free had free. She wur small an yung wiv a furry chest an slender fingurs. The woom-men fed her, but nun remembered birfing her or when she cum amongst us. This wur our dim, clowdy way then. Fowk came an went, carried away by death or their legs, an there wur nothing strange in that.

Flames had a tangle of red hurr an a hot way about her . . .

'My muvva?' asks Blind. 'She the same Flames?'

'Yes an no,' I say. 'I tell it all later. The passed won't be hurried. She only confides when she's good an reddy.'

Potto got the pot belly of a pecry, the gulp of a guppy, the bobbing hed of a crake. But uvva ways he looked the spit of a potto, cumplete wiv swagger, whiskus an black-tunged smirk.

Duk had a busy, wide-legged waddle, her thys so brawd she cudn't bring her nees for meet, so yu always knew her prints apart by the spred of her futs.

Green-eyes had a cool, mocking look her own. Moonsik took herself off sly-eyed, moaning wheneva the moon wur full, an offen when it wasn't, but the dark wur sumwhere in it.

Wurm's legs wudn't move him, but Broke wur broke all over. Raw's chest wur a dripping, weeping wound. If he wur sum small parts rotten, he wur still good by an large.

Carf, my muvver, wur bony. She looked kindly but startled. Hare's mouf wur split up for his nose – an seemed for smile a deal, most when he got sorrurs. Towd's skin grew scabs an warts. But the blemishes on Coot's speckle chest wur soff, an her breasts wur smoov, freckled delickut an prutty as coot eggs. So yu offen felt moved for stroke them. No reasun, sept yur fingurs wud reach for them fond, sins yur eyes wur drawn for them luvly.

Crow had the skwawk of the burd, an a long crest for his hed where his hurr rose up as a rij.

Bruvver Mows wur small an skweaked plenty. But he had a strong hart an sharp hurt inside him. There wur a hole inside his chest the very shape an size of anger, so it always found a perch.

I went nameless a long while till fowk ansur for my shrieks, calling me Hoots, becaws of the noise. But then they took for calling me Gob, by way of my mouf. Then they changed it for Gobs. As I sounded for have more than wun, an cuffed me ears for kwiet me, which struk me as a fine name, sins a mouf is a good opening, an there are wurs bits of a body for be named after, an I neva minded being sevral, being better pleased by me calling than uvva chiles, called Flewk, Lowse or Leech for being small, suckly an clingy. Or Egg, who wur slow, plump an smoov.

But we barely noticed the slinking Shadow. An seldum spoke his name.

'My muvver Carf . . .' I mumble.

'Yes?' Blind asks.

'Got taken urly . . .'

I wur still small an low. She wur scarcely grown.

The drips cum thin her, then the shrinks took her.

Wun red-dawn she topples over by the trunk of a Yurra tree. The breff gon from her. The gust of her spirit blows out in a final grunt. She slumps, legs splayed. Her redded eyes stare still an ded. Her mouf sags open. Growing tired of her weary body, an famished, her spirit has flittered out.

The nobbles of her nees are wider than her thys.

Mows an I crouch close for looks.

'She wur wasted by hunger?' Blind asks.

'She wur shrivelled by sickness. But food wud have helped . . . yet she wur too prowd for ask us.'

'But?' Blind asks.

'No,' I explain. 'She wur too far gon, too weak for forrage. Soon she lost the will for steal. That wur her mistake.'

'Ha?' asks Blind.

*   *   *

'Hu?' asks bruvver Mows, poking her ribby chest wiv a stick, for see if she wud move. Becaws she's sprawled strange an still.

'Agh!' I advise. 'Gon!'

'Whaa?' he asks of the britening sky.

'Whaa! Whaa!' I agree. Indeed. I howls.

Sumthing fills me – thick, clotted an black. In my hed I see her live, plump in urlier times. That woom-mam nursed me at her fat wetpaps, sat me on her soff lap, an led me by her callussed hand. An thruw the cold moons she had tossed me scraps of food. Offen, I'd turn for find her watching me, a far interest swivelling her eyes, following my tottering steps, till I grew strong enuf for feed myself. She has given me my first pokey stick, shown me how for suck an egg, sepert out the seeds an chaff, peel a locust, crack open bones, smile an larf.

The same sadness spikes us both. So Mows an I fall on each uvva an weep our loss. We smear each uvva wiv hot, salty tears. We howl. We frash our legs in the dirt, nash teef, chew filth, an crack our heds on stony ground.

This is rite. Fowk gather round, an chuckle till they cry. For see small tottering childrins greefing so, lowd, hart-felt an trickly wet.

'Fowk larfed?'

'So they needn't cry,' I explain. 'Well, better mockry than misery. They had trubbles their own, wivout shuldering ours.'

By the time the sun burns overhed, all the wet hurt of it is skweezed out of us, like water from a gord. So Mows an I fall still, our faces dried, scabbed salty. Then we think of ourselves. An consider Carf's left-overs. We know we muss show our respecks, by tending her remains.

'What did she leave yu?' Blind asks.

'Only what her bones stood up in.'

'Yu neva . . . ?' Blind gulps while she gesses, han for mouf, as thow gagging.

'Fowk thort diffurnt then. Manners wur ruff. We showed luv in our urly, clumsy ways . . .' I spred my empty, innocent palms. 'I wud neva have thort it for myself . . .'

*   *   *

We'd seen elders care after their ded. We know what shud be dun.

But I fear a fite will cum of it. My bruvver is my flesh. But his spirit is spiteful an no kin of mine.

So it is, we scowl an skwabble, disputing our muvver's left-overs. As she had no way for promiss or porshun what she had for pass on.

Mows reaches for his cutting stone, slashes out an shakes it at me. His face is twisted wiv rage an hate, as thow he's defending from sum buzzurd a hare he's juss slayn. So I step back. Mows is a wilful hed taller, an a nose less. He knows Anger better than me. An I can neva wressel his Greed, so I stand aside an watch Mows take his pick.

He hacks off Carf's nose an digs thruw her ivory ribs. He tears her chest open an plunges in his hands for pluck out her hart. He knew juss where it was.

'Aaah!' says Blind, drawing her hands tite for her chest. 'Why?'

But I knew well enuf what Mows ment. He want for clutch all a muvver's luv for himself at last. An, then again, cumplete his face.

It is pityfull for watch. He holds her nose for the gape in his face, trying for make it hold, panting, snuffling eager thruw nostrils not his own. As he gnaws on the uvva handfull – a black ball of gore.

Myself, I muss make the best of what is left.

I neel shaking by the stiffened body. Sun is high an hot, but I shiver low an cold.

'Don't!' Blind says. But her warning sounds an age too late.

Strange. It's only a carcass, torn an ripped. But it still looks most parts like Carf on the outside, all thow she's long gon out.

Taking a crushing stone, I split open the skull an scoops out the grey, red-rippelled jelly of brain. The mouf is set firm in a yawn. I have for crack the jawbones, for sever the tung at its fibruss root wiv a cutting ej of flint. An I think long an sad of Carf as I chew on this an that, still warm.

But I have small hunger in me. As sorrur has gobbled my appetite.

Yet I can't bear for be alone or leave her there outside me.

Yes, I took her wisdum into myself. So part of Carf lives on in me. Now she thinks for me in me hed, effen as I sleep. Sum nites I can't stop her feeling thruw my dreams. I can tell yu what she knew. But I won't say the full of it, sins much is secrets between a muvver an her son.

** | The dumb

'Gob . . . Gob . . .' The wurd's flown across the lake, thruw the woods, up the slope, finding me in my hidey place, crouched behind the rock. Wurd flutters down, perching on my ears. It cum upon me kwick as an eagil swoop, an thow no eye cud see me there, hugging stone, cowerd in a wrap of shadow.

My name had stuck close by me all summer. So it knew my ways an where for find me. Yet it didn't call for me frendly now, but had turned harsh, skwawking against me.

'Feef! . . . Flea!' Yes, too more wurds followed in the wake of my name. They'd cum bad-moufing me too, accusing. They wur angry, nipping me sharp, like talons on my scalp, an my teef slice into my lip, as I mutter, ansurring back for the nips of them.

Frets follow, warning what cums, when I meet the mouf that spat them out.

It's Potto who shouts me, I know. I cud hear the brawd chested ruff in him, reddy for hurt. Anger clung spiky for sound.

He'll be wanting the hare he cort. But it's gon missing an can't be had. As my hands passed it over for me mouf, which let me teef have their bite of it, befor passing it for my throwt, which gave it for my belly, which cud neva look out for itself, or feel itself eva full enuf.

Wurds bred an spred kwick as lice. There wur biting, itching, scratching, picking, soreness an bickering. The shrill barbed sounds wudn't let us forget.

Wun wurd's slite enuf an lite. Juss spit it out – like an ant strayed onto yur tung. But when yur hed is a crawling nest of them, they hevvy up for a load yu can't litely shrug off.

Yes, wurds wur waying me down. My neck ached, cumplaining the strain. My shulders slumped. My back wur bent from the carry-

68

ing. The burden slowed me. I cudn't move so nifty now, laden down wiv Talk.

Uvvas felt it simlar. Yu saw peepil paws puzzild in their tracks, gon all swivel-eyed an dreamy. Becaws a wurd had howled out in their hed, like a chile screaming for muvver. Or muvver bawling for her chile.

But it wurn't the wayt of wurds that trubbled us most, nor their wet-eyed screams. The itchings wur the wurst of it.

Wurds cum crawling thruw our thorts, in prickly, winding lines. An wud stop at nothing, knowing no barrier. Then when yu try for block their path, there sudden cums a swarm of them, gnawing away, insisting for chew a way thruw.

Yu have a site in mind. Like the face of yur bruvver Mows. Then wurds cum trotting out for chew it up, swarming all over. Each nibbles away like a termit, biting off a snip of the site, having it off in its pincer jaws.

Yur scowling bruvver in mind has lost his missing nose. Then the red-blotched ears are gon. Nex the tite mouf. After, the glowering eyes. Till there is a bit-up mess. Then no site left at all. Juss hunny-wax holes in yur murmury, an a trail of termits, trujing hed for tail, then slid away down a dark crack in the parched ground of yur mind.

Then yu knew, sure, that Talk had taken against yur eyes, snaffling yur sites from spite.

Yu think yu are free of wurds. But, sudden, anuvva line of them scurries out, for search out sum new seeings for eat. An yu wince from the drum-beat of the tiny pinching futs, inside yur frobbing hed.

Bruvver Mows wur trubbled bad. By wurds in his hed. Offen I came upon him banging his brow, or wiggling a fingur in his ear, for try for ease the scratchings an kwiet that russling noys.

'Itchit?' I ask.

'Shh!' he hisses. 'Wurss!' he whines, rolling his eyes, whimpering soff an hurt as he clawed away at his bludred lugs. Then he's taken for dropping his hed on his shulder, clowting his brow wiv his fist, trying for shake them out. Still he cudn't loos them, the wurds from his ears.

I saw there wur no soov nor cumfort bin had this way. For him, for me, for yu. Be warned. Lurn by Mows. When it cums for trubblesum wurds, scratchings only makes it wurs.

Of caws it wur bad for Skinks.

'Go on, then . . .' says Blind. 'Spit it out. If yu muss.'

Skinks's sunken eyes an swollen cheeks gives him a peeved, puzzild look. Anger offen stings him. Yu see the same spit-face when yu surprise a gowfer at the mouf of his burrow. Yu neva look long at Skinks. He sees a taunt in evry stare. Cum on him dripping by the lake, best look away sharp. Yu know he's bin ignorant again, an cum away vexed – from stalking his insolent, unblinking look-back thruw the shallows, befor leaping for seize it, wresseling it for the silty bottom, where the slippery prey turns watery between his grasping fingurs, an he splutters up empty-handed, which is sure for turn his temper wurs, as the same face cums scowling back at him, only more furiuss than befor.

A restless, windswept spirit stirs Skinks. He isn't wiv us when we first start talking. He'd trujd off wun sunrise, when the lemin grass wur sprowting. The frushes wur warbling shrill – sum crazy joy their own – but we fowk wur still days away from it, chattering ourselves. We'd watched him leave. We felt the loss of him, as he shrunk out from our site. But by sun-hi we'd kwite forgot him. His mistake wur for leave us no wurd. For remember him by.

So that nite Crake looked about her puzzild, finding herself alone wiv herself. She ambled round in circils as thow looking for sum thing she dropped, then settled herself by sprawling down wiv Broke insted. An it wurn't long befor they lay low, lowd an eager, an wur both glad, fore times. But as they hugged together, an the fire lit their frusting flanks, an twitchy faces, we neva saw nor heard them. Which wur rite. As they neva heard nor saw us nyva, gathered round them, unblinking, blive.

We're glad enuf when Skinks returns in the Willow-Moon. He stands glowering at our ej, waiting for our smiles for wellcum him in. We swarm for sniff him well, good an close, front an back, mouf an muddel, an fingur the bumps of his brow, smile at his lost ear, an admire him all over, reminding ourselves of our lost parts found. We feel entire again, an are content. Sept Broke watches thruw slit eyes, growling kwiet, an crawls apart, while Skinks swaggers, wiv pride alongside, face wrinkled smug. As he's hunted strong. Over his shulders hang rabbut pelts an a deer skin. From each hand he swings a ded howler by its stiff claw futs.

Crake beams, seeing his face again, an remembering the suckullens of howler from happy eatings long befor.

'Howler,' says Crake warmly. 'Howler.' She counts them. 'Pelt. Pelt. Skin. Skin. Pelt.' She eyes his catch, approving. 'Tired? Laywe? Jerky-pokey?'

Now Skinks knows he's in trubble, sunk over his neck. Becaws fowk are joined together in sumthing skwijy he neva firmly grasps. So his face goes ox-arse crinkly. Besides, he's blinking scared. It's as thow he doesn't know us. Sins we are sounding off so kware an shrill, gon rawcuss wiv our Talk.

He'd left us befor we spoke, an cum back for find us skwawking like hungry crows.

We don't see it rite off. Our new soff wurds are old firm frends for us. It felt as thow we'd always known them. So it's this mute man who seems the stranger.

'Giveus,' offers Hoopo. 'Sharem,' he invites, stroking a howler's furred ears, then sniffing a drip of its blud, fresh curdled. 'Slugs?' He offers up a ripe, ded handful. 'Towdstool?' he tempts.

Having gobbled so much large meat, Skinks mite hanker after small fare, for a change, glut on our admirings, then gorge on our gratitude too.

'Feastwe!' says Flames. 'Rowstem,' she offers.

But Skinks rocks silent, jerking his bewildered hed. I seen the same puzzild fury on a face wunce, much later, when I give a booboon a stone appel I carved. An he threw it back, hurtfull, my way.

Yes. Skinks got his meats. We got our wurds. Only we can't pass wun for the uvva.

Then we see the dum gape of his mouf, hear his hurt scream of silence, an then we understand.

So we're cackling wiv larfter.

Skinks screws his redeyes shut. A howl cums, which sounds his sorrur clear, but juss can't talk our common sense.

He turns, barging us aside, flailing out, battering us wiv the ded wayt of his meats. Then he's fled.

When he later shuffles back for view, he circils us wide, scowling, slumping a stone's throw beyond us, gon surly. He turns his face from fowk an took a long lonely meal. But too full-grown howlers are too much for the most cavernuss belly. Those meats gavè him no joy. It brort him only solitudes an numbaless separations.

Only Crake left Speech for join him. We saw her whisper in his ear. This wur her mistake. The skwawk of wurds wur too much for Skinks. Envy an Anger rose in him. Becaws thow he wur strong in body, he wur booby-puny in his tung.

He buffets Crake ruff on her nose, making blud spurt. He bit a lump from her lip, then clamped a hand over her mouf for have it stop bludding an skwealing.

He muss have gessed we wur talking about him, behind his back. But he neva knew what we wur saying.

We wud have called him names. But wurds wur wasted on that wun. How cud we talk for a man who wudn't lissen?

As Mows wur grown, in teef, temper an tall, so fowks took for calling him Ratz. Naming him after all rats, sins he wur not so much like any sepert rat, but like sevral cum together.

'Hed-sore?' I asks him. 'Fowl-mouf?' There's a suffuring slicing the brow of a bruvver, as urf-breff spat sky-tears into our wincing faces, an I'm frowning, startled by the new sense I've said, savurring the tingling taste of sounds, cuppling in me mouf, suddenly uncertain – wheva it wur I speaking wurds, or wurds speaking me.

'Hard-hurts!' Ratz sniffs. 'Stony-greef.' He shows a crustblud hand. Yes, flints had struck back at him, while he wur crushing them.

'Of caws, it was Wurm who wur hurt hardest by wurds . . .' I sigh at the murmury. I wince at the eckowing splinter of bones.

'Wurds gave him greef?' Blind gesses.

'Juss the wunce,' I say. 'When they bit his hed off. In a manner of speaking.'

Wurm an Potto had cum on a cash of hunny, after watching the cummings an goings of bees. Sweetness wur hid high in the hollow of a Yurra tree. Yu got for be cleva for find it. Bees are jellus sly. Wheneva they find hunny, they hord it for themselves.

Potto stood on Wurm's shulders, pushed damp leaves in the hole, lit them for a smulder, then both went back a way for watch. Shortly, the bees wur stunned by smoke. A bee got prick an he's brave. He fites fierce, in force, for the death. But a swarm of singed bees are no match in strenf or wit for too men wisely slid from site, hid from the stings of blame.

The fire had give a warmf an smokey savurr for the hunny, an scared it enuf for run. Wurm an Potto wur licking hot trickles from sticky fingurs.

They wud have wrapped it up in fronds, bringing it back for share wiv us all, an neva eaten it all themselves, but hunny sticks, an tugs apart in eager hands. Yu lick a fingur, then anuvva. Shortly, yu're up for yur elbas in it, bogged down in sweetness, gummed up wiv joy. This wur their mistake – neva hearing the cat cum, till he's snarled behind their backs, for win their ears. Potto turned an fled, only pawsing for look back from the upper branches of a weeping Ocka.

He saw Wurm still sitting, sunk in the ground. Wiv his broke-up legs, Wurm wur always slow for shift himself. His licking slows an his smoov brow creases wiv wurry. Then his face lites wiv a twisted smile.

They eye each uvva – the stout, frobbing cat an the ribby, twitchy man. Both are gon kwiet wiv their sepert thorts. Cat smiles his glissening teef, then coffs, for clear his throwt for sumthing els.

Wurm can't flee by fut, but he races ahed in his thorts.

'Ha! . . . Raa! . . . Faa! . . . Stkk!' He breaks the hurt of silence at last, an gurgles an unsure larf, then swallows.

These are urly wurds, lost, best forgotten. But in the urly tung, Wurm wur giving warning for the cat – 'Hello there, Rabbut. Yu'd best be gon. Or I'll slap yur ears. Or maybe wurs.'

It's the way wiv peepil still. We twist talk for say things are better than they are. It's a cunning of sorts. An wit wur all Wurm had for spook a cat.

If he cudn't fite the cat wiv fists, perps he cud better it wiv wurds, shrinking it rabbut-small.

Wurm had spoken strong an plenty befor, wivout any seriuss harm. Loos talk had neva killed a man befor. But Wurm had a weakness. His site wur twisted. He had for strain for see clear. While he wur kwick for make frends of things, he wur slow for see their harm. An he supposed that when wurds wresseled things, names overcum, being stronger than stuff.

But it's a mistake for larf in the jaws of a cat. Lion's spirit is savage, an frendly wiv Pride.

Not-a-rabbut sniffed the air. His amba eyes drew tite for slits of surprise. Then he growled slow, opened his mouf in a lazy yawn, an seized upon the man, shaking the stiffness from his neck, an the hed from the shulders, an started chewing thortful on the skull, like a howler wiv a caribnut. Not becaws he's hungry, but becaws he wants for get inside the shell. So, soon the frewt's cracked open, broke an crushed, an all its jooses spilled. As it is wiv a howler an nut, so it wur wiv the cat an the man. The lion crunched on curiuss, for find whateva lay beneef the skin, clinging round the bones.

There wur trubble both ways. Yu wurn't safe. Talking or staying dumb.

Pride sticks for Skinks, an loiters wiv Crake – those dumbs. They sit beyond our reach, backs turned, shulders twitching wiv flys an disdain. When they turned our way, it wur for throw us red-faced glares.

Skinks takes for wandering a wide circil, burbling lowd, flicking his fat lips wiv stubby fingurs – for show us the folly of Talk, the crazy way of wurds. He waves his latest catch of game – a hare, piglit, or crow – in a shaking hand. He wants us for know he's the clevarest, despite he's dumb.

An we see he eats good an offen, now he has only too moufs for fill. As he all ways lays his fire upwind so that his smoke drifts thruw us. An we hear the spats an spits of fat, dripping down, bickering wiv embers, an sniff the smoke an scorch of crackling meat. An we hush for catch those satisfied clacks of teef slicing thruw suckulent flesh, an see bulging jaws grinding on bones. Then cum burps, an groans of content. As we munch thortfull on wriggling bungo grubs, or suck grasshoppers out from their shells – as wurd-napping had held us from our hunt.

We'd cort only a prickle-ball that day, an wur a long time peeling it, sins it went stubborn sulky, an curled up tite for hide its soff underbelly from our hungry curiussity, an juss skweaked pityfull when we tried for pry it open wiv sticks. Then it took the rest of daylite for us for search our heds for its likely name, till we agreed on Pork-yu-spined, caws it had prickles enuf, an tasted like pig, a littil, but wur small meat, wiv only a trickle of thinblud for it, wunce we'd peeled it from its rind, an it didn't share itself generuss amongst so many moufs, an the bowels of it wur stringy, bitter, so cum dusk there's nothing left for us for chew on, sept a nest of mows pups, an a scattering of bugs, grubs, an a scattering of spines – tiresum for teef an spiky on the tung, which made us think of Crake, an her full fat belly, which cost her no more than her silence, an a bit of lip.

We pretend not for care. Our larfter cums lowd. But brittil, dried of joy. The smoke of Skinks's fire trubbles our nostrils. Besides, his blowted grunts, burps an farts burst hurtfull on our ears.

It's not juss meat he's gobbling. He's chewing away at our contentment too. An gnawing our tie for Talk.

On the third nite, the scents of clay-rowst duk are teasing us crewl. Yu'd have for sink yur teef infor the crackling greasy skin of it, chew on its breast, swallow its hart, crunch on its futs, for understand this. Leaving aside the fevvers, only the beak can't be ate, an effen that yields a savurry tang for a stubborn suck.

Towd thinks for go befor the last morsel of the second duk is gon. He rises, shrugs his scabbed shulders, makes a move wiv his fingur of sealing his lips, an is fled from us wivout a backwuds look, gulped by the dark between us, speakers an dumb, till we see him hop in amidst the shady shapes round the oranj glow of Skinks's fire. Then Starling frowned, skwealing, jumped up an scampers after him. So their numba's swelled for fore.

Well, all we had for say for them wur wurds. An the only thing we cud take from them wur Talk. At sunrise Crow calls out for them, crewl an cutting. Becaws Potto had bin calling out for the mutes, trying for beckon them back. 'Whygo? Cumback! Bringbones?'

Crow shakes his hed. 'Hzzk!' he says, all disdain for Skinks. 'Crrrk!' He moves his eyes for Crake. 'Uurp!' an 'Gwaaa!' he mocks the uvva purr.

We understand, of caws. Crow's returning their beast noises for them. An taking back their names. If they won't share their meats, we won't share our wurds. If they turn their back on Talk, Talk will shun them back. They will be dumb, numbaless things unspoken. No more than animul grunts.

So Skinks is un-named. An the uvva free struk senseless.
The loss ain't slow for show.

Yu can't tell them apart now. When they amble into the distance
for hunt, all fore look alike. Hugging the horizun, they are no more
than dots, an hardly human things. When they return at dusk, for
make their fire, we wonder which is who, having lost the wurds
for tell them apart. An they hunch alike, juss as beasts, lurking in
the dark. An they sound senseless their jibbers an skwawks.

Now they lost their diffurnt names, their sepert ways merge an
twine. Till the fore pursins becum wun pack, like wulfs. So yu
cudn't call them fowk. Not when yu heard their bickerings, skwab-
blings over bones.

An yet we felt a wrench for split. Our wun flesh wur torn. Each
nite they stray furva from us. But still both camps keep the uvva
in site, an well wivin smell, near enuf for lissen.

It wur like nyva side cud bear for part. As they are our passed.
An we are their future. But Talk wur tearing us apart.

* *–> | Storys

We wur closer an furva then, seeing shallower into each uvva's heds, but touching deeper thruw skin. An flesh clung closer for flesh, an fingurs felt more, wiv each eye privy for the pores of evry cheek, the wurls of evry ear, the creases of evry nukkel. Each nose knew evry breff. An our tungs cud taste apart the tang of evry hide. An when yu saw a damp patch, ocha in the yella sand, a breef sniff wivout lowering yurself told who it wur that peed. Or when yu brushed a strand of hurr tangled on a branch, yu knew who'd got snagged crawling thruw the spiny bush. An there wur sevral uvva sepert signs, whispering who dun what.

In the dark, the curv of sound wur touchable around, hard an sharp as rock, wiv mounds of snores an scarps of groans. An the bursts an drifts of scent wur patterned clear an brite as the fevvers on a gawdy duk. So yur nose an ears told who lay where, wiv who, an what wur going where.

So there wur close flesh an closer flesh. An Ratz, my bruvver, wur closest for me. We belonged for no wun but ourselves. Too yung for any woom-man but a muvver, an Carf had gambolled off, for browse Beyond. So no wun reached out for ruffle our hurrs, stroke our heds, loj us in their lap for pick away our lice, whisper our names soff, or palm us tids of offal.

Tredding a path for the lake we followed no body, effen when we scuffed close behind. An no body took after us, effen as they clipped our heels. We scavenged alongside, alone, together, digging vishuss, for unurf grubs an roots.

When fowks clung together, I hugged for Ratz, an Ratz cleaved for me.

As a carcass wur cut, we hooted for be seen, skwealed for be given for, tugging on arms, puckering our baleful faces, rolling wide our pleading eyes, till Potto or Crow tossed us sum small bits

– of bitter spleen, pink-froffed lungs, or chewy scarlet gullet – when most of the best wur gon.

Fowks wud not have us starve, nyva did they think for blowt us fat. So we slinked, too cowering lean things, too parts hungry, like scavenging wulfs, following evry glister trail of spatterblud.

I neva said we wur fond, Ratz an I. Our tie wur titer, an binding wiv pain.

It bickered for food, scoffing on skwabbles an tears. It stung befor it sooved. It ruffed us up more than it smooved. Ratz wud give his last breff for me, but kindness neva held him from clawing berrys out between my clenching teef. I still swallow kwick. It's a lurning I made yung. Wunce the food is deep inside yu, it's all yurs for keep. No wun wants it back or see it eva again.

'Cum?' I ask Ratz.
'Naa,' says he.
'Stay?' I ask.
'Naa,' he sneers.

Becaws Ratz wur as close but prickly wiv wurds as he eva wur wiv me. He kept their cumpany, an gave them no peace. He begged of them, then spat in their face. He called them for him, then howled them gon. Whateva they said, he ansurred back.

Which wur how he cum generuss for Talk, giving for it neva wanting for, wiv his delite for deny, an joy for dispute.

Yes, *no* wur first his wurd. It cum kwick an reddy for him. It fit his mouf exack, like a snail for its shell.

Ratz begun it. I copied kwick.

It bickered an fort its bruvver wurds. It ignored yur name, defied a cummand, denied whateva it cared for refuse, hated whateva it liked, twisting wurds round for face themselves, for snap at their tails.

We wur held in a hard hand, grasped in a fierce grip, as our will wur being emptied from us, like the jellys from an egg.

Wurds wur sucking us insides out. It hurt Ratz hard. He'd all ways splutter an snort if anuvva made him yield or bend.

'Naa! Ratz!' I skweal, as his futs an fists are striking me wild.
'Naa stop. Naa Ratz.' Ratz snorts.

This is stubborn Ratz. He won't stoop for the bidding of a wurd. An he is what he is. Not what sum name calls him. His pride won't have him shrunk for splutters of sound, or breef flickers of sense.

The spirit of Ratz hugged No. But then he had a hed start. Being parted urly from his snout. The taking of his nose tort him loss an hurt. Besides, it made his voice snuffle indistinct. So he had trubble saying 'yes', wivout ending it in the mockry of a sneer or grunt.

He wur fond of saying what things wurn't. He'd neva do a thing befor saying what he wudn't. Uvvas cum kwick for grasp what's ment. After plenty practice, he shorted it, saving needless breff.

'No!'

Or 'No?', which wur Ratz's sideways 'may-be', or 'perps'.

Or 'No-no', which wur a backwud, grujing way of saying 'yes'.

Or 'Neva!', which said no for dawn an no for dusk, denying days ahed.

An 'nyva', which said no for too things all at wunce, while scowling at much els.

An befor long, it wur a habit that spred. Uvvas took for it too, as their own, thow Ratz all ways knew no better than all of them, an spoke no better than anywun.

But Ratz hadn't thort it thruw. No wur a wurd itself. An wurds are wun flesh. They stick together. When a mouf turns on them, they always outflank it. An the more yu shrieked against them, the lowder an angryer they swarm waspy back.

I saw the snare of it too late. An knew we had bin cort.

Wurds skwirmed wivin me, lissening for my thorts. If I wur for speak ill of them, effen kwiet, between me ears for myself, wurds wud know, an tell each uvva. Maybe striking sum harm in me, in revenge.

So I woke screaming wun nite, howling that sumwun had stolen my name, an dropped it under a distant stone that covered a bottomless drop.

Awoke, I shivered silent thruw the nite on it – neva twitching me lips, lest wurds shud hear my thorts.

'Whereme booby?' Flames reaches down, shakes Ratz by his shrugging shulders.

'No-say,' he says, pointing up for his parted kwivering lips. His pinkeyes are welling up wiv tears. Refusal speaks him, an ain't slow for cumplain.

'Wha?' asks Crow.

'No-worss,' Ratz says. 'Mouf-close.'

'What-say?' demands Gooz, scowling at the defiant chile, twisting his ear purpil sore. Yu cud all ways see when Ratz wur clutched by feelings. The pink gaping scar where his nose wunce wur darkened for a bluddy frobbing flush.

'No say. No see . . . Whaabooby?'

Fowks gather close round Ratz, twitchy for hear him speak so, neva having heard so many wurds blow from a mouf, together, in wun breff, an all cum skwirmy, stung by feelings.

'No! No!' Ratz spouts his rage, then invents it a littil more. 'Tung-no-talk. Ears-no-hear.'

But sumhow Talk wur speaking itself, thruw his very own mouf for spite him. He stands bulj-eyed an startled, clamping a hand for his gob, surprised by his bursting wind.

'Where booby?' Flames hisses, narrowing her eyes, gripping Ratz. 'Sayit!'

'No-say-worss . . .' he stammers after the sense of it. 'Worss-say-us. Talk-snares-fowks . . . We worss-food. Worss-hunt-fowks.'

They gaze down at his twisted, straining flush face, urgent for know. Fowks' brows creased, their hands wresseling, scuffing their futs in the sand.

But I understood. Yu muss be a chile for know it. Behind yur back, against yur will, things are decided for yu. An yu are crushed for submit. Fowks force chiles for obey. Now wurds doing it too. Asking what we neva want said, concerning sum lost booby we'd neva see again.

Wurds seem soff enuf, then stiffen hard as flint for prise yu apart. An yu're slashed up, spred open, limp an moist, like a mussel shelled.

Crow bends down for Ratz, staring into his face. He lets out a gust of breff, nodding solem.

'Fowks . . . eat . . . pigs . . .' He says it slow. 'Pigs . . . neva . . . eat . . . fowks. Not-that-I-saw.'

Wurds are scampering fast now. For the slow of ear, their dance wur merged for a blurr.

Crow an Ratz scowl at each uvva, man an boy, locked in their struggle, wresseling wurds an each uvva.

'We-hunt-eggs,' Crow goes on, nodding at the easy way his wurds are running all together now. 'Eggs-no-hunt-us . . . No, I neva see it.' He skwints at the flowing sense of this. His wurds wur froffing out, a pissing stream.

'We speak wurds . . .' Crow taps his lips for show so. 'Wurds neva speak us!'

'No. Worss talkus. Talkus bad.' Ratz shivers. The prey is near now. They've stalked a sly sense a long way. Now they're poised for the kill.

'Cack-mouf-chile!' Crow shakes his hed wearily. He slaps Ratz's ears. 'Piss-hed-boy!' He clowts him on his brow, swatting him down for urf, kicking dirts into his dripsy eyes.

'Whereme booby?' Flames wails on. No, she doesn't care about the birf of storys, or the dance of wurds. She only howls for her missing chile.

'Is that *me* my muvver's missing?' asks Blind.

'Not yu,' I say, 'but yu cum out of it, far behind. In a kware way. Cum the Ice. An for that, yu'll have for wait.'

So I, this old Gob, becum uncle of all storys. Sins Ratz, my bruvver, wur their farther.

Ratz it wur who spoke the first tale, joining wurds together.

'Talk snares fowks. We're wurd meat.'

Blame Ratz if yu will, but he wur only a chile, an neva knew what he wur saying, nyva what wud cum of it. An if he hadn't spoken the first story, anuvva wud have talked it insted, soon enuf.

Sins that day, in my seffernth summer, Talk took over our heds, clogging the darkspace between our ears. An only disputes, deceit, moruls an chatter have eva cum of that.

'We've cum a long way now,' I tell the nodding Blind.

'We have?'

'Oh, yes,' I explain. 'Now fowk can say whateva they like.'

Peepil wur rawcuss wunce storys wur cum into their heds. Tungs wur tiresum. Inventings wagged them. Tales cum thick an fast, small but insisting for start, like a buzzing clowd of flys around a gawping mouf.

* * *

'Yu want for hear the first story eva?' I asks.

'Tell me, then,' she yawns.

'Itchit bad.'

I tell it all. Start for finish. That wur the oldest tale, an got told
offen, lowd wiv feelings, whimpers an scratchings. 'Give me!' wur
anuvva, urly story.

'Ha! Pig.'

Wur anuvva story. But it tricked Potto's stones by running crooked,
that long-lost mottled sow, then hid itself in a tangled thicket. So
it wur lost for the killing. Its happy end escaped us. So we neva
heard the last of it, skweals, snorts an death rattle.

'All gon dumbs.'

That wur anuvva tale. There wur always sumwun moufing off round
our fires. Then anuvva wud lissen, or join in. An talk is juss a
torment of noise, if yu don't see the sense. So the drift of our
endless chatter muss have driven them off – Skinks, Crake, Towd
an Starling. Wun dawn they wur gon, wivout a goodbye wave or
backwud look, leaving only a scattering of charred bones round a
steaming piss-damped fire, an retreating futprints in the lakeside
mud. We stared at the hollowed marks of them lost, trotaway futs.
Then we wept till we stopped.

We neva saw them again for sevral summers. An when we met
again, they cum terbly dumb, an awfull changed.

'Fox killed Bok.'

That wur a longer, later story – tasty too. A big rowsting an many
meats cum of it. We gorged for days on that wun, till the carcass
went fowl, but 'Skull madeit bowl', 'Bladder madeit waterbag',
'Bowels made twines', 'Tail cum a fly-swish'. An such. The storys
are endless when such a cumplete beast gets slayn, holding as it
does so many obliging, hollow parts.

Then Fox gets called Bok, in murmury of his famous slaying.

But 'Bok kills Bok' muddys the trewf of it. Which is the trubble telling storys. Becaws meanings twist an change, effen as yu speak. So for tell it trew, yu muss say it false.

'Sky rained frogs.'

Wur a mistry story. The sky pissed on us all thruw the nite. We thort it rained waters. But when we woke sodden, we saw it had pissed down frogs, sins the shore wur a kwake of shimmering green croaking, all along the rim of lake.

'Locusts chew it all away.'

A trajdy, that wun. The sky darkened as the swarm fell. When the black clowd had lifted all wur chewed away – the bushes, the grass, our hides, the twine binding stones for wood, sum of the hurr of Broke's hed. So Broke went bald as a booby for a while.

'Bald mates buzzurds.'

Wur a ly. But wunce a man asks for mockry the whisperings neva stop.

Whateva a story told, thow, the most part went unsaid. So the more got said, the less wur known. An evry wurd thickened the clowds of dowt. Plenty fog got blown about this way, on the gusts of careless talk.

Yes, it wur like running a path of powdery urf. The faster yu went, the less yu saw, as yur pounding futs kicked up dust, clowding yur eyes. Or chasing a fish thruw the shallows.

The furva yu wade, the more yu muddy the waters, the less yu knew of the fish or yur legs.

No, it wur more like wandering a deep cave. The furva yu went, the darker it got. Wurds wud neva tell the whole story, but laid dark shadows over trewf.

Or, perps, it wur like staring out the sun, which always won. It wur yu that had for blink first. The longer yu looked, the less yu saw, as the dazzle of it all grew blinding.

★　　★　　★

Wun nite, Hare made hystery – raking the cold embers of days gon. He juss plucked passed times, rite out of his hed, an had them moving in wurds.

All thow yu barely saw him move, his eyes rolled upwuds an he wur gon in the inkling, for anuvva place, hills away, moons befor.

'Carf ded. She shrunk,' he grunted sorry, 'an cat chewed up Wurm.'

'Ha? Wher?'

'Passeds. Times gon . . .' Hare tells.

'Wher yu see it?'

'Inside . . .' Hare says, tapping his hed. 'Murmuryns . . .' he brags.

It moved me too. Sudden, I wur back there. His wurds took me back.

Yes, he'd raised the ded. Then had them snuffed out wun more time. We nodded, while our eyes wet our cheeks. Afterwuds we snuffled as we hugged each uvva close. Our thorts wur cum together, the sad same. It wur a trajdy, that story, digging up fowks long buried, near forgotten.

An Flames chilled us by looking the uvva way, forwud for things cumming.

'Leefs falling,' she says.

'They falled wunce befor,' says Crow, 'moons ago.'

'Hottime gon, cooltime cum,' Flames says.

'When?'

'Happen . . .' She shrugs. 'Maybe. Days for cum.'

'Ther many days cumming?'

'Ha!' she smiles. 'Enuf for me.'

But she neva knew, not for sure. It wur gessings mixed wiv hopings, stirred by feelings. Still, pangs of cold touched us. I shivered an screwed my face, looking over my shulder, for chill days slinking up behind us.

Flame cud be rite. Nun cud remember clear, or imagine past tomorrow. Maybe there wur always a cold following on from hot. We'd taken the wevver as it cum. It wur not ours for call or change. Yet there mite be a patturn for it, much like the stripes on an oruk hide. Lite, dark, lite. Like day follows nite. Cud yur mind peer so, around plenty days an nites between, for see so far ahed?

Out of this wur wurry born.

From there, it wur a short way for knowing what-for an how-nex, seeing how things happened, wun first, then the uvva. An we wurn't slow for see the becaws. For things wur tied in nows, an linked by thens. Bound for happen. As an when.

'I neva walk alone . . .' Potto tells. 'Moon follows me . . . I turn an she's cum behind.'

'She follows me,' Crow says. 'Stars too. Whereva I gon.'

'My Moon shrunk now.'

'Mine too. She not all there.'

'She hungry. She hunts sum stars. Then swells again.'

'Yu seed . . . Sun?' Crow asks.

'Up . . . there?' Potto peers up into the thickening sky. But Sun is sunk below their site now.

'Sun gon lay down. She sleeps herself,' Crow confides of his frend. 'She hate it dark. She only show her face when it cums lite.'

'An she hate it cold.'

'She do?'

'When it cold she hides. She wrap herself. In clowds.'

'Keep herself warm?'

'That so.'

'Yu hear that blow?'

'Brr!' Potto slaps himself against the chilling breeze. 'Blow restless. Blow angry.'

'He got no place for stay. No home. No fire. No frends.'

'He pushes those clowds around.'

'He jellus.'

'He bends them trees. Shakes them ruff.'

'Trees is slow. Only wind stirrs them.'

'But rocks is slower.'

'Rocks is hard. Rocks is lazy.'

'They lay still. Nothing moves them. They're hevvy wiv their sorrurs.'

'Ha!' Crow nods wise for them.

'Yu seed those . . .' Potto struggles for grasp the wrigglers. '. . . fish . . . fishus . . . fishusses?'

Crow gulps like a guppy, staring cold, for show he knows them too.

'They breff water, not air.'

Crow nods. 'Got no legs for walk them. Juss flap about on land.' he tells.

'An burds!' Potto says. 'Yu eva seed them?'

'Hu?' Crow flaps his arms in fevered copy. But he can't raise himself, lacking a burd's cunning, sincerity an fevvers.

'Those them,' Potto agrees. 'They skid on air. They slide on sky,' he says.

'They move cleva, but think stupid.'

'Ha?'

'Burds shriek plenty. But they neva lissen.'

'How yu know?'

'See those burd-heds.'

'Hu?'

'They got no-ears!'

An both men shake their heds in pity at the folly of burds. For thow we fowks are urfbound, at least we paws for think in our ears.

My tired hed heard much first said, deep into nite, as the fingurs of sleep reached out for clutch me.

As the lids slid for shut my eyes, I heard tell of the wants of water, the soffness of air, desires of lizzurds, the sowls of snails, the hevvy harts of oruks, the rumbulling of skystones, the malice of ice, the slyness of shadows, how thunder all ways chased litening, but neva cort it, the tacky luv between hunny an bees, how murmurys are scars an scabs in our heds, cut by the sharp slashes of time, why lice luv peepil an will neva leave us, why the porcupine's kwills point out, why fish all ways go slimy an cold for us, an how yu know the clowds are cuppling, for yu see them layn dark an thick together, till semen falls, clear as rain.

Then dreams have cort me up.

∗∗–>> | The wurst

Blind's face is a hunter's powch, swirmy wiv live rabbuts. Her fingurs gon flickery as silverfish.

She bobs her hed, twisting her ears for catch the skwawks an skrieks from below.

'Fowks skwabbling,' she says.

'Again?' I ask. 'But they dun that day befor.'

'Ain't gossip this time.'

'About hats, then? Whose is gaudiest an such. Or who stinks best?'

'Not hats, nor prutty smells. Not necklaces, nor bewtybones.'

'Then they found Blew-Nose in the bushes again? Doing it wiv Gote?'

'Not them, nyva. Peepil skwabbling about Rock-fowk, if I hear rite.'

'Rock-fowk! . . . They took Skwirrul-boy long ago. We saw his futprints led up for a fire an charred bones. But them legs of his neva walked away.'

'They stole Bud,' says Blind, 'brewsed her ruff, used her bad an offen.'

'They're no better . . .' I paws for ponder the wurst. '. . . than us,' I conceed.

'We snuffed free of them,' Blind reminds. 'It's tid for tat, fum for tow.'

'But the look of them . . .'

'What about them?' Blind asks. 'In purtickler?'

'They got brown teef. Hurry faces, brissly stumps – like tails.'

'Well . . . evry family's got its diffurnt look,' Blind says. 'Fowks aren't all ways wun shape.'

'They got few wurds. An littil sense.'

'Sum peepil talk more than uvvas,' says Blind. 'But they wave their hands. They're neva slow for grunt. Pursins can speak sevral ways . . .'

'Where's their music, then? What their moruls?'

'They sing together. They wail for the ded. They gard their yung. They share their meats. They paint their flesh.'

'No,' I say. 'They roll in mud. They larf at blud. An calling them fowk neva make them so. They ain't us. Not for my eyes. Not for my nose. Yu can ly wiv a River woom-man, but Rock-fowk . . .'

'Yu bin wiv them, then?'

'Neva.' I wince. 'Not me.'

Only the wunce, when I lay down wiv a Rock woom-man, lonely after the Flud. I brort her a gooz-wing hat for prutty her hed.

'Huhu,' says she, grabbing it, pulling it apart, an starts for eat it. But it stuck its fevvers in her throwt, so she coffed it up, matted, sticky.

When we cuppled, she wud not cum well pleased, juss rolled her eyes, skwawked her surprise an larfed.

'Huho, haa, haa,' she says, like she's being fevver-tickled, fluffy lite. Thow I wur swetted by my struggle between her legs.

Her thys rubbed me raw. An her paps wur brissly as ratskin. Her armpits smelt of ded crabs.

When she'd had enuf, she sat on me hevvy as rocks, crushing all the breff from my chest. I wake yelping. She's tugging my fingur nails out wiv her teef, smiling for herself, happy as a chile plucking berrys from a bush. She wur the only woom-man who eva left me sore an brewsed. I wur sum small bits the looser, by lying down wiv her.

'Shame's a stranger for Rock-fowk,' I warn.

'Fowk are talking of going for them, making them frends. Taking sum gifts, smiling soovy, talking nice.'

'Not me,' I say. 'My legs won't have it. Yu won't get me walking harf a day for be clowted by sum ruff booboons. Then rowsted on a spit. Not at my time of life.'

Blind hushes me, straining for hear. 'Smile says fowk shud go. Flints says no. Mist can't decide.'

'The Passed warns plenty,' I say, 'but fowk won't hear.'

'We made frends wiv the River-Peepil,' says Blind. 'We cum wun blud.'

'Yes,' I conceed, 'but remember the hurts that cum befor that –

trying for shame the Bears wiv our generuss gifts, then friten off the Ice.'

Yes, there wur plenty fowk neva knew when we wur fresh – why pain? Why winter? How we are cum? Where go we? How will it end?

Wivvered for cracked levver, I know better. All is repeated. But evrything gets changed. This is snuffed. That is born. We are each a skinful of offal. An soon we will die. But at first this wur hidden as the morning from us. An the ignorance served us well. An hopes swarmed thick an furiuss for it, like buzzing flys for fresh, steaming dung.

An sins we fowk wur so fresh born for this Urf, our spirits had neva bin befor. An so we tottered dazed as childrins, awkward, unknowing, unprepared.

Yu don't have for be wise for see it. The most pityfull sowl on Urf is an egg's. Becaws an egg knows what's cumming for it in life. Its spirit has bin crushed too offen befor. Egg has no legs. He can't see nor hear, nor run an hide. He has no mouf for feed himself. He got no sticky parts for cupple wiv. All he can do is wait, until a burd cums for sit on him, an plant its seed wivin, for gobble him from inside. So the egg can neva grow. An only a pest of a burd can cum of him. An a crushed scattering of shell. So egg juss lys there, langwid melancholy. He neva effen trys.

It's the same wiv stones – their bodys so hevvy, the only way for them is down. So they only tumble or slumber cold. Their spirits have no enthusiasm, for they can make nothing of themselves. Only breaking for smaller pieces. So, howeva hard yu move them, they ly again for rest, an soon are fell for sleep.

Pleshurs an pains cum an went as they wished, mistrys then as now. Plenty got shared an felt together, so when wun cuppled, too did. An when the man wur finished, the woom-man wur.

If wun pursin wur hungry, we all felt it. For food wur taken an given for share.

But we knew there wur only a thin spred of pleshur in the wurld, for be shared about. An not enuf for evrywun for have sum all the time. So, if yu took too much for yurself, sum unhappy sowl wur sure for be going short.

*　　*　　*

89

I wur loaf for smile when Ratz wur about. He'd gon grabby for my feelings, greedy for seize any joys for be had.

'Yu got happy, muvver's-blud?' He sniffs suspishuss.

'I have sum happy in me. A smear of it. It warms my hed, calms my belly, shivers thruw my legs,' I giggle. The sun wur high, the breeze wur kind. The scent of buds an grass wur fresh an sweet.

'I had sum happy . . .' He jerks a hand at me. '. . . until I saw yur face. Then it wur gon like a slippery fish. Yu took happy from me. Yu stole it for yurself.'

'No!' I wail, gessing what cums nex. Then he's slapping my face too-handed, till I sob.

'Ha!' A smirk lites his face. 'I have it – happy – now. I took it back for myself.'

An, trew for his wurd, he had. While misery wrenched my face.

Hare wud slouch off downcast alone. But cum back happy enuf, wiv rolling eyes, staggering, facing back our stares wiv smiles. An gurgled, rocking back an forf, when he thort we'd stopped watching him, which we hadn't, getting wise for him.

So we took for wondering where he went, an what joys he snared an where. How he wur cum so happy wiv himself, when we cudn't squeez much pleshur from him.

'Where he get that smile?'

'He find hunny? Keeps it all?' Duk suspects.

'He cupples sumwun?' asks Crow. 'He found a new way for do *it*? But he ain't said.'

'Cort a piglit? Ate it all himself?' Broke cluks.

But Hare juss lay there, in a snuffling sleep in the circil of our gathered futs. Then we sniffed his evry part as he twisted snorting.

But it wurn't a woom-man, not that we cud smell. Thow a taint of pepper-grass clung all over, most suspishun attached for his lips. Fife noses wur lowered, sniffing curiuss his face as he panted his stale breff, an ten eyes watched. There wur a sour sweetness we cud not name. An sum secret joy had slackened his twitching mouf, so spittle trickled out a murky purpil.

'What?' Potto swept up a daub of dribble on a fingur an sucked curiuss on it.

We all took a taste of the mouf-joos, as Hare twitched on, obliv-

90

iuss. There wur a frewty, musty, rotting taste, wiv a tart bite, back of throwt.

Then we knew he'd found sum sleepy pleshur he'd clutched secret for himself. But thow Potto kicked his ribs, for wipe the smile from his face, still Hare neva woke, juss snuffled on, curled up for a booby-ball, sucking a fum.

'Sleep good?' Crow asked Hare nex morning. 'Dream far?'

'Good an far,' Hare agreed. But he winced an rubbed his brow, then felt tender his brewsed belly. 'Fell me down. Ground tripped me . . . Thirst me strong.' He stumbled down for the lake, an lay gulping a long while, oddly dry, shaking his hed befor lapping more.

Fowk threw hard glances at his back. There wur muttering an scowling. But still Hare wurn't telling. Which wur why Crow an Potto took for following him, slivvering behind thruw the grass, lying long behind bushes, watching Hare's doings.

'Why he?'

'What it?'

The whispering watchers cudn't see the sense. It seemed a spoiling of ripe frewts that, any ways, shud be shared. But it's well known now, how for do it an why –

Berrybrew

Take wun large shell an empty out the mush of turtul crawled inside for hide. Eat the turtul. Keep the shell. Its use will cum again, an more. Take ekwal palmfulls of water an berrys until the shell is full. Pound the mix into soup wiv a stump of wood. Have care not for spill round the ejs. Lay on the surface a Yurra frond an sum leefs from a bush of pepper-gorse. Dig a shallow hole for hold the shell. Cover wiv a sprinkling of dried grass, for hide it all from yur fellow fowk. Leave the mulch free days. When the bubbling stops, joos is reddy. Return for drink alone. Sup yurself silly on berrybrew.

When yu go back amongst fowk, walk as steddy as yu can. Say nothing, els yur slivvery wurds an slidey legs betray yu.

We drifted out of the shadows that dusk, surrounding Hare from all sides. He raised his gloomy gulping hed from the shell, showing first a trew surprise, then a poor pretence of wellcum.

'Juss eat me old frewts,' he slurrs. 'Yu want? It well rotten.' Then he twists a face of disgust for diswade us, spitting the joos out lowd. 'Ugh!'

We gathered round. We all scooped a thick handfull in turn.

Yes, it wur rotten frewt, an musty an fusty. But there wur a sweetness in it. An shortly a warmf for the gob. Then a spred of hot for the belly, after a weakening of the legs. But a happy thort slid thruw in its shadow.

My eyes blurred over, an I saw odd hazy shapes as if in a dream.

It took us all diffurnt. Crow began warbling an strode off into the lake. Gooz an Potto wur frendly lowd together. Flames chattered like a fritened howler, scuttling, hooting. Bok an Ratz took for butting heds like musty ox. Only Hare sat sober an still, eyeing it all solem sorry, now all his brew wur drunk.

That's the power of berrybrew. Out of the rot, fresh pleshurs cum born.

Hare found much more later of the powers of roots, berrys an leefs, frendly wiv pleshurs or familiars of pain. But being Hare, he took care neva for be followed again.

But we lurned a strong thing from brew. The rotten wurn't all bad, an deserved its place wiv the raw an the cooked.

Pleshur tort us less than pain. It wur out of hurts we lurned of Bad.

Bad is a twisted, tangled knowing. The senses in it are sevral. So the lurning of it cum hard.

It's all ways Bad for fingur flames. The blame cums burning kwick. It's Bad for hurt a stronger pursin, they will maul yu more blows in return. It's Bad for fall off a rock, for yu can break yur bones as yu tumble down. It's Bad for eat rancid meat – for yu're sure for retch for regret it soon. The Bad in those wur always known.

'Suppose I tell yu my chile's wurst mistake . . .' I paws. 'Yu mussn't blame him too strong or soon.'

'I can forgive a chile most things,' says Blind, 'as long as he's gratefull an shows respecks.'

'No . . .' I suck on it, considering. 'Rude an ungrateful it wurn't. So, be payshent an lissen. It sounds norty enuf . . . Yet it wurn't as bad as wurds have it sound.'

★　　★　　★

Bruvver Ratz an I did it. But only wunce. Not that anywun warned we shudn't. Most men had tried it wunce at least, thow they wur sly in the taking. Our mistake wur in being small, then getting seen. For if there's no wun watching, there can be no telling. Nyva shame.

'But, yes, it wur Bad of Ratz an I for do it . . .'

'Do what?' cowxes Blind.

'Eat it . . .' I paws.

Perps it ain't wise for tell it after all. But it has for be said. So much hangs on it. An if I neva dun it, things wudn't be as they are.

'What did yu eat?' she asks.

Well, that wud be saying.

Still, if I say it kwick, an give her sum cullurs an shapes for think over, perps it won't sound so bad.

'Bruvver Ratz an I . . . we ate wun . . .'

'Wun what?'

'Booby. Son of Flames. Name of Fluke. Remembered long. Plump wun. Blew eyes. Wun hot day in the Dust-Moon. It wur very long ago.'

But the wurds stumble into a sudden silence, shrieking their fall lowd in our heds.

She slaps her ears, then wiggels a ear-hole wiv a fingur. 'I thort . . .' she giggles, 'yu said yu ate a booby.'

'A small wun . . .' I gulp. 'That wur the size of it.'

'Flames's booby?' Blind howls. 'My muvver's chile?'

'That's anuvva story.' Let's not get too blame too kwick. Let's hear things wun by wun.

'Yu ate my bruvver?'

'No . . .' I swallow hard on my sour regret. 'It all cums out, in its turn. I gave back in full for all the Bad I dun. It wurn't harf bad as that . . .'

Trew. For it wur Good in parts, for we wur ravenuss, an we thort no wun saw us steal the howling thing, an we tapped its hed for part it kwick from its breff an pain, so there wur wun less skinfull of suffuring in this wurld, which wur Good. Then we haggled how for split it. Sins Ratz wanted the top for himself, an me for have the bottom. But I said that wurn't kind or rite, as he'd get most soff offals. So, in the end, we shared it down the muddel, after we had washed it clean, becaws it wur sum small parts smeary sticky, but it had too of most bits, being both sides the same, which helped us share fair after our skwabble, which wur Good, thow there wur only wun of sum parts – like nose an hart, that an the uvva – but there wur enuf still for fill too yung bellys well, an the offal of it wur joosy an delickut for taste, but the sweet liver an marrow-jellys pleased us most.

That much wur the Good in it. But the Bad wur sevral more. We ate it raw, for fear a fire wud draw uvvas for share, so we did not enjoy it tender an hot, an the chewy obstinit grissels of it, nyva proply hard nor trewfly soff, wearied our jaws for ache. An sum hard parts wud not be swallowed. An we felt uneasy in ourselves, as thow the flesh wur sum way tainted, an kept looking over our shulders, wheneva we heard a russel in the grass, which soured the pleshurs of the sweet meat . . .

By the end, I'd ate too much for my stomak for hold. An sicked the face an gullet back.

'Aagh!' says Blind, rocking, heaving for retch.

'Yes!' I agree. 'That's how it was. Juss so.'

'Yu animul,' she splutters.

'Yes, evrywun know it's bad *now*. Only we didn't have the moruls then. Not the wuns we got now.'

We thort no wun had seen us catch it. But Flames had bin skwinting down from the hill, shading her eyes from the midday dazzle. So she saw us steal up an take it. Which wur Bad. For she neva forgot nor forgave us. We made an enemy for life that day, juss by eating her chile, an sevral Bads cum after, so the eating of the small thing wur small reward for the trubbles that followed.

A life can be shaped by wun breef yung doing. It dogs me for this day. Flames wur big in herself an close wiv strong men. All of which wur hard an Bad. For fowk flung us for the ground, kicked us, picked us up, hurt us bad wiv fists an hands, sticks an stones. Thow we limped moaning, they gave us no food. So it wur a stupid, impayshent eating, for in the long of it, we lost more food than we'd scoffed in that booby.

*   *   *

'Beast!' Blind hisses.

'Yes, an yu're not alone in saying that,' I agree. 'Uvva said simlar. They made us suffur too.'

There wur no spare pity for us. Thow we wur chiles. An knew no better. Thow we wur swollen an pained. An I wur wun weeping sore from scalp for fut. Then flaky as a lizzurd after, crusted all over in scabs.

Fowk shunned Ratz an I all that hottime. When we spoke they neva lissened. When we walked up for peepil, they turned their eyes away, but barged thruw us like things unseen, sending us sprawling. An neva heard our crys. It wur a hard time, gon invisible, an sent silent so long. The Bad of it lingered, long after the breef eating.

Then I knew that what we had dun wurn't so much bad as *Wurs*. So I spoke for myself strait. An warned myself off it –

'Neva again will I get myself seen amongst those rocks by the stream, no, neva, not eating boobys again. Least, neva wun of Flames's, not wiv my bruvver Ratz – the animul.'

Which wur a well ment morul, far as it went. But wurdy, being a big mouffull, wiv too many nots an nevas for remember. All together. In a row. So sumtimes I cum confused, or forgot the start or the end of it. Remembering only parts – that there wur sumthing I muss not be cort doing. Or sumthing sickening about those rocks. Or I recalled that there wur sumthing strong for know, concerning the eating of boobys. An sumthing terble disgusting about the habits of my bruvver Ratz.

Still, I neva ate anuvva. For the crys of them boobys cum for sicken me strangely. An I cud neva again look wun in the eyes an trewfly see it tasty. For a fowl taint cum into my mouf, an the sour sting of vomut rose up in my throwt.

An Ratz an I wur well cumforted when the Mussel-Moon cum an peepil opened their eyes an moufs for us, cuffed our ears, tripped us down, spat an called us bad names. For at least they spoke for us again.

'Hyna. Booby gobbler.'

'Jackal.'

'Buzzurd.'

Which wur their way of wellcuming us back, as gossip, for the chatter of human kind.

Eating Flames's booby wur the first Wurst thing I did in my life. But I knew no better then, having only too manners, an no moruls for speak of.

Yes, I share the blame wiv Ratz. Moruls wur partly our making. A good wur lurned by it for all. An boobys now sleep safer, becaws of us – lost textures, forbidden sweetmeats, forgotten flavurrs.

Blind's cheeks twitch. She's eyeing me odd, swaying away.

'What?' I ask. 'Yu gon bone-cold?'

'Yu trewfly did that? Ate a booby?'

'It's wurds say so, not me.' I flush at her accusing, all the stinging shame's cum back for me. 'Wurds all ways speak things stronger an wurs than they are. Wurds ain't got the delickussy . . .'

'Yu said . . .'

'Lissen. Or don't.' I soov for explain, 'If yu can't stomak Hystery, I can't speak it. So say now. Becaws there are ties between us that shud be told. They cum out of this . . .'

Any ways, boobys then wurn't like boobys now. They wurn't so dear for fowks. Most died kwick any way. We neva gave them names till their second summer, for fear of wasting wurds.

It wur befor we knew exackly what wur food, an what wur not . . . An when yu think of it, in its old time an far place, yu'll see it wurn't me, nyva, but sum long-lost boy. He clung round my yung bones, but he left my skin long ago. There's no join left between us. Fore or fife diffurnt pursins have lojd in my hide in between. I'm juss an old empty burrow now – plenty foxes have cum an gon, lived an died. All I have left of the boy are the scars. Like this scab on my nee where he fell on sum rocks, being careless wiv my legs. So now I muss suffur, for the sins of that chile.

'But it wur *yu*.'

'That's juss what wurds say . . .' I sigh for explain it. 'Yu, me, I, we . . . As thow fowks neva change or grow, get moruls, cum nice. That's why peepil starting changing their names, wheneva they'd dun anything bad . . . Becaws if we wur still for blame for the yung ruff wuns we wur, fowk wud curl up an die. From shame.'

There's a thick, long silence befor Blind speaks again.

'Didn't yu have any sense in yur hed?' she asks.

'Strange yu shud ask . . .' I say. 'I'm juss cumming for him.'

∗∗−>>> | Over my hed

I offen felt it close, befor I found what it wur, its wants or its ways. A kware itching presence, hovering behind my hed, peering over my shulder, or ruffling my brow.

Like suspishun, it wud not show itself clear, nyva go away.

An I felt a prickly touch for my neck, or hevvy hand sinking thruw the hurr of my scalp. I shiver, stroke my hed, an twist around. It ain't a pursin. Nyva fleas, nor flys.

There's nothing for be seen, but I hear a knowing cluk in my ear.

'What that?' I ask. 'Who there?'

'Juss my self,' a small voice confides. Of caws, most wud say as much, only this wun sounded purtickler, confiding, muffled between my ears, but insisting for be heard.

It offen cum for wake me wiv the greylite of dawn, its chill fingur plucking me from warm sleep. I'm sprung alert by its touch. My ears prickle an my eyes narrow, but there's no more afut than a restless, lost roach, crawling the desert of my chest.

'Ha!' I say. A thort cums for me sudden, as thow wriggled into my hed from sumwhere els. 'I am urf for this roach, as Urf is home for me.'

Then I blow on him an see his legs tug for hold steddy in the gale. An I sneeze lowd as thunder. Then cup my hands over him. An wonder how he explains it, that nite is fallen so kwick.

'Poor dumb bug,' the voice whispers. 'He neva understands.'

Itches an whisperings woke me offen. But I sensed the jittery, gobby stranger ment me no harm. No, I felt its concern for my safety, its kwiet content in my well-being, its keen eye for my surrounds. So when it touched my back, drawing an iced fingur up my spine, I wur warned for look about. For then there'd be sumthing well wurth knowing – futsteps crackling in the bracken, maybe, blud spatters on the grass, or sumthing warm an telling for the nose.

Befor long I'm grown used for my twitchy cumpanyan. I took for sensing its cumming. An felt a warmf I wurn't alone. An the more I wellcum it, the longer it stayed. Sum lazy days it clings wiv me from my waking up for my laying down, hovering behind me, or gazing down over my scalp. So soon we cudn't split us. An for greet wun of us wur for talk for both.

'We are wun,' says the voice. 'In this.'

'This?' I asks.

'Life,' he says.

'Frends together,' I gess.

Not that we neva skwabbled. Becaws he grew restless if I slept long, or kept gnawing a bone long after the flesh wur gon, or basked on in the sun, or I kept on counting my fingurs over again, when their numba wur settled all reddy, beyond any dispute.

'Fife!' voice mutters. 'Now let's move on.'

He wur all ways a curiuss wun. For the more he saw, the more he had for know. So sumtimes I'd find myself sniffing a blossom for tug its sevral smells apart, or gazing on an ant's leg, wondering how its nees wurked, or fondling a rabbut's fur for feel it soff an plush, thow there wur nothing for eat in this, but juss becaws the uvva dawdled wiv the tasteless whim, an wur neva satisfied, but muss find out, poking for see what wur beneef, an then reaching out behind that, for clutch furva beyond.

'Who wur it?' Blind asks.

'A mind,' I say. 'My own. Cum a littil late.'

'Mine gessed as much . . . It takes wun for know wun.' She grunts an nods, palming me a sand-hopper for suck skwirmy from its shell.

Yes, this curiuss cumpanyan wur the cleva in me – searching, an sussing – but it took me time for see as much. For I swear by my last, lingering toof, a creaky, wobbly backwud stump, which I don't care for use, for it crushes my gum, that our minds wur nameless strangers for start.

It's this way.

Close yur eyes. Use yur hed. Think of a dog wiv flees. Or a large fish gobbling a smaller wun. Or a snail clamped on a stone on a rock, clinging on for its crunchy soff-centred life.

But, better, think of a man wiv a rock an a hunger, eyeing a nearby mottled pig, rooting for sum hognuts.

When this man crouches for spring on the pig, he sees only the pig. He don't have a thort for himself, he's so rapt up in his prey, single minded in his hunt. Meanwhile, the pig grunts hopeful. He only has thorts for his nuts. Now all his sense is slid down for the tip of his snout.

An minds are simlar in this, like rooting pigs or hunting men. They don't have a mind for themselves. They watch hard an sharp, neva remembering it's them that's watching.

So, when a man watches a hog, he only knows the hog. An when this man's mind watches the man watching the hog, it only sees the man an the hog. It's too busy for watch itself.

So what is, is more than is known. For what's seen is less than what's there. What wiv the watcher always blind for himself. Our heds being for blame for this.

An eyes don't help, nyva, looking out an away, neva watching themselves, which makes them knowing, an ignorant, but that's the dark hole we fowks are tumbled in, so it's a hard climb scrambling out, an only the beckoning lite at the top keeps yu trying, an that's the sun, all ways beyond reach.

So, becaws our minds wur watching, but hid for themselves, an any way wivout a name for call themselves, we got lost in our thorts, sum ways, so cudn't tell what wur out there in the wurld, an what wur stumbling the gloom between our ears, so there wur stuff insides we thort wur outsides, an things outside we thort wur in, an such as wurds an dreams that wandered between, an suspishuns an fears that trickled in, an urges an pleshurs that fluttered in aimless, befor they flit away kwick, an things that cum for all us minds, an rare thinkings that only reached into a single hed, leaving odd ideas.

Pain tort me this. Yu first felt yur mind by the ache of it, as its mussels strained for grasp on stuff. Yes, our minds hurt our heds hard.

It felt like a feeble hand, folding into a fist, for crush a hard, unripe frewt for skweeze out the joos of sense. But however much wet cum out, yu knew that most still clung in the pulp. Yu strained for harden yur grip. Then furrows formed on a brow. Eyes screwed shut. Grunts an gasps of effort sprung from a gaping mouf. But still yu cudn't crack it, being weak between the ears. So much stayed closed for us. An plenty trewfs wur barely brewsed.

There wur more talking than hearing, for start, at least. The speakers being more than the lisseners. Fowks talked most of themselves, neva needing anuvva's ears.

There we wur, sprawled together on the rock in the sun, fed an safe, wiv only our heds an fleas for wurry about.

'Go on hand.' Crow points for his pocked belly, sending wun mit out for guide the uvva. 'Scratch it good.'

'Louse in me fleas,' says Flames, picking curiuss thruw her lap hurrs, nibbling them bugs that cum for hand, popping them an sucking the jellydrops.

'Toof broke,' Potto shows us, smiling gape-moufed.

'Where me chile? Name it Egg,' asks Moonsik. 'I leave it . . . sum place.' She remembers.

Crow eats strong an runs kwick but, dizzied by the twists an turns of speech, he wants for do evrything out lowd, by way of wurds, effen if he has for cum afresh for what he knew well enuf befor, which had him confiding for his legs how walking got dun, or have his mouf tell itself how for eat, then his gob, doing both at wunce, confused itself wiv its spluttered cummands, an misled his parts, so yu cum upon him choking, his cheeks smeared wiv misguided food, or he's fallen in a tangle, bickering wiv his grazed, bluddy nees.

'Lissen leg!' he cumplains. 'Hear clear. Stay till yur bruvva leg is first gon . . . then bend a nee an cum.'

But the knack is for tell yurself clear, not lowd. An legs need time for steddy themselves when yu've first bound them up for wurds.

'Hungry,' says Bok. 'That man.'
'Which man?' asks Potto.
'Big man. Good man. Strong man. I like him plenty.'
'Where?'

Bok looks down. He pats his hollowed belly. 'Here!' he says. 'This wun.'

'Yu!'

'Ha!' Bok nods. 'Yu.'

'See it?' asks Potto.

'What?' demands Crow.

'Rabbut!' Potto says. 'There!'

'Where?'

'Gon now.'

For the too, facing each uvva, saw diffurnt ways, thruw sepert eyes, so wun's front wur the uvva's back, an Crow's view wur Potto's shadow, which led for dark confusings.

'See it thruw my eyes,' Potto urges, pressing down on the uvva's shulders.

An Crow stoops by his side, an they smile, nuzzling ear for ear, close as they can, looking the same way.

'Yes,' Crow agrees. 'It's low down here. It smells strong of yu. Thruw yur eyes. An rabbut's gon, like yu say . . . Now! See it my way.'

So they turn about for see it diffurnt, wiv Potto jumping up an down panting, for get a higher view, like Crow sees, as a taller man.

Becaws it wurn't clear, who saw what, what heds held diffurnt, what we kept for ourselves an what we shared. Until we felt it on our own skin, heard it thruw anuvva's ears, felt it between the uvva's legs, or smelled it up anuvva's nose.

Urges twitched us, dreams gripped us, feelings stirred us, anger burned us, voices sounded off in our heds. Things got heard when no wun spoke.

'Who says it?' Bok leaps up, an glowers at our startled faces. His hands are clenched for striking fists.

'Who say what?'

'A man says I dun it.'

'Dun what?'

'That bad thing.' He scowls. Enuf said.

We shrug. We neva heard any accusing.

'I neva do it,' Bok hisses. 'What that voice says . . . Not yesterday by the lake. Not today in the wood.'

'Ha?' we wonder.

'An yu steal my fur . . .' Bok remembers, turning on Potto.

'Which fur?'

'This wun.' He pats the oruk hide, draping his shulders.

'But yu got it. That fur.'

'Yes? Then sumwun's sly!' Bok scowls round. 'They leave it on my shulders, but take it from my hed . . .'

Yes, sum had found their mind kwicker than uvvas.

'Saw new burd,' says Ratz.

'Dark burd?' I ask.

'No.'

'Lite burd?'

'No.'

'Then it's red burd?'

'No.'

Then I'd shrug, bewildered by Ratz's tangle of lys, or this burd's unspeakable cullur.

Yes, we'd gon fancy, finding the taints for cullur things. Cullurs had bin there a long time all reddy, but we'd only juss thort for call on them. Firstly we had lite an dark. Then we saw red when blud got spilled. Uvva cullurs wur there for see, but we hadn't thort for call them names.

We took us time for say it yella, green an blew. Then we rested us sore eyes an weary heds. Befor we saw any thing brown an purpil.

Wiv numbas it wurn't so diffurnt, nyva. At first we knew nothing best. Then cum wun, too, free an many. But we felt most sure counting a gon or single thing, for the larger numbas made us giddy.

'Gard them eggs,' Gooz tells me. 'Gard em good.'

'Gard em,' I agree.

When she cums back, she scowls at the broken shells by my futs, besides there's smears of yolk on my chin. So she slaps my ears, gessing good. Suspishuns cum into her hed, which moves her for count em eggs.

'Wun . . . too, free . . . many!' she says, but she looks bemused, sucking in her cheeks, eyeing me wiv plenty distrusts.

But the fault lay in wurds not me. For there wur still more eggs by my futs than numbas in the wide wurld, so we hadn't the names for count them all.

'Look! Many then . . . Many now,' I protest. 'I gard them good. Best blame many, neva me.'

For I'd bin thortfull for eat only wun an wun, leaving too more eggs than free.

'They cumming.' Potto ran panting towards us wun dawn.

'What?'

'Bruns!' he howled.

'What bruns?'

'Bruns wiv claws.'

'Buzzurds?'

'No . . . Bruns wiv claws. Wiv fangs. They bite.'

'Ratz?'

Potto's eyes roll side for side, pleading for our slow heds for know, then he blurts again, 'Nah. Yellabruns wiv claws. On their futs. An fangs in their moufs. They fore legs. Too front. Too back. Got eyes too. An tails.'

'Ears besides?'

'Too each hed,' Potto agrees.

'Them hynas, then?'

'Not them, nyva. Yellabruns, black noses, wiv fangs, claws, fore legs. They roar. They big.'

'Lions?'

'Yes, those!' Potto shudders. 'Sept that's juss the name of them. The chew of them is wurs.'

'Where they cum?'

'There.' He waved at the far peaks. It wur a long way off an misty. We cudn't gess how he saw them cumming.

'Many?'

'Plenty many.' Potto nods, shivering. 'Plenty angry wiv us. Chew free fowks. Rip out throwts.'

'How yu know so?'

Potto looked puzzild breefly, gazing around him for remember the cumming of his knowing. Then his gnarled face smooved.

'Fear it,' he confides, tapping his scalp. 'In my hed,' he explains.

Well, that wur no cumfort for him. But it cum sum relief for us.

We lurned by it. Yu had for know how knowing wur cum – feared, gossiped, heard or seen – an wheva the knower wur asleep or awake, sober or drunk, when the trewf cum in.

Els we'd wake for anuvva's nite-frite, an find ourselves climbing peaks, swimming lakes, for flee a plague of tigers or pestilence of buzzurds, juss becaws sum old man wiv bellyache had slept himself bad, an woken screaming, for friten us wiv the horrur of his dreams.

Most, we spoke of ourselves. Which helped us understand. But we wur sorry hapless tumbleweed, blown about by fierce feelings, fluff fevvers on the blow breff of Urf.

Fear an Hunger clutched us. Wurn't much we cud do.

Anger wur all ways there, an took us by turns, burning, twisting the face for scowls an twitches. The feva raged breef.

Then the face cleared. Becaws anger wur restless, gon into anuvva. Most times thruw the ears.

'Why yu ate my meat?' Ratz wants for know.

'Hunger dun that. It push my hand. For grab yur meat. Befor I can think, it's ate.'

'Yes!' Ratz nods, then clowts my brow.

'Yu hit me,' I say. 'Why?'

'Anger cum into my hand. Twist it for a fist.'

'So?'

'Wur anger hit yu . . . not me.'

'Oh.' I scowl, rubbing hard for soov the frob. But too late. Sum anger, gon out of him, has cum into me.

Then we're a flurry of flailing arms an legs, wiv jooses spilled out of us both.

But nex day all's healed an forgotten, until the nex time. An nothing's left bar the scars.

Befor wurds there wud have bin a scuffle alone. But wunce elokw-ence wur in us, a story cud cum of it too – a tale for tell after the bludspills. This way, we remembered more, an the past clutched us wheneva we went, clinging like burrs in fur.

****–>>>>** | Wunce fowk

Most things had bin told all reddy. Wurds spoke them. Mists rose. Shadows lifted as langwij lit things, scowls an smiles. Most things took for their names, settling as they wur said.

Sept the thorn bush, by the twisty path up from the lakeside, which wud not be told, thow we'd warned it hard an plenty. It wud not lurn or change, give up its frewt wivout a scuffle, or be a fond nearby, thow we neva meant it harm. Till we slayd it.

'It bit me again.' Potto showed us the spike marks on his hand. 'It trips yu when yu pass.' He made a lurching for mimic the sly, silent pounce of a gorse bush.

'It slash my leg,' Flames told. 'When I picks its berrys.'

'It waits in the nite, for tug yu down,' says Ratz.

'It hates us.' Crow spat.

'Yu thort bushes had hard feelings?' Blind swivels her rheumy eyes for the sky.

'It seemed so *then*.' I confess, 'We thort it wur the crewlest bush on Urf. Wiv the stubbornest of sowls. All ways prickly in our path.'

There wur sumthing for its still, mocking malice that brort Anger in us all. Now, we'd had enuf of it. It has pierced us wunce too offen.

We wur an unhappy, skwabbling band that day. The sky wur pissing cold on us, lashing us pimpled an blew, while the wind whipped us crewl. If we cud not stop the bitewind, we wud do what littil we cud. Which wur why we hunted it down, surrounding it, reddy for the slaying. It wur well trapped as we gathered round an howled out at the clutching barbs of that spite bush.

It russelled in the wind, bending back from Crow's raised fist. It seems for shrink an shiver, now we all faced it, wiv rage an each uvva. But we wur circilled round it, an there wur nowhere it cud go. So it juss trembled there, rooted.

'Yes!' Potto mocks. 'Yu not so brave now, spiky twigs.'

Ratz struk it first. Wiv an ox rib. Hacking away the topmost leefs. Then sumthing wur loosed in us all, an we fell on it together, feeling our strenf in numbas. So we wur all slashing an swiping. Stoning an kicking. Till Bok hacked its stem. An it wur split apart, root an branch. An we trampled the scattered pieces an flung them for the gusting winds.

It grew again the nex Leef-Moon, cum its time, but furva along the lakeside, safe out of our path. So all wur lurned by it, bush an fowk.

For we'd no longer take the wurld as it cum. We'd ansur for its insults, an bite back if we cud.

We wur smaller than oruk an ox, kinder than the cats, slower than dik-dik an deer. An yet we had our strenfs an wit.

There wur plenty weaker than us, less knowing.

So it pleased my bruvver for stalk snails an slugs, larfing at their slow, tacky trail, then smear them on the rocks.

'Sshhlssh!' Ratz sounds the skwelch an gurgles. 'He neva see me cumming. I slayd him wiv wun fut.'

'Why?'

'Well . . .' says Ratz, '. . . a man muss hunt.'

So it was he'd bite the heds off burds he snared, snap the legs of rabbuts for see them slowed for a mewling, wriggling crawl, an swallow a frog in wun gulp. Yes, he offen looked down on lesser things, broke up weaker beasts. It pleshured him for show his strenfs.

An still we held our insides darkly, unseen beneef our hides. Nostrils, navels an ears barely broke the surface. Yu cudn't reach in. But down a gullet, yu saw the darkening burrow where a wild thing nested, nursing its skwirming pups. There wur a litter wriggling wivin. We knew not what. Only we felt their trembles, kwivers an shudders. An, if we cud not have them out, we wanted them calm an fed.

Effen when a body looks sooved on the surface, this an that sounds unstill wivin. Yu hear a steddy frob, an strange gurgles of flewid. But neva a sensible wurd.

This wur the mistry – of what trubbled our insides. An the ded wur neva showing. Whereva yu looked for them, or poked about inside, yu found no more than tangled offal an tubes, like a slayn beast. So whateva had stirred in them had slinked out wiv their last breff.

'Angry water runs,' I tells Ratz, raising me ear from his belly, 'deep inside.' Yes, there's more for him than meets the eye.

'Ha!' He smiles at his flowing, froffing jooses.

'An sumthing says "wish . . . wish . . . wish . . ."' I tap my hand for its reglar murmur. '. . . like sniffles ansurring tears.'

'What?'

'Sumthing there, sobbing,' I say.

Now I know better. It wur the sound of the sorry spirit tapping for be let out – that frob that neva stops till a body dies.

We wur lissening. We wur lurning. But there wur secret understandings, signings we neva saw, whisperings we neva heard, senseless smells, an such. Things wur calling out for each uvva.

The sprowting grasses drew the deer. As soon as the magguts wur gon, flys wur cum insted. Then the warblers wake, fly out of their burrows, knowing there wur easy eatings. Yes, the plants an beasts wur babbling lowd for each uvva. But we neva cort their grist or grissel, only speaking wurds ourselves.

'Water hate fire,' I say.

'Fire burns her. So water smuvvas him,' says Ratz.

'Water hisses. Fire spits.'

'They fite kwick, till wun gets snuffed.'

'Water kinder than fire. Unless she's hard as ice.'

'Water runs cleva, all ways.'

'Try for catch her . . . she breaks for pieces. Runs round fingurs. Then joins up again.'

'Water all ways run down, like gowfers down their holes. Fire reaches up. Burds fly away.'

'Smoke flys. But slower than burds.'

'An Urf lys still, most times.'

'Water wanders. On the lake. Back an forf. Air strokes her.'

'Lake soff for us. She likes me. She carry me. On her back.'

'Air neva flowt us.'

'Air don't want us.'

'She gobs on us. She blows hot an cold.'

'She drop us kwick. She lifts burds thow.'

'Duks are liked. Frends wiv water, urf an air.'

'Ha!' I agree. 'An the belly likes them well enuf.'

'Breast is best.'

'Guts is delickut.'

'But futs are levvry. An fevvers too dry.'

'. . . Ratz?' I ask him. 'Do yu eva think wiv yur mouf shut?'

His eyes wrinkle closed. His mouf draws tight. He nods, silent. He has.

'Me too,' I say. 'Got wurds in my hed. Silent voices. Howling kwiet.' I wince at their shriekings. 'Me guts are asking eager now.'

'My belly wants rabbuts. Mine does.' Ratz nods, rising.

Yes, the wurld wur strange an variuss. There wur much we hadn't tasted yet. An plenty still for lurn.

It wur the Crab-Moon. An we felt well glutted an trusted Urf wur well fond of us, sending up the crabs, scuttling out from the lake, black-pincered, red-bodied, hugging sweet bunched beads of crimson eggs beneef them. They cum in packs, stone legs clawing scratches in the sand, stalk-eyed yet blind for us, rite past our fire. We neva thort for ask how they knew where for find us. Juss thanked them in passing. Eats are seldum so forfcumming. Yu neva had for rise for yur futs for for catch them. An most, bar the shell, wur chewable. But effen the shells had a use, being shaped exack for hold a crab snug for the cooking.

Yu cud crack open their backs an gobble them salt-skwelchy an raw. Yu cud lay them on their back on embers, till their legs stopped their heated frenzy of twitching. Then leave them a littil more, befor nibbling them steaming, stiffened but flaky.

For days we neva hunted or forraged, but skwatted round our fires, reaching out for food as it shuffled by obliging, surrounded by flame-licked cracked shells an broke beckoning claws, munching contented, belching into the fish-rotten air.

It wur a fine time. Till a distant smoke drifted the dusk air for scare us.

There's wildfire – blazing thruw dry grass, scorching the sage, flaming the lavendur, seering the bushes – an tamefire, held in a circil of stone, fed by fowk, rowsting meat.

This wur tamefire. Its drift carried many mixed scents – oke wood, scalded flesh, scorched fevvers, burnt fat.

'Rowst dipper?' asks Bok.

'No.' Potto's nostrils twitched. He sniffed delickut, savurred his saliva an spat. He smiled, for it left a good taste in his nose. 'Bake blackburds. In clay, wiv rosemurry.'

'Who?'

Crow shrugged. 'Shadow?'

'Shadow went that way . . .' Potto pointed flankways for the sunken sun.

'Then who?'

We cudn't gess. Nun but Shadow, an the ded, wur gon missing. So, together, we wur the only fowk on Urf.

But piercing the clot of nite we saw an oranj glow, an faint yellas flicker, liteing the pines on a far rij.

'Booboons cort fire. At last?' asks Potto.

Crow shook his hed. The wurds escaped him. For wunce he cudn't say.

In the nite we heard a strangled, near-human shriek. Then an ansurring moan. But we neva spoke back into the nite, but shivered mute. We did not care for the sound of the voices. We feared for draw wild moufs for us.

Nex day they cum, hobbling dots on the farside of the lake. No more than a handfull. An as we saw them, they saw us too. They stopped. We heard them start up a fritening noise, a growling mixed up in a humming.

We gathered up sum crabs an spiny frewts, flung our hides on our shulders, filled the bladders wiv water. We clutched our cutting an killing stones, reached for our pokey sticks an striking clubs. Then scurried up for the peak of the crag.

Free slouchers cum, an free skwealers on their heels, trujing along the lake. Their reek carried for our twitching noses. Well-rotted pig, sun-baked fish, stale pee an mud, fusty damp hides.

'Oohoo,' said the leading wun, whacking the spiny bushes wiv a man's leg-bone as he hobbled on, 'hahoo.' But these wur no wurds of ours. His darting eyes took the lenf of the rij, where we crouched. He seemed for have no site or care for us.

'Whaa?' asked Potto.

'Men? Woom-men?'

Then passed-times stirred our minds, murmury spoke, old fing-urs reached for us, an fowk long gon cum back for us, shadowy befor our eyes.

'Not-Skinks-One-Ear?' Bok whispered.

Yes. His rocking walk an missing ear told on him. It wur the man who had bin Skinks, until Crow took his name back. But time wivout wurds had changed him terbly, blowted his belly, whited his hurr, bent his back, an took an eye. For he had no name for clutch at, for hold him whole, strait an steady.

'Then that old woom-man?'

'Wur-Crake.'

'Wunce-Starling!' I saw.

'Then they are . . . ?'

'Wild chiles?' Crow gessed.

Picture us in our swetty distress. We had no manners for grasp them, for hug the occashun. We'd neva met departed kin befor, returning as animuls wiv a skwawk of jibbering chiles. We smiled down as we shivered, savurring their wafting stench, pretending we found them all parts peepil, all smells sweet.

They grimaced up. We cud make no sense but fret of their grunt-ing. They hadn't the nous for be scared of us, thow our numba wur many more.

We had stayed. They had gon on. But now we wur together again, we saw we'd gon furva. An left them far behind.

Only now they wur in front of us, an held us trapped on our rocky perch above them.

Hesitashun kept us from rushing down for wrap them in our arms, hug them for our bussoms. Seperashuns hadn't sooved their tempers. Befor they'd seemed kinder. An thow they'd cum by chiles, wun of the grown wur gon missing. Not-Towd wurn't wiv them. Unless in small part, an that wur his leg-bone that Wur-Skinks brandished, an his lower jaw bone on a fong round his dumb throwt.

'Ha, bruvvers! Ha, sisters!' Crow called down from our hite. There wur a kwaver for his voice that told of a stronger tremble wivin.

'Yu speaking yet?' he asked polite, hoping they'd cum for our senses, despite the ruff looks of them.

'Hach . . . urk . . . ssptt,' Wur-Skinks told us. 'Huhoo. Och. Och.'

He said it lowd, hevvy wiv feelings. It seemed for mean a lot for him. But for us it sounded senseless.

He wur rocking, each time his hed butted the air higher. An he made wide sweeps of the air wiv the long-bone, as if swatting at low-flying duks. His upper lip twitched, for bare oranj teef. An spits gobbed out as yella flecks. An he kept repeating himself. In a harsh, unfrendly voice, as thow he'd neva known us. An it mite have bin in his dumbdark mind for scare us. Which he did.

'Good hunting?' asked Potto. 'Fife summers we neva seen nor smelt yu . . . So we wondered where yu gon . . . Nice here. Plenty crabs. Hot sun . . .' He smiled, gesturing open-handed for the sky. Then he realized his mistake. 'But better over them seffern hills . . .' he waved. 'Yu go there? Take the best place . . . We stay here.'

But the only ansur wur the roar of the beast.

'He still not speaking.' Crow turned, shaking his hed for advise us. 'Not a wurd. He's dumb still.'

'But Anger stays wiv him.' Potto winced.

'He's not going.'

'He's staying?'

This wur our wurry. They wur kin. An we wished them happy – if they didn't take ours. But we had neva invited them back. Time had torn our tie for them. Fife years' rain had made it musty. Fife hot summers had rotted it. Our luv for them wur long gon. We had nothing new for say for them. An their manners wur neva ours.

'Why he cum?' said Sly. 'For us? Of all peepil.'

'He want woom-men?' gessed Crow.

'We cud give him *wun*,' says Potto. 'An old, broke wun?'

'Yu want him?' Crow asked Gooz. 'He eyes yu fond. He want yu plenty.'

She hugged herself, shivering. Her eyes blinked fast. She jerked her hed wunce. It wur a kwiet 'no' but a strong wun.

'Anywun . . . ?' Crow smiled at woom-men turned away. We looked for them for help us. But no woom-man rose for go. No, nun wur eager.

'Not-Dumb good-killer,' Crow cowxed. 'Catch plenty meats . . . strong . . . nearly a man . . . kind too.'

But then Skinks's growling frets betrayed him, an he began a swaying, swaggering rise towards us.

Kin is kin. But fear is fear. An Skinks is dumb. An wurds won't do.

Our scared sounds didn't stop him. So we loosed sum stones insted. Thrown small an soff first, for discurage him. Then hard an large for hurt. It wur our way of telling a wurdless man not for rise for our hite. But for wait till we wur reddy for drop down low as him.

Wun cutting stone struck Skinks's temple, which brort blud out in spurts as he slivvered down the slope on his belly, futs first, his hed bowncing after, cracking on stones, his face all the while screwed in a startled rebuke.

Skinks struggled for stand, but his nees wudn't straiten, as he swivelled for look about·him. An whereva he looked, gobbets of blud spat the ground befor him. His kin backed off as he howled.

'Haaa . . . Huhu.'

Skinks sniffed the air. He had the scent an trail of fresh blud. Spatters lay all about him. He looked for the sand then up for the sky.

'Whaa?' he brayed. He struk out for both sides of his hed, but still he cudn't feel his prey. An he slumped, a slidy elba struggled for jerk him uprite.

He looked less fritening now. We slinked down the slope towards him. Crow, Potto an Hare crept close.

'He's weak,' said Crow.

'He bluds bad,' said Potto.

'Bind it wound?' asked Hare.

Becaws if too much sap drips out of a man, the spirit drifts away. But when yu bind a bludding arm or leg above the wound, the flow slows for a trickle.

'Bind it where?' asked Potto.

'Neck,' said Hare. 'Below the bleed. Between the hed an the hart.'

Crow narrowed his eyes. 'Can't do no harm.' He nodded his agreement. '. . . not for us.'

So Hare wound a strip of hide twice round Skinks's throwt, an the uvva too men tugged it tite, so it bit into the straining cords of the gasping neck.

An the bludding slackened for dribbles, as Skinks's jaws clenched, an his eyes buljd, an his strenf cum back for him kwick in a rapid jerking, an twitchy stretching fingurs. But the moving soon drifted out, an his redded face darked, blewblack an sickly, befor the ends of hide wur loosened.

'Gon . . .' says Crow, neeling down for peer into the still staring, unforgiving eyes.

'It neva help him,' said Hare, turning for us, shrugging, tossing the hopeless strip of hide for the ground.

Caws, curing knows better now. An arm-bind wurks well, but a neck-bind snuffs more than it saves, wheva the harm is bludding, spusms or snake-bite.

Wunce-Starling, Wur-Crake an the childrin wur fled, melting into the bushes, hugging the ground, well hid. We called for them but they neva ansurred. Not in wurds. But only russelled like wind-blown leefs, hoping for confuse us.

An they neva cum back for bury their ded wun. As wud be Good an proper. An sweeter-smelling in the hot days cumming. But we heard they wur nearby by they moonlit wailings. So we knew they had luvved Skinks wiv their own ruff reasuns in their wurdless animul ways.

'Skinks's spirit is near . . .' Moonsik shivered an sniffed, warming her palms at the fire. 'Feel it close an angry.'

'If we're peepil . . . what are they?' Crow asked our flame-lit faces.

'Wur-fowk,' said Flames.

'We're fowk . . . they aren't,' said Hare. 'All can see it . . . Deer, trees, burds, fishes.'

Yes, suddenly we wur wurried, how those nearby saw us.

'How, any know us diffurnt?'

'So!' Gooz spat on ashes, drew a fingur thruw the paste, then marked her chest wiv a gray line, so –

<

'Ha!' Gooz chortles. An, having pleased herself, smeared her uvva breast too.

Which wur how-cum our first hand-made cloves. Befor that we'd borrowed off the backs of beasts. Now the wurld cud see us diffurnt, apart from all pretenders – wunce-peepil, nearly-fowk, almost-beasts.

'But they neva kept yu warm, those cloves?' Blind says.

'No,' I agree. 'But they covered us enuf – stopped us shivering wiv shame. They showed us apart. Least, we wurn't slug-nakid any more.'

| # Trubble. Between the legs

I made it – the first dog – out of no more than a wulf pup, cowxing it tame wiv food, clutching it wiv kindness, knapping it wiv clowts of my hand. It wur the finest thing I eva shaped – apart from the woom-man I wunce made – an the most finished thing I eva carved. Evry hurr of its hide glissened apart an brissled sepert. Grown, it wur sharp as flints, fast as blow, sly as a starved chile, crewl as ice.

It came harf-way for Langwij. I cud neva teach it for speak out lowd, but it lurned for lissen well, twitching up its ears, holding plenty wurds in its hed – 'choke, bite, kill, give.'

Like me, Dog wur small an lost its muvver yung. I found it whining by the stony knoll trying for scratch its way thruw tumbled, grimgrey stones. Rocks had fallen hevvy an muss have blocked the den. They lay lazy an stubborn. Having cum so far so kwick, those stones had no urgings for be moved again.

'Ha, littil wulf,' I say, swinging my stick for crack its hed hard. For wulfs an fowk wur neva frends. An it turns, staggering on splaying legs, lifts its jowls for snarl at me, but juss skweaks a puny fret, then topples on its side, panting, like it's all reddy clowted down. It wur no longer than my hand, no fatter than my fist.

'Stand,' I say. 'Where's yur spirit? Fite or run.' Then I larf at its reedy wails, for effen its misery wur shrunk ribby thin.

It juss jerked twig legs, heaving its flat, mottled, wispy belly. There's no more pleshur or hunt in it than cracking a stone. So I stayed my hand, crouched an watched. I gessed it wur well starved.

When I'd dug a mows, I twist the neck an it lays limp, then I push the mowsmeat close for the snout of littil wulf. He raises a wobbly hed, sniffs an sneezes, scenting me, a danger tainting its fur.

Then the pup twists its hed an eyes me sideways, nuzzles mows again an feebly nibbles the neck. Yes, he's too weak for chew. So I take the mows, tear the skin, gnaw the meat from back an thys, an spit out the pulp. Then the pup parts his jaws, weakly lifts the flesh. After a weary paws, he gulps. The fur of his throwt rippels as the bulj slides down his gullet.

The pup looks up for me for more. He takes anuvva mows an a frog, but the sun is slid low befor he finds the strenf for stand.

I know I've dun an odd kindness for a strange kin. For I see a boy in the pup, an the pup in me. It being a bony, hungry, snarly thing. An its spirit fierce but sly.

When I walk away it makes a whine, like it's calling me back. But when I'm turned back it slinks away, hissing me gon, a rij of fur risen behind its stretched-back ears.

So it wur – free times. It wud not let me leave, nor have me near.

This wur pup's way of telling me his thirst. For when I brort water in a crab shell, he lapped it dry, pink tunged.

Then it whines again, but strong an pityfull now, twisting its hed, pleading more.

I shake my hed an show my empty palms. Pup's asking me for his muvver back. But she is gon, an neva mine for give. No way.

'Ha, wulf!' I console. 'Mine's gon too. She's Beyond, but her spirit lives.'

This cums no cumfort. Pup sits on his haunches an sounds a thin warbling howl for the sky. 'Ow-wow-wow?'

'Look . . .' I ask, 'have yu no kin?'

But he wails on. So I gess he has nun. Els they wud cum.

'Kwiet,' I say. 'Yur sorrur is give for yu, an yu alone.'

It's the same wiv chiles, who want for share their weakness, while they suck away yur strenf. Boobys are our burden, but it's neva bin our task for feed the wulfs.

I trujd away, leaving the pup sniffing, scratching at the fallen stones that held him from his crushed kin. I neva gave him any cum-on. I neva looked back. But when I wur gon behind the rij, I heard a snuffling behind. Pup cum padding round the bend, tail swinging from side for side, sniffing my prints, depressed in the urf. As I scowled down, he sat payshent, cocking his hed, as thow asking –

'So? Where do we too go from here?'

*   *   *

I've shared a sleeping-hide wiv plenty odd wuns, an all sorts in my time. But when yu lay down wiv a wulf, yu'll find he has nite-manners all his own.

He is furry an warm when still, an the hot pants of his breff waft gentle on yur chest.

But, be warned, yu'll find plenty bones in bed, slivvers of gibluts, beaks, webbed futs, an such. Then beneef it all is spred a tacky damp of clot-blud.

Wulf is a restless sleeper an keeps diffurnt times. He crawls out from beneef the sleeping-hide an starts for howl, like woom-men sumtimes do. Or wakens yu anuvva way, chewing yur ear, but frendly, or licking between yur tows wiv a rasping tung. An when yu both at last find sleep, he dreams of chasing rabbuts, clawing yur belly wiv jerky legs, as if it wur the ground. But wurst he gnaws yur ankils or nips yur buttuks, as thow tugging a deer for the ground.

An it's scary for wake at dawn for find chill grey eyes watching yu above a wide grin of pincer teef. Then he nuzzles yur nose or licks at an ear.

He is a puppy for his frends by daylite. But when the moon is up, a savage hunter's spirit wakens wild.

We'd fore seckses for start, those urly days, befor wit an progress gave us choice an seffern.

Shemale wurn't born yet. Nor Nyva nor Both, an Imaginings hadn't tangled wiv Desire.

There wur men an woom-men, an by seffern diffurnts yu knew them apart – by size, their faces, between their legs, their moon-tugged tempers, their chests, the smells of them. Then there wur too sorts of yung, unripe – budding woom-man, or twisting male.

My flesh wur pulling me upwuds, sprowting me a man. But in my hed I held no hurry, for after growth cum the wilting, I see, then the going Beyond. For I've watched the strong men of my fresh days gon bent, teeflost an haggud. An seen plenty woom-men wivvered, snuffed, dug under.

I watch the many of man an the many of woom-men, an see the men are more. An they hunch taller, stouter things, for they eat more an better, coff less yella, an last the longer. The woom-men are foreva swelling or nursing. Sum tiring of the struggle, heaving for birf a thing, knowing only a booby will cum of it, or a clotted mess of less.

An the shrinks wivver them when food gets scarce. Yu see the legs of woom-men drawn slender, the cheeks hollowing, as their belly blowts, or a booby sucks the joos from them. This bulging, suckling an shrinking slows them. Getting weak, they go tottery, dizzy, neva wandering far for forrage, for tiredness an childrins tether them.

An I saw that men trod the surer path. An so I thanked me spirit its wisdum. The weasel. For howeva we body twisted an warped, it always stayed a man's. Unlike Contrary whose spirit wur fickle, laying him both sides of the sleeping-hide.

Grujs had built their nests in wurds, hatching clutches of skwawking cumplaints.

There wur kwarrels beneef the sleeping-hides, skwabbles circilling the fire, cumplaints between men an woom-men, disputes between the legs.

Dog, Ratz an I sat curiuss, narrow-eyed, aloof. The bad wur nun of our doing. We wur innocent at last. The grown wuns made mischif now. An secks wur at the root of it. Wiv meat, mating, an chiles all mixed into a sour mash.

'Itch between me legs,' says Potto. 'See!' He spred his thys for show the split an redded flaky scabs. He spoke for no wun in purtickler, telling all who care for hear.

'I hungry still,' Flames sighs. She spoke for the gloom, any open minds, the embers of fire.

'A hungry woom-man . . . she cud catch herself . . . crabs.' Fox looked down solem, advising his skwirmy tows as they wurry the sand.

'All gon crabs,' Flames says for the fire.

'When I hungry, I hunt . . . I hunt for . . . food.' Bok spoke for himself an the wind, but lowd enuf for any nearby ears for hear.

'Look at me!' Flames slaps her bulging bellyful. 'Booby growing in me.'

Men turned for eye her sorry lump, swelling befor their eyes.

'It's trew,' Crow said. 'She makes anuvva booby . . . Why?'

'An my scrotum hurts me,' Potto confides. 'Between my ears.'

'Woom-men do like those boobys,' Crow declares. 'They make a booby. They ly wiv it.'

'It's woom-men's way,' Fox explained. 'Men neva think for grow chiles inside them.'

'I'd neva let nun suck me nipils.' Crow screwed his face, scowling disgust. 'I keep my bussoms flat. For myself. I keep my nipils dry.'

'My belly swells. My legs going thin.' Flames whimpers for pity's sake.

'So?' says Potto. 'We all got our trubbles. I coff up yella flems. An there's green gissum cuming out of my nose . . . See!' He spred sum in his palm. But no wun chose for watch it shiver close.

'I like a woom-man, I bring her meat,' Bok advised. 'I cupples her good.' He offered.

But Flames juss gobbed again on the fire. Nun moved. But it wur as thow a space yawned between them then, Flames an the uvvas.

'Men . . .' she muttered, an as if all wur the wun an same afflicting, like sum pox, on the face of it.

It wur juss that those men wanted cuppling. An Flames wanted feeding. Misunderstandings lay at the roots of it.

When a man cum home wiv a limp carcass hanging off him, he'd strut his dripping flesh. He eyed woom-men. An woom-man eyed him. Nor wur she blind for his meat. So when it wur shared out, a woom-man who got a choice piece mite go sprawl wiv a hunter. But mostly she'd finish eating first. Which wur Good. For then man an woom-man pleased each uvva by turns. Which doesn't all ways happen.

But the woom-men wur fewer than the men. So sum men had for wait their turn. Then they knew Impatience, sniffed the air, stamped their futs, scowled an muttered. Or els they met Refusal. Scuffles an tangles cum of that.

But it wur changed kwick as the season. Thow we had only seffern seasons then, going short, befor wisdum an wevver cum full stretch, giving us eleffern moons.

When the mussels, eggs or crabs wur plenty nearby, woom-man saw man wiv a cooler gaze. Then she mite turn her back, shun a proffered rabbut, cross her legs an smile, or favurr a man's face the more than his food. So Fox got cuppled more when food wur plenty. Bok found favurrs when game wur scarce.

Dog an I sat on the knoll. We watched the grim dance, its dim twists an turns, gessing at the tangled reasuns, as my bruvver Ratz gnawed a bone, slinked thruw the shrubs, or lazed scratching by our futs.

'Hare gon wiv Gooz,' says Ratz. 'Jerky pokey, pokey jerky.' He thrust his hips in eager copy, grunting like a busy man. 'He on her belly now.'

'He gon wiv her nite befor,' say I. 'They cupple slow. Then he growns good. Then he jerk fast.'

'He slow for start. Then finish kwick. The same wiv Flames.'

'What he do in there?' I call on Ratz's older wisdum for explain. 'What he looking for? What's in it for him?'

'Man get itchy pokey stick . . .' he supposes, 'so he rub it back an forf.'

'Why he stops?'

'Itch gon . . .' Ratz says, 'for a while.'

'An why them all want cupple Green-eyes?'

'She give more scratch,' said Ratz. 'Her wrigglings good. Her moanings eager.'

Yes, he had his inklings. But there wur much we had got wrong, more we had for touch upon first hand.

'Anuvva thing . . .' I ask. 'How them chiles cum?'

Ratz rolls in the sand. Now he's the spit of a newcum – all splutters, dribbles, howls an skwirms – for the dismay of growly dog.

'No,' I say. 'How they get up there for start?'

'Spirit wriggles in, up a woom-man's nose. She neva knows. Until she swells.'

'Ugh!' say I, patting me belly. Then think for sneeze. I wudn't have it happen for me.

'Booby bad for a woom-man,' Ratz says sagely. 'Juss want for drink woom-man dry . . . Swell her plenty. Then shrink her more.'

'They bad, them boobys,' I agree. 'They neva care.'

We nodded at the sense of it. Woom-men laid themselves open. Men trujd the cleva path. An had a crewler cunning.

*　　*　　*

'When am I born?' asks Blind.

'Between the Pox an the Ice.'

'An tell me,' she asks. 'How old I wur when I stopped seeing.'

'Fore summers. No more.'

'Then tell me again. How sites are seen.'

'Well . . .' My tung paws for summon it. I have for liken it for what she knows. 'It ain't a pain. Pain is wivin yu, body an hed. Touch presses down on the skin. Taste is mouf an mind. Smell is mist, a swirl of fog tite around yu. But sound is furva, out there, beyond in the wurld. Yu sense the way it cums. An where its centre lys.'

That way, site is like sound. Out there. All around. But it is fiercer an briter than hearing. There is more diffurnce in it.

'Is it lowd?' asks Blind.

'Lowder when the sun is high. Kwieter as it dips. Only murmurs when it's set. When it is lowd, it sounds steddy, like the hum of a bee. But the touch of it is firm yet lite. It is effen as the heat of embers. There's no smell for it but the freshness of breeze. It is muddling warm. It neva hurts the eyes, sept when it sounds too lowd, or sees a fritening thing. Then it skweezes the innards an sends rippels up the spine. Yu can ease the hurt by closing the eyes.' ·

'So, shapes?' she asks. 'How are those? An are they many?'

'Much as yur fingurs feel them. Jagged as broke stones, curvy as roots, sharp as flints, blurry as fevvers, smooth as eggs, spiky as gorse. Large as bolders. But small as grits of sand.'

'Cullurs, then?'

'Plenty, sepert an diffurnt,' I say, 'but mixing an merging like fowk. White is soff as fleece. Black is hevvy as sorrur, sucking as mire. Red is hot an fierce, but pleasing. Yella is frendly, warm an kind. It smells like dry grass an pollen. But there is a tartness for the taste of it, like sour berry joos. Green is fresh an calm. In its hart it's melon cool. Blews cum hevvy or lite. There a coldness in their sowls, an an indiffurnce in their harts. But they're pleasing enuf in their place – which is offen far, like sky or hill tops. Brown is close, thick an clotted. There's a rot for the taste of it like over-ripe yaw.'

'That's all?'

'Remember wun thing more,' I warn. 'Cullurs rest themselves

122

at nite, like fowk. All bar the oranj of flames, an the black of dark. Shapes sprawl lazy, but they stay awake.'

'What els?'

'Sites are telling, but they ly like wurds, an can't make up their minds. It looks a far hyna, then its a near fox. It changes shape as it twists an turns, long as a fingur, then stubby as its tip. An seeings shrink as they leave yu like the sound of parting futs. Also sites cover each uvva up. The top cloves the beneef, like a sleeping-hide an its man. But the hed an futs of things offen stick out, so yu know what lys wivin.'

'Then . . .' Blind is gon jerky, open-moufed, clawing her scalp. 'I have a site in my hed after so many dark summers.'

'What?'

'A seeing! It's cum loos. There at the front of my hed.'

'Tell it.'

'A hot round, size of my mouf.' Her lips stretch wide an round, a fingur circils the inner rim.

'Is it strong or weak?'

'Strong as can be. An hot.'

'Then that will be the sun,' I gess.

'An there is a flatness behind, curved, smoov an cool as the brow of a skull.'

'That will be the sky . . . purbly.'

'Ha!' Blind cackles, slapping her thys, peering down, blinking at the ground.

'What?' I ask.

'I see the red sun an green sky again . . . beneef my futs, after so many dark years.'

I don't know what for say. Shud I tell her? That her wun good site in mind is gon discullured by a rot of age, an spilled upside down.

But purbly that's how girl saw it – reflecting up from the water, when she wandered by the lake, that long ago day in the Egg-Moon, when she stumbled on sumthing terble bad.

An saw No-wun doing Nothing.

Which we neva spoke of sins.

But still I got for tell her. That.

**–*–> | A dog's life

Perps I wur lurned as well by Dog as Dog wur tort by me. My eyes wur sharper, but his nose an ears wur keen. He heard far scents drifting over, long befor they told for a human nose. For he'd always kept his snout moist an fresh by pressing it into whateva wet, an small sounds buzzed lowd in his pricked-up twitchy ears.

So when he cowered low, eyes fixed, an started slinking towards a distant shape downwind, it swaying like a dazed beast fit for topple, I cud spare him a needless stalking. An save him foolish loss of face.

'Ha, Dog!' say I. 'That's only a skweaky tree, bending for the blow of wind.'

But when his puppy lollop stiffens old, an he sniffs the ground, his grey eyes narrow knowing, an he looks up for me, then his kwivering snout snuffles, then I look for him, for he's found the track of sumthing fresh, that a dog an boy mite care for follow, so wun cud chase it towards the uvva, who waits crouching aside, an ground it wiv stone or teef, an part it from its breff, then share its eats, thow a wulf likes for gulp it down soon as he mite, while I prefur for chew my share slower, rowsted hot.

Ratz kept on growing, all ways, in temper an tall. Now fowk called him Too-Jackl, telling how they minded their backs when he wur about. Becaws they thort he's gon befor, but turned to find him crouched scowling behind. Maybe there wur sumthing in his hand that had belonged befor for sumwun els. But, for me, he wur still only Wun-Jackl. Knowing his ways better than most, I'd lurned for hear him cumming.

He an I had slept together beneef wun hide, then Dog joined us, cumming between, an Jackl wud not be happy nor leave, cumplaining Dog's gnawing woke him, an that cold airs rushed in when Dog's hed peered out from the hide, so Jackl picked nitetime tussles wiv Dog, which he mostly lost wiv blunter teef, so he took the sleeping-hide for himself, an slept aside.

Given a choice of cumpany, I prefurred a frend in Dog for the kin in Jackl. It wur my own kware taste. Uvvas mite choose it diffurnt. But a wulf is kinder than a bruvver, until cums the time for kill. His temper is steddier. His wit is briter. His legs are swifter. He catches more meat, an he's more reddy for share. For he prefurs the innards an bones, which leaves me happy chewing mussel.

So we took for rowming, alone together, an knew darker times than most fowk, taking dognaps thruw the day.

A wulf is evry bit as curiuss as a boy, I saw. He asks plenty wheneva he meets anything new –

Can I eat it? How does it smell up the arse? Cud I chase it? Is it wun of us? Do I know it from befor? An is it worth a care? Or shud I cock a leg an piss on it?

Jackl offen saw it simlar. But Dog had the more reddy bladder, an the more knowing nose. Still, he likes for roll in ded stuf, so smears of rot fowl the air, clinging for his fur.

But it wur thruw Dog's suspishuns that I got inklings.

That we wurn't alone.

For in the copse, beyond the crag, past the lake, near the cave, we cum across futprints an spaws that looked like fowk's.

An yet Dog neva knew them. His snout trembled, his jowls kwivered, he sneezed an whined, backing off, ears stretched back, tail stowed round beneef his belly.

'Who?' I asks.

'Aaaagrrr!' Dogs tell me. Which speaks his wurry.

'Fowk,' I tells him. 'Look!' I place a fut in the mud tramped print. Wun by wun, I match the tows for my own. 'There! Wun, too, free, fore, fife,' I tally.

But I see it is a brawd fut, an a hevvy body stamped it down, an the space between the prints shows the long pace of a high man, also the futs don't step strait, bending inwuds.

'Hog,' I gess. 'Carrying hevvy on his shulders . . .'

'Aoww,' confides Dog.

'. . . running . . . a kware way . . . nocking his nees . . .'

'Grrr.' Dog speaks low, an lifts a paw back slow. For there is the crackle of dry grass under the tramp of a hevvy tred. Then we're scampered off.

When a wulf is fritened, who am I for be brave?

Dog an I slinked apart, between the snares of wurds, aside from the tugs of kin, beyond fowk's suspishuns.

Dog heard wulfs howl in the nite. He parts his jowls an whimpers soff, then twists his hed for me. An when I heard peepil's chatter I'd mutter, looking first for Dog.

The puppy wur parting him, but the full dog wurn't cum yet. The boy wur nyva yung nor grown. The dog wur nyva tame nor wild. I slouched along wiv him, restless by the fireside, uneasy in the dark. An becaws there wur no names for say what we'd becum, now the wulf wur part in me, an sum pursin's sense wur sprowting in him, we wurn't seen clear anymore, so fowk seldum called for us, sept for have us gon.

We wur kwiet an foxy in our wulfish ways. It wur a pryvut bond, sealed by mixing bluds. There wur nyva dog-howls nor fowk's-wurds for what we did, where we went, what we lurned. Flesh an teef got used, led on by gile an stelf.

Men barely bovverd for us, an woom-men scarcely cared. We went whereva we liked, lazed apart, neva watching or lissening. This way we saw an heard.

The woom-men gathered by the lake. They had started calling themselves *we*. It wur the name they gave themselves, for mark them apart from men, but together in themselves. They talked by turns. They told on their insides. They spoke of themselves an men. They had purtickler names for men. Which men neva gessed. Dog an I wur the only pricks who heard, being there unseen or low, els sprawled in the hollow of a prickle-bush.

'There's hurt,' says Gooz. 'I feel it burn. I smell it sour. Taste it bitter. But I juss can't say it.'

'Where it cum?' asks Flames, wincing.

'In my guts. Between men an us . . .' Gooz struggles for the sense of it.

'Big pain?'

'Big in hurt. A moving pain. Spredding up. From belly for hed,' say Gooz. 'It cums evry day. It bring Anger wiv it.'

'Kwick burn or slow scorch?' Green-eyes asks. 'Flames or embers?'

'Scorchme kwick, then burns on. Smulders slow an smoky.'

'I know it too, that wun,' says Flames. 'It cums in me.'

'It's what men do . . .' Gooz gazes wide, straining for the far site of it. 'There's sumthing they do that hurts.'

'Men . . . they eat, they sleep, they jerk on yur belly, they poke below, they howl at chiles, they slap ears,' Coot reminds her.

'They stink. Air all ways bursting from them. They snort as they sleep. They tug the furs off yur belly an back,' Flames tells.

Gooz nods. 'Trew. This hurts. An it's part of it . . .' She taps her brow for loosen thorts. 'But there's more, beyond.'

'Past the lake?'

'Past there. Befor now. It's about men's cumming . . .'

'Yes, how they cum?' asks Flames. 'An why they cum? What they for? An when they going?'

'What brort them?' asks Coot.

A silence wraps woom-men. They struggled for remember how men wur cum amongst them, so big, so lowd, so many. An what wur woom-men's need of them.

'Men I know . . .' Green-eyes ponders. '. . . befor they wur men, wur changelings . . . befor that they wur chiles.'

'Chiles wur boobys for start,' Flames explains.

'. . . from *woom-men*!' shrieks Gooz. 'Think back! Men cum from us. We muvver them.'

'Those boobys.'

'Yes,' Gooz agrees, following the same path back, 'all men wur boobys wunce . . . if murmury tells me rite.'

'Men juss growed boobys.' Green-eyes rocks an chortles. 'Whaaa! Who'd gess?'

'Ha!' Flames grunts. Her mind wanders time passed, thruw all those summers, the tally of her tows an harf her fingurs. She creases her brow, chews on the trewf, gobs out the rind. 'We make them. They cum of us. But they neva asks . . . they neva thankful.'

'We feed them big. We grow them strong. Then they bite the tit that feeds them,' says Gooz. 'They leave us weak.'

'Ha!' says Flames. 'They suck a body thin.'

'They bring food at least,' says Moonsik.

'Sum do, sumtimes,' says Gooz. 'Sumtime neva.'

'Neva enuf,' says Green-eyes.

'Not when we need,' adds Flames. 'Sum days they eat all they cort. Then we chew roots. An we sleep hungry.'

'We do!' Gooz shivered. The cords of her neck strain. 'Rage in me now. It prickles my chest. It scalds my ears!'

'What we do?' asks Flames.

'We?' asks Coot.

'Woom-men, together,' says Gooz. 'Graze together like dik-dik. Then we stay strong.'

'Dik-dik chew grass,' says Green-eyes. 'It blowts yur belly. But it gives yu wind.'

'No,' says Gooz. 'We *stay* together. We *help* each uvva.'

'I can see that dim.' Green-eyes smiles. 'Juss behind my eyes. I see men an woom-men, besides dik-dik an deer. There are hogs too.'

'What does it show?' asks Gooz.

'Man catches deer . . . he's happy,' says Green-eyes. She screws her eyes tite, imagining. 'There are plenty deer . . . but woom-men are few.'

'It's trew,' says Gooz.

'There are more piglits in wun litter than woom-men in this wurld,' says Flames.

'We juss the fingurs of wun hand,' says Green-eyes. 'Too an free an fore.' She points for the uvvas. 'And . . . wun more.' She peers around. 'That's me.' She pats her chest, finding herself, close by, 'the fum.'

'We preshus meat. We are so few,' says Gooz.

'We're rare flesh.'

'But, if we're so rare . . . how cum men catch more woom-men than deer?' asks Gooz.

They ponder it a while.

'Deer run faster . . .' Coot concludes. 'They got cleva legs.'

'It's so.' Flames nods at the sorry trewf of it.

'Yes,' says Gooz. 'So what we do?'

'We cud go scarce,' says Green-eyes.

'Hide?'

'Hard for catch,' says Green-eyes.

'We cud tell men this . . .' says Flames. 'They want rare woom-men, prime flesh, full flank, between the legs. They first catch plenty, easy meat.'

A contented silence fell as they thort on this, till Dog starts scratching his belly, then all heds turn startled, our way.

'What's that?' Flames whispers. 'Man cumming?'

'Juss lousy boy. Flee-bit dog.' Gooz sees our fore eyes thruw the branches an turns away her careless gaze. 'In the gorse bush.'

Up on the crag, the men wait woom-men's return, imagining their embraces.

It will be a long unkwiet nite.

Dog an I rise stretching our legs for slope into the dark, for do what we have for do, as our appetites stir, for nite always kwickens us.

All that summer I knew sumthing wur missing, but I cudn't remember what. It nagged an itched like a louse between the shulders I cud neva reach for scratch.

Then Crow asks me wun day, 'It's kwiet wivout him. No wun bites the childrins, steals eggs, throws stones or fires the bushes. Do yu know where he gon? . . . the uvva?'

'Who?' I ask.

'Boy wiv no. . . .'

'Nose,' I gess.

'Ha! Him. That wun.'

'Jackl . . .' I looked over my shulder. But he wurn't for be seen. 'He went wun place . . . or anuvva.' I shrugged. I cudn't tell.

So I'd remembered what I'd forgot. The thing gon missing wur my bruvver Jackl. The nuts an spiny frewts had cum an gon. The yella an red berrys wur all eaten. We'd had more than our fill of snails. An all this time I had not seen him. So I wurried for him. I called out for him for cum, sevral times. But he neva cum, juss stayed gon, whereva.

Moons passed wivout seeing him, so it cum for me I had lost him. Which made me cry, more than wunce.

But Jackl wur neva lost, juss mislayd, but it wur years befor I knew this, for when he wur returned I wur gon, an when we met again we wur diffurnt peepil, grown bodies an fuller minds, so it wur only our names an murmurys that told us each uvva's, an remind us we wur still blud of wun muvver.

When we wur met again as men, he told me his story, that he had fallen down a deep crack in the ground, while chasing rabbuts. The sides wur sheer, an slippery wiv loos urf, so he cud not climb out, wiv wun leg crooked an bendy, beside wun arm broke. He heard happy larfs above, then a crewl silence.

But there wur food of sorts, there in his hole – beetils, slugs an slime wurms, fallen leefs. Wun moon he cort too moles. An acorns tumbled in, out of an overhanging tree. Which wur his good lukk. An there wur windblown seeds later. The rains left puddles. An in the dry times he cud suck the sap from roots or skweeze out the joos from skwijy slugs.

Sum days he heard peepil passing near. But becaws he wur so deep an dark no wun saw him. An becaws he wur so low his sounds wur muffled an carried strangely, like a whimpering wind, or far panting deer.

The food gave him strenf. His wunce broke leg wur hardened, curvy. He cud reach for a stout root growing out from the side of the hole. He thort on it, then tugged it hard, found it fast, an clambered out.

But it wur dazzling brite in the wurld again. An the Urf wur fritening open an brawd. He missed the damp, the walls an the dark. So he climbed back down for find peace an rest.

After a few days an nites, he changed his mind an wunce more climbed out. But it wur days befor he felt safe apart from his hole. An longer still befor he wandered back amongst fowk. He had lost trust in them. An they found him strangely changed, kwiet an pale.

As wurds came back for him he took for blaming his kin for leaving him so long in a hole.

Which surprised peepil. For it wur them who'd pushed him in. An they wud have gon for fetch him out of his hole, juss as soon as they felt sum need of him again.

'But we do not want yu back. Not yet,' they said. Els they blinked in surprise an asked him strait, 'What did yu lurn by it?' or 'Aren't yu grown? Taller an thin' or 'Who are yu, white-wurm?'

Blind cluks. 'Wur there much pushing into holes?' she asks.

'Sum,' I say. 'It wur harsher than stinging wiv hornets, an kinder than ambush-by-cats.'

'Cats?'

'It happened for a few crewl wuns who cudn't be tort. If yu bite an claw, so yu get ripped an chewed. By larger or more.'

We'd find the body at dawn, all ripped. An thow there wur no cat prints, we knew what muss have bin, feeling sorry but safer now a ruff wun wur gon Beyond.

Blind nods her understanding. She is prowd in an old fowk's way. She has seen all of life, thow she has no eyes. She has gagged on the tuffest trewfs. Nun have suffurd hard as her. Nor bin so kind. An no chiles wur eva ungrateful as hers. Still, she has thorts for forgive. I hope. Becaws there's wurs I've got for tell her yet.

Got for say about her muvver.

Got for tell her about the cat skin.

Got for tell her about her eyes.

****–*–>>** | Spirit in man, spirit in woom-man

Bok crept behind Green-eyes thruw the long grass, then jumped her, neva asking, neva minding her refusing. She howls lowd as he clutches her wrists, holds her for the ground, an lays hard on her belly, an jerky between her thrashing legs. She bites. He hits. Gooz an Flames cum running, ansurring her shrieks.

Bok's bigger than any of them, but free woom-men bleed him pale, break his jaws, splinter his teef, wiv a stone, an so he neva speaks that summer, an no woom-men talk for him, nyva lets him ly wiv them. An his blurt cums wurs than his bite.

An thow men larfed at the livid gape in Bok's face, that befor had bin his mouf, an passed him hard things for chew on, an called him gorey names for being spilled between a woom-man's legs, still men eyed woom-men diffurnt after, grew hesitant for grab, more asking an less taking, an lurned a littil more of numbas, for while each man wur more than any woom-man, he wur only too futs an too fists in himself, so he looked over his shulder when the woom-men gathered about him wur more, an their arms wur dubble that, besides they cud kick, an a man has tender parts about him, thow he is harder than woom-man, he is mostly skin on the surface, soffer than stones, more tender than teef.

We saw the loss an lack in Bok's eyes, which rolled dull an slow. An all the larfter went from Bok's mouf. Now a new, sad spirit wur cum into him.

Hare wur hare-crazy. He looked it too, his upper lip wur split up for his nostrils, giving him a wide-toofed smile when he scowled.

He walked apart, stumbling sideways, or striding backwuds. But carrying himself drunk wiv pride. He perched in trees, sum days, or flowted on his back in the lake, staring at the drift of clowds. He had his reasuns. But they wur all his own, sepert from ours, an changed day by day, depending if he'd bin smoking weeds, or what he'd brewed or chewed.

Hare knew spirits better than anywun. He cud sniff them passing, an tell them apart by their diffurnt scents.

He'd yawn silent, his twitching nostrils flared. Then yu knew he smelled a ded wun near, but he neva spoke till it wur gon an the air gusted fresh again, for Hare had secrets an knowings he didn't want the ded for hear, an understandings wiv spirits he didn't care for the living for share.

'It's an old cum-again,' he confides. 'I cud smell it stale. Struggle an despair. Them unborn smell of hope. Clean as balsam. Sharp as lemin grass.'

'What it wants?' asks Crow.

'Not us,' Hare smiles. 'It try for cum born again. So it want a woom-man. It's looking for an opening.'

Hare follows the moves of spirits. When he smokes the smuldering weed, the fumes gust his mind Beyond, for talk wiv the ded. But he leaves his body behind. His eyes stare wide, puzzild. His legs stretch out jerky.

Sumtimes he goes stiff, pale an cold. Then we gess he's died again, loitering Beyond. But fowk leave his bag of bone alone, knowing it will twitch alive again befor anuvva dawn has cum. For Hare has died more times than we remember, an always risen again.

Fowk buried him, juss wunce, which wur their mistake an wasted digging, becaws having clawed a hole, laid him down an covered him, Hare wriggled out spluttering thruw the thin cover of sand, an Potto an Crow had all reddy wept their greef, bled his arm for drink him sum drops of kinblud, shared out his fire-flints an hides. So harsh wurds wur spoke by Crow, who wur not a man for be put under.

Woom-men will let a frendly spirit in, an let it grow inside. A booby, els madness, cums of that.

But a man's spirit ain't so generuss, or obliging. It wants for fite any strangers who try for enter in.

'Go out!' it says. 'This skin can only hold wun of me. I cum here first. These bones, these meats are mine. By rite.'

This way sickness cums. If the spirits are matched then the struggle is hard. Then there's feva an babbling. Nothing sensible gets said. For too spirits are twisting the wun mouf babbling together as they wressel for the single tung, both tugging for wun hart.

When the fevered rage is over, the man wakes cool an calm again. Yu know wun spirit has bin ousted, an wun has stayed. But yu don't know which. So yu watch the glister of the eye, as a spirit shines out from wivin. Or yu give a frendly greeting, juss for see what a sowl has for say. Yu ask him for sum rabbut he promissed yu, or not, or wheva he's slept well.

Maybe a new voice ansurs. Or he blinks – not knowing yu from befor. Then yu know a new spirit moves yur muvver's bruvver.

This way frendships break. Kin vanish. Or cum again. Promisses go lost. Or hatreds drift away. For yu can neva blame the arms an legs, or sack of offal, for its old spirit driven out.

This is the adventure in being a pursin. Yu neva know what spirit will move yu at dawn. Perps yu fall tangled asleep wiv wun woom-man, but get stirred awake by anuvva. Or yu open yur eyes at dawn for find yurself a stranger, diffurnt man, or ded.

'Bok . . . he lost his old spirit,' says Potto.
'When them woom-men broke his skull,' says Crow.
'Old strong spirit gon out. New sorry wun cum in,' Hare sighs.
The men look at Bok, rocking solem, droning sadly, a yella joos trickles down his chin from his broke-up mouf. Flys wur gathered for feed on the wound, a twitchy black glistering smile.
'There's a way . . .' says Hare. 'For help him.'
'Yes?' asks Potto.
'But it's hard . . .' says Hare. '. . . for bear.' An he whispers how it cud be dun.

'Aah!' Bok whimpers, tugging from Hare's clutch.
'See!' Hare cluks. 'New spirit whines. Sad!'
So the men had for seize Bok an bind him wrists an ankils, becaws his new spirit feared a cure, knowing he'd be driven out.

First they had for hold Bok's hed steddy, so Hare cud bore the hole thruw his scalp wiv a pointed flint, twisting it for a blurr between his rubbing palms. An the spirit in Bok howled against the new hole, screaming he had enuf about him. Wiv the wuns he got all reddy. For, besides the hurt of it, the hole wur there for skweeze him out, like pus from a fester.

'We scared it now.' Hare claps his hands. Medsin's good. 'Now we fear it bad, then hurt it out.'

An Bok's spirit howls, gessing what's cumming nex, wresseling for be free of them.

'How?' asks Potto.

'Fire,' Hare says. 'Is best. Becaws it's wurst.'

'No!' Bok wriggles for loos his hands from the binds.

'See.' Hare nods sage. 'Like I say. Spirit hates fire. We smoke him out . . .'

So Hare holds the flaming stump of wood beneef the soles of Bok's jerking futs. Then lingering up for his ankils. Nex slow along his shins. Then behind his nees. Befor scorching blister streaks up his thys.

Then I turned my back an fled. Howeva it helped Bok, it hurts me sore. For watch an smell. But still I have for suffur on, as his wails an scorch smoke carry far.

Bok's spirit draws all the strenf of his body, struggling for cling on against the pain, while his body crackles in bubbles an blisters beneef the embers. An the smoke of rowst meat an scorch fat is sweet when it rises from pig-hide, but foul on the nose if yu know it cums from a manskin, effen thow the crackling smells much the same.

They burn Bok up his belly as far as his nipils befor the spirit is gon from him, fled out in howls of hatred, ending in a whimper of despair.

'Aah, naah, whaa . . .'

Then the body jiggles kwiet, wobbles calm, spiritless an free.

'Cured now. The spirit's gon out thruw his hed.' Hare smiles, an slumps, tired but content by the untrubbled Bok, who sleeps snuffly as a suckled booby, for only his eyes an mouf twitch now.

'Bok spirit! Cum back now!' Hare calls out for the dark, cowxing back a hidden frend.

But it neva did. Cum back. The old spirit. Purbly it wur gon Beyond. Maybe it wur wandering far, an neva heard Bok's screams. Or it didn't want a broke-moufed scorch-skinned body no more. Maybe it'd wurmed its way up a woom-man insted.

But, still, anuvva spirit cum into Bok. Yu cud see soon as he woke. It wurn't like his old self's sowl. But a pitiful, bitter, sorry, mumbling wun, that flinched away from fowk, feared fire, an jumped at the sound of his own fritened larfter. So we wud have prefurred the wun that wur driven out. At least that wun wud talk an hunt, an wurn't spooked by rabbuts.

Cures wurk odd ways. An thow yu wurk a remedy, it's offen not the wun yu sort. But yu cudn't dowt Hare's power, only fear it. He wur the first curer. An most that cum after lurned their medsin from him.

There wur plenty this boy cud have told – kware knowings, hidden places, strange pleshurs – if fowk had treated him kinder, tossed him tastier cuts off their kills. An if they'd spoken soffer, they'd have stretched his mouf for a smile, an prised apart his gritted teef for tell. But men hooted an called the boy Mows or Maggut, or slapped his ears, or dropped him hed down in the lakeside mud, or handed him rowst yaw for eat, but stuffed wiv glowing embers, as sum scorching joke.

So this Gob fell closed, sullen an silent, an skirted fowk flinching.

'Peepil don't like yu much, chile,' Blind warns.

'No,' I agree. 'Becaws the boy's gon wulf-wild.'

So, as fowk turned their eyes away, an hid their kindness too, seeing the boy passing, he clutched his secrets close for himself, an wurn't tempted for tell – where the sago roots grew fat, or how for blud a tree for sap, where turtul eggs wur buried, where nearly-peepil lived, beyond the crag, or uvva knowings worth the hearing. For secrets filled his belly, an hidden things pleased him well.

Dog-sniff rooted out things long buried, I-site saw things being hid. An our pricky ears heard from all sides, seizing at whispers, snatching at russels.

We saw how Fox an Coot wresseled together, what got bit, who won, an what senseless skweals cum out. An where Crow lay wiv Flames. An a certain way Moonsik took wiv Hare alone. Which wur kware. For while they touched upon evrything in the bracken, an nothing passed unfelt, their gazes neva effen grazed when uvvas wur about.

Dog dug, an I ate, where woom-men laid caches of seeds, nuts, an dried roots, hidden from men's eyes, for feed themselves thruw cold times cumming.

We saw Duk straining, whimpering for birf the too harfs of Both. An ded offal cum out after. She ate sum. An buried the rest, which Dog dug up an snaffled after.

We found the hollowed out rock where Crow took himself alone, an took for our care the cutting stones he knapped there, an wulfed the charred remains of a rowsted tortus.

Dog an I found rabbut burrows no uvvas knew of, ate ratburds, odd eggs an strange crawlers no uvva fowk had tasted. We found where Urf passed water, in a froffing torrent, cascading out of her stony piss-hole. An we found where the clowds wur born, drifting out from the peak of the far hill.

We cum for know the slope well. From the ferns by the crumbling rock, oranj wiv lichen, I crawled for the swell befor the dip for the lej. An thow the curv of crag cast its long shadow across us, I feared they mite look up an see us.

They nested below, between too beech trees at the frinj of the copse. Free, they wur. That's all.

The nock-need wun wur taller than a man. His stooping step wur pained, buzzurd-towed, as the futs of him splayed inwud. His lean face wur creased by wurry. An he wur always looking over his shulder, for his sowl took frite at his shadow.

His mate waddled stiff backed, wiv too full breasts above a bulging belly. She wur near for birfing sumthing.

An I gessed the small wun muss have cum out of her befor. This wur a slender, willowy legged, unripe wun, mean hipped, who wud reach no higher than my shulders. But she'd grow herself woom-manly, if the breff stayed wiv her. This thort cum for me, wivout reasun, by moonlite, as my snorting, snuffling kin lay wrapped together in armfuls.

Each time we watched, Dog an I cum bolder. They didn't friten me now, but drew me curiuss, as they slumped fireless, witless, an few, wiv only grasses for cover themselves. Their hands wurn't cunning as fowk's. Yu cud not help but pity them. An I neva saw them eat larger than bukrabbut or fiercer than gowfer. Still, by moonlite, generuss eyes cud see them most parts peepil.

I neva wearied of watching them, but Dog tired of lying still an wud slope off sniffing, while I wur slid over the crag, crawling down the long slope towards them, till I wur close enuf for hear the wheezing strain of their sleeping breffs, their sickly coffings an splutters.

I heard the yung wun whimper – 'ow . . . ow . . .' An the sound tugged sum soff inside me, an a thort cum in me that I cud leave a sleeping-hide or food nearby, for her for find, an thank the darkness.

Stony thorts sounded round the nitetime fires, as fowk spoke feelings. Wurds wur for blame for this.

'Who wants I cupple them? Now?' Potto asks woom-men, but no wun ansurs, so he asks again, of each an evry wun.

'Cupple we?' he asks Coot. 'I poke yu plenty.'

'Hu!' she grunts, neva raising her eyes.

'Cupple we?' Potto asks Duk. 'Fat woom-men good.'

'Ha!' she spits, neva turning.

'Cupple we kwick?' Potto asks Gooz. 'I like yu wun tit, wrinkled.'
She shook her hed disdainful.

'I cupple yu, then,' he told Moonsik. 'Yu best.' He glared for the uvvas. 'I like a woom-man crazy.'

But Moonsik only giggled, rolling her lost eyes too sepert ways.

So having circilled the woom-men, Potto starts over again. Yu can tell he knows his wants, an ain't shamed for plead his need.

'Cupple we?' he asks Coot wunce more. But she only sounds a sharp, barbed larf.

'Why no woom-man ly wiv me?' Potto demands, slapping his chest, stamping the dust.

'Yu slug-stupid,' says Flames. 'Yu are.'

'Yu stink like lepud-shit,' says Gooz.

'Yu stone-lazy,' says Moonsik.

'So?' Potto conceeds. 'Evry wun diffurnt.'

'An yu don't bring us food enuf,' says Gooz. 'We're hungry still.'

I knew this wur cumming. I'd heard woom-men's whispers.

Potto slouches away an sits rocking, hed between his nees. I wander for him, crouch on my haunches an tap his furry nukkels, for advise him, as only I cud, knowing woom-men better.

'Whaa?' He screws his hurt eyes, disbelieving the touch of my small paw on his bulging shulders, my pokings in his sorrurs.

'Yu want I tell yu trew, old man?'

'Whaa!' He bares oranj teef, rolling bludshot eyes.

'Lissen,' say I. 'I know woom-men best. They're seffern ways diffurnt for men. An then again, purtickler for themselves. I know why they larf at yu. It not juss yu stupid, lazy, buzzurd shit. Trubble wiv yu is . . .'

But he cuts me short, butting my hed, wiv wun swift nod, sending me sprawling into the dark. From the warm spatters raining down on my chest, I know my num nose is spewing out blud.

No, nun lissened for me when I wur yung. Which wur their mistake. An loss. For thow I didn't hold myself prowd, I wur the cleverest human-being on Urf. Then.

I had made a numba name for each of my fingurs. I'd lurned most wurds eva spoken, an grasped their evry sense. I cud spark fire. I knew how for knap the most cutting stones in the wurld. I cud tell men an woom-men apart in the dark, an gess what stirred in their dim minds. I'd travelled furva than anywun, having trujd fore days for the far peak. I had tamed a wild thing for a dog. I cud think free dawns ahed, an sicks summers behind. I cud chew my way wiv weeds from gloom for joy. I cud outrun most rabbuts, an throw trewer than any howler. An still I wur growing, cleverer, bigger.

Yes, the boy in me wur dying. The man in me wur hatching out. Yu cud hear it in his uncertain voice, squeaky yung an rumbully old. Also there wur prickling inklings between the legs, sprowting for suggestings.

∗∗–∗–>>> | Blind site

Blind taps her fingurs, peevish on the rocks. 'Day's passing,' she says.

'Hed an shulders,' I agree.

Still, there's a long way for say. I muss carry on telling until the day's haunches an tail are cum, then the long shadow.

But grujs against Hystery are welling up in Blind's mouf.

'When do us living cum into yur passed?' She swipes my chest wiv a fly flecked melon rind. 'Sun's dipping. It is warmer on my shulders than my face. Still the past ain't crawled near enuf for touch me yet.'

'Yu cum in yur own . . .' I paws. '. . . lifetime.' I console, 'Juss wait anuvva seffern summers. Hystery don't skitter Hare-crazy. It juss stumbles towards us backwuds. Evrywun has for wait their turn. No wun can cum into time befor they're born.'

'Pizzle . . .' Blind twists away.

'When yu cum . . .' I cowx, 'there is plenty about yu, all in a rush. Yu tally up for a tale in yurself. Yu cud be stretched out for a morul. At the hart of yur life is a hard hurt, wrapped up in a mistry.'

'I'm big in Hystery, then?' Blind turns back my way, the lids kwivering hopefull over her jelly eyes.

'Yu are *blind* in Hystery.' I cannot hide this from her. 'An smaller there than now, being a chile. But the passed can neva forget yu. Evrywun had site but yu. This makes yu special for our eyes. As yu stumble into the gorse bush, or tumble into holes, we are there for look on an lurn. Any ways, we're moving for it. An it's now that sumthing kware happens for me . . .'

'Hystery's like that,' Blind agrees. 'It sticks close for yu. Pawsing for yu for piss. Following close on yur heels.'

I nod. 'Trew. Wheneva sumthing strong happened, I wur nearby the time, or close for the place of it. Till my legs went from under me. Then Hystery strode ahed.'

'There wur plenty lowd moufs, an broke legs. But there's only wun blind. An she barely gets a look in.'

'Lissen,' I say, 'yu'll cum when yu cum. It's Time that has it so, not me.'

I wur always wivin my body, which always clung tite around me. It's how we wur, inseperable, at wun, wivout any tie or join. I'd bin as much in me legs an arms as I eva wur between me ears. An I neva strayed far from me belly, nor turned a deff ear for my hart.

But now my spirit wur drawing away for watch apart, curling up tite an small behind me eyes, peering down perplexed at my parts. For the flesh of me wur sprowting, growing a stranger for myself. Tufts of hurr peeked out thruw the pores of my skin. There wur brawdnings an thickenings, swellings an bulgings. Thow the bulk of me wur larger, sumthing inside me shrank back, yawning a hollow wivin. An I sniffed rank scents new for myself.

So I cum awkward walking by fowk, fearing they wur larfing at the changeling. For I wur nyva wun thing nor the uvva. The boy in me wur scuffing out as the man cum, slouching sulky in. But them grown neva seemed for care, sept when they slapped me for eyeing them close, but most they minded me skwatting beside them, casting my shadow on their cupplings, as I found a new pleshur in it, an looked for lurn by the watching.

Then closed eyes wud blink open, or a glazed gaze came sharp. Then a busy hand wud wriggle itself free for swat me away, or a mouf lift for shout me gon. But offen they neva heeded me, unless surprise or interest moved me tung for ask them why.

'Yu put *that* . . . ?' I asks, '. . . there?'

'Hu . . . hu . . . hu,' they juss go on, an on.

'But ain't it tiresum?' I ask. 'Repeating yurself so?'

'Go!' shouts wun, peering over the jerky shulder above. 'Far!' says the uvva.

'Go on then,' I say. 'Fuk away. Neva mind me.'

They wur racing breffless ahed of themselves. But neva getting anywhere.

For, when man an woom-man lay down together, there wur all

ways more ansurs than kwestyuns. Nothing gets decided. An reasun cums tangled as them legs. It's only pulling apart those flickering eyes see they've dun anything foolish.

A hungry time we'd had of it. The berrys wur eaten. Roots wur shrunk. Small beasts slunk into their burrows. The deer had fled the thunder.

Hare staggers towards me wun dusk, an slumps rocking by my side. 'Ha?' he asks, laying a chill arm on my shulder. 'Wha?' His smoky breffs reek of smulder herbs.

He's mistaken me for sum man, or a frend.

'Ha!' I agree, an look him full in the face. His pupils shoot up beneef fluttering lids, so I'm blindly observed by the pinks of his eyes. He cackles. But the larfter is cold as the claw of his fingurs. An the clutch titens for talons as I move for pull away.

'Boy ded,' he cluks, sorry enuf.

'Who?' ask I.

'Yu.' He palps my pimpled cheeks.

'I? Ded?' I ask, concerned. Wurds from Hare cum as a warning from the wise.

'Man cum born in yur skin. Boy ded.'

'Ha!' I shrug, relieved. He only means I'm grown.

He tweaks my thy then, gentle, slaps my ears. Dog growls by my side.

'Grrr!' Hare mimics, an bares his teef. Then Dog cocks his hed an whines.

'Wulf,' observes Hare, 'grown too.'

'Pup no more,' say I. 'He's killer now.'

Dog lays his hed between his paws an whines, watching us eye him, panting keen.

'How yu made that?' asks Hare. He flicks the tips of his fingurs, in a rasp an click. Dog rolls over, closes his eyes, shows his speckled belly for be rubbed.

'Kindness,' say I.

'Kindness . . . ha!' Hare cackles long at this till a coff stops him.

'It wurks,' say I. 'Kindness does. Try it.'

But he juss rolls his eyes. For he's a hedstrong man, an best admires his own advice.

'I got sum leefs. For yu,' Hare confides wiv a moist, throwty whisper. 'Good chew. Show strange sites. Take yu far . . .' He waves loos at the empty air. '. . . behind things, Beyond.' A curled fingur reaches into his mouf, an brings a sprig of herb, glissening dewy wiv his spit. 'Chewit.' Hare holds it for my clenched teef. An I'm scared for take it. An afraid for refuse. But wurried for do nyva.

So I takes the leef an sucks at it, pretending for chew, but stowing it beneef me tung. But suspishun is slower than weed, it being a strong herb, new for me, that has me away, kware an kwick. Like a kick for the hed.

My mouf goes num, I remember well. An blossoms swell befor me eyes an I'm swallowed wivin. They had cullurs I neva see befor, or sins. An there's a dizzying odur I'd neva scent. I'm gon small, hard skinned. An there's more for my legs than I counted on or felt befor. I'm moved by savage wants. Nothing will stop me. If any fwart me, they'll feel the sting in my tail. Then I'm sunk deep into a flower, an I'm pushing down between the hevvy press of petals. Which is when I look down my lenf, an see my arms are wings, frobbing at my sides. Besides my legs are sicks.

So I'm a bee, but neva mind. Cud be wurs. An I'm well placed. For there's nectur below, gobfulls, an yu neva knew such slit-joosed pleshur for slide into that soff moist hunnyd split, for sink into the sticky warm of it. So I'm shivering wiv joy.

Then it's chill an I'm tumbling. An I like it less for find myself wriggling, changed – into a maggut in the rotted eyeball of a pig. An a crow cums, plucks me out, an gulps me down. Such are dreams.

An if yu think it harsh in winter, trujing thruw the lakeside mud, reaching thruw the slime for siltwurms, then think of drifting slow down the intestines of a crow, awash in stinking sluj which bites yur soff parts, an eats thruw yur skin. An there's low, wriving cumpanyans yu don't want for know. An time drags slow, aflowt in the bowels of a burd. An the future don't promiss much. But it cum as a relief for pass out at last. Thow yu're no more than a pip in a smear of cack. An the fall thruw the air is fearful dizzying, if yu don't care for hites, befor yu strike the rock, splattered by the flattening blow.

But it's hard for keep me down. An I'm shortly risen again in life, as a puffball fungus, swelling up from a dank patch of Urf. Yet no sooner have I pushed myself prowd thruw the mulch of leefs, leaving the woodlice below, than I get snaffled by a pig, who chewed me up. Then thort again, an wiser. So promptly retched me back.

Many lives I lived, animul an plant, by turn. I wur mussel, newt, sage-grass an wurm. Befor spending stubborn years as lichen, clinging on sum chill rocks, eyeing the frenzid cummings an goings of grass, watching the busy generashuns of moss.

When I woke again a pursin, I wur racked by shivers, wet from swet, I wur more understanding of the plants an beasts, sorehedded, ages older. Wiser too.

Only a tow of nite had passed amongst my fowk who, by the scorched smoke on the air, had ended their long fast at last.

Having made a late, dark killing, they'd rowsted sum meat.

Hare looks up at me as I stumble for the fire.

'What beast?' he growls.

'What?'

'The animul yu dream. Yu dremt yu wur . . .' Hare slurrs.

'I wur bee,' I say. 'Then maggut.' An I'm wondering how he knew I'd dreamed myself a beast.

'Yes . . .' he cackles. 'Trew enuf. Yu'd neva be an eagil, scorpyun or cat.'

'No?' I ask.

'Wur it good, wriggling down there . . . as a maggut?' he asks. 'Or perps not?'

'Starts well, gets wurs,' I tell.

'Wur it a long time or short?'

'Terble slow an stretched,' I says.

'What plant wur yu too?'

'Fungus. Then lichen.'

'So?' he asks, picking a sliver of meat from his teef. 'Do yu want for know what's cumming for yu? In life an death?'

'Yu can tell?'

'I can.' He nods. 'I see it, in the first dream of the man . . . What do yu want for hear first? The good, the bad? Or wud yu like for know yur end?'

'The good,' say I.

'Yu will live long. Yu will see much.'

'But there's sum bad, yu say?'

'Plenty sorrurs an pain,' he cluks. 'Starting now. But it don't matter much.'

'It don't?'

'No,' says he. 'Not for us. Becaws yu ain't a man for remember, fear or respeck for much. Uvvas do. Yu watch. An feed on their leavings. A hunter yu ain't. But yu do go odd places, where uvvas don't. An yu keep cumpany wiv stones.'

'An my end?' I gulp.

'Wriggling on, wivout any legs,' says Hare. Then he closes his eyes. Which is his kwiet way of saying he's all reddy told enuf.

Fellow feeling an fondness wur mixed up in men's faces. As if they saw the hungry suffuring in my eyes, an had took for me at last.

'Eat then, Maggut . . .' Fox beckons. 'Yu man now. Our meat is yurs for share.' An he passed me sum ribs of pale meat. There wurn't much fat about it. It trubbled the teef an wur strong on the mouf. But I wur famished an gulped it kwick.

An then Crow handed me a hollowed part of hart, scorched an firm.

'Yu want sum bowel?' asks Potto. 'It's good. If yur bite is hard an yur throwt don't mind.'

'We flavurr it wiv sage, for cover the taste,' says Crow.

'An rosemurry,' adds Potto. 'Helps the bitter offal go down.'

So this wur being a man. Taken for, spoke for, sharing an liked.

'What meat this?' I ask, gnawing busy. My teef wur sunk deep in it. My thorts barely skimmed the skin.

Now I'm grown, they share the best of the kill wiv me. But, still, I'm a speckle surprised. Neva having felt this fellow fondness eva befor, nor eva swallowed this purtickler meat. It's a thing I ain't chewed upon befor. The flesh is grey, fusty like hyna, but soffer for the bite. The bones are thinner than pig, brawder than bajur, shorter than booboon. The taste wur musty, all its own. Hunger helped it down.

But nun ansur me. Only they look around, or down for the dancing shadows on the sandy ground. There's sumthing stirring their faces that looks a mite shy. Skittery as shame.

'Hungry time we've had,' says Fox. 'We needed eats bad.'

Then, as Crow slumps, I see, over his shulder, the grey an black specked pelt of Dog, stretched out for dry, staked down where his fore kwick paws shud pad.

'Aaa. No,' I moan. 'Not my frend!'

'Yu dreaming yur man's dream . . .' says Potto. 'We can't wake yu for ask . . .'

'If yu mind,' Fox explains.

'But we save the fur,' says Hare. 'For yu.'

'It keep yu warm,' soovs Crow. 'At nite.'

'So!' Flames cackles, slapping her belly, rolling her gleaming eyes. 'Yu eat my baby. So I eat yur dog – snout an brains.'

But I juss scream. A long, throbbing, wulfish howl, that fair rattles the teef from my gob.

Then I felt sumthing tugged cum ripped apart between me ears, like levver being rent. It wur the bind in me mind that had tied me for fowk.

An I'm stumbling away from the stabs of firelite into the thick nite, retching up along the lakeside path. But feeling the prints of fowk's futs, hardened in the dry mud, I leap away thruw the bracken. I like its hurt, lashing cold an wet on my maddened legs.

An I think I hear Dog bounding aside, russelling the stalks. But I know it cannot be. It's juss the rasp in the tail of each panting breff.

I had taken nothing, an left nothing behind. I wur running for sum fresh place where fowk had neva smiled, thort, ate, dreamed or spoke.

But over me shulder I still see red glow of their fire. An up my nose I still cort the drifting stench of their smoke. It wur the scent of my only frend well scorched, flavurred wiv sage an rosemurry, basted in duk fat.

An on I ran, out of Hystery, dog-lost, far from fowk.

* *–*–>>>> | I go wild

So begun my wilderness years.

I wur fled strait thruw that nite, past the woods, thruw the nex day, across the plains, into the deep dark stretching beyond. I wur still howling out at peepil after I'd left them far behind.

'I ain't wun of yu!' I shrieked. 'I neva return,' I fretened. 'Yu lost me now,' I wailed.

Neva thort where I wur going, or what I wud becum.

There wur neva a gowd as strong in me as my giddy loafing of peepil then.

I turned for go back. For tell fowk I'd neva return. Els they'd neva know. Until it wur too late. But I gessed wunce they saw me, they'd think I wur cum back. An I wurn't going for leave them wiv the pleshur of my return.

Fowk wur gon bad. The rot wur spred into evry frewt. The whole bunch wur spoiled putrid. There wur no sound piece left, bar me. An I wur gon from them.

I saw no binds but hate an greed. Fowk burned the skin off their bruvvers, an drove their spirits out. They ate dogs. Chiles wurn't safe from them, nyva. They stoned their own. Men an woom-men battered each uvva. Food got hid from famished kin. When they wurn't tearing yu wiv fists an teef, they sliced yu open wiv wurds. Ask why they do it, they gaze puzzild, then smile an speak. But all their reasuns wur waytless an pointless, sounding empty, blown away on the breeze of talk, woven of no more than wurds.

An wurds carried no kindness, but juss puffed pride, self-pity an hate.

The beasts wur all beneef us now – for hear peepil talk. An cumplaining neva stopped. The sand wur too dry. The rain wur too wet. The ice wur too cold. The sun wur too hot. Nites wur too dark for them. Days cum too brite. Duks wur too few an small. Cats too many, an their bite too sharp.

Peepil craved hunny wivout bees, caves wivout walls or dark, pigs wivout the gile for escape, hard stones that wur soff for knap, nuts wivout shells, berry bushes wivout the thorns.

There wur wun Dog on Urf. An they had skinned an rowsted him, my wun trew frend.

No, fowk wud neva be satisfied till they'd gutted an ate all that moved. Yu cud neva trust them, for wurds had turned fowk strangers for themselves. They'd gon wurdsik for a man, neva mind the woom-men.

Hug them back? I'd sooner scavenge wiv buzzurds, hord scorpyuns up my nose, an have gowfers burrow up my arse. There's no pretending wiv the savage, bruvvers in blud, whose teef are honest, ripping at throwts, for at least a jackl stays trew for his jaws.

But there's no telling how the tung will tug on a pursin's hed. An fowk wur gon wanton wiv wurds. An had no inkling what crewlty wud move them nex or what wild thort wud slink their mind, sniffing for gore, stalking sum wounded fellow. They cud not know who they wur, for evry day they wur changed.

No, I knew no need of fowk. Their touches, their smiles, stung like gouging spines.

Yes, I hated peepil more than any wounded pig. I cud live wiv them no more, but wud find myself sum tite, dark burrow.

'Wur yu eva so alone?' I ask Blind.

'Too nites an a day I got lost as a chile. It wur terble fearfull on my own. Anuvver nite wivout touch or talk, I think I wud have died. My spirit wur thinking for leave, for return for find its own.'

'I didn't care so much,' I say. 'After fife moons or so.'

'I need peepil like a fish wants for water,' says Blind. 'I'd rarva spend my time lissening for a prattling fool than sit a day alone.'

But it's no easy thing for leave peepil behind an wriggle away from their clutch.

I took fowk as my guide star. I turned my back on them, for keep them far beyond. Each day I wur trujd farva away. But whereva I wandered, I knew there lay a strait path back, joining them for me.

So fowk crowded close in my thorts for have them far behind.

Evry futfall of my way wur a mistake. For I saw I wur walking like a pursin, still striding for their step. An I wur muttering an waving like a man, thow only for myself. For their sayings an signings wudn't leave my mind. So, as I willed myself rid of fowk, their voices kept sounding off, cackling lowd in my hed.

'Eat!' says Hare. 'It yurs for share.'

'We save yu the fur,' says Crow.

An their flame-flicked satisfied faces leered out from the gloom in my lonesum mind. An the gloss of dog grees shone their smeared fingurs.

An I cud not shake off the scent of them, for their stenches leaked from my very own hide. So I plunged into white water, an wur swept along by a furiuss pull, clowting the rocks, scraping their skin from me, wiping their stink away.

Then the thort cum for me that fowks wash themselves too, splashing thruw the shallows of the lake, for have the water drink their dirt. An in spurning peepil, I wur only copying them.

I wur running from hate, as uvva men did. Fleeing till the fire of rage wur burnt away. But it wur diffurnt for me, I knew, becaws I wur gon for all time.

'Yu see my trubble?' I ask Blind.

'Yes,' says she. 'Yu're gon dogsik crazy. Yu're barking mad, chasing yur tail, howling at the moon. Yu're a lone wulf, an no mistake.'

There wur cunning ways peepil still clawed at me, clutching me in, tracking me from afar, neva leaving my solitary mind.

'Be gon!' I howled at them. 'Leave me be.'

Crow's face formed in the shadows. Flames's cackle sounded thruw the breeze. A hollow of urf, sprowting wisps of grass, wur the shape of Hare's hurry ear.

So, I realised the only way for be free of them wur for shun them, pretending they wurn't there.

'Ha!' I shout them gon, each an evry wun. 'It's no use cumming. I don't see yu there. I can't hear yu any more.'

An I went cunning, gon contrary, but in an animul way, growling insted of talking, sleeping the day, but keeping my eyes open, waking for nite, for close my eyes, crawling a winding way, or scuttling on all fores, washing myself in dirt, drying myself in the rains, eating the rind an pips, an throwing the frewt away. Becaws peepil did it all diffurnt. An I wud neva be free if I clung for their ways.

But when I wur sleeping, they crept into my dreams, jibbering an skwabbling. They spoke out that they luvved me well, begging me for return.

'No!' I'd howl. 'Neva!' But still they cum back for more.

My muvver Carf offen found me out in my dreams. She consoled me that my suffuring wur nothing, nex for hers. An her eyes saw clear where mine saw blurred. An what I thort wur wrong. For she had neva thort it the same. So it cud not be so. Then she reminded me for pity her. She asked me for help her. Then wailed it wur too late. An told me she forgave me. That I wur no better than a louse. Which I did not want for hear.

So I took for dozing open-eyed, for keep fowk away, the living an ded. An wiggled me fingurs in me ears when they howled in my hed. Effen then, they wud not leave me be. Their faces formed in the drifting clowds, smiling down, an their voices gusted in the winds. An their scents kept cumming. Yes, effen out of me. An I retched for smell the small porshun of pursin left in me.

I wur gon strange an no mistake, fritening the beasts. Booboons froze at the site of me, then chattering wur fled for the tops of trees. Jackls turned an ran, when I charged them snarling. If cats crossed my tracks they sniffed an hissed, the hurr on their back risen brissly, as they slinked away wiv a startled backwud glance.

I wur turned for a fierce thing. An not for be crossed. Besides, I wurn't a pursin now, any ways. I'd found the ansur for my trubbles. My mistake wur being me. I wud be nothing from now on. That way, I cud be no wun, free.

Slowly, I cum for be wun wiv Urf. When the wind gusted fierce, I panted strong. Where the waters drifted calm, I flowted kwiet. I wur hot wiv sun by day an cool wiv moon by nite. I wur wet wiv the rains, dry wiv the dust, hard wiv the stones, an skwijy wiv the marsh.

I'd stopped struggling against the ways of things, an bent their way. So I cum content.

Then the more wur drifted out of me, the more I saw beyond. Evrything wur evrywhere, mixed up in evrything. There wur the flicker of deer legs running in the waving of the grass. There wur wafting grass on the windblown fur of deer. Sticks wur bent gnarled like antlurs. Rocks wur pimpil-pocked like the snouts of ox. Eyes saw river, which glinted eyes. Yes, the water saw evrything an cast back evry shape an cullur.

It wur then I first began for see them – hidden shapes of things wrapped in bark, or bulging out from rocks.

'Yu carving now?' asks Blind.

'I am. Sept it seemed easy as skinning a rabbut then. Juss tugging the cover off stones an sticks for show the flesh beneef.'

It wur the cleva eye of a fox, watching out from a smoov stone, that first showed me this. Nearby wur a flat piece of bark, curved an rijd like the wing of a dove. Soon I saw evry stone an wood wur showing me sumthing in its buljs, clutching uvva smoover shapes, trapped wivin.

'Juss give me time, an I'll let yu out,' I told the nipilled belly an fore-legs of Dog. The hed wur crusted by stone, twisted sidewuds, but I cud see the prick of an ear, an tip of his panting tung.

It wur slow cowxing the full shape of dog from stone. An when I got him most parts out, I saw it wurn't the like of my Dog, but sum bruvver wulf, wiv wun back leg bit off below the nee. Yet I wur pleased for let him out, an have him watch an hear in spirit, in his still, chill, stony way.

Thruw the passing moons, my face an lap grew themselves beards. An it wur gon dank an furry in the pits of my arms. When the breeze fell, I winced for find myself alone wiv my ripe, sour stench. The deep threat of my voice still scared me when I growled unawares. An those pointy clawing nails drew blud when I scratched, too eager for be rid of a louse.

My look-back in still water wur a fine disgusting site for my cool grey eyes, gazing crewl an unblinking. Them greedy lips parted on a warning glint of strong, unbroken bite, glissening wiv fresh blud. While the wispy tangle of beard wur matted wiv clots of old bluddy eats.

No, I wudn't want for fite me. I looked a dirty vishuss beast, hardly a pursin at all, wivout a freckle of frendliness in my challenging stare.

I had bin up the long vally between the breasts of Urf, then across the flat of her chest. Still Sun an Moon seemed juss as far. The ground wur crumbling rock, low shrubs sprowted out tufty from narrow, grujing cracks. The salty breeze of Urf's breff blew wetter an fresher now. So I gessed I wur cum near by her mouf.

I heard the roar of water as I trujd over the rij of sand. Man had neva seen the like of this lake. It stretched out furva an brawder than the eye cud tell. There wur no end in site. Curls of water rose up white, taller than men, an flung themselves down on the shore of sand. Then a rippel ran up, casting stones at yur futs, then ran back. But only for trick yu. For it turned, rushing, soon as yu cum, an sent yu sprawling wiv a harder blow.

An yu didn't know where for start eating. For there wur small crabs, long wurms, water grass, stone mussels, drowned burds, stranded fish, scuttlers an wrivers, red frobbers, spiny shells, purpil skwirm-bladders.

The wet air sprayed tangy an ripe, speckled wiv white spume, as if the whole wurld wur rutting, skwirting jooses. Whateva yu put in yur gob tasted savurry an salty. An the soff slimey meats slivvered easy down a gullet. Which gladdened a mouf used for the fur, the mean fusty meat of shrews, the fevvered grissel of hatchlings, or the dry crunch of beetils.

But the water of the lake, whereva yu tried it, wur tainted sour an stinging. An dried for a flaky white scab on yur skin.

When I found the stream of clear water trickling down thruw the sand, I knew I wudn't go thirsty. I had wandered far an found the best patch of Urf. I thort that spred of water wur wun of her moist glissening eyes.

'Look . . .' I gasp.

'But there!' I tug myself anuvva way.

'Speckled eggs . . .' I see, layn on a bed of grass in a curv of rock.

'An burds too.' They screech all around.

★　　★　　★

'Yu happy now,' Blind asks, 'by the Sea side?'

'No,' say I. 'I'm trubbled still. Bin crazy an all.'

Befor a moon wur gon, sadness had crept into my nest of delites. Frowns tugged smiles for the ly of my face, an tears skwirted down while I cackled lowd.

The thort cum for me how Dog wud have liked this place. There wur so much for sniff, wurry, roll in, gnaw on an eat. Or juss rip up from joy.

An in my solitude I knew I wanted for show, for tell, for share. I wanted anuvva for touch on my skin, heed my voice, walk at my side.

'This ain't Hystery,' says Blind, pitiless. 'Does it last long?'

'Free years, no more. Unless it wur fore. But lissen on. In a way yu're in it too.'

I wurn't thinking clearly. Wurds an numbas wur sluicing from me. I thort most in my belly an skin. My dreams wur neva sensible now, but a tangle of sites, tastes an smells, as reasun wur wafting out of me.

I wur barely speaking for myself at all. Wurds no longer explained for me. I knew things best by pulling them apart, eyeing them inside out, sniffing them, chewing the bits, spitting out the sinews, grits an grissels.

I took for the stunted bushes, an the few trees, as frends. They wur payshent, stout-harted, long-suffuring, reliable, cover by nite, perch by day. They dropped me nuts an berrys. I hugged them branch an stem. But their pawses an silences wur awfull long. Yu cud wait moons for a reply. An when it cum it wur moved more by lite an the seasons than it eva wur by me. So, they'd only talk of the wevver, an their ansurs cum terble slow.

'Yu eva tried make frends of a fish?' I ask Blind.

'Not I,' she says. 'I neva knew the need.'

Wise. Fish are cold, gulping, scaly things for a man. Still, no wun cud have tried harder or more hartfelt for cowx them for frends. In the water they flee yu. On the land they thresh wild an scared, frantic for be gon. They loaf yur touch, flapping wild. It's no use offering food. They'll neva feed from yur hand. They juss gaze wide, startled, an will neva look yu in the eye. Then the last twitch is gon from them. Yu've scared them out. An there's nothing left for be fond wiv, bar a spoiling smell an fly-flecked fillets of fish.

Turtuls had no desire for me. Clams an mussels wud close for my touch. Yu may think yu are getting fond wiv a crab, stroking its shell soff an kind, murmuryn this an that. Then crab turns on yu spiteful for pinch. An yu have for smash it up on a rock, breaking it for parts, befor it lets go its crewl grip.

Yu try for be kind an cumpanyanable. At the end of it there's nothing for cling to. Yu're left holding sum crab claw. Face wiv shattered pieces, cold eats, an a ded-eyed rebuke.

So I'd taken for watching the booboons. They skwabbled, had yung, ate frewts, frollicked, cuppled, picked each uvva's fleas, warned wun anuvva when danger wur cum, dug up ants wiv sticks, gathered for romp at the water's ej. I saw they had the pleshurs of peepil, wivout the dark desires, free of the rot that cum wiv wurds.

So offen I went close, for show I wur eager for be their frends, sitting beneef their trees, smiling up, tossing back fallen frewts. But they did not want for know me. They wur loaf for have me near. They chattered, an gobbed, showing slicing teef, flung sticks, an spat out rinds an stones of frewt my way.

'Heehee,' I'd calm them, 'huhu,' for this wur how they spoke soff, for soov each uvva. But they muss have heard a strangeness in my voice that stopped them eva cleaving for me, hugging me as wun of them.

They'd swing away for a furva tree, then sit chattering at me from their new, far perches, a brissling, hooting chorus of red-eyed, moufy hate.

When I cum towards them, arms outstretched, they moved again. I muss have followed them there an back thruw evry tree. The strain of a smile neva left my face. Still they cud not find it in their harts for take for me, or suffur me near.

The only booboon I eva get near is a sick old silver-hurr. She has the twists an staggers so can't run fast, an only in circils.

'Look,' say I, reaching for her hand, as she soon cums round again. 'Shall we be fond? Or what?'

But it is a breef, unhappy embrace. Perps I cum on too eager. I hug her hard, stroke her back an nuzzle her neck. She gave me greef an fleas, then bit my neck. An, in passing, tore an ear.

I hear the booboons chattering thruw that nite, badmoufing me. At sunrise, they cum for ground an gathered in a ring around me, howling, slapping the air, teef chattering, faces screwed in disgust. Then, as wun, they wur turned an gon, a scampering pack, over the mound of rock. Yes, they cudn't abide me any more. I've spoiled this good place for them. They'd gon for live elswhere.

All I eva got from them wur hoots, throwings an fleas.

When the yella blisters sprowt over my face, I know for sure my sowl is finally taken sick. Days of feva cum after that, wivout any nites between. Then sum nites all together, wivout any break for lite.

Then I'm taken by stumblings an mumblings, lumps in my neck an groin, walking circils, an falling flat. I shiver a lot an pick my scabs for keep my skin clean.

Yes, the sickness wur my spirit's. It wur the yella-feva of loneliness. If my body wurn't yung an well-fed, I'd neva have survived.

One day, rubbing on stone, I found sum smoov shapes wur swelling out from it that I remembered dimly from befor. I breefed on it, blowing the dust away. Sure enuf it wur a woom-man. Cum into my hands. Out of nowhere.

'Hello hips,' I say. 'Wellcum tits.'

'Who wur she?' asks Blind.

'She wur no wun I'd eva known befor. Her face was blank an smoov. But her body had the parts of evry woom-man.'

'Prutty?' Blind asks.

'Prutty. But cold an hard. Still as the ded.'

'Yu need a frend,' says Blind, tapping my hand. 'If it ain't too late.'

'I thort of that. For myself,' I say.

*   *   *

Nex nite I dream it cumplete. If I wur for have a mate, it wud be best for carve up my own. Cum the grey glimmers of morning, I knew how it cud be dun.

I had made Dog from a wulf cub. I cud shape any stone for an animul. So I cud surely make sumthing good from *that*.

Yes, all reddy it wur grown an warmed for a cumpanyan in my mind, pieced of warm imaginings, swelled by desire. I cud cleave for it fond. It wud clasp me warm at nite. It cud gather frewts an roots, rowst my meats. An it cud feed the flames I gave it. Yes, an keep them always alive.

Purbly, I cud teach it sum small wurds. Enuf for ansur my cummands. It wudn't need for speak itself, juss cum when I called. Only lissen, an hug me fond.

∗∗–∗∗ | I cort it raw

'Yu gon hartsick?' asks Blind. 'Yu looking for luv?'

'I am, so,' I agree.

'I had many luvvers.' Blind smiles smug. 'When I wur yung.'

'Yu did,' I agree. 'Yur face wurn't much for look at. But there wur plenty good for touch upon. Yu wur lithe an sleek as a fawn. Yur breasts wur swelled as firm as downy frewts. Yur hurr glistered, hunny yella.'

'Neva saw it myself,' she says, 'nor my luvvers. But I felt them all the same. An I knew them all by touch, effen those that neva spoke their names.'

'There wur men who tried for trick yu. Becaws yu cudn't see.'

'They tried . . . But I all ways knew. What my tung didn't taste my hands felt. My ears wur sharp. An my nose cud tell.'

'Crab wur kind. He liked yu well an luvved yu offen.'

'Peepil said his looks wurn't prutty. But my fingurs neva saw him so. So I neva blamed his face. His neck wur short an firm. He had large, soff ears. He had the smoovest elbas I eva met in a man. There wur plenty for him, an most parts firm an warm.'

She thinks of her luvs. I think of mine.

'Much of him went into me. Plenty of me wur gon into him . . .' Blind sighs. 'We nearly cum wun . . .'

I wud have for catch it first. Then train it well, for show it how I cud be liked. An be fond an giving back.

I thort a female wud suit me best. They're calmer, kinder, an warmer by nite. They take less pleshur in a fite, so I thort. I'd have the yunger wun, if it still lived. It wur smoover an smaller, more wellcum for the eye. It'd be the easiest for tame.

Having plucked her in my mind, I wanted her kwick in my hands. But for have her, I had for take her. There lay the seffern dangers. I'd need for go back, nearby fowk.

∗   ∗   ∗

157

For reach her I wud have for cross the white water.

For reach the white water, I wud have for cross the wide parched plain.

For reach the plain, I wud have for climb the high crags.

For reach the crags I wud have for leave the place I wur. That I luvved so well.

I wur sicks days an nites on the jurny, guided back by moon an the dim, dumb tread of my futs. The return wur easier than the cumming had bin. The distance wur less, the ground smoover, the vallys shallower, the hills lower. An it wur desire not despair that tugged my legs.

Their place wur there still. But time had moved on, dragging them along. They wur gon from their frinj of woods. An I wur fife days circilling, in widening sweeps, befor I found the prints of their futs leading for an empty nest of grass. But hope carried me then, as I scented her sweetly stale in the hay, layn amid the stench of the older too, an I stroked the smoov hollow where her hips had sunk into urf. Furva along glissened too fair strands of her hed hurr. I drew them fine thruw my fingurs, sniffed their lenf, then sucked the scented oil from them.

I followed their meandering path, by the scattered rinds of their frewts, the broken husks of their nuts, their dug-over spores, snapped stems, yella spits, damp spots. It wur as thow they sort for be found. So I thort if I hadn't cum upon them, sumthing crewler – cats, wulfs or fowk – wud have found them soon enuf.

I heard them, cluking an grunting, befor I saw them, neeling, grubbing for roots, in the clearing between sum pines. I peered out, bulj-eyed, throb-chested, thruw sum ferns.

Yes. It wur. She. I last saw her nearly a girl. Now she wur nearly a woom-man. Grown an swelled, breasted an tufted. But my eyes liked her better for that. An the grunt of me breff an kwiver of me hands spoke me impatience for have. An for hold.

She stayed her rummaging hand, twisted my way, gon still, suspishus at sum scared scuttle thruw fallen leaves, an warning skwawks from the trees.

Seeing her face only made me want her more. The lips wur

parted by a pink flick of tung. Wide-eyes looked past me, neva taking me in. Nostrils flared. Her eyes neva saw me, thow her nipils pointed me out, shuddering shy on swaying breasts, of which she had too. Wun on each side.

I saw she had legs for the walking, arms for the carrying, tipped wiv hands, finished off wiv sly fingurs. All I wanted in a cumpanyan mate. An if she wur no pursin, I liked her more for that. She'd do well enuf for me. I'd neva wanted for catch a beast so much, sins I stalked an stoned my first hog.

As the free sat chewing on roots, I wriggled back an lay myself low in a sodden dip, scattering myself wiv a covering of leefs.

I thort how for do it. They wur more an wild. But I had gile, desire, an a handy stump of hardwood. Also I cudn't be seen in the gloom, wunce I'd smeared myself wiv clay an dirts. Wiv me cum surprise, a blink behind.

Slink a distance, then slivver close, then pounce. Too hard blows an a soffer wun. Then have her away. That's what I planned.

I waited till the nite-ones moved. The owls flew their perches, the foxes wur padding. A bajur scuffled past, eyeing me harsh, grunting rude.

But I slipped at the ej of their nest. The ground wur tacky where they'd trod an spilled, an I wur toppled down onto the sprawl of them. The old male wur rising up as I clubbed him, the old female wresseled my slippery legs. So I had for batter her bad, as the he-one crawled dazed, split-nosed at my futs, dribbling bluddy. An it wur gon all slidy under the soles of my futs from his wets. An the wun I cum for sunk her teef in me neck an clawed at me eyes. So I wur striking out about me, wivout aim or check, as we wrived about in a howling heap.

As I wriggled away, they wresseled on, blinded by blows, fear an the nite. The hemale wur throttling the she, an she wur blujenning him wiv her fists. They wur terble crewl for each uvva, like bludded jackls, tugging each uvva apart.

Then there wur too things still for be dun. Befor I cracked the yung wun gentle on the back of the hed, where an ugly wound wudn't show beneef the prutty flow of hurr.

Then I wur off into the dark, wiv She on my back.

*   *   *

An I wur pleased, panting from the wayt of her, which neva seemed a load. An glad for have saved her from a dumb, dark, fireless life wiv the beasts. Now I cud make sumthing of her.

I carried my catch all thruw the nite, as far as the dawn.

An yu'll grasp my kind respecks. She wurn't an animul any more. Not for me. I bore her fond wiv care, holding her mouf above the rushing waters when I crossed the river, mindfull neva for crack her hed against trunks of tree or the bumps of the crag.

'But what is she?' asks Blind. 'Yu ain't said clear.'

'Becaws she's shadowy. Time will tell,' I say. 'It's up for me. She's whateva I can make of her.'

It wur easier than I'd supposed, making wun – a cumpanyan mate – but harder than I thort.

The raw stuff wur good but awkward for shape, soff as clay wiv spikey bits, hard as flints. Sum ruff ejs smooved easy. But a sharpness lay hid beneef that pliant skin, an it cort me unwary, cutting thruw for the bone.

So she turned out sum ways less than I wanted, an uvva ways more than I ment.

'But wur she a woom-man? A pursin?' Blind wants for know.

'She did lean that way,' say I. 'In her looks an ways.'

Trew. A likeness wur there, strong from the start. She as much resembled a woom-man as a rabbut is like a hare, or a dik-dik cumpares for a deer. She wur fairer, leaner, sleeker, sliter, wiv a sharper nose an smaller tuck-back ears.

Her hide wur too pale, a mallow pink, an her eyes a cold stony blew I'd neva had watch me befor, except in the bobbing hed of a crake. The hurr of her wur hunny yella. It mostly lay on her hed, being sparse an fine on her belly an thys, thow it sprowted again, a thick tussock in the cleft between her legs.

Like those pale cavecrabs, the cullurs had bled from her. Still she stood out brite from the dark, when her swells glissened moonglow. Yet her vallys hugged shadows, an her crevisses swallowed lite.

If she wur smaller an flatter than a woom-man – more curvy

slopes than buljing mounds – still I liked the ly of the land, an knew it wur ground I'd be happy for tred.

I saw she wur well made of all the parts I'd wished for, placed where a man wud hope for find them, an in the numba he'd expeck, all smoov joins, sheeny skinned.

Her smells wur as close for a woom-man's as the scents of a carf are those of an ox. The muskiness wur soffer, the nosetickle cum sharper, the sour stung less gamey, the milky whiff of hay lay sweeter. An there wur the tugging sniff of sumthing new an strange she carried all her own, like frewt ripening slow an sweet.

Of her insides I knew nothing at first. She didn't have the human hedful, so far as I cud tell. Nor any sense of good an bad, or any sensible sounds. For which I wur glad enuf.

So at first I thort her a pale copy. An wur plenty pleased. For have found this body for cleave for, an hed for fill wiv what's rite.

So I mused as I carried her on, thruw dark for the lite. She wur pressed moist an warm on my shulders. Seffern diffurnt scents of her wafted heddy up my nose. Yet I only knew the names of fife.

'Ow.'

That wur the first sound she uttered, by way of a moan, as she woke snuffling, wriggling for be off my back. Then I crouched low an let her slip from my shulders, rolling onto a flat of pebbely ground. She wudn't try for escape me now. Not now she cud see I wur kindly. An not when she wur bound up wiv twines of birch bark, ankils an wrists.

I saw I wur wise for keep her tied. She wur woken hissing, spitting, thrashing out wiv her legs.

She shivered kwick, teef clacking, as she lay on her flank. She panted fast, like a far-run dog, or a well-trapped hog. Her eyes stared wide, then screwed tite in her shaking hed, as if she cudn't trust, not for her eyes nor for me. Becaws sumthing disagreed wiv her.

'Look at it my way,' I say. 'An understand.' An I smile.

'Ow . . . ow . . .' says she. A moan soff but hartfelt, as if she wur trying for mean sumthing, out lowd, by way of her mouf.

'Ow. Yes. That cud be yur name.' I grin. I prefurred it so, that she'd chose her own. Myself, I'd had for take what wur give for me.

But there's pain cum into her moufings, so I gess she hurts, on her bludcrusty hed, or purbly inside, below the purpilling marks of my hands. Yes, yu cud see my fingurs an palms on her sides, I'd held her so tite, so fond.

'Tsst . . . tsst.' She's started spitting now. Which, cumming from an animul, is neva a wellcum sound.

'But I'm yur frend,' I tell an reach out a testing hand for stroke her hed an pat her blud-flaked ears. But she twists her hed an bares white teef, as if for bite. So I tap her snout firm as a warning.

'Prutty . . .' I say. 'Wild . . .' For I've cort me a ripe thing, fine smelling, teasing for me eyes, suggesting for my mind. But wivout a pursin's taints, an wiv a raw spirit unspoiled.

I knew she wudn't cum for luv me good till I'd fed her plenty an offen. It's the same way wiv muvverlost wulf pups. Yu reach for their hart by filling their belly. An I knew for bend her sharp like willow, but not so far she'd snap.

'Stay!' I pointed down an tapped the ground. Of course, she cudn't wander away. But there wur a few strong wurds she cud know from the start.

Yes, wurds wur cumming back fast into me, now I had sumwun for tell, an sumthing for say.

I gathered spiny frewt, pine nuts an yaw for her an laid them by her futs. She twisted up, sat on her rump for beg, rubbing her bound wrists together, asking for be undun.

'No!' I said sad enuf, then shook my sorry hed. So she cud lurn the sound an sign of refusal together.

'Wahaha-ga,' she said, 'haza-haza krk . . .' Then spat hard an snarled. Like she wur trying for speak.

This warned me. She had a pinch more wit than I needed of her. Maybe the seed of a mind in her hed, an perps an inkling of sense all reddy.

Still, her home wur lost for her, an her kin far behind, an hedsore I gessed. So I wur all she had. But it muss have cum as a cumfort for her for see my smile. An she'd see I had no thort for harm her, nor eva use her for eats.

'Yu no thing yet . . .' I tell this nameless, senseless, skwirmy thing, '. . . but I cud make yu good, if yu juss let me. Nearly a woom-man,' I promiss. 'Or all most a dog.'

Well, I didn't know then how she'd turn out. Or what I'd find beneef the skin.

She ate. She scowled. She spat. I untied her legs, ringed blew an red where the binds had bit above her ankils.

Well, I cudn't carry her foreva thruw life.

We moved on. She walked sum steps ahed, my hand guiding her, resting in the hollow beneef her spine or on a jut of hip, or fingurring the sun sparked strands of her hurr, els sliding my palm down her spine, then stroking her flank. As she hissed, over her frail freckled shulders, like a trapped beast that loafs for be touched.

All the talk wur up for me.

'Yu're firm as a water-melon. Smoov as doe belly. Soff as a booby. Sleek as Yurra frond.' I smile my delite. Juss the site of her drew happy thruw me.

I wanted for feel her more. I wanted for lurn her for like me. An I knew her animul spirit wudn't be forced. It had for be cowxed or led. But the raw smells an touches of her tempted me strangely. I wanted her more than flesh an drink, warmf or safety, bruvver or dog. Only I didn't know, juss yet, for what.

'Yu smell salty as a new cort fish, fresh as resin, heddy as balsam.'

Senseless urges haggled in me hed, an me mind wresseled me will, an me face wur tormented by spusms, an I grunted much. An on we trujd.

By the time the sun wur overhed, I'd cort too lizzurds an stoned wun hare. I unbound her hands an pointed for my meats, for her for carry.

Well, I cudn't do all the wurk.

She looks regretful back along the flats, knowing she cudn't out-run me, then turned wide eyes on me, like a trapped fawn. Knowing she wur well cort, she wur trying for charm me for let her run free.

'Nowhere for hide,' say I. An I think she understands. For she clutches up my food. But it's wurs for her for go along wiv me untied, as if she has agreed. So I hear her sniffles an see her face blowt red an moist.

Yes, all reddy she'd lurned for cry like a pursin, wivout me showing her how or why.

Later – when the time wur reddy – I wud show her how for larf an be glad.

She watched as my palms spun the rod into the groov of the flat-wood. As smoke rose she frowned, then skwealed as a spark flared the dry flakes of leef. Then she watched thruw the splits of her fingurs as I built a crackling nest of fire. The darting flames lit her startled face. She shuffled back, feared of this heat I'd strangely tamed.

I clubbed down too notched stakes yva side of the fire, an skew-ered the meats on a stick which I balanced between.

Then I watched her thruw the drifts of smoke as my meats cooked. An when I'd fed well, I let her chew on the rest.

I'd known evry woom-man that walked on Urf – Gooz, Moonsik, Green-eyes, Duk, Crake, Carf. I'd seen evry patch of evry skin. I'd clung for them when I wur small, swayed from their clowts as I grew tall, ansurred back when I cum strong. I'd seen woom-men do as woom-men will. I knew what they shared an what told each sepert. So I didn't expeck this wun for surprise me much, shaped as she wur much like anuvva, only empty of reasuns inside.

But I jerked uneasy, me buttuks skwirming in damp cold sand. It wur the site of her. For while her mouf say nothing but angry silence, her body wur signing for mine, suggesting oddly. An I sensed she wur perswasive. For my body ached for cum agreed wiv hers.

Her skin glowed sheeny in the firelite where woom-men showed dusty dull. She wur smoov where woom-men wur puckered, pocked or flaky. Her breasts swelled out hard, unripe, small but stubborn. The nipils peered prowd ahed. Whereas woom-men's paps wur bladders, hanging stretched an flat when empty, downcast for the ground, or swollen fat when suckling. An her flat belly wur tugged inwurd wiv her evry breff, where folds of skin bounce or kwiver on a woom-man.

Those swollen petal lips wur split by a flickering tip of tung. The cheeks wur curved in, not blowted out like a gowfer's. The brow wur unwurried by any cutting wrinkles. No, this fresh face told its fear by the flitter of gaze, the jumpy whites of its eyes. An the tite clench of those thys. But the sly gard of that hand, curled over the fluffy wisps of fleece, only drew me curiuss. As if she cud conceal from my imaginings whateva lay beneef.

She wur a dewy, unblemished bud, reddy for unfold.

So I sat twitchy, in the thrall of what her body told, wondering what surprises it had still for reveal, an when it wud confide.

An I understood in my hed the tugs I felt below, the pull of man for woom-man, the mute sayings of her shapes. It wur a thing between our bodys, that hardly glanced up upon reasun or sense, but glissened silent in the glimmers of her skin, swelling curvs, clinging in clefts.

All the while her body went on shouting itself for mine. Them dark nipils darted in them amba rounds, eyeing me odd. Them breasts swelled prowd. Between long shimmery thys yawned a small dark smile.

An if I wur confused between the ears, me body below knew well enuf. An my hand reached out for her shulder. For my hand well understood.

But she juss flinched away, neva understanding that her body wanted mine, beckoning strong behind the back of her skittery mind.

'It wur crewl an ruff for take her,' says Blind.

'Wait,' I say, 'an yu'll surely thank me by the end.'

★ ★ – ★ ★ – > The purr of us

Dog wur diffurnt. We understood, sharing the same tastes for secrussy, rabbuts, dark, blud an chase. We wur moved by the same slyness an slinking lope. He took for me from the start. As I cleaved for him. Trew, we bickered. But if he nipped me, I bit him back. Then, wivin too snarls, the tussle wur settled. Then, wiv a smile an wag wur forgot. We'd curled up together the first nite, trusting for the uvva's warmf, wiv no suspishun of their teef. He delited for me for stroke his fur, rolling onto his back for have his stomak scratched. If he scampered from site, I knew he'd soon be bounding back. He licked my cheeks. He found joy in my smile, panting his content, narrowing his eyes. When he sniffed my hide he snuffled glad, kwivering from haunch for snout.

But my new cumpanyan wur pieced of tuffer, chiller stuff. She wur sorrurful an surly. Her affeckshuns she held shaded, as a dog stows a sorry tail between its legs. Her enthusiasms wur breef an few. She cringed from my touch. She flared her nostrils, all sniffy at my smells. She hissed when I patted her hed or rubbed her belly, growled when I reached out for stroke her fur. When she slid from my site I knew she wur gon for hide. She licked me nowhere. She scratched me where I neva itched. She insisted for ly an arm's lenf apart at nite, hissing if I eva rolled close. But when she thort I wur sleeping, she wriggled near. Then I woke hurt, for warn her neva for hit on me. Nyva on the hed nor my body. Not wiv stones, wood nor fists. An when I had slapped her snout or ears – but soff, mind, neva hard enuf for wound – she whined a long while after, then silently nurrished a gruj, which she wore all the nex day, in creases of hurt on her face, being loaf for forget.

Of caws, I knew the diffurnce an how they spoke. Wulfs are luvving for any they take as their own. Dog wur yung when I first cum on him. This wun wur nearly grown, an had many years for

166

lurn distrust. An Dog wur male, while this wur female. An there's always a tussle when the seckses mix.

So I kept myself payshent, an suffurd long. 'Taming takes time,' I told myself. 'A rock won't be smooved in wun day.'

An I wur tugged by urgings for Ow that I neva felt for Dog.

My hands wanted for touch, my mouf yearned for taste, my arms wur shivering for hold. An uvva parts of me wur oddly moved. All by the parts of her. Unfelt, but telling for my eyes.

Yes, coils of want wrived like snakes wivin me. But I wur afraid for have them slivver out, for fear of their winding crush, venom an bite.

I had given up my pursin's ways. An she wur an empty nameless thing. I didn't know what. But far diffurnt for me.

Like only mates wiv like. Duks wiv drakes. Doe wiv buk, sow wiv boar. Yet a kware thort wriggled in me mind for tangle wiv her, as a man cupples wiv a woom-man. Yes, still I wanted to, effen thow I'd left peepil an their ways far behind.

I thort of it as I looked her way, an looked her way too offen. So I stumbled an tripped. Or ripped my legs, neva seeing the dips or thorns on our path.

For she wur good for look on. Yes, I liked nothing better than for watch her befor, behind, aside, uprite, bending, layn on the ground – slate eyes, flush face, salmon tung, fire lips, freckled shulders, berry-brown nipils, sandy thys, hunny bush.

We wur many days on the way for the great lake. Her steps wur meandering an slow. She offen stopped, looking over her shulder, the way that we wur cum, gon away from her own, or gazed down at her spiked shins an blisterd futs.

'Cum!' I'd call, an she'd grujingly slope on. But I knew wunce she'd seen the place I had for give her, she'd neva want for leave.

All the while we walked, I pointed for things an spoke their names – water, bush, berry, blud, hill, arms, legs, brews, lips.

If I wur telling too much, too fast, for her for lurn, I knew sum sounds muss pierce her ears, an loj between.

'Wulfs,' I say the fird nite. 'Hungry. Free.' We wur slumped apart by the fire. I showed my teef an ground them, for help her understand. An I yelped my ansur for the dark, for tell them wulfs I wur nearly kin, an held no harm for them. Not in my hart.

She muss have known the howls for herself, an what muss slink behind. For her face wur twisted by spusms, an her shulders went twitchy, an her breffs cum blustery, short an fast.

Nex happened a strange thing.

Wivout looking for me, she wriggled her buttuks my way, so she wur skwirmed close for my side.

An as the wulfs panted nearer, ansurring my call, so she cums closer still. So the gulf between us wur shrunk for the nearness of frends. Till I cud feel the warmf of her skin on mine, prickly across our narrow divide. So I supposed she wur wun of those who'd neva seen the good in wulfs, neva fed them scraps an bones, or taken wun as frend. An neva having had fire about her befor, she wudn't know that flames held wulfs in the shadows, sevral leaps apart, effen if they ment yu harm.

'How, wow, wow, waaa-aaaa,' I tell wulfs plain enuf, as Dog himself wur fond for say. They pace around us whining, brissle backed, sparkil eyed, pawing the ground, free pounces away.

But she is clinging for me now, her arms round my chest, the nails of her fingurs clawing eager for me, like a woom-man clutched by fondness for a man.

All those days she wudn't suffur my touch, now she won't leave me alone.

When I stretch out for the rabbut bones an fur from by the fire, for fling them for the wulfs, she mistakes my moves, thinking I'm going for leave her there. An her hands are clasping hard for my calves, tugging for me for stay.

Then cums the kwarest thing. No ly.

Believe it or not. The animul spoke.

She says out lowd. For me. Using the very wurd I've told her most.

'No!' she says, kwiet an kwavery.

'Ha?' say I, peering down at her dancing eyes, sparked by fire, glinting me back. 'No? . . . No what?'

'No go!' she shouts. 'Stay!' An she's smacking the ground by her side wiv wun hand, tugging on my nee wiv the uvva.

Dog neva spoke wunce. Which made this wun slyer in her purtickler way. She'd bin lurning from me all the time. Cummands, fears, likes, an such. But she'd bin too grujing or shy for say.

'Yu want . . . *me?*' I ask.

'Here . . . wiv me,' she conceeds, sad for say.

So now she wur moved by a desire for me. As only Carf, Dog or Ratz had eva felt befor. So a need in me cum met an matched by her want for me.

Then the strenf in me is splintered. I'm crumbled weak, broke open, crushed moist, like an egg trodden by sum fowk's fut. So my eyes wetted my cheeks. An I shrieked for the dark.

But I didn't howl like a wulf this time. But sobbed out like a pursin again.

Understanding lay between us that nite. We both grasped at it, an so we cum joined.

She knew me better than the teef of the dark, an having thort on the diffurnce liked me more, an trusted me kinder. An looked for me for gard her. For she had no wun els. We wur amongst biters in a strange land. The wind wur gusting cold, russelling the bushes, an the scarps of rock wur whisseling, an the vally ansurred in moans. An the nite wur a thick curdled black, clotted dense wiv her fears, an arms reach from our dying fire. So it cums as a cumfort for touch. Thow she had nothing better for cling for than me.

So she neva pushes me away. Our rolling eyes watch each uvva. We're lit by the pulsing glow of embers, as we ly cheek for jowl. My arms reach round for the back of her, drawing her close, so we meet belly for belly, ruff for smoov, brissle for down, an her legs part, then clench tite on wun of mine. She's warm as a shaft of sun when yu blink out from a long dark cave. I'm rapt in the scents of her, fragrant as a muskrat, as my fingurs press her, frail, rib thin an nobble spined. Then I tug her titer, warm breasted, as her tears wet my neck. An I rub her hard for warm her from the shivers an smoov her gooz-bumbed skin. An I lick her salty cheeks, tasting the zest of her rind, sour appel sharp. An smell her, all fresh shelled scallops, ox rut, an fox lair.

My fingurs rove curiuss, an much of her cums closer for hand, warm an cool, bony an soff, fleecy an smooth, dry an moist, permitting an resisting, open an closed, kwivering an still.

'Ha!' I gurgle delite at my find. 'Haha!'

There being much more for her than I eva gessed. I reached places about her that had shown for the eye, an touched upon sum things I'd neva felt befor. An all of them spoke thruw my thick hide, urging on the flesh of me.

But still we wur not nakid enuf. For our hides cloved us, holding us raw flesh apart.

'Skin!' I wail. 'It cum between . . .' an I'm wresseling for be in her.

Then they wur wriving together. Body of mine an body of hers, wiv a frenzid ruffness all their own, juddering together like butting deer, hips clattering, fingurs scratching, all crushed in a tangle of wresseling limbs.

My body is flinging itself into hers as if it has for be in. But I'm watching apart, above, startled, thruw harf-closed eyes.

After, I patted her outsides fond, bumps an curvs. I wanted for talk of the wonder. How her body moved mine for a thrusting fit. How we wur matched so exack.

'I juss fit in . . .' I say, 'tite . . . wiv a push.'

For we'd cum together so hot, wet, fast an trew.

'Yu draw the very jooses from me . . .' I gasp.

But Ow don't say, being moved by sum new sorrur her own. Sadness cums weeping like winter rain over the empty flats of her face. So she shakes on, by my side, back turned, shook by blustering sobs.

'Be happy.' I pressed her wincing face between my firm, kind hands. 'I've made yu like a woom-man. Yu're nearly a pursin now . . . I'll call yu Made.'

For I'd knapped her wiv my own too mitts into sumthing handy, well-shaped.

'Whaaaa . . .' she juss sobs on.

I'd had her clean, unblemished, only handfulls of days. Then her face grew those yella blisters, like mine had worn befor. Then I knew the same sickness of spirit wur cum into her, as had cum into me. It wur the yella pox of loneliness. She'd gon ill, her spirit sickening, yearning for her kin.

I raged as she fevered. She cud not find me cumpanyan an cumfort enuf. I feared she wud be spoiled befor she wur cum ripe. That smoov face wud go livid an pocked. I wur worried she wud die on me as soon as she wur tamed.

Free days I watched her thruw the shrieking feva. Then I followed her thruw the staggering days, an picked her up, when she cud not raise herself. I chewed food for her an spat it down her mouf. I washed the hot sour swet from her wiv sooving waters. I lay by her, till her spirit cum strong again.

But the sickness had ate her insides, whittled her thin, an rattled her shaky.

'Yur legs are gon spindly. Yu gon scrawny an ribby. Yur face is bit up like a wurmy blossom,' I told her, 'but I will still cleave for yu. I like yu well enuf. There's no wun els for me.'

Perps she didn't understand all I said, but she knew the frust, for she wur lurning wurds kwick. For my teaching tung had found a telling ej.

I neva forgot her first wurds, scarred in my mind.

After she'd told me 'no' an 'stay', she nex says 'ffetch', 'ffire' an 'ffish'. 'Yes' came slow an grujing after. Then there wur 'crab', 'water', 'me' an 'mine'. 'Go' an 'bring' followed. 'Kwick' wurn't slow behind.

'Good' an 'bad' she spoke offen, but not for say what wur needed or shud be dun. Rarva for tell me her wants an tastes. Of which she had many, an plenty felt strong.

She took for poking into my hed wiv her tellings, stirring round in my feelings, wiv her scowls, smiles, sulks an chortles. So her pleshur wur my delite, an her pains becum my sorrurs.

Becaws I didn't know then what I know now. That when too are long together, the woom-man melts into the man, an the man trickles into her. So nyva are eva what they wur befor. But a tangle of this an that, him an her. Like lizzurds merged into their rocks. An, if yu leave them alone long enuf, each is so mixed up in the uvva yu can't know them apart.

Which gave Made strenf, an took it from me. While lending me her kindness, an making her ruffer by the day.

Lurning as much, an faster, she wur using the looks of her face for get under my skin. I wur a nut for the crack of her stony gaze,

171

a peeled yaw for the bite of her glare. Her pout sucked me out, snail nakid from my shell. My temper wur still as a pool, till the stamp of her fut splattered my calm, an muddied the waters. So I wur grass that bent an shivered for her blustering blow an suck. An when she tossed hard wurds thruw my ears, I had a sinking, falling feeling. My face showed the rippels.

** – ** – >> | Too much, too bad, too fast

'There's a mistake peepil make in Hystery,' Blind says. 'Fowk look too much at the wurld outside, neva peering into themselves. There's things wivin them they think are layn outside.'

Yes. Mite be. Easy for her for say. Blind had a hed start, missing eyes. The sites of the wurld neva misled her from lissening for the slivvers an rumbuls of her insides.

'Trew enuf,' I nod. 'We wur stuffing our moufs a long time, befor we realized it wur hunger had us do it. We had fire befor we talked of the burns wivin. We'd gon deep down caves, befor we found the damp, winding tunnels of our desires. We ansurred the skweals of animuls, eckowing thruw the vallys, befor we thort for talk for ourselves. Rowst pork cum befor luv. We got brew befor we got drunk. Many things in our heds wur a long time in the finding . . .'

'The wriggle wurm of hope,' says Blind.

'The eckowing caves of murmury,' say I.

'The snake of revenge.'

'The twisty burrows of yurning.'

'The tangled briars of desire, the shivry ice of regret,' says Blind.

'The hog of obstinassy. His snuffling snout of greed.'

'It's a deal for skwash in a single skull,' says Blind. 'It's a wonder there's space enuf. It's no surprise the beasts of mind skwabble sum, crowded so.'

An suppose yu're stung all over by the prickles of need, while the leeches of luv are blowting on yur blud, sucking yu pale, drawing yur hurt insides out.

'Yu eva hear . . .' I ask Blind, 'of the man who swapped his chile for a cat skin?'

'No,' she says. 'Why he do that?'

* * *

I wur hedsik. I wur shivring terble. Skin wud warm me. Chile cudn't. I owed a chile for a woom-man who wanted mine. She'd care for the girl, feed her, an hug her fond an warm. Seemed it wur for the best, for all. Only it left me sunk in a midden-of-shame. So my nose wur gon sniffy at the stench. An my tung neva liked for sound it.

'He got his reasuns,' I explain.

As Made got wurds, she took for bragging about what she had.

'These my futs,' she says, scuffing the sand. 'I got me hands too . . .' She stoops for fingur a shell, rijs an whorls, then casts it aside. 'I got eyes, ears, mouf an all. I is Me.' She taps her belly. 'Me is I. An myself too.'

'Ha!' I agree. 'Yu all together wiv yurself. An together too wiv me.'

'No! We sepert.' She draws back frowning. 'Yu apart. Yu . . . grunt,' she says. 'Yu animul.'

'No I'm . . . a pursin.'

It juss cum back for me, despite neva seeing anuvva pursin so many summers.

'No. Yu Grunt.' She nods. 'Umm . . . umm . . . umm.' She chuckles, making sum sucking sounds she supposes cum when I eat.

'Can't be,' I explained. 'Only fowk give names. Only peepil can change them, or take them away.'

'What those . . . peepil?' she demands.

'I fowk . . . Many more, over there . . . like me.' I waved for the hills. Yes, I found myself prowd, calling up my kin.

'There *more*, like yu?' She frowns.

'Plenty! Alike as the fingurs of a hand.'

She considers, scowls an swallows. 'I Uman,' she says or sumsuch.

'Yu Uman?'

'Ha!' She nods. 'We fore. Far. Over there.' She pointed the same way.

'They talk?'

'Umans talk? Nus parlys. Cum wossus.' She shrugs an grins. 'Ruwin retnus, cumprin? Nus, jackassus, crius, chuchotus, gemissus, surrus, rirus, chantus, marmonus. Parly vrays, men-songs, sentimens, idys . . .'

'Stop that babble,' I say. I'd heard enuf. For it wur empty of any sense, but prickly an hissy on the ears.

'Umans cum soon,' she says. 'All free uvvas. They catch yu. They tie yu, like yu tie me. Then . . .'

'Kill me?' I ask. 'Eat me?' I challenge, unafraid.

'No!' She shook her hed, winced hurt in disbelief, then spat. 'We . . . larf at yu,' she warned, 'whole day long. Maybe too . . . Then yu'll be prickled sorry . . .'

'Larf, why?'

'Look at yu!'

I peer down my lenf, belly, shins, futs. All seems perfuck, in place. 'What then?'

'Yu animul,' says Made, 'but yu *talk* sum!' An she wur turned away, her hands for her face, her ribs kwivered by mirf.

But if our moufs saw things diffurnt, our bodys wur cumming better frends, in the muddel, between the legs, wheneva they chance together, wiv less struggle an more clasping, more clukings an less spittings, more spredding an less clenching. An the bitings an claw-ings wur fewer too.

I look down at her face, seeing her lids closed, an her mouf twitches unspeaking, like she trusts, an there's nothing needing seeing, becaws our bodys are cum for an understanding, an our minds need neva mind so much.

She wur cummming more like me, an I wur cumming more like her, for there wur looks we found that spoke wivout wurds, an knowings we found together, an expeckings shared, an kwiet touch-ings, brushing hands or bumping hips or stroking of heds, that wur only for show we conneck.

There wur a Shrimp-Moon, then a Bladder-Moon, then a water-grass time, befor I saw she wur growing plump again.

'Full belly,' I say. 'Good. I stuff yu fat. I stuff yu offen.'

She narrows her eyes an shakes her hed. 'I grow wun,' she says.

'Grow wun? What?'

She juss shrugs. 'Wait . . . we see.'

I think of woom-men an how they swell. 'Whaaa?' I gess, sounding off like a booby.

'Ha.' She nods. 'Like that. Cud be . . .'

Sure enuf, she wur gon vomutty evry morning, cramped an blowted the rest of the day, wiv her breasts swelling tender, nipilsore. There wur a dark rij down her belly. An when I lay my hand on it, I felt wrigglings beneef.

It lasted sevral moons. But I bore it like a man.

An it wurn't juss annuvva she wur making nyva. She'd started bringing up wurds.

'Good wurds?' asks Blind.

'More use for her than me,' I say.

'Like?'

'Like . . .' I ponder back. '"Thatall? Fish-off!"' I remember that wun well. 'It wur said wiv a rolling of the eyes. It ment – Call that a meal? Where's the welks? An where's the flesh? Do yu think I'd be happy wiv bladder grass? Catch more! An bring me better. If yu eva expeck a smile from me.'

Then there was 'Hocum-yuneva-wunce . . .' which was for encuraj me for do diffurnt nex time, no matter what I dun befor.

An there was 'Wha-haaha!' which cum more frendly. Being a glad greeting for rowst crab's claws, well met at the fireside by moonlite, after a lean, hungry day.

Or 'Getoffme-now'. Which wur a surly turning away, wiv slaps an pinching.

An 'aaah-urrh'. Which wur pleased an sorry by turns, wiv swallowing an spitting, saying sum of this gote leg is savurry, while sum parts taste rotted terble.

The grasses wur wivvering when Made wur swelled full stretch. She lay down whimpering for birf it. I fell by her side panting. Becaws the hurtful push wur starting. An it came slow for start, then it wur like a mitey rolling rock wur coming for burst out between me legs. But there wur nowhere for it for cum. So it wur wurs for me. At least Made had an opening. For let the swelling out. But I wur a frobbing absess wivout a hed.

Yet still she's whimpering on.

'Kwiet . . .' I howl. 'Be still . . . All yur pain . . . gon into me.'

This way I wur lifting the hurt out from her. I wur all cries an wails, clutching me belly, wriving on the ground, knowing I muss burst soon or die. So Made knew only pleshur. Murmuryn an yelping her delite.

Then the small thing wur born. Blew eyes. Tufty hed. Beneef bluddy smeary gizzum. Female, between the legs.

'Aaaah!' I scream.

'Whaaoa . . . aaa,' it says.

'Owww,' shouts Made.

An it is cum out skwijy, steaming in the chill air, wrapped in tangles of offal, wiv a grimace of regret.

'Ha!' I shriek. 'A littil . . . pursin.'

Yes, its arms an legs wur too. An the hed of it wur human, cumplete wiv eyes, nose an ears. It looks as much like a booby as any booby can, being itself alone, an new. Which surprised an kwarely pleased me. Thow I'm puzzild how sum stray spirit has cum upon Made an I in our lonely place, for ask her belly for be grown.

'We birf wun!' I whimper. Me teef have sliced my lips. I'm sore stretched, weary an pained by the cumming of it.

But she juss hugs it for her, prattles an gurgles for it, but neva ansurs me.

Now it's cum, it's like I neva bin there. She only got eyes an bussom for chile.

So I'm cum the stranger. An they the purr. It neva leaves her, clinging like a barnacle for those breasts that befor wur mine. An when I go for ly wiv Made, an hug her sum, she's pushing me ruffly away.

Made says the small thing is wun of her. But I can see the signs. It wur growing like a pursin. Wiv a spirit old an wise. Soon it wur shrieking, taking in an giving out, wivout us eva showing it how.

I called it Girl. Becaws its spirit wur so sharp an previuss, it wur like a pursin from befor, having lived many lives all reddy.

Girl fattens at Made's paps, still she neva does much, sept demand an skweal. The free of us live tite as wun. Only I sense, we're torn for they an me.

Still, I wur happy for have them, there, an mite have stayed so, but a wurs, terble split was for cum between.

We wur layn for the nite on the flat rij, among the wire grass, in a sandy hollow, behind the windbreak of rocks.

The gowfers know first. An the knowing sent them crazed. They sprung skweaking out of their burrows, hed over tail as if thrown, scurrying past our fire wivout a sidelong look at us, moved by a terrur of sumthing wurs.

The burds lurn nex. Their dawn screeches an skwawks wur scared too lowd. They swarmed thick an dark above us. Then they wur flown. An the grey morning air glowered empty an still.

Too turtuls lay belly up, unstirring, playing ded an cold, so the killer cumming wud pass them by.

The waters knew too, slapping the rocks. But wiv a new, kwicker, shallow swish, like a fritened hart.

By the shore, the crabs wur warned all reddy. They clung in their rock pools beneef the gurgling waters. An the barnacles wur clamped tite. An the mussels wud not open the merest crack. The skwirm bladders throbbed scared on the slimy stones. Kelp wur strewn limp an broken over the sands.

The wind wur warning us, panting hot an fast, tainted a smoky yella, rotten on the nose.

Then it cum.

The eye of Sun blinked closed.

We wur swallowed into the hot belly of dark.

Urf wur shivery beneef our skwirming startled futs.

Then She shuddered. Nex She yawned open. An the rocks thundered an screamed as they cum ripped apart.

We kwaked too.

As the sands swayed like waves, I clung for Ow, an Ow clung for Chile. An over the ripping of Urf's skin we barely heard each uvva, sobs an howls.

Time wur gon. For the Sun neva came. An Moon neva showed. But we lay smoked by the hot brown air. An effen when it thinned, it wur juss long deepdusk, then longer nite, by turns. But hotter than day. An we thort we'd lost lite. An wud neva be sooved by cold again. Nor did we expeck for live.

This wur the longest nite on Urf. When Sun came back, it glimmered tired an weak behind the smog. It rained hot, sour an yella. But at least we cud drink.

In the gloom we saw that mounds wur sunk, an dips rose up, rocks wur rent, flats buljd cracked. Urf wur ripped thruw her hide, for mussel an bowels, all gaping wounds.

Nothing knew its place any more. The trees wur plucked from the ground, crabs crawled over splintered trunks, the bushes wur fallen into crevices, lizzurds flowted belly up in pools, fish wur burrowed in holes, clowds hugged the urf, dust hung in the air, wind gusted up from holes underground, wurms wriggled lost on stone.

'We go.' Made said.
Baby howled.
'Wha?' I cried. My place wur torn apart.
'We go sumwhere els,' said Ow. 'This land is broke up an can neva be whole.'

We trujd free days an saw nowhere strait, nothing whole. All the old paths wur gon, an the old places twisted, tangled. An we cud not walk wun way any more for deep cracks split the land, an wur too wide for leap. So we snaked this way then that, an lept over the splits. But any way or reasun we followed wur soon broke up by deep cracks.

When we saw free pines, swaying slanted but still rooted, we gessed we wur cum a good way, or things, thow bent, wur getting strait. An thow it wur long befor nite, we lay down on green, living grass. An slept.

We didn't know where we wur hedded. We juss walked on. More days than we cud tally, far as we cud from Urf's gaping wounds.

We knew we wur wandering unsafe. We shud have slept by turns, only offen we wur too tired by the long day's truj. Uvva times we trusted.

*   *   *

I wur layn on that damp shore between the sea of dreams an the drifts of understanding. Warm sleep wur lapping me an slivvering back. I sensed the tide wur drawing out. The cool wind of sense wur rowsing me, russelling my hurr. Soon, I dreamed, I'd cum awake.

Their sounds carried first for my drowsy mind – a clack of bones, whispers an soff wissels. Then their smells wur drifted for me, warm an sharp – a hot soursweet rot, an a musky pissdamp ecko. Shortly they wur cum themselves, in their bodys, becaws I felt the touch of wun of them nex, in the prod of a horny townail in a soff place juss below my ribs.

Much cums kwick into my hed – a fond disgust, a fearful relief, a knowing surprise. My throwt gulps for retch, my nose twitches for sneeze, waters gush out between my legs. But my bladder neva consents. An my hart is thrashing like a stranded fish. But my mind warns me for ly still, as I shiver an pant, for pretend for sleep on, while thinking what wur best for do, peeking up thruw part-closed, startled eyes.

They wur free, looming tall an black against the gold glare of sky. My eyes wur not reddy for the shock of sun, after the dim sites of sleep.

They look down for me, as I look up for them. They are peepil. What isn't changed in them has stayed the same. I am back amongst my own.

'What those?' asks wun. A man.

'This an that,' a second shrugs. 'Bits like peepil, parts like beasts.'

'I seen sumthing like the ruff wun wunce . . .' The man's eyes flicker closed. He strains for the wurd for snare me.

'There's sumthing for its hed . . . I seen a smaller, smoover wun befor. An we had a name for that . . .'

Made jerks awake wiv a startle, wrenching on my arm. The chile skwirms an splutters by our side.

'Ha!' I sway up for skwat, talking as calm as my panting breffs allow, hoping for soov us all. 'Hello there, fowk . . . I am Gob . . . This is Made . . .' I pat her hed. '. . . an the small wun is a chile.'

Fowk jump back, sneezing, wide-eyed.

'Well?' Wun says. 'Yu hear that?'

'It's trying for talk!'

'Like it straining for say.'

I reach out a hand an drag a fum line in the dust – of the shape daubed on their levvry brows.

'<,' I sign it, an nod for the wise.

'It scratches the dust.'

'Like a hen, clawing for grubs.'

Their faces show clearer for my eyes, now I'm woken for the day. There's no mistaking that flat crab scowl an noseless drawl.

'Jackl!' I shriek, bringing up more pleshur than I know. 'Bruvver Ratz . . . Mows . . .' I name him all the way back for the tottering chile who still had a snout.

'It babbles out those names yu lost!'

'Yu're Jackl,' I say. 'I'm Gob . . . We're bruvvers. Wun muvversblud . . .'

'No . . . I'm not Jackl.' He spits the name for the ground, wiv a dollup of sumthing els. 'I got no bruvver,' slurrs Jackl. He speaks for the uvvas, then twists scowly on me. He shakes his hed, bemused for find himself speaking back for his catch for wunce.

'My name is Kinder . . . Kinder-than-he-wur. Neva-speak-of-his-nose. Brown-eyes-owns-the-duks. Ear-bone. Bent-leg.'

'A good name.' I suck, tasting the full lenf of it. 'It drapes yu good, an yu wear it well. It covers much of yu.'

'Only murmury an the ded eva call me Jackl.'

'Carf . . .' I remind him. 'Our muvver wur Carf.'

'Gob?' Jackl's eyes roll. Pain pinches his face. It's like his tung has found a sour pip lojd in the back of his throwt.

'There wur a Gob . . .' his frend reminds. 'But he wur a boy. Wun of us . . . long ago . . .'

'He ate childrins.' Jackl winces.

'Then a wulf ate him.' They consider this kwiet befor blustering lowd into larfs.

I thort they mite have remembered me trewer, fonder, for more.

I know the uvvas now, thow their faces are aged, dug deep wiv wrinkles. Hurr has fled. Teef are shed. An arm is wivvered. A limp has leeched itself for a leg.

'Yu're Potto . . .' I wag my knowing fingur. '. . . an yu're Crow. The cleverest an the strongest . . . The best men on Urf.'

'No. I'm Big-Pig,' says Potto, 'an this is First-Mouf . . . Peepil know us as The Pig an The Mouf.'

They step back, looking at me narrow-eyed, heds cocked, then sway together for a whispering huddle.

'He talks ruff an slow, but sum he says is nearly trew . . .' Crow tells. 'He is not of us . . . but he knows how we wur. He sees behind us, for where we are cum. His hed is in the passed. His manners too.'

'An Wurm . . .' I babble on. 'Broke an Bok . . . I knew them all.'

Their faces turn, twitched an wincing. Hurt rolls their eyes.

'He knows the ded . . .' I heard Potto whisper, 'an by their old, ded names.'

'Shud we send him back, then?' asks Jackl. 'For those Beyond? Those ded are purbly missing him all reddy.'

Crow leans down, sniffs me, then turns away kwick, sneezing. 'I muss ask this of yu,' he says. 'Are yu living? Or maybe a ded wun?'

'I live,' I say. 'I can piss, weep an bleed.' For it's known well

enuf that thow the ded may sumtimes walk an talk, they're gon all
dusty dry, like a haze of pollen shaken from the grass – so yu can't
skweeze any gobs of jooses from them.

'Sum of yu's like a pursin. But yur face confuses my eyes. An
yur tung muddles sense . . . Are yu sum mixed-up chile of a man
an a beast? Els sum rotted pursin?'

'He's wun of those twisted birfings. Purbly his muvver wur a
woom-man, while his spirit wur sumthing wurs.'

'A bear or hog, or such. Which ruffs him up.'

'I am a pursin,' I protest. 'Thruw an thruw. From scalp for tow.
Inside an out.'

I ain't seen my kin for fife full years. Soon as I'm cum back for
them, they're bad-moufing me again. Neva mind a frendly wellcum,
befor they start.

'Yu are?'

'I am that. I can swim. Knap stones an snare rabbuts.'

'If yu wur a pursin . . .' says Potto, shaking his hed, 'yu wudn't
look wild. Yu'd know fowk's ways. Yu'd have numbas an moruls.
Yu'd wear sum charm on yur face.'

'Wun, seffern, fife, free,' I brag, saying sum numbas I knew
from befor. 'Those are sum I remember well. They got bruvvers
born between. I know sevral more, many by name. But, perps the
family's grown, while I've bin away.'

'It's got a thinking hed at least,' says Potto, tapping kwick on
his. 'An lissening ears.'

'Yes,' I confess it, 'I've got a mind in this skull of mine.'

'A spirit too?'

'An old wun – cunning an sly like a fox,' I confess, 'but kind as
a cow for its own.'

'Yu've got moruls too?'

'Sum. An I'd like for cum by more. A man can't have enuf if he
hopes for be agreeable.'

'Can yu make fire?'

'I call it for me . . . by rubbing woods.' I spill fowk's secret. His
eyes glare thruw slits of concern.

'Why are pigs?'

'Becaws fowk muss eat,' I gess.

'So . . . who are these?' He points for Made cowering by me
blink-eyed, hugging her snuffly booby between her breasts.

'The big wun is nearly a woom-man, as yu'll see by her shapes. The small wun is much like a chile.'

'Where they cum from?'

'First I made the woom-man myself. Then the woom-man made the chile. I neva ask her why. She had reasuns all her own.'

He sneezes, eyes crinkled, clowting his brow in disbelief.

'Look, I wur lonely,' I say. 'I needed a woom-man, I wanted a frend.'

They look sharp for each uvva. Whateva they'd lurned about woom-men wivout me, they hadn't found how for make their own.

'That's a useful medsin – making woom-men.' Crow sucks on the joos of this idea. His voice joins envy for dowt. 'But easier said than dun, I gess.'

'How many woom-men yu got now?' I ask.

'Seffern,' Crow says. 'All shared out. All told.'

'I cud show yu how for make sum more,' I offer. 'Yu muss know where for find the raw stuff, an how for knap it kindly. The secret is knowing which parts for rub an which for leave well alone. Then yu muss smoov it up the rite way. Like wiv wood, yu mussn't bend it far against the grain.'

'An how did yu cum by those wurds of yurs? They're ours.'

'I wur there . . . when the very first wun cum, that Dust-Moon, gurgling out from the rib of rowst pig.'

Crow is silenced by his sneeze of surprise. He's used up plenty kwestyuns, still he can't understand. He starts drubbing his brow wiv his fists for disloj the clinging ansur.

'There's sumthing here,' he says, 'that needs looking into, closer, more . . .'

Potto nods. Jackl scowls.

'Perps we shud open it up, look under the skin?' my bruvver says.

'No!' I say. 'See it thruw my eyes. Smell it thruw my nose . . .'

'What?'

I sniff the air. I see how they have painted their hides. I eye the gloss for their heds.

'Is that duk grees on yur hurr? An ashes on yur chests? Becaws if I dirty myself the same way . . . Stained my man's parts oranj wiv lichen . . .' I watch their dowt-tugged faces sagging for imagine. '. . . I'd look juss as fine . . . a pursin, like yu.'

But they aren't perswaded. They aren't at peace wiv their wep-urns yet. Jackl swings a clubbing bone at his side for the spusms of his blinking distrust. Crow skweezes a round stone in his clenched palm. Potto holds a rock in both palms. It cud be dropped for shatter my skull.

'I don't think yu're for eating,' Crow confides, 'becaws yu ansur back . . . We better not kill yu. Least, not juss yet.'

'Thanks, frend,' I say. 'Good thinking. An yu won't regret it nyva . . . Becaws if yu ate me, yu'd only enjoy me wun day. While now yu've got me for life.'

'Whateva they are . . .' Potto nods, 'we shud share up the bits . . .'

'But I smelled them first,' says Jackl. 'They're mine.'

'Wrong again, bruvver,' I say. 'We are our own.'

Jackl juss ignores this. 'The best part's mine, at least.' An, for sum reasun of his own, his eyes wur on Made not me.

They push us ahed, poking our backs an buttuks.

There wur much I itched for say for my kin as we walked. I wanted for ask if sum bitter greef had fled their harts, now I wur cum back for them. I wanted for tell Potto that there wur a dried deer bladder stuk for his scalp. But he purbly knew well enuf all reddy, for it wur tugged tite down over his brow, hugging his mind warm.

I wanted for ask Crow how, by what sorry happen-chance, the leg bone of a chicken had cum lojd thruw his scrotum. I wanted for ask Jackl why he no longer walked strait, but hobbled along bent-legged.

There wur new wurds they spoke – like *owe, own, shud, ort*, an *suppose* – an I wished for suck their sense. But I knew it wud be a mistake for show ignorance of their ways when I wur so recently cum, a dowtfull pursin, suspishusly taken, hardly well-cum. So I spoke only frendly an familiar, of things I knew all reddy.

'So, Jackl.' I smile back over my shulder. 'I can tell by yur face, yu neva grew anuvva, then.'

'Nuffa what?' he growls ruff.

'Nose,' I say. 'Or found anuvva's snout for fit?'

But he says nothing. Only snuffles thruw flat, gaping nostrils.

An looking for Potto, I say, 'Yu're gon fat an slow, old man. Yu grunt as yu walk like an oruk.'

But they don't want for hear such as this. They're gon shy for talk, prickled by my old, odd knowings of them. So they juss hiss, prodding me for hush.

By sun-slip we've trujd over the far rij, thruw the low vally, across the plain for the lakeside. Thruw the rising mist an dank mud, I smell rowsting rabbuts, charring bones, sinjing hurr, an gusting over it all the dung-heap of my kin.

'Smell it!' Made splutters, then starts spusms of sneezing.

'Yes . . . Fowks do smell,' I tell.

'Whaaaa!' howls booby. Her old spirit remembers the stench from lives befor, an wakens her for the happy strenf of it.

'Ha! Home!' I sigh.

The scents an sounds wrap me around, clinging familiar as a sleep-ing-hide, still plenty more is changed. It is more, lowder, wider, stronger, more pressing for the nose. Skulls of dik-dik, pig, booboons, cows are perched on poles, clacking for the gusts of wind. The paths are sunk deep by the tred of so many futs. Stripped bones ly all around. Drying hides are staked down. Rats scamper. Crows peck at droppings of offal.

Fowk leer close, their faces crusted by grey masks of ash. They jabbed an pinched, calling out. An my murmury ansurs back for them, as if I'd neva bin away.

'Hello, Gooz, wun tit . . . Ha, Moonsik crazy too.'

But those I returned for wur not as I left them. They had bin hard dried an cracked like yaw roots stored thruw sevral summers. Skin wur wrinkled. Suffurings had gouged into wunce smoov faces. Flesh had sagged, bones had slipped an bent while I wur gon. Teef wur spilled. Sum ears gon, cum away in sum angry, grabby hands.

I don't know her at first. For her hurr wur a shock of white fleece. An wun of her eyes looked past me, mussel-shell clowdy, lost. But she sways befor me blocking the path, breefing hot an bitter into my face. As she steps aside she slaps my cheek.

'Yu ate my booby,' says Flames. 'Yu ain't wellcum back.'

'See!' I turn an smile for Potto an Crow. 'Sumwun remembers

me from befor. Ask Flames. She knows me well enuf. An for what I am.'

The men drag Made away. I saw they layd her for urf beyond the midden. I heard her skwealing rage as they took for her. Anger flared thruw me, dying back for ashes of helpless regret. They haggled what for do wiv her, befor they wur agreed.

I had made her for clutch as my own. I'd neva thort for have uvvas share her out. But I heard men hug her strong an soon, juss as they wud for a woom-man, which wur their human wellcum. So I wur sooved she wud be safe. For what a man enjoys alive, he's loaf for snuff.

Crowding women took thick round me. They clutched at me, patted my back, tugged on my ears, peered close into my eyes, prised my lips apart for see what I held in my mouf, burrowed fingurs up my nostrils, licked my skin for know my taste, sniffed my hurr, waggled my fingurs for see how they bent, poked me all over, for see what wur hard an which wur soff, an pinned me down on my back, tugging my legs wide for see what I had, cluking an cackling, till all of me wur felt by evry set of hands, as I skwirmed thin-skinned an touchy, as their faces came an went above me, an their bodys pressed down on me, so I knew woom-man had taken for me as a man, becaws fowk have their moruls, an will only be so familiar wiv their own.

Fowks had a special test of strangers. If they cud fuk it, it was wun of them.

So I wur embraced back as a man, while Made wur taken as woom-man, while I heard from yung chants an the screams of our booby that the chiles wur cum firm attached for her, showing her how for wressel, jump, tumble, an scream.

So that long nite the free of us wur taken for as fowk. An if we wur sore an brewsed from hugging so many, so tite, so soon, they fed us plenty after getting for know us, an there wur many bluds drunk, clotted an fresh, an plenty berrybrew gulped, an strong weeds smoked that tangled our minds, an a crackling fire stacked high, an fowk pleshurred themselves plenty, wiv humming an howling, gobbing an retching, larfing an mocking, jigging an falling over, trewftelling an lying, embracing an falling out, slapping an butting, stroking an tickling, until they toppled for exhausted heaps at dawn.

Many spirits had wandered back amongst us. For find what the clamur wur for. Sum long deds wandered thruw. An Gooz passed away. But it wurn't till the sun wur high that we saw the pink shimmer of her back, an dark drifts of her hurr, as she flowted belly down, bobbing out in the lake.

Wulfs had howled thruw the dark at us, an the duks skwawked peevish, an the towds croaked, an dik-dik bleated, an starlings chattered, all calling on us for hush, for we shattered the sleep of the beasts. But fowk wurn't minded. Being drunk on berrybrew, or gon out of their heds on smulderweed. For it wur a celebrashun. An all for Made, the chile an I. Becaws it is not evry day free new wuns cum born for fowk, all helfy, an too of them all reddy talking, full-grown.

∗∗−∗∗−>>>> | Born again

'Peepil changed,' I tell Made. 'I don't remember them this way.'

'They gon ruffer?' she gesses. 'Too lowd, too many, too ugly.'

'No!' I say. 'Older. Sum parts kinder an clevrer. But stranger, many ways. They've all gon wurdsik, I think, for hear them speak.'

They'd gon off, a diffurnt way in their heds. Becaws yu can't leave fowk alone, fife years, wiv wurds, an minds for play wiv, desire an leshur, an expeck them for stay still, juss the same.

Still, they wurn't moved from the lip of lake. Water, fish, mussels held them. They'd juss cum as well attached as lichen for pock rock, as rooted as gorse for their small patch of urf, as well shaped for their place as crabs for their shells. Heds poked out an looked about. Legs scuttled sideways. But when they wur startled they'd kwickly pull back. But if they'd barely travelled in their bodys, they'd wandered far thruw their heds wiv wurds.

As we wandered past fowk, by their ej, I told Made what wur what, saying which wur who.

'Fox an Bud. Man an woom-man. She's nibbling his . . . chin fluff. She's tuggin the hurrs out wiv her teef.'

'Why?' Made asks, curiuss enuf.

'Don't know,' I conceed. 'It's sum smoov morul, thort up while I wur gon.'

'Maybe that's why men's faces ain't brissly like yurs.'

'Cud be . . .' I say.

'An the woom-men smell of sage grass.'

'An rosemurry,' I say. 'They got a paste of the leefs an wipe it on their skins.'

'That's why their chests are smeary green?' says Made. 'An they smell like trampled bushes.'

'Yes. Sweet, ain't it? Ain't fowk cleva?'

'An the man got a rat leg thruw his nose,' she's noticed.

'Sumwun muss have put it there,' I gess. 'Purbly it means sum-thing solem . . . Prutty ain't it, thow?'

Becaws I wur encurajing her for look kind on the face of fowk, an see the better cheek of it.

'They scratch a lot – peepil.'

'An not for nothing. It's flees, lice, frips, crabs, lap wurms, ear-wigs an nits,' I explain. 'Evry body's got theirs. Neva wurry. Yurs cum soon. Then yu'll be cumplete.'

Yes, fowk had taken for smearing themselves sevral cullurs, pluck-ing their eyebrows an chins, making as much of bowels an bladders as their imaginings wud allow, skweezing smells from leefs an roots for spred tacky on their skins, shaping powches out of levvers for hold this, that or their heds, piercing themselves wiv bones, finding seffern new uses for beast skulls, each cleverer than that animul's mind, making snares of rawhide, slings for kwickening stones thruw the air, furs for clutching chiles kwiet, pastes for poisuning prey, powders for enticing rain an fritening lice, leaps of face for eyeing a pursin hard while seeming for look the uvva way. They'd found few ways of saying 'yes' that wandered between 'if-yu-muss' an 'neva-if-yu-please'.

An there wur sum new ways of fuking, I saw, embracing many ways. Yes, much that wur fresh an cleva had cum into their heds.

Tungs wur swifter, sharper. Talk flowed out in longer streams, carrying new wurds I didn't know. There wur so many names for kin that evrywun wur tied for evrywun twice at least, by sharing a muvver, or having the same cullur eyes, or lying together offen enuf, being born the same season, or both being yunger than sumwun els, having a penis, or not, or wearing a bone in yur same soff part. An there wur manners for meeting whoeva, wiv greetings that muss be spoke. So when yu met after too pizzles apart, yu'd have for tell evrywun yu met what held yu together or showed yu apart, no matter it wur yur bruvver, or the very wun yu lay wiv most, saying –

'Hello, fatbelly, brown-eyes, nipil-bone, wurn't yu born when the duks wur cum, an don't we share a sleeping-hide?'

Thow yu knew the ansur all reddy, it spoke a frendly tung. The uvva wud say sumthing back. Soon it led on for uvva things.

Sum fowk had gon, dug under. But childrins grew for fill the space of the ded. Louse an Egg, who I'd known as chiles, wur now grown for Lips an Stone, swaggering tall.

It wur hard for numba them all. For they wur neva still wiv their itchings, torn wiv their cummings an goings. Those together wun nite wur moved apart, backs turned, the nex. Becaws of sum raw-cuss or skwabble. But at dusk there wur fife fires, wiv fife or sicks fowk round each, wiv movings an stayings, men an woom-men, clinging childrins.

We'd cleaved a long time together, Made an I, an she wur twined like wrapweed around my trunk, so we'd grown sepert together, limp an firm, coiled an uprite. We'd had pryvut signs an silent sayings all our own, gripping us tite, rapt in each uvva.

'Don't . . .' she'd warn, juss as the thort cum into my hed, '. . . effen think of it.'

No wun asked us for join round their fire, so we lit our own lite, at the ej of fowk. It wur kwieter there. An the air gusted thinner, sweeter.

This woom-man had bin all me kin so many seasons. I'd forgotten most about being wiv peepil, while Made had neva lurned.

She winced an shrank back, her nose twitched sniffy, as peepil idled near, so they saw most of her hunched back, as she peered out thruw the slits of her fingurs, an we kept close for our flames, an she clung close by me, an her chile blinked out, snuffly between her paps.

Curiuss eyes are all ways watching. Fowk ambled close, looking the uvva way, stumbling over us wiv a show of tripping careless, sprawl over us, idly fondle our shulders, an sniff us, mouf, under-arms an laps, fingur our tows, stroke our scalps, lick our necks, yawning their langwid smiles.

'Hello, scrawny blew-eyes, dumb-skin, cum wiv wur-Gob, whose bruvver got no nose, why yu freckled, is that a booby, or what, wur it born in the Melon-Moon, ain't yu got a bone of pity in yur body, where are yur smears of frendship, an wud yu like for fuk wiv me, becaws here's fevvers for yur hurr?'

*　　*　　*

191

'Whaa?' Made only grasps a tid of it, besides she understands too well. So she winces an draws back, snapping closed her nees, slapping a hand that had strayed aimless for touch upon those prutty freckles, shaded on the inner slopes of her thys. She wur cool for peepil, no mistake.

'Fowk . . .' I say, 'are fond an curiuss. They like for know, they lurn by fingurring things, they're always fond for feel.'

It wur wearying for Made. Men wur as avid for her as she wur shy of them. An woom-men had for see her suckle, needed for press an ear for her chest an belly, for hear how she sounded inside, an wur kwick for joggle her breasts for feel how hevvy, an talk curiuss about the tints of her hurr, or shapes of her nipils.

'Sniffem. Lickit!' I whisper, as a new face smiles close by hers. 'Be frendly . . . stroke its cheeks. Pat its ears.'

For manners wur cumming back for me kwick. I wur fondling fast, grunting good, an snuffling agreeable enuf.

'Oh, yes, she likes yu well,' I nod an smile, for cover Ow's coldness, 'she wants for pick the lice from yur lap . . . But she's shy.' I felt a need for explain her oddness. For there's only so much stiff distance fowk can abide.

But, as it wur, I knew less than I thort. For there wur things layn hidden beneef evry surface.

It wur a good patch I'd found for build our fire. But Fox crouched near grimacing, sneezing, clacking his teef.

'Yes, burn a fire there. If yu muss,' he says. 'If it is the only place yu can be warm. I neva say yu muss be gon.'

'This ground hard . . .' I patted it. '. . . wiv a dip for hold the embers. It is a good place. A spirit moves me here.'

'Yes,' he agrees. 'Spirit is my muvver's. She lys beneef. Muss yu rowst her, bones an sowl?'

The childrins watched us offen too. The boy Lips wud cum sit wiv me. I liked him well enuf. He reminded me of the chile I'd bin myself – greedy, sulky, sniffly, gobby, sly.

'Peepil talk about yu,' says he, looking hard thruw me.

'Yes?' I say.

'They ain't sure – if yu're stupid or sly.'

'Stupid, me?'

'They say when yu wur a chile, yu wur cleva as a man.'

'Yes?'

'Now yu're a man, yu're stupid as a booby.' He smiles. 'Sumthing gon missing from yur hed.'

'Plenty new things cum, while I wur away. I need for sharpen my tung. My wurds gon blunt.'

'Yes!' He nods. 'Yu're slow. But purbly yu'll lurn.'

The littil wuns have gathered round, babbling, making faces, sticking out their tungs.

'Why those childrins all ways watch us?'

Lips looks me up an down, from scalp for tow. A sad pity soffens his voice, moists his eyes. 'They like for larf,' he says. 'It gladdens them.'

'Larf? Why?'

'Yu stone nakid.'

'*Nakid?*' I ask, stalking my mind for the sense in that. 'Is that a wurd of frendship, or maybe respeck?'

'Nakid.' He nods. 'An yu neva know it.'

'What, then?'

'Yur skin's silent, uncovered. Yu go bare as a beast. Yur woomman too. An yu got no splinters of bone between yu.' He clacked the rat skulls swaying between his thys for show how a man mite decorate, while obscuring, an so revealing, the splendur of his parts.

Which was why Made an I painted sum marks we'd seen, copying fowk, culluring ourselves sum, wiv smears of ashes, lichen an berry joos. I did her, then she dun me. But when they saw our coverings, the childrin grew lowd, calling for the grown wuns, who gathered skwatting around us, muttered, sneezed an blinked.

'Wellcum for cloves,' says Potto. 'An not befor time. But do yu mean for cover up this way?'

'It's wrong?'

'It tells yu're carrying a booby.' Potto points for the lines on my belly. 'An those marks on the woom-man say she slayd sicks bok this moon. But all the hunters say she brags.'

'Ah, yes!' I nod. 'Then we've made too mistakes. There's plenty new for lurn when yu've bin away.'

'No.' His eyes wander past my shulder, weary for look at me. 'Yu are a pursin. It makes yu better than any rooted, fevvered or furred thing. Be as yu will. Do as yu choose. Only . . .'

'Yes?'

'Behave like a man. Be better than a beast.'

'How?'

'Urf watches us. The sun, the moon, the wind, the rains. We are neva alone. When yu act bad yu bring shame on us all.'

As he told it, peepil thort they wur at the centre of this Urf, an the rest of creation, ancestors, enemys, a chorus of spirits, wur gathered round for watch.

'Got for do Rite.' He looks concerned for the blew sky, fearful for a change of its temper. He confides kwiet for my ear behind a curled hand, 'When there is wrong-doing, mischif happens, spirits go surly, things cum apart. Snows fall, or the deer flee.'

'What muss I do?' I ask.

'We ask only wun thing . . .'

'Yes?'

'Piss proper. Sneeze polite. Sleep good, an cupple decent.'

He'd seen me showing disrespeck – pissing into the face of wind. An he'd heard me sneezing rude or indistinct – so all fowk cud make of it wur whateva cum out of my nose.

'An I sleep wrong?'

'Yu show the soles of yur futs for the moon. It shows her no respeck. An yu twist away from peepil, turning yur back on our dreams.'

'I've dun bad, then?' I look down for the dirt.

'An when yu mate . . . her . . . yu grunt like a rutting hog.'

'I do?'

'It is not juss me that says so. Uvvas hear. Chiles copy. It is not a delickut sound. Perps yu shud cupple sum proper woom-men. Lurn how it's dun. Skwirrul's neva as shy as she pretends, an Owl's more prutty than her looks.'

'Yes?'

'Now!' He smiles wide an spits full in my face. 'Be a frend. Show there is no offence.' An my spittle cums kwick an eager, a froffed glob between his eyes, then slivers down his nose.

'Good.' He turns away beaming, having tort me a small thing. 'Tomorrow I will show yu properly how peepil breef thruw their nose an walk on their tows. Which are good things for a man for know.'

* ★ *

194

Now Made had seen how fowk wur, she liked me more than she'd thort befor. I looked well shaped beside them, kind too.

'Why we stay here?' she asks.

'We got cort up,' I say.

'When do we run away?' she whispers for the nite. 'When they sleep?'

'Fowk neva sleep,' I say, 'there'll always be wun awake for see us go. An effen those asleep can follow us wiv closed eyes. They clutch us tite in their dreams. Wunce fowk have fingurred a thing they like as much as us, they'll neva let it go.'

'Ha! I hear that!' Potto calls out for us from the dark. 'It's trew enuf.'

'So . . .' Made shivers.

'There's no escape. If peepil can't tame a thing, they kill it as it fleas from them.'

'So if we stay?'

'Yes,' I nod, 'we'll have for cum like them.'

Made only moaned.

'Sumtime they'll forget us,' I console. 'Then we cud be gon . . .'

'Ha, but yu neva alone wiv fowk,' a nearby voice ansurs us brite thruw the dark.

Nor wur we eva left all alone. There wur always a man crouched nearby, unsleeping, watching us. Fox, Potto or Crab took turns, following us whereva, wriggling close, a hand curled for an ear for clutch our whispers.

Each day the men an boys tramped together over the crag, down the flat towards the woods.

'Cum hunt?' asks Potto. 'Like a man?'

'I rest sum more, swat sum flys, scratch myself an watch the woom-men,' I say. 'I prefur that. But if yu can't sleep, go catch what yu like.'

'I neva say yu are idle an greedy,' says Potto, 'or more Gob than legs.' An the men walk off, wiv backwuds glares, in a furiuss fit of sneezing.

But wun watcher wud stay close by us. The woom-men an childrins went for the lap of the lake, sang, lazed, forraged. I wud go for stone sum rabbut or catch us frogs, the silent shadow close on my heels. Made an I wud have eaten by dusk when the men returned. Most times they carried the carcass of a large beast. They had found a reglar way for kill larger than a man. The carcass wur cut. The meats wur cut an shared. Our silent gard always brort sum pieces for us, dropping the meats by our futs. For our second supper. Thow we all ways had for cook it ourselves.

'What?' I ask. 'No liver today? No marrow or brains?'

So he'd take our share back, wivout a wurd, only sharp intake of breff, followed by whimper, leading for a long pleading moan, an bring sum better piece in its place.

'Good,' I say. 'Kind man. But Made she'd like a share of kidny too.'

Fowk wur generuss, at first. I had only for ask, an it wur brort.

'Ha!' I nuj Made. 'Fowk are kind enuf. They feed us good.'

'Ho!' she glowers. But she eats as eager as anywun. Yu cud neva fault her chew or bite.

We cud have bin happy so, at the ej of fowk, facing peepil wiv a backwud view for the hills, in the shadows of their doings, for the eckow of their sayings, as they fed us an watched over us well. But they wudn't let us be.

Only fife nites had passed when fowk gathered in a circil around us at dusk. They had cumplaints on their minds. They spoke lowd amongst themselves. Hard wurds carried our way about the moruls of the beasts.

'Wurms eat meat, but they neva hunt,' says Crow.

'Fleas suck yur blud,' says Flames.

'Dung-beetils take but they neva give.'

'Buzzurds eat what uvvas kill,' says Potto.

'If yu got lice, yu want for scratch,' says Jackl.

'Hogs like best for roll in mud.'

The accusings flit busy round our ears, like a whining clowd of gnats, an made a few small bites, which swelled a littil after, when we reflected on them, rubbing against the stings.

We'd cawsed offence, Made an I, having smiled when we shud look away, an looked away when we shud have smiled. We'd shown what shud stay hidden an hidden what shud be shown. We soiled what wur clean. Our fire wur built too high an wide. We took too much wood from the wurld. We shud burn our bones. We'd howled against the wind. An said sum ill of the rain.

I knew I needed for know sum more things. I thort it best for ask a chile. The yung don't believe all they're told, but they see what's going on. They've thort it out.

'Look, Lips . . .' I say. 'What's this *shud*? An why's this *ort*? Why won't fowk leave us be?'

He tells that shud an ort are bossy bruvvers. Ort is yunger, but the stronger wun. Their muvver is Rite, an they help yu shun shame, *if* yu do as they demand.

'I understand most of what yu say. But what's this *if* in peepil's minds?'

He says it cums befor *then*, saying what follows what, like as not, or purbly so.

'If sumwun ifs me, then? They're saying what I'll do, then telling me what'll happen nex?'

'That's it.' He nods.

'But it ain't for them for say,' I protest. 'An if yu if me again I'll slap yur ears.'

'If yu hit me,' says the unblinking boy, 'I'll tell fowks what's on yur mind.'

'Yu know about that? An the uvva?' I'm flushing trubbled, deep an hot.

'I can see yur thorts,' he gurgles, pleased wiv himself. 'Nakid on yur face.'

I clench my teef. I smile at him. Thruw tite lips.

'That's better!' he says. 'Ly like the rest.'

'Yu bin watching my face, wivout asking?' I ask.

'I have,' he agrees. 'It ain't a prutty site.'

Which warned me for keep sharp eyes on myself, an pull my face strait, an firm up my lip, so it shudn't leak too much.

'Yu such a small man?' Crow asks wun day. 'That yu only want wun woom-man?'

I smile. 'Understand this,' say I. 'I made Made juss how I wanted her. An there ain't eva bin a better nearly-woom-man. I like her better than the real thing. Her skin is smoover than carf belly, soffer than a rabbut's ears. She is warmer than summer sand, an gentler than a moff. She smells sweeter than cornflowers. Her hurr is fine as fevver-grass. Her eyes shine brite, pearly as mussel shells. Her lips are red as poppys.'

'Yes, all woom-men are like that,' says Crow. 'They all got cullurs, smells, parts an such.'

'Eva look at Skwirrul?' asks Potto. 'She got wun grey eye an wun brown wun. She can look too ways at wunce. Her tung's a furry yella . . .'

'An there's Moonsik,' says Crow. 'She smells like hogberrys. An her hurr is thick as briar.'

'Or look for Duk,' Potto suggests. 'Her legs are brawd as Ocka trunks. She's eager as a warthog. Her paps are like too ox bladders, brimful wiv water. She can crack bekelnuts between her nukkels.'

'It's juss as yu say,' I agree. 'But Ow is woom-man enuf for me.'

Still, they'd got me thinking.

'But there ain't enuf women,' says Crow, 'for a man for have wun all for himself.'

'An there ain't enuf men, nyva,' says Potto, 'for a woom-man for have wun of her own.'

'We got moruls. So we look at it this way,' says Crow. 'It ain't rite for a man for have more than free woom-men, or a woom-man for have more than fife men.'

'Not when there are juss ate woom-men in the wurld, all told. An the men are only twelf,' says Potto.

'An the chiles ripen so slow,' says Crow.

'So there has for be fair shares for all,' says Potto. 'Wiv nun left out in the cold.'

'An so evrywun's joined up proper. So there are tys that bind,' says Crow. 'Him for her for him for her.'

'But Made an I only want for each uvva.'

'Think what wud be, if evrywun did as yu do,' Crow warns. 'Fowk wudn't hold together. We'd scavenge lonesum as jackls. There'd be only too around each fire.'

'If men an woom-men stayed together – like yu an her – fowk wud fall apart,' says Potto.

'I don't want anuvva,' I say. Whateva my fife cumplaints against Made, I won't have uvva peepil know she's marred.

'Yu don't have for *want* them,' Crow explains. 'Juss ly wiv them sum. Frendly, like a proper man.'

But I gessed they wanted Made for themselves, for have her for themselves, much more than they eva cared for my pleshur.

Fowk wur decided how show we shud live, eat, sleep, cupple, take breff. Men had decided. Woom-men too. An what wur decided wur soff an gentle as the breeze for them. But hard an cold as rocks for me. I cud nyva live happily wivout peepil nor wiv them. They wur in my mind an I cud neva have them out. I'd struggled hard for escape. But I'd neva really left them. Only in my hart, neva in my mind. An my body wur a pursin's. An my spirit wun of theirs, a few lives used.

Yes, my sowl an I wur back wiv our own.

✻✻—✻✻—✻ | But the rabbuts wur mine

Made's body all ways drew mine. The looks of it, swells an dips, all beckoned, cumforting an familiar. Until sumthing terble cum between.

It happened while we slept. By the nite fire her face glowed pleasing. She fell asleep wiv a spredding smile. But when I woke at sunrise her face wur froze for a terble frown.

'Whaa?' I wailed. 'No . . . can't be.'

But it wur. Sure enuf.

'What?' asks Made, eyeing me harder an colder still.

Trewf for tell, her face wur much as befor, but the look of it wur most parts changed. The fondness wur gon. Her spirit wur turned cold for me. I saw it in the scornful flare of her nostrils, her slit eyes an tite narrowed mouf. All the while, she looked at me, like I wur a crusty puff-towd crept onto her sleeping-hide.

'Uugh! Yur face is turned against me,' I wail. 'I can't ly wiv yu no more.' I wriggled out fast from beneef the skins. The morning air wur sharp an stinging. But the look of her chilled me wurs.

'What?'

'Yur nites are yur own, then,' I says. 'Take yur body too. I can't desire yu any more. Not if that's the way yu look on me.'

'But . . .' Made starts for explain. But her scowl's gon wurs.

'Kwiet!' I mutter, stepping back. 'Can't yu feel my hurt? Misfortune has struk me hard. My woom-man's face is set against me. I muss be alone – an howl my loss of her.'

So I lay elswhere that nite.

Made's pleasing looks cum an went, drifting across her face. Wheneva she looked prutty again, or smily from afar, I'd wander back. But it wur juss distance muddling the eyes. For her look wur turned scornfull, scowly again, soon as I cum near.

✻   ✻   ✻

Yu cudn't pass a day amongst peepil wivout hearing sevral wishing, mostimes for themselves.

I wurn't slow at gessing what they ment. Wishing wur wanting – for sumthing that can't be had, ain't there, cudn't be, neva wur, els bin lost in time.

Lips wished for the rabbuts I'd promissed him, thow they wur still scampering thruw many burrows, waiting for be cort.

But I neva minded giving him what I didn't have, an seldum sensed a loss. He only had himself for blame, for trusting in what wurn't.

'I give yu the nex carving I make, insted . . .' I promiss.

An like a fool he agrees. Saying he'd prefur a duk, or maybe a deer.

'It's yurs . . . kwacking away,' I chuckle. 'Here in my hed.'

'Thank yu,' says he, like it's in his hands, all reddy.

So pity strikes me sharp, seeing his yung face split for a smile of trust.

'Look . . .' I warn, 'yu're only boy, an I'm a man who's seen more, stumbling far. Can I give yu sum advise?'

'Well . . .' He looks sly into my eyes, wondering what it'll cost.

'I give it yu for nothings.'

'Then nothing's purbly what it's worth,' says he. Sly chile.

'No.' I tug his arm. 'Lissen, this is solid trewf.'

'What, then?'

'I got where I am today . . .' I shuffle my futs in the dust, I slap the mound of my belly, brace my too strong legs, an shake my mows skull necklace, 'by seeing what's what . . . But yu talk of things that can't be touched. Yu believe in things that ain't. It don't speak well of yur sense. It'll only get yu nowhere, lost . . .'

'What,' he asks, 'yu babbling about now?'

'These un-rabbuts an not-carvings. Things for cum, that ain't yet bin snared or made . . . *iffing, thenning, becaws* an wurs. The un-ded, the not-living, the *maybe sumwhere*. Where's the sense in those?'

'Maybe when yur hed's cort up,' says the boy, 'then yu'll know well enuf.' An he winces pity. 'There's things yu wudn't believe. That only I've seen. In my hed.'

'Like what?'

'There's no end for the things fowk cud still find . . .' Lips says, 'if only they look hard enuf. As juss care for believe in stuff unseen.'

He's supposed all sorts, in his yung mind – burds that don't fly, an fishes that can't swim, dukrats, wun-horns, free-legs, tree-crabs an waterhunny . . .

'Now stop rite there . . .' I say. 'Now yu ain't juss talking nosense. Becaws I've seen towds wiv tails. An there are powches that swim, an skwirt black, an got sicks legs instead of fins. They carry their shell inside them – so they wear their insides out. Besides there are jelly-fish, made of no more than see-thruw gizzum. But they prickle wurs than spines.'

'Where those?' demands the boy.

So I tell him about the lake, that stretches furva than an eye, bending up for join the sky. An how it cums an goes, juss as sun pleases, twice a day. An goes high an low as the moon chooses. An there are diffurnt plants, odd fishes, long crabs, water-snails an snakes . . .

'Knew it. Seen it. Bin there,' Lips skweals. 'Wur there also wurms wiv legs? An rock eggs too?'

'There wur . . .' I gasp. 'How did yu gess?'

'I seen this place. It wur in my sleep,' says he. 'Tasted it too. Ain't the water salty? Ugh!' He spits.

'Yes,' I agree, 'that's the verysame place.'

Cleva boy. I had for walk seffern days for get there. He found it wun nite in his dreams.

'Lissen,' he says. 'Yu've told me. So I've told yu. This is how things is –'

Evrything's got a top an bottom, he says, a start an finish. Hunger is stuffed at wun end an famished at the uvva. Warmf has a scalding scalp an icy tows. Fellow feelings stretch from hate for luv. Lite goes from dazzling brite for thickest black.

'Perps,' I conceed. I hadn't thort it thruw an thruw befor. Or looked underneef. Or peered behind, down the dark crinkled arse of trewf.

'So there's an uvva end for evrything, but sumtimes it don't show. Then yu got for go an look for it.'

'Like busy rocks, or frendly cats?'

'Purbly.' Lips frowns in thort. 'A pursin cud find those things. But most cums in the muddel. Like most of a body lys there between

202

hed an futs. So it's inbetweens that show themselves most – like muddeling hot, nearly enuf, belly an chest, so-so far, nyva big nor small, not this or that. So, howeva diffurnt too things are, yu know there's sumthing, sumwhere, for join them up.'

'Like waists, nees an elbas – connecking things.'

'Those are the wuns,' he agrees. 'Evrything gets mixed up. In the muddel of it all. There's above an below. Sky an urf. Lite an dark. Life an death. The kwick an the still. But most is scuttling fast in between. Falling rain, rising dust, getting old, cumming born, crawling out of the water, digging into the ground, lifting into the sky.'

'Frogs, from water for land,' I say. 'Neva mind crabs, passing them the uvva way.'

'Duks,' says Lips, 'from sky for urf. An water-rats. An flying fish.'

'Flying fish?'

'Cud be,' the boy supposes. 'Sum burds swim. So there's purbly fish that fly. Secret's knowing where for look.'

'Flapping low, between the water an the air. That's the way they'd cum,' say I. 'An if we cort wun?' I ask. 'What then?'

'I'd look at it good, an think on it long an hard,' says Lips. 'An call it names.'

'Yu cud have it first, then,' I promiss. 'If I cud have it nex. Becaws I'd prefur for pluk its fevvers. Then rowst it kwick. Having sprinkled it wiv garlik grass.'

Yes, I cud smell it all reddy. Taste it too. Only, the solid bite of it wur missing.

Crow said he didn't mind me using his wurds. Not as long as I spoke them rite, an used them kind.

'Wurds yurs now?' I ask. 'I neva knew.'

'An old story,' he says. 'Happens while yu wur away.'

'There wur fites,' he says. 'Skwabbles over water in the dry time. Haggles over the meat when game wur scarce. Tussles over eggs. Teef wur loosed. Blud got spilled. Angers clung thick around us. Fowk said *my* an *mine*. They clutched things tite for their chest. Or swallowed more than they shared. Sumthing had for change . . .

'Wun day a man catches too duks. His eyes are bekel-brown.

He is yur bruvver. It is best forgiven. I'll mention no names.

'We gather round as he lites a fire. We watch him pluk the fevvers an draw them shiny sweet innards out. We watch him smear the breasts wiv a pulp of lemin grass, an skweeze on the joos of spiny-frewt. We watch the plump meats rowst. Smell them too. We pat our stomaks. We smile his way. We gather round his fire. We belch, expecking. We grin as he pulls them steaming burds apart. Then . . .' Crow spits in disgust.

'Yes?'

'He shuffles round, for turn his back on us. We watch him eat both burds. There is nothing left for us but fevvers, too nibbled necks an crack-boned nees.'

'Ha!' I cluk a kwiet, well-mannered sympathy. I've tried for share wiv my bruvver too.

'So I says for him, "Jackl, do all the duks in the wurld belong for yu?" An he burps all satisfied. An says, "Yes, Crow. It's trew." He shows no shame, but juss licks the grees from his tacky fingurs, wipes the smears from his flat snout an smiles. But his face is turned odd an ugly for our eyes.

'"If all the duks are yurs, smurk-face . . ." I say.

'". . . All the pigs are mine," says Potto.

'"An all the paths are mine, fart arse," says Flames.

'"An those are my wurds yu use," say I.

'"Neva forget the waters are mine," says Gooz.

'But this man has no mind for care, now his belly is full. So he lys down grunting an closes his eyes. But we are payshent peepil. We watch the dreams jerk his lids. We sit an wait for him for wake.'

'He's thirsty . . .' I gess, 'when he wakes. An strangely tired, for he hasn't dreamed well.'

'An restless,' Crow agrees. 'He tries for wander the path for the lake. So we trip him up. For remind him, kind as we can, while being clearly understood, that the paths belong for Flames. An we pull him away from the lake becaws the waters belong for Gooz. Then when he cumplains I slap him sum, an clamp my hand over his lips, becaws he is taking my wurds.'

'Ha!' I nod at the sense of it, grunting my approval.

'We tell him, "Eat all the duks yu like. Those are yurs, an yurs alone. But eat only duks. For, if yu take anything els, yu steal what is ours." We follow him all day. We sit round him at dusk. For make sure he doesn't take what is ours. Or drink, or speak, walk the Urf, or such.

'When we wake at dawn he's gon. He returns at dusk, clutching fore ded drakes. He builds a fire an cooks them. Then he offers us the meat. But we say we are not hungry, an have him plead, then whine, nex weep. They are fat drakes. An savurry. It is a pity for waste. So, at last, we eat. All is good. We let him drink at the lake sum drops, then say a few wurds of gratitude, for slake his thirst for speech.'

'Ha!' I larf. 'It's a strong lurning. Spiky too. Yu show him nothing can be owned. For Urf gives evrything. The water is given its wet. A duk is given for the burd, for be itself.'

'No . . .' Crow shakes his hed. 'Do yu neva understand?'

'What, then?' I say.

'Soon as fowk owned, they felt it wur good. They look about them prowd. Bent backs sprung strait. They felt taller now. There wur a bounce in their stride, a new strenf moved their legs.'

'Yes?'

'So now most is shared or given away. Wurds are mine. Potto takes the pigs. Moonsik has the fish. Duk's are the nuts. Jackl still has the duks. Gooz had the lake. Now it is passed for her chile. The paths are Flames's. The roots belong for Mole. Owl has the nite. Green-eyes has the eggs.'

'If I want for drink at the lake, or eat pig?'

He smiles at a chile's kwestyun. 'Catch what yu want. Only share the meat. An be grateful for whoeva gives it. As for water, Skwirrul lets evrywun drink at her lake.'

'I do,' she agreed. 'There's all ways more than enuf for me. So, juss go wheneva yu thirsty. An be grateful. Juss say "Thank yu, Skwirrul, dawter of Gooz, muvver of the waters, kind frend, whose eyes sparkle like leaping carp, whose hurr gleams like yella grass in sun, whose teef are white as snow."'

'But the lake's for all,' I say, 'fowl, fish, fowk. An pigs are their own. So they understand. They can be killed, sure enuf, but in their spirits they stay their own . . .'

Crow shuffled an scowled. 'This is how fowk have decided it,' he said, gon hawty. 'If yu don't like it, feel free for go. But neva cast a shadow over us, breef our air, or steal our game.'

205

I cud tell it wur decided wivout me. Most of Urf wur divided up, shared out, all reddy.

'Now most is owned, nun feel want, becaws each has his own, but she wiv water has no meat, an he wiv meat has no drink, so evryone muss give an take. Now things belong, evrything muss be shared around . . . So yu may take what yu want, if yu give what yu have.'

'But what I got – for give?' Yes, I realized I had missed out. My woom-man an chile too.

'Yes . . .' Crow pawses an nods. He clowts his brow, feeling my lack for himself. He eyes me wiv a solem pity. His eyes gon moist misty. 'Yu are a sorry man. Yu have nothing. Sept yurself, an that's a poor, ignorant thing.'

So that nite, when the family of fowk wur gathered for gabble around wun large fire, I sneezed, for show wurds wur cum into my hed, an I shud be pleased for spit them out, when all uvvas had had their say, but I wur glad for wait my turn, an any way it wur only a small matter.

So when they had spoked themselves out, I coffed for get their eyes, then asked what I mite have, what they wud care for give me. So I mite give it back for them, an share in what wur theirs. If they see what I mean.

There wur a hurtful hush. Reluctance gagged fowk's tungs.

'Yu bin taking all this time, an neva giving,' says Flames. 'Now yu asks for more.' Spite sticks bitter in her wurds. Becaws I owe her a chile still from wunce eating her booby, summers befor.

'There's littil left for give,' says Green-eyes, kinder. She smiles her regret. 'Urf's grown short of most things now. Yu're free new moufs for feed.'

'Perps if yu wander far away, yu'll find anuvva glut,' says Flames. 'Urf mite have a sister.'

Potto smiles. 'Yes . . . take all those far away places yu like so well,' he says. 'Have them all for yurself.'

But I knew it wur a slender giving, more grissel than meat. I wanted sumthing for fill our bellys. I wanted sumthing fleshy nearer for hand. An my woom-man elbad me sharp in the ribs for nuj my curaj.

'There's Made, too,' I say. 'She's all most a woom-man. She deserves sumthing at least.'

'She can have our regrets,' says Flames. 'Or the spiny bushes. Or as many beetils as she wants.'

'She ain't our blud,' says Coot. 'She got amba nipils, so we can't spare her much.'

'I will take the sun,' Made says kwiet an modest, yet firm, as if merely asking for wun pip from the core of the frewt, after the flesh is chewed. 'My chile will take the time that draws us on. Gob can have whateva is left.'

They cluked an shook their heds, whispered amongst themselves, sneezed a lot an sevral spat. Then Crow spoke for them all.

'Yu can have the blow-flys. Gob can have the lice. Yur chile can take the wurms.'

'No!' I protested. 'We'll have the Seasons, Hope an Pleshurs.' I demanded no less for myself an mine.

'Those are too much.'

'What els, then?' I scratch my lips, rub my ears for have them think hard, wondering what worthwhile remains for be took. 'What's left?'

They huddled again. There wur a waving of arms, shaking of fingurs, scowling an muttering, befor they soffened for our needs.

'Take the rabbuts, then,' says Crow. 'The woom-man can have the clams. The chile can have the melons.'

So they becum ours. There an then. An nothing cud take them away from us, eva, bar death. Unless I later make a thortless swap wiv the boy Lips, giving him all my rabbuts, for teaching me how for think clevarer.

'Yu neva did?' Blind whissels. 'Swap yur birf-rite, for sum wurds?'

'Suppose I did, it wur for the best. Them wurds of Lips wur sharp an cutting. They all ways stayed wiv me.

'Any ways, after the Ice we shared out the Urf an all its rabbuts again.'

——*—> | Yella

Sumtimes I passed Fox deep in the nite. We neva spoke. I wud be going back for Made. He'd be going the uvva away, hed turned, pretending he neva saw me passing, near enuf for feel his heat, an the scent of woom-man on him.

An when I reached my own woom-man an lay down besides, she wud twist langwid, still awake, looking up at my shaded face, asking where I'd bin all nite. I think she'd gessed all reddy, but tact had neva rooted in her.

'I bin wiv uvva woom-men,' I say. 'Her an she, here an there.'

'Doing what,' she asks.

'This an that. Fuking too. Standing up. On my nees, or laying down,' say I.

'Why?'

The ansur wur plain enuf for any man for see. 'There's pleshur for be found in woom-men. All over.' I told her trew. For she ort for know. 'On their chests, between their legs. There's always plenty prutty for look at. An much for touch upon. I can't enjoy them enuf. There are too I neva gon wiv yet. Perps I try tomorrow.'

'Aah,' she says, all solem, her hand stroking smoov hollows in the sand. Her looks for me ain't so eager now.

'I like the grasp an hug of them. The smells an tastes. I like it best for be inside . . . It's good for spill up woom-men.'

'Yes?' Made nods. Elokwence has left her. 'That so?'

'Skwirrul skweaks. Sow has fat, soff udders an thys. There's too of Both, together. It's good cuppling woom-men,' I explain. 'Yu shud try it. There's a lot for feel. Plenty for hang on for. They more eager than yu. They smile an larf.'

'Yes?' she asks. 'Yu take them things?'

'Myself . . . an rabbuts, eggs, yella stones, cats' teef, blew fevvers.' Yes, for be sure, I take them small givings. They like me better for it. It's neva proper for ly wiv a woom-man unless yu

208

leave her happyer for it. Offen she asks befor the start. What I got for offer her.

Made's eyes roll suggesting – that all my givings shud be for her. I had cum for lurn of late her spirit wur neva a generuss wun.

'Yu like uvva woom-men more?' she sniffs. 'More than me?'

'Blame me,' I admit. 'I made yu like a woom-man, but I neva finish yu rite. Yu please the eyes an hands. But there's all ways sumthing missing. I feel it when we fuk.'

'What?'

I think awhile, bite my nukkels, mumbling for it.

'Joy.' If I remember rite. 'Small pleshur in yu. An yu lean meat.' I skweeze the thin fold of her belly skin, for show her what she's lacking. 'Yu sad face.' I hold her cheeks in my palms an twist her hed for face me. 'Plenty tears. Few larfs. An that chile's all ways clinging for yur tits.'

Trew enuf. Her eyes gon pinked, moist, an she sniffles sum. The bite of a chile on her breast pains her again.

'I'm all man,' I explain. 'Dick-hed an bollock-brain. My mind's between my legs. Uvvas say as much. But *yu* . . . yu not kwite a woom-man yet.'

'No?' she asks.

'All that time I only lay wiv yu. But now I see what I bin missing.'

'What?' she asks.

'Fife.'

'Fife what?'

'Uvva woom-men,' I explain.

Yes, I wur warming for the cumpany of woom-man, sum men too. While Made kept herself apart an kwiet, spurning their touches, pushing fowk away. Effen me that made her. No, she wud not join in an show herself a pursin. So I thort.

Sumthing wur lost between us. The binds that tied wur loosening.

Her misery clung bitter around us. Her cold darting eyes stabbed at me. The ground felt ruff on my buttuks, prickled my legs, wheneva I sat beside her. The sun wur paler an cooller in any spot she chose. For shadows hung over. The wind blew harsher. I had only for ly down by Made on our prickling sleeping-hide an a chill

wud cum, or ants wud crawl beneef. She tugged dark clowds
towards us, spilling rains.

'Yu hungry?' I ask.
  'No,' says Yella.
  'Treat her kinder,' warns Blind, 'or yu'll loose her.'
  'Yu thirsty?' I demand.
  'No.' Yella scowls.
  'Yu got dik-dik hides for sleep on?'
  'Yes.'
  'Maybe she wants kindness,' says Blind.
  'Yu got legs for walk yu?'
  'I have,' says Yella. 'So?'
  'Then yu got all yu need. Let a smile know yur face. Let happy
trickle thruw yu. Have joy split yur mouf. An stop drawing down
the rains on us.'
  'How-cum . . .' Yella mumbles. Then shakes her hed for silence,
as the trail of her thorts cums for a briar bush of confusion.
  'Yu trying for drive her away?' asks Blind.
  'Me?' I ask. 'How?'

Wurn't me but her that wudn't be satisfied. This woom-man
neva knew what she wanted or how for be glad. Larfter shunned
her. Her puny booby whined. A gloom clung around the purr of
them.

'But ain't she gon wiv uvva men?' says Blind.
  A whimper cums back for me. Strangled in my throwt. After all
these years.
  'How yu gessed?' I ask. 'An why am I the last for know it?' I
wail. It sticks bitter in my gullet, effen now.

'Yu happen for know yu got horns on yur hed?' I ask Made wun
day in the Melon-Moon.
  I'd sensed there wur sumthing changed about her. Now I saw it
for what it wur. She wur wearing the scalp of a dik-dik on her hed,
wiv short spiky antlus branching out from her ears.
  'These?' She shrugs, an her velvert doe ears wiggel too. 'A gift.
Ain't they prutty?'

'Where they cum from?'

'Fox brort them for me. He likes me well enuf.'

'Fox! An yu got cats' teef on a fong, round yur neck.' I point them out for her. 'There!'

'Those cum from Crow,' she says. 'But Egg give me the fevvers.'

'Fevvers?'

'These!' She turns. An sure enuf, there's too gooz tails, waggling on a fong. Wun waggling above each buttuk.

'. . . an Rabbut,' she says, 'lissen!'

'*Rabbut?*' I ask. 'Rabbut . . .'

'It's what fowk call yu, Bunny, behind yur back. Didn't yu know?'

'They do?'

'Yes, Rabbut. An understand this. My name ain't Made. It's Yella. For the cullur of my hurr.'

'Yella?'

'Well . . .' she says. 'There's anuvva who calls me Crowcus. An wun who calls me Clam. But those are fond, pryvut names. So don't twist yur clumsy gob round them.'

'Clam!'

'Tuff outside – but soff an sweet, when opened up.'

'Crowcus?'

'Yella, sheeny, smoov, sweet smelling – prutty.'

'Yes?'

'So, Rabbut, if yu an I are for stay speaking . . .'

'Yes?'

'Yu muss call me by my proper name.'

'Neva *Rabbut me*, nor *muss me*,' I warn. 'I made yu. I call yu Made. Or whateva I like.'

'My spirit grew me, Rabbut,' says she. 'In a muvver's belly.'

'No, I made yu. Myself. Out of less than an animul.'

'Yu snatched me ruff, from my kin. For which I neva forgive yu. Eva.'

'Yu're mine,' I tell her strait. 'Yu're Made. An if yu don't do as I tell yu . . .'

'What?'

'I'll unmake yu, or shape yu into sumthing els.' I bluff. 'A towd, or wriggle wurm purbly. If yu don't do rite.'

'Yu can turn me angryer. Nothing els.'

'Yu bin talking wiv fowk too much,' says I.

'Yu lived too long wiv booboons,' says she.

'Yu do as I say.'

'I'm a pursin. My own. I'll do juss as I like.'

'My mistake,' I tell her strait, 'wur lurning yu for talk. Yu've bin ansurring back, eva sins.'

Now wurds had gon for her hed. She got sum reply for evrything.

'Now, don't go cleva on me,' I warn.

'Don't be a Rabbut all yur life,' says she.

'Yu bin wiv uvva men?' I gess at last.

'Suppose I have? Yu jellus?' she asks.

I frowned an scratched my hed. It wur then I knew, at last, she had me wresseled.

'Jellus?' I mutter, scorched by rage, while twisted by yurning. 'Remind me of the sense in that.'

It wur a wurd I hadn't seen the use of.

No, I neva knew much need, till then.

Now I got no dowts. This woom-man wur changed from the wun I'd made, sins she'd taken for chattering wiv peepil, behind my back, while I wur fuking elswhere, or catching foods. She'd lurned evry last wurd there wur for be said. Getting for if an suppose. Neva telling me. Wishing this an that. Letting peepil change her name. Sharing in their reasuns. Wearing their antlus. Wiggling their fevvers, dangling their fongs, rattling their bones, an more, I gessed, besides.

So I turned my back on her, there an then. I stamped my futs hevvy on the urf, so she cud see my rage rise, in the puffs of dust. There wur wurs I'd have like for tell her, but fowks wur gathered round, in a smiling circil for lissen an advise.

She wudn't ly wiv me for a while. That I knew. I'd take myself for uvva's arms.

I saw the first blister, glissening on the upper lip of Sow. Nex day, Skwirrul shows on her brow, Both on their cheeks.

Terble lukks wur dogging my tracks. I only had for lay wiv a woom-man an sum sickness struck her spirit low.

I sidle up for Yella. She scowls.

'Yu seen those yella blisters?' I ask.

'Shh!' says she. 'Not a wurd.' Then she's blushing for me, again. Like she ain't for many a moon.

'They're like the wuns yu had.'

'Don't speak of it, Rabbut. Or it'll be the wurs for yu.'

'Yes?'

'I'll say yu gave them me,' she says. 'I'll say yu bin mixing spites wiv magiks.'

'Me?' I protest. 'Evrywun knows I'm stone-stupid.'

'So,' Yella smurks. 'So don't wressel me for cunning.'

Potto an Jackl are nex. Then Flames an Crow. After that evry face seems blotched wiv yella weeping scabs. So yu began for notice whose face wur clear – sum chiles, Hare, Yella an I.

Those sickened yella faces eyed each uvva an moaned.

'How yu feel it, inside?'

'I burn. I shiver. A fog inside clowds my eyes.'

'It's hot as rage, chill as terrur. There's buffalow stampeding in my ears.'

'There are prickling thorns in my guts.'

'Lissen!' I tell them. 'If yu got for screech so lowd, yu cud at least howl sum sense.'

Sumthing evil wur cum into fowk, burning the body, shading their site, muttering in their heds, gouging their soff parts, blistering yella bile out thruw their skins, wresseling their spirits, choking their breff, as they gulped in hot sharp bursts.

Pity hurt me bad. It wur as hard for me for watch as them for suffur.

An unseen enemy wur cum wivin, but we cudn't name it. We looked about us fearful. Whateva did this wur watching us close. Yu neva knew what it wur that ment yu harm, sum slayn beasts, angry ground, ancestors defamed, peeved spirits, a rage in Urf.

There'd bin sum Bad dun. An sumthing fierce wur wronged. Now it struck back at us. So our eyes wur cum suspishus of each uvva, looking for the culprit. We back-tracked our paths in our minds, searching our trails for find the offence.

'Is this a punishment,' I ask, 'for sum Wrong dun by most?'

I wurn't feared for think so. My conduct an face wur clean an clear, unblemished.

'Perps there wur an insult for Urf, a disrespeck for cats, or a bad-moufing of the ded?'

'Angry spirits,' says Hare. 'Their spite bubbles thruw the skin.'

'I see they speak a yella pus,' I say. 'What they mean for say by that?'

'It strikes the grown wuns first,' Hare drawls. His tung is slurred by stronger than confusings. 'An the older sicken wurs. Perps there's an urly wrong, buried in our past.'

'Did yu make sum new enemys?' I ask. 'While I wur gon?'

'No. An the pox cums juss after yu. Close behind.'

This feels like a prickle of blame. Like he's meaning a smij more than he says.

'But it doesn't hurt me, my woom-man, her chile,' I protest.

'No,' he agrees. 'It only strikes the woom-men yu ly wiv. Then the men who ly wiv them. Then them that go wiv those.'

'Then it's a strange sickening,' I agree. 'Is it a pox of envy-between-the-legs?'

'Not that.' He shakes his hed. 'Those are the white blisters. They show on crotch an mouf.'

'The drip-drip of jellusy, then?'

'No. That is pissing pain wiv yella lumps.'

We fed the sick, wiped the pus from their faces, watered them an cleared their dirt from the sand. We did this kwick, wivout kind wurds, smiles or larfter.

Then we kept apart, the helfy an the hurt. We, the clean, calm-spirited, feared the touch of those fevered dirty. We didn't want for anger the pox, by showing ourselves frends of its foes. An those sickened suffurd us wiv bitter eyes an mad dark mutterings. Perps it wur us still standing, they rambled hot, that had brort them low an sick.

'Look . . .' I shake the shivering Moonsik, for loos the babbling spittel spite from her mouf. '. . . see who is clear. The childrins, Hare, Yella an I. Neva blame them innocent.'

Nex day Hare has a new understanding, from watching the sick for study their signs.

'Mite be monkey spirits. Peepil jibber an howl, walk on hands an nees. Spit an chatter. Bare their teef.'

But there'd bin no howlers, nor booboons, near these parts for years. Fowk had eaten the last, long ago.

'The ded warn of fleas . . . I don't know . . .' Hare shakes his trubbled hed. 'The tracks of it all muss be sumwhere near,' he mumbles. 'I muss find the prints, then follow them. Perps in the spaws of lions, or in the bellys of frogs.' An he's stumbling off sideways, stooped, eyes glazed in his wallnut face, the frog skulls tied for his ankils rattling his puzzild retreat.

We, who had our helf, took for trickry, blotching our faces wiv mud, staggering, moaning an wriving, for show the sickening pox that it needn't fingur us. Becaws we wur touched all reddy. But those angry spirits kept cumming. First they saw thruw Fox, an then blotched Gote.

Hare nex tried for fite boil wiv boil, yella wiv yella – using bee stings an poisun Ocka.

'They don't wurk this time, yur cures,' I tell him strait. 'They don't soov the suffuring. If anything they make it wurs.'

'Spirits see us cumming,' he says, 'hiding from our medsin. They fear it. Becaws they know it's strong.'

After swelling for the skin, there cum nubbins for the neck an nodduls for the groin.

Hare took himself into a cave, away from the eyes of the pox, for prepare a paste of crushed galls. This way he'd strike like wiv like, lump wiv lump. But only vomutting an tumbling came of that. An old Sow coffed her last.

Fearing the lake wur poisuned, we neva drank from it for too whole days, but lapped from dirty puddles. But this neva helped us much.

Then, fearing the air wur tainted, we burned stink weed for days, breefing only choking smoke.

Fasting wur no more help than eating, but wailing eased the pain. Walking brort the staggers on, as offen as it shook them out.

'I seen a trubble among peepil,' I tell Hare. 'But I don't know if it brort the pox.'

'No,' he says, shaking his hed, sure at least of this. 'I dowt it. This pox is foxy cunning. While yu're cleva as a snot . . .'

'Juss so,' I agree, for Hare got a sure way wiv wurds. 'I'm like a snot in the nose of fowk, nyva proply in, not trewfly out. I bin wiv fowk an wivout them. So I see things diffurnt. Becaws I bin apart.'

'What, then?' He frowns.

'Peepil gon . . . wurdsik,' I tell. I wur pleased enuf wiv myself, for have seen what uvvas cudn't.

'Wurdsik?' he asks.

'Hear peepil babble,' I says. 'The wurds in them gon furiuss, vain an crazed.'

'Vain?' He smiles sly.

'Wurds neva stop talking about themselves. "Lissen," they say. "I ment this" or "Hear me rite" . . . . Where's the help in wurds,' I ask Hare, 'when they only chatter about themselves. They get all the gossip. But it's our moufs that have for do their wurk.'

'So wurds bin gossiping on each uvva?' he smurks.

'There!' I say. 'Look for yur own gob. They juss dun it for yu. Wurds bragging about themselves again.'

'I hear what yu say,' says Hare, 'an it's wise as a booby's fart.'

'Trew enuf,' say I. 'A booby's arse speaks lowder than wurds. It says as it finds. An neva needs for be tort.'

He screws his eyes, an shakes his hed weary. 'So . . .' says he, 'yu cleva as an arsehole?'

'Well . . .' I smile, 'I'm not wun for brag. But I do my best. What's inside got for cum out.'

'Yu eva think on yur wurds befor yu speak?'

'Try not to,' say I. 'I don't want for give wurds the upper hand. I want for speak my sense. Not theirs.'

'Trew,' he nods. 'It shows.'

'Tell yu anuvva thing about wurds . . .' I offer.

'Yes?' he scowls.

'Sumtimes wurds all ways try for hurt.'

'They do?'

'They cum out unkind. Like they mean for wound. They gnaw a man's respeck. They turn man against woom-man. By calling a pursin what he's not.'

'Like when they call yu hog-pizzle, whelk-brain, or wurmhed?' he gesses. An he gesses rite.

I think on this a littil. 'Yes. Ouch,' I say, an swat my hed. 'They hurt a smij. Those wurds did . . . I don't mind them telling me what I am. But I won't have them call me what I ain't . . . An anuvva thing, wurds making fowk greedy. It's all "I want this" or "Give me that". An there's no time nor place that's safe from them.'

'That so?' He blinks.

'Becaws wurds started talking about the morrow – thow they've neva bin. An changing all our yesterdays. So yu can't trust the way yu've cum.'

'Haa!'

'They're liars an braggarts, wurds are . . . I'd sooner trust for hynas. I'd rarva lissen for rutting frogs.'

'Yu bleat like sum gote,' says Hare. 'Yu gon crazy as a coot.' He's turned away, jerking his hed loopy, like he's shaking out lice.

Good. He understands at last. 'Trew, juss so.' I shout for his back, 'It's wurds dun that. They wurmed holes in my hed. They making us mad.'

For sumtimes a man sees clear when uvvas can't. An those in the fog won't be led out, an those in the kwagmire wriggle deeper in.

So it wur for me. I knew what wur wrong, but cudn't help. For fowk wudn't lissen. All I cud do was turn a deff ear for the rest of them, an heed the small kwiet sense in my hed. I clung for my helf by holding my tung.

Cum the Crab-Moon, the wurst wur over. The ded wur ded. Free. Dug under. Killed by vishuss talk. The living wur cumming steddier, gathering flesh for their wasted frames, growing helfy dry scars where the wet scabs had bin.

I wur stronger than my wivvered, weakened kin. I hunted better than many, more eager than most.

I don't speak well of the yella-pox, but it neva did me any harm. Not the second cumming.

——*—>> | Girl

Yella still shunned me, an lay herself wiv uvva men.

I offen asked her why, when I'd be glad enuf for clasp her back, beneef my sleeping-hide.

'Fox is strong. He makes plenty kills,' she says. 'Crow is cleva. An knows how for give me pleshur. He makes wurds dance. Also, he cares for me. He's kind. Besides, Egg's smile pleshurs my eyes.'

'So?' I say. 'That's nothing. I can carve animuls. Out of stones.'

Yella blinks slow. 'I looked long an hard for the good in yu,' she says, 'but my hart wants more than rocks.'

'But I brort yu a granit frog I made.' An I hand it for her.

'What use that?' she asks. 'What frog for?'

'Use?' I ask. 'For?'

Neva thort of yva of those.

She shakes her hed. 'If I eva need stone frog wiv a smurky smile . . .' Yella lays it aside. '. . . I'll reach for that. An think of yu.'

My hart wur frobby, happy. Now I've given her the very best I got.

'Shall us, then . . . like we used . . .' I stutter for ask, dry-tunged but prickled by swets.

'Neva,' she says, short an sure, turning away, twining a gooz fevver into her long yella hurr. Becaws she still see into my hed, all thow she doesn't want me near. She wur starting for scorn me. I knew that now.

'But, don't yur yurning still howl for me?' I call after her. 'Becaws mine still shrieks for yu.'

But I wur speaking for her deff, dusty heels.

I don't say she began it, but Yella wur cum close wiv the woom-men now. An they'd started spinning a spider's web of wurds, concerning boobys, for snare a fly.

They wur sly about it. They did not tell the whole ly for start, but spred false trails that wud lead men for it. An they prepared it well from wurds, shaping, smooving an polishing their tale. So when it wur finished it wur so sharp an cutting, the trewf wur split apart by it.

'Look at Girl,' Yella says wun day, when I brort her meats wiv seffern smiles. 'She look like yu.'

'Like me? . . . What way?'

'Those towd eyes,' she says slyly, 'fat lips, greedy mouf, flat nose.'

'Her eyes like my look. So she copys me good.'

'An yu both got speckled backs. An hurr like dry grass.'

The likeness wur small an dribbling. It didn't please me much. 'But that chile lazy an stupid,' I say.

'She watches yu,' says Yella, 'she copys good.'

Duk had bin taken curiuss, kware, watching the animuls mate. 'The deer rut,' she says. 'Moons later, the doe drops her carf.'

Potto an I ponder this an nod. But the push of her wurds doesn't prod us hard.

'The hares mate,' says Duk. 'Too moons later the levrets run.'

'They taste sweet, levrets,' says Potto. 'But they're small meat. Rowst them in clay, an then the fur cums away in yur hand.'

'The porcupines cupple an the yung cum soon,' Duk tells.

'Manhog takes care how he mounts,' I say. 'There's spikes for prick his pleshur.'

'First there's the mating. Later the birfing,' Duk tells.

'She watches them beasts terble close,' says Potto, 'when they're jigging an poking.'

'If they go jerky-jerky, she knows it. Afterwuds, she tells on them,' I agree. 'She knows all the rabbut gossip. An gote doings. Animuls got no secrets from her.'

'After the cuppling cum the yung,' Duk tells. She's stuck fast for it, like a hyna for carryon.

'First the crabs scuttle, then the berrys swell,' says Potto.

'Sum things run ahed,' I agree. 'Sum things crawl behind.'

'Cats an snails,' says Potto.

'Rabbuts an wurms,' say I.

'Men an boobys,' Duk agrees.

We nod at the smeary, slug slowness of boobys, but the snail's pace was ours. We neva saw till late, but woom-men wur leaving a glissening trail of story for snare us, concerning their insides.

We wur gathered wun nite after a bok-feast when Green-eyes led us thruw the web. She spoke kwavery wiv juddery breasts. As thow she got a wriggle passion inside. The uvva woom-men wur watching close, an nodding at her, agreeing all reddy, for what she hadn't said yet, as thow it wur cooked an ate.

'Moon calls for a girl. She's wounded for bleed. It's the death-blud of girl. A woom-man's cum insted.'

Yes, woom-men offen bragged of it. How they stood well-connecked wiv the sky, being blud-kin wiv the moon.

'There can't be no booby till the woom-man bluds. Then she muss lay wiv a man. Like it or not.'

'Yu saying men are in it?' asks Potto.

'Making chiles cum?' asks Crow.

'Yes,' says Green-eyes. 'It so.'

'How cum?' asks Potto.

'The joos cums out of a man . . .'

'Yes?'

'Asks the woom of woom-man for swell . . .'

'Yes?' Crow's eyes narrow, then look down for his lap. He shakes his sleepy part. 'Yu cleva enuf?' he asks it, dowtfull. 'Yu say all that?' But it juss sprawls back idle, blind an limp. Not a sound leaks out. 'Yu bin up for things, wivout asking, neva telling.'

'Yu sure?' Potto scowls his suspishun. 'Mine neva says. He wants plenty. But he neva asks. He's eager enuf . . . but talk he don't.'

'They got their own ways of telling, men's an woom-men's parts,' Green-eyes says. 'They talk kwiet an sly. They speak wet an slow, like snails. All yu eva hear are skwijs an gurgles between the legs.'

'Boobys a long time cumming,' says Potto. 'An woom-men slow for swell.'

'Ate or nine moons if the chile cums live. Less if it cum urly, ded. Becaws the man's joos ain't strong enuf. Or tells a woom-man's insides wrong.'

'How many men it takes, then?' Crow asks. 'All told, for make a booby?'

Yu cud tell woom-men had bin counting on this. They'd knapped a neat ansur all reddy. A glance skims over their faces like a flat stone bouncing over the lake. It plops thruw Green-eyes in the rippels of her spredding smile. She sounds the smoov ly.

'Too, free, or more.' She nods solem, tallying her men off on her fingurs. 'The first for suggest. The uvvas for perswade.'

'Then I'm . . . part a muvver?' Crow asks. 'For this an that.' He waves for the skwawk of chiles, fiting for bok's ears. 'Becaws I've cuppled plenty.'

'Yes,' Green-eyes agrees. 'Yu fuk around.'

'It's so,' says Skwirrul. 'Yu're the furva muvver.'

Yu can see woom-men don't mind sharing chiles now. There's a swelling silence. Yu know sumthing new will burst from it.

'It's trew.' Moonsik nods, smurky.

'I hear an eckow of sense for it. That men make chiles cum,' says Potto.

'I all ways thort . . .' says Crow, 'it wur asking too much of woom-men. For make those boobys . . . all by themselves. Wivout men telling them how.'

Coot's risen eager, clutching her chile.

'So, here, take!' she offers. 'If yu made it, it yurs,' she tells Crow. 'An yurs too.' She turns for Fox. An she lays a skwirming chile between them.

Fox's face puckers. On second thorts, he don't want it. He pushes chile back, the way it cum. The littil wun promptly howls its rage at being passed over, by ruffer, colder, levver hands.

'An this yurs.' Duk passes a small wun for Potto. 'Crow's too.'

'This for yu. An anuvva's . . . I forget which man.' Yella lays her chile for my chest. 'Feed it good an plenty, fife times a nite.'

Then woom-men wur turned, as wun, scampering away empty handed, down for the lake, chortling at sum woom-men's joke they've told.

But they had dug a pit an hid it well. So men had tumbled in.

Those boobys mite be shrill an puny. But the ly wur deep, strong an eckowd long. An powerful, being oddly pleasing for prowder men, who liked for think they brort chiles into this wurld, all wivout their bellys swelling, an by no more than a sticky sneezing of gizzum.

But it wur neva the same after, between men an woom-men. Soon evry chile had a farther or too.

For what a man helped make wur partly his, howling for his caring.

This wur the twisting tug of wurds. It didn't matter if what they said wur trew, so long as it wur pleasing. I wud let men believe what they liked. Myself, I wud believe what wur trew.

Yu'd think men had neva looked at boobys close befor. Now they wur man's handywurk, they seemed better shaped, more cleverly crafted.

'Look!' said Crow, smiling, poking a fingur into a small wun's gob. 'Them tiny white teef.'

'Mine got teef too,' says Potto. 'Mine got small bendy legs. An blew eyes that smile up at me.'

But I juss felt a warm wet trickle in my lap, as Yella's chile pissed down on me.

I didn't have the muvver no more. Still, I wur left holding the chile.

'How wur yur chile?' Blind asks. 'Yu neva speak of her.'

Yes, if eva there wur a time for tell it . . . Still I cannot say.

Girl looked hard on fowk an thruw them. She stared wivout smiling or fondness. In this she wur like her muvver. She peered for secrets wivin, hidden beneef faces. She knew all reddy peepil wur more but wurs than they said.

It wur like being stared in the pryvuts. Offen fowk turned away, blinking from the look of her, flushing or blurting, at the flicks of her gaze. I looked the uvva way, offen as I cud.

The hed on her wur prutty enuf – yella hurr an pleading marigold eyes. An older, wiser spirit lit her gaze.

She wur growing sly. No sooner had she walked into a bush befor yu she cum down from a rock behind, an we neva saw her pass between.

She cort rabbuts by sitting still as stone, whispering like russelling grass, her pale face sad as winter. Beguiled, those rabbuts hopped close, peering up at her forlorn blew eyes. Then she'd reach out for them gentle, an fluff their hurr. Then her face wud wrinkle wiv pity. As she wrung their breff out from their fur.

222

When she walked behind, her legs took yur step, an yur spirit wur mocked in her moves.

This wur her sly kwiet way. But it wur wurs soon as she took for talk.

She'd watched silent free summers, sitting alone or whispering in her muvver's ears, befor she began for speak her mind. An terble lowd.

I'd thort she wur slow an weak in her tung. But all the while she'd bin watching an dowting, hording small grits of kwestyuns in her cheeks, like a cavy stores his seeds.

When it told at last, this chile's mouf wudn't stop. She demanded for know. While the wit all reddy in her eyes pierced me thruw like burins.

As I skwat gnawing the rib of a carf she buffets me wiv kwestyuns.

Why do I sit near them, when I cud be sumwhere els? Why are Sun an Moon neva together? Do they hate? How many are snails? Why do I smell so? Why is water colder than land? Why are fleas? Where are dreams gon when we're awake? An where are wurds fled after they're spoke? How do hands know more than futs? When will I go? How do tears know their sorry time for cum?

While her askings slap round my ears, her mouf still has the leshur for mock mine, burps an grunts, an her slow eyes stroll her muvver's way, an her fingurs wurry an invisible bone, copying mine. While her tows are busily stripping the leefs from a willow stem, for she's whittling prongs wiv her futs, pointed as her mind. An she has harf a mind lissening for sum nearby talk behind.

'Ha . . .' I chew on grissel. 'Good kwestyuns. I tell yu all the ansurs tomorrow.'

'Today is tomorrow,' she say.

'No, not yet.'

'Today is yesterday's tomorrow,' chile says, an yelps her pleshur at snaring me.

'Whaa . . . ?' I mumble. 'Today cum back all reddy?'

'So yu muss ansur for yesterday,' she demands. 'Like yu pro-miss.' An the wurst of it is, she remember it all from befor.

When will I die? Why aren't men prutty as woom-men? Why is blud warm? Why do hogs curl their tails? Where is summer gon? Why does ice sting fowk's hands?

'It is a year's telling . . . Yu ask in wun breff. I will tell yu when
. . . the frogs are croaking again.'

So I muss turn my back, so my mouf can stick for its wurk wiv
its bones. But behind I hear her shrill, asking on.

Why do I have thick brissles growing out of my ears an nose?
Did I lurn for eat by watching the hogs?

Still, she makes her muvver glad enuf.

Yes, this chile is part mine, for care an gard, juss becaws I lay
down wiv her muvver, moons befor she wur cum, a tiny lowdmouf
for suffur an feed, until she's grown thy-high.

✳ ✳ – ✳ ✳ – ✳ – >>> | Desire

There wur soff warm years for peepil. Fife or sicks, all joined in a row, grinning, glissening brite, like crow skulls on a fong, below a smiling face.

Hystery wur dawdling then. These wur good seasons for fowk. Perps they wur the best times for me. There wur plenty meat for the moufs on us. The Kwake wur far behind us. The Ice wur yet for cum. The yella pox wur gon. We had sum innocence still. Fear wur drifting away like a morning mist lifting from the lake. Wishing wur freshly cum for us. Now there wur more hope in our heds than dred.

I had most I needed – rowst meats at nite, a deer skin for drape my shulders, then a dik-dik skin above an beneef for sleeping warm, smulderweed for smoke me calm, berrybrew for slews the grits of wurry from my mind, too slicing stones an a smoov hard crusher, made from buffalow bone, a woom-man or anuvva for hug me darkly, a chile of sorts, a lowd clattering necklace of duk-bills, for sound my cumming, too dried cats' ears an a striped hyna tail for prutty up my loins, a bull-bladder powch, a nipil ring of polished bone, strenf thruw all my body, most of my teef, a sharp tung, sevral strong ded family, whose spirits clung around, fire-stones, a long, strait piercing stick, wiv a tip hardened by fire, an ax shaped from the jaw bone of an oryx, far-seeing eyes, a mind that wur cleverer than many supposed, an a stubborn spirit for move me along. I had plenty time for carving. Yes, an evry last rabbut in the wurld wur mine. An I had ten good, long-lasting sayings for guide me, that I'd bort from Lips for no more than a mouffull of eats or handfull of stones.

I kept them for myself, but yu can have them now.

> A scratch in time saves plenty later, in yur hurr, between the legs. But if yu sleeps wiv fowks yu wakes wiv fleas.

>> It's the urly wulf that catches the carf. Then jackl steals it from him. Then buzzurds take it from jackl. Nex, sum cat drives off them burds.

>>> Wunce bitten, twice clawed. If yu're born for be gobbled yu'll neva be drowned.

>>>> Blud is thicker cold. Famine is the best sauce. A hungry belly has no nose.

* All cats are black in the dark. It neva stop them biting thow. Out of site, into wurry. Jaws are the nearest bones.

*—> Neva speak bad of them ded. They purbly lissening close. An childrins shud be seen, not ate. It's a wise chile that knows all its own farthers. It's a cleva mouf that can name all its chiles.

*—>> Evry dark clowd has a bruvver.

*—>>> A man is as old as his teef, unless his legs are gon befor. What can't be cured will kill yu. Yu're neva too old for die.

*—>>>> Don't put all yur eggs in wun numba. Harf a crow is better than no duk. First catch yur hare.

* * Free into wun don't go.

Those wur my ten wisdums. They've stayed wiv me, an carried me on, longer than my nees. They dun me well. An better, they tell the trewf of it.

They wur good times for telling storys, swapping insults, dressing up, making hats, carving stones.

There wur a hat season when evry man wur straining for strut more gawdy than the nex. Potto wore an oruk hed. Fox wur fevvered like a flite of duks. Wherever he cud stick a gooz wing or duk piece on himself, fevvers sprowted out. An he left a trail of down in his sneezing wake. But Hare wore a tall dark hed-piece bound together of seffern rotten bats.

Then there wur fong moons an a bone time. Men clattered round wiv as many skulls, teef an ribs as they cud hold, which wur tiring for carry, but made a rattling good show. Only yu had for take them off when yu went for hunt, els prey scattered urly, hearing yu cumming.

An woom-men smelled prutty an fierce like they neva smelled

befor or sins. Becaws they wur skweezing the joos from sage, rose-murry, lavendur, lemin grass, unyun bulbs, for daub all over, which made them sharp an pleasing on the nose, but flaky or sticky for the touch. An there wur fancy stains for wear on yur face an thys, or prutty patterns for paint round the nipils. An there wur cunning ways of twining the hurrs for yur pryvuts, after culluring them blew or red, an pebbels yu cud tie in, which wur prutty for the eye, but lumpy when yu humped.

An becaws we had plenty time for idle hands, there wur a deal of strutting an swaggering, admiring or mocking, wiv gossiping about who dun what, an desire wur stretching itself wide an strange, as we tired of the tried.

An becaws there wur plenty for eat, peepil went sniffy, choosy about their foods, an had fads, which cum an went, saying they only wanted fresh fish heds baked in clay, or skwirrul legs smeared wiv unyun, or dik-dik bowel stuffed wiv Ocka frewts, or sun-dried frogs. So much that wur good eats befor or after got wasted – tossed away, pecked by burds, nibbled by rats.

Talk wur gon fancy too – wiv firteen wurds for fuking, eleffern names for hats, seffern for diffurnt types of necklaces, an fife sepert names for peepil who acted prowder than they shud.

I whittled thruw the hot of the day. So my carvings cum better as they improved. Now, I cud make things bigger than they really wur. Or smaller if I chose. Becaws there's sum satisfying if yu can shrink an oruk for the size of a fist. An the more I looked for the shapes of things, the more stones wud confide for me what they clutched beneef. I cud do all shapes of animul legs, lithe, stumpy an curved. By ruffing up the smoov again, I cud scratch the look of fur, or give a fish its scales. Then, by etching circils round, I cud raise eyes for a bulj. I made animul faces that showed their spirits an feelings, so they didn't all ways smile or smurk, but showed their cunning or pride besides.

Wun day in the crab-moon it came for me I cud effen carve peepil I knew, shud I wish. But better if they didn't know. Becaws sumtimes the way I shaped them changed the way they wur. For after I'd broke Fox's arm, whittling too hard, a fall broke his elba. Kware. But trew. Which made me think sum. An hide any peepil I carved in my pigskin powch. This wun. Which I carry for this day.

*   *   *

227

Yet sumthing wur missing – for me – besides Yella, who'd gon hawty for my site an touch. An what I cudn't find then stays missing still.

'What yu burbling about now?' asks Blind.
'Don't know,' I say. 'Wurds won't say.'

It wur sumthing I desired, that always outran my stuttering mouf, leaving me gaping, empty wivin. So my happiness wur flimsy, bent empty as a wind-blown reed.

The wurd for my want escaped me. Sumtimes I felt it tingle the tip of my tung. I thort purbly the sound of its name began wiv an *ss* or an *ff*. But it neva got itself said. Not by this Gob.

I chased it hard thruw sense. Late into nite I wud mutter for myself, following the faint trail of it, saying evry wurd I sensed lay near . . .

'Smoke, snake, sand, sawfly . . . yella, fox, frog, fore, forest . . . sicks, sick, secks, suppose, spaws, spows . . . frite, fury, furry, frenzy, fuk, fog.'

But there wur too many wurds for chase down. An befor dawn I wur fallen for a mumbling daze.

Sumtimes I heard the russels of its retreat, like fut treds thruw dry grass, or there wur the distant eckow of it behind the sound of anuvva wurd. They wur fast, darting an slippery as a scatter of fish those wurds, when yu reached into the water yur hand deceeved yur eyes, reaching in befor, or clutching out behind, then they wur turned swift away as yur fingur felt for them, an there wur neva a solid grasp at all, only a slimy passing glance, like the shiver of a fish.

There wur a yawning hole in me which I cud neva fill. Becaws I cud neva say what I yurned for. Not knowing the elusive name of that sly stuff, my own trew want.

I took myself for brew most evenings. Whoeva I lay wiv, howeva we passed the nite, by morning the want wur yawning in me again.

Not for the first time, I saw that wurds wur playing tricks wiv me, neva meaning what they said, or saying what they ment.

I wur not where I spoke. An I spoke where I wur not.

Wurds had led me on. Then stranded me lost. So I cud neva tell where I wur. In my hed. Wiv my self.

I thort of all that wurds neva reached or said, that stinging an skwirming in me, the frob of my insides. I knew that wurds wur no more than the shadows of things, a darkness that touched at ejs, a gloom they cast for their sides, or a dimness lying behind.

When I thort a woom-man by name, she juss flittered by flimsy in mind, unreachable an cold. There wur neva the warm frob of a chest, nor the wrap an tug of her arms.

Hunny dripped into mind. Jooses ran for greet it. But I neva savurred a sweetness. Only the lingering sourness of lack. Or I promissed myself rowst rabbut, but the wurds gave me nothing fleshy for chew. They juss spoke empty – taking the solids from our moufs, casting shadows on walls in the caves of our heds.

'Yu're all Rabbut,' peepil said, 'yu shud . . .' But it wur neva me they spoke of, but a hollow thort of theirs, made of arms an legs an orts. As thow men wur wun an the same.

No, wurds juss said what they wurn't, neva what they wur. Man wurn't woom-man, she wurn't he, fish wurn't fowl, water wurn't urf.

So I yurned for sumthing beyond, that talk had neva grasped or spoiled. I wur missing a stuff, that wud split my face wiv mirf, bring the warmf back for my belly, soov my mind, an fill the empty powch of my desire.

Perps, yu saw the pleshur of it cum into the serene smile of sum ded, whose faces wore a strange, still content. An I gessed they had found what they sort at last. But it had cum a breff too late.

'There's missing things. An things missing,' Blind snaps. 'Yu can find yu don't know what. I've lost my eyes an harf my tung.'

'Payshens, chile,' I cowx her. 'All these things cum in their time. They're layn on uvva things beneef, resting on furva things below. They are freckles on the face of it. First yu muss look on the flesh an bones.'

When the meat wur in our bellys, the grees still on our hands, an the fire still blazing, we'd speak of what we wished for the morrow, an tell it out lowd as thow it wur trew. So that Urf an the spirits wud hear what we wanted, so they mite choose for give or help.

'The sun rises again tomorrow,' I hope.

'It is hot,' says Potto.

'There are no clowds,' says Egg, 'not tomorrow.'

'We eat well,' I say, 'on duk breast an deer liver.'

'The duk are fatter, tomorrow,' says Egg, 'so they fly slow an low. An pigs run onto our stones.'

'There are no cats for cum steal our kill.'

'Yes.' Potto sucks lowd. 'That's so. I see it clear.'

'No wun is hurt tomorrow,' I tell. 'Not in their flesh. Nor pained in their mind. Wurds are fond.'

'Urf likes us well.'

'Becaws we are good, an behave rite.'

'We're well-mannered.'

'Wiv strong moruls.'

'Kind,' say I.

'I dreamed we lived . . .' Egg's hand reaches over his hed then sweeps down. '. . . wiv rock or urf around us. It wur like a long large burrow. The wind did not cum in. It is hot an smoky. The air is clotted thick wiv our smells.'

'We happy there?' asks Potto.

'We are that. Snug as rabbuts, safe an warm.'

'We are plenty?'

'Plenty an lowd. We shriek together . . .' Egg narrows his eyes. His upper teef nibble his lower lip. '. . . we shout an clatter stones. Ha-ha-ha-ha. He-he-he-he. Then we are all larfing together.'

We savurr things cumming, gon kwiet.

'I dreamed a new beast . . .' I tell. 'It is like a fat pig, white fleeced an slow. It stays when yu walk up for it. It is happy for die. It neva thinks for run an hide.'

'An when it cums?' asks Egg.

'We cut its throwt. It bleats, rolls over ded. Then we cut it apart. The tastes of it is rich an sweet. The rowst flesh trickles plenty grees.

'Also I see frendly ox, black an wide, wiv swinging udders. They cum pleading for us for drink their milk. They want peepil as their chiles. They yurn for suckle us all. An I see burds like sandhens, sitting all in a line, waiting for us for twist their necks an rowst them.'

'Nurrishing dreams. An savurry.' Potto nods an cluks.

But they wur juss my fancy. Pieces of hope. I passed them on.

No, I neva told them I dreamed them running scared over the splintering surface, falling thruw the yawning crack.

For fowk wur hedded for a fall.

| # The Ice

'Time's cum . . .' I say.

'For what?' asks Blind.

'For what yu want for know. But are scared for hear. So lissen best yu can. Yu waited long enuf.

'It's hard for tell, but it got for be said. It's about yu. An it's terble bad. There bin so many eyes in Hystery. But yurs saw strangest, most purtickler.'

Sun is dipping. It is the Berry-Moon of yur forf summer. Yu run amongst us howling. Yur eyes are weeping. Blud not tears. An yu've swallowed the tip of yu tung, becaws yu mussn't say . . .

'What?' demands Blind.

'Yes!' I agree. 'Puzzil, ain't it? We asked the same of yu. Thinking yu cud tell.'

'What?' We gather round. We demand of yur distress.

'Whaa . . . aaah,' yu splutter, an deep, dark blud trickles over yur chin, an yu coff sum clots, then totter, fallen moaning for a jerky sleep. We lift the lids of yur eyes. First they are gon dull-dark, hollow, swallowing lite. Then they turn for black jelly. When yu're woke, too dawns later, yur eyes are lost for us, for yu. They juss won't see no more.

When yu walked, yu clowted trees, brewsed the ground or tumbled into trees. For yu had a mind for wander off wivout lissening for site.

Hare put wasps on yur food, stones befor yur futs, for warn yu for see. But yu wud neva be tort. Yur spirit had gon obstinit blind.

'She's seen sumthing terble bad,' said Hare. 'Now, her spirit is scared by site itself. It's too fritened for look out for itself . . .'

'Ain't there no medsin for that?' we ask.

'Perps . . . if we pierce a fird eye in her, the lite will flud back into her hed.' Hare narrows his eyes, while his mouf gathers for a smile.

'No!' Blind winces, clutching her hed firm an fond in her hands, like she was protecting a sick booby. 'Don't let him touch me.'

'We thort . . . for help yu,' I soov.

'Then this?' Her fingur presses the nobbled blew scar on her brow.

'Yes. Hare bored a hole in yur hed for yu, for let the sunlite in.'

'It neva wurked,' she mutters.

'It closed itself up again, yur fird eye. Hare's cures seldum wurked,' I agree, 'but his wur the best medsin we had. An the only magik.'

Blind is rubbing her eyes.

'So?' I ask. 'Yu remember? Anything cum back?'

'There's a storm in my hed . . .'

'Yu saw,' I say.

'Saw what?'

'Sites,' I say, 'when yu wur old enuf for walk an watch, too yung for understand.'

'There's fires in my hed . . . an a deep dark hole, spewing out darks. Hurts wivout names.'

'Yu saw sumthing yu shudn't,' I say.

'What?'

'The wurst there eva was. The wurst man eva did.'

'What?'

'Only yu saw it being dun. Besides the wun who did it. Yu wur a curiuss chile. Yu offen cum where yu wurn't supposed. Yu stumbled on it, past the long crag. Yu saw him doing it . . . We only cum on the spurting remains, days later, on the ground. Then we gessed the wurst. But howeva long we looked at it, we cudn't piece it back whole in our minds. Or eva make good the harm that wur dun.'

'Who did it?'

'No-Wun.'

'No-Wun?' asks Blind.

'Yes, we'd warned him plenty. But he neva lissened . . .'

'Warned him?'

'For stop. For leave her be. But he juss kept on. Doing what a man shud neva . . .'

'What?' Blind demands.

'Hurting her. Ripping her. Clawing her open.'

Yes, he wur all ways at it. Effen as a boy.

Mole was.

Piercing her, making holes, leaving scabby mounds. We told him for stop. We knew wun day he'd go too far, dig too deep.

'But my eyes?'

'When No-Wun saw yu watching him, doing *that*, the terble thing, he dug out yur eyes wiv his fums.'

'Why?'

'For stop yu seeing, of caws. For hide from our blame. Becaws the site of him, an the Wurst, lay glissening on yur chile's eyes, for anywun for see. An purbly he thort he cud push out the sites befor, juss gon in.'

'An my tung?'

'He cudn't leave yu speaking, cud he? For tell on him. So he bit on yur tung for have it out. So yu cudn't say. But he didn't get it all. But left the root an stump. It wur free years befor yu spoke again. Then, when yu started telling wunce more, it wur slow an slurred.'

'Who wur this No-Wun?'

'Yes,' I nod, 'it's trew. He wur . . . a man. He had a name.'

Mole did.

'Who, then?'

'He wur wun of us, shame for say. Until he did it.'

'Who?'

'How can I tell?' I splay my helpless hands. 'His name wur snuffed. Nun have spoke it sins. It's lost, taboo.'

'But he wur punished? For what he did for me.'

'It wurn't what he did for yu. What made us shiver sickened was the wound he made for anuvva.'

'What? For who?'

'It wur a thing unspoken. We neva told of it. We neva said. For fear of wakening sickening thorts. Hystery is dumb on this. Only No-Wun knew for sure.'

'It wur bad?'

'It wur terble, the wurst . . . *Nothing*.'

234

'Nothing?'

'Nothing at all. Becaws we pushed it from our minds. Threw it from our thorts. As much, as best we cud.'

'A killing?'

'Wurs. More than that I neva say . . . So, shh!' I clamp my levver hand over her mouf. 'Don't effen gess at it. Lest yu shud remind fowk. It's a dark hole in Hystery. More than that I'll neva say.'

'But what?'

'It's hard for a good pursin for think, for carry that terble wrong in their hed.'

Well, wurs I eva did myself was scoff my muvver's brains, harf-eat a booby, an give away my only chile.

It's bad enuf seeing the blud spurt from a dying beast.

Imagine how it looks for see the jooses gushing out of wounded ground.

'He pierced her,' I say. 'He hurt her bad.'

Urf blud spurted out in a torrent. Hot. Watery oranj. An juss kept cumming. Seffern days it was befor the wound stopped bludding.

'Who?' asks Blind.

'Her!' I whisper.

'Her?'

'Yes,' I nod solem. *'Herself.'*

'Yu mean?'

'Urf!' I wince.

'How a man hurt . . . Urf?' Blind splutters.

'Muss neva tell. There mite still be a bad man living. They mite think for do it again.'

'But . . .' she gasps.

'Suppose . . . yu pierce a pursin.'

'They'll blud, hurt, an sicken.'

'So! Think on that. No-Wun made a hole in Urf. Dug thruw her skin. For her insides.'

'How?'

I shake my hed, purse my mouf. Lips are sealed on this. Can't say. How he dug an dug wiv an oruk's shulder bone. Till he went thruw her hide.

'Urf's joos cums spurting out . . . an wudn't stop. So Urf wur bludding weak.'

She shakes her wrinkled hed.

'We're all fleas in the fleece of Urf. No hurt in that. Evrybody's got fleas. Ain't whole wivout sum. We juss prickle her a smij. We wurn't doing no harm . . .'

Till No-Wun smote her deep, like a hunter fells an ox.

Blind shudders. She knows now why it's best left unsaid.

'It's terble,' I nod, 'but trew.'

We sit shivery kwiet, an consider this.

'So No-Wun dug a hole?' She snuffles. 'An juss for that . . .'

'Man hurt her. An she wur gon chilly, weak. So wurs was for follow. For us that live on her warmf.'

'What yu do for No-Wun, then?'

'Evry wun of us slew him evry day. We killed the very site of him. Whoeva he wur.'

'How?'

'When he cum near we neva saw him. When he spoke we neva heard. He wur no-place amongst us. He wur no-where for be seen.'

'Yu shud have broke up all his bones,' says Blind. 'Or torn out his throwt. For taking my site.'

She thinks her chile's eyes wur more important than the helf of Urf.

'He wur too bad for that. So we cudn't fingur him.' I try for shape it for sense. It's important she understands.

'If we had fingurred him, we wud have shared in him, touched on what he did. The taint wud have clung for our hands. We wud have had for know him. An remember what he did . . . So we juss threw stones – where he mite have bin, if we cud've seen him.'

'So yu let him live?'

'Not us,' I protest. 'We killed effen the thort of him. We made him fade away, wivout trace. The sun shone thruw him. He went flimsy an thin as the membrane of an egg, befor he wur disappeared. His howls went kwieter, like the skweals of fleeing, pierced hog. Then there wur no more than a putrid smell in the gulley, where the buzzurds pecked at a crimson mound.'

Blind is gulping breffless.

'So the Wurst remains only wun place, now,' I say.

'Whaa . . .'

236

I stroke her hurr. 'Yur burden. Hidden scared in yur fritened hed. A terble site for yur lost chile eyes. Let's hope yu wur too yung for understand.'

'I don't see it,' she mumbles, chewing her lip.

'That's best.' I stroke her shulders. 'But if yu glimpse it again, chile, effen glimmers . . .'

'Yes?'

'Keep it for yurself. Neva tell me. I don't want for hear. Becaws it ain't a fit thing for a pursin for see.'

She sobs sum more. I stroke her shulders.

'Yu saying No-Wun took my eyes? For *Nothing*?'

Yes. She knows it all at last.

'Terble sad, ain't it? It's a hard an bitter trewf for swallow. But at least yu gulped it down.'

Pity claws on me. Blud feels for blud. This sobbing old woomman is my own lost family.

'Whaaaa!' she howls, rocking, like the first chile on Urf.

'Weep on, Girl,' I encuraj. 'Till yu're all cried out.'

The cold cum urly, fast, befor the wivering.

Crow said the Wurst had brort it on us. A man had made Urf sick.

We shuddered shamed. Peepil wur gon ugly for the eyes of Urf. For No-Wun had bin wun of us. Sun looked kwick at fowk then blinked an turned away. Yu cudn't look her in her dazzling eye. A gloom was fell on us.

The briar berrys wur still on the stem, but the warblers wur flown. Those cunning burds all ways knew urly. Urf whispered her hurts for them. Trees wur shedding their leefs hevvy an kwick. Blustering winds whisseled an whined over the rocks, ruffling the lake water for whirls an whitened tufts. The bushy herbs wur wivered scrawny an snappy, hugging the soil. The grasses wur brittil brown, cringing back into the ground. The hares had run crazy urly. Now their mating wur dun. There wur no bugs left but beetils. The wurms had slivvered deep. The few deer wur skittery an startled, passing kwick, having gazed forlorn on our dim, dying place.

Powder snows cum befor the gorse berrys. Futsteps wur iced over at dawn. The sky wur rockgrey clowds. We draped ourselves in all we had – sleeping-hides, dik-dik furs an rabbut pelts. Still it wur too cold.

The fallen snows neva melted, juss stayed. Then more cum on top of that. Then plenty fell above. So Urf wur gon all white, except the lake wur blown ashes, drifting speckly grey an black. There wur no cullur, unless yur chillblisters bled, sept our legs wur purpil, an sum tows went blew-black – too of them wur mine, an cum off in my rubbing hands.

Tears clung for yur lashes. The sniffles froze in yur nose. Yur piss cut yella rounds in the snow, gon hard soon as yu wur dun. An yur parts shrank back into yur belly as icicles hung rattling for yur hurrs. Yur teef clattered, an the shivers moved yu lively. The air wur clowded misty by yur breff.

The fires gave most of their heat up for the air, so we crouched over the flames an sinjed our hurr, an blistered our num hands.

Fowk wur gon jellus for their flames. Try for skwat by anuvva's fire, they'd push yu away. 'Go!' they say. 'There's not hot enuf for us in these seffern embers, wivout we share wiv yu.'

We thort we'd suffurd most, until we woke for see the boy Flints sliding, skwealing across the lake.

'Walk on water!' he shrieked, as thow there cud be pleshur in that.

Yes, the lake wur flat an hard, crusty wiv ice.

'It's neva dun that befor,' Potto says. 'I neva knew it wud go hard on us.'

We wondered at the temper of the lake, an what it ment – closing for us, holding us out.

'It's not firm it wants for be ice,' says Lips. 'Yu can break it open wiv stones. It's still most parts water beneef. But terble chill.'

'It feels like old Urf's gon cold on us,' Moonsik sighs. 'Pale as a sick wun, chill as a corps.'

'She's hurt an cold,' says Crow, 'but there's life in her yet. The pines are growing, the crows are circilling, the martens are running. There's sum brite for the sky. An soon the cold will melt away.'

But the ice kept cumming, harder an burrowing deep. Each morning it took more an harder blows for break the surface up, till yu cudn't see clear water below, only the mussel-shell sheen of ice.

★   ★   ★

Hare shivered, gooz-pimpilled like the rest of us, but the smoke of sum smuldering tree-bark kept him chuckling, an glazed his eyes against the dazzle white.

'Wulf . . .' he splutters between coffs. 'Hunts rabbut. Snaffles it . . .'

'What?'

'Fire,' he says.

'Yes?'

'Ice!' he tells an shrugs, as thow he's said the full of it.

We stare at him, waiting for the finish. He offen speaks the front an muddel of a suppose, then leaves the rest for us for gess.

'Fire . . .' Hare says, '. . . it's stronger than ice. Chases it for water. Then fritens water for mist.'

'Sun too,' says Potto.

'But Sun shines weak,' says Lips. 'She looks away.'

'Then make yur own,' says Hare.

'What?'

'Sun,' he says. 'An make it hot an round. Make it out of fire.' He chuckles. He reaches for pinch of snow an drops it in the fire, for make it spit then puff up mist. 'So!'

'What?' asks Potto.

'So fire the lake,' Hare larfs. 'Burn it hard. Burn it bad. Tame it soff.'

'Yu mean . . . ?' Lips's face twists in thort.

'See who the strongest, who cleverest.' Hare is swaying, a smile for his cracked-nut face. 'Fowk, Fire or Ice?' Then his lids fall an he's back in himself, alone in his hed.

'He's gon again?'

'He has,' I say, moving my hand across Hare's unblinking eyes.

When he's woke, we ask Hare what he ment. But he's sore-hedded an sobered, having used up all his smulderweed, so can't remember what he said an, any ways, he doesn't care for talk. Juss keeps slapping his hed, for shake loos sumthing itchy.

But Lips dreamed on it, an says he saw it, an felt it warm. 'We build a fire an melt the lake. We show it fire's strenf.'

'It wud need a . . . *big* fire,' Crow supposes.

'Have for be big,' Lips nods. 'Tall, wide, wiv plenty wood, above slow-burning bones, kindled by splinters.'

I don't want for snap his twig of hope, but in my hed I'm not convinced. There's a taint of sumthing weak an fusty for the plan. I juss don't believe it's strong enuf. I fear it will break apart an spill its load, like a wurmy carry-pole.

Crow an Lips try out a way, how it cud be dun, stacking a fire over a frozen puddle.

We gathered about, watching as a pile of sticks crackled alite, roared up, flared for leaping flames.

There wur spitting an hissing at the base of the fire. We watched the embers smoke, then steam. Most ice wur gon for water. An the water wur warm for our touch.

'See!' Lips claps his brow an dances.

All for a futstep of water, flowting blackened sticks.

'So?' I ask.

'See, then!' says Crow. 'How Fire slays Ice.'

Yu cud see in our sunken eyes, an ice-bit faces, there wur the dowters an the believers. An Hare who swayed between, stumbling, cackling.

'Suppose we don't melt the whole lake?' says Lips.

'Still we burn a warm hole in it,' says Crow.

'Where we cud drink an fish,' says Potto.

'Dunk in it. Get warm.'

'A circil of summer,' says Crow, 'in the centre of winter.'

'Juss make a fire big enuf,' says Egg. 'Melt all the ice off the lake. Then drive away the snows around.'

'Sun melts the snows evry Berry-Moon,' says Lips.

'An sun ain't so hot,' says Moonsik.

'An sun ain't so big,' says Lips.

'A fire rowsts meat,' says Lips. 'Sun only warms it sum, an makes it stink.'

'It's warmer by a roaring fire than in the hottest sun,' says Crow.

We toss more wood on our sputtering blaze, an shiver, nodding.

Potto said hard wood burned hotter than soff, an white wood hotter than green.

They knew they'd need a big fire, burning fierce, for drive off so much cold.

'Ants . . .' Hare cackles.

'Yes?'

'Chew trees away . . .' Then he's sunk for deep thort again. An his tung wur flicking silently, like a lizzurd rapt on flys.

'There's sumthing wrong . . .' I tell. 'We're wishing too strong an thinking too weak.' But I cudn't say my wurrys, which wur tangled, spiky briars in my mind. 'Can't we see for this wivout wurds?'

'Who made the first hat, Rabbut?' Potto demands.

'Yu did.' I admit it.

'Wur it a good hat? Did it cover a hed warm enuf, but still let the eyes see an allow a mouf for breef?'

'It wur,' I agree. 'It did.'

'An who spoke first wurd?' asks Potto.

'Crow did,' I conceed.

'Did it sound strong? Did it say what it ment?'

'Yes,' I say.

'Did it lead a mouf for more?'

'It did.'

'Who tort yu for hope an suppose?' Lips asks me.

'Yu did.'

'Then perps we free together know better than yu,' says Crow.

'We can do this wivout yu,' says Potto. 'We don't need stragglers. For whine behind or clip our heels.'

'If yu don't eva want for be warm,' says Lips, 'then leave us be – go shiver alone.'

'Flys . . .' Hare slurrs, woken again an lissening now, swaying side for side.

'What?'

'Can move an ox . . . if they bite it rite.'

'Where?'

'Nibble it back side . . .' An he's breffless, racked by coffs. '. . . chew its scrotum.'

Perps Hare wur advising, or taking sides, but we cudn't tell wiv whom or how. For we cudn't cowx his opinion – what wur the bollocks, or which wur the flybite.

'Where we make our fire, then?' I ask.

'Yu wiv us, then?' asks Lips.

'I am,' I say.

'Yu slay kwickest thruw the hart or throwt,' says Crow.

'Fire the hart of ice,' says Lips.

'In the chest of the lake,' says Crow.

Well, I wur wurried still. But at least a blaze wud warm us. So I thort.

✳✳—✳✳—✳✳ | The pyre

'It ain't a warm or wise fire, this wun.' Blind shakes her hed.

'We know now,' I agree. 'Hindsite cums easy. Yu warn us now
. . . Yu said nothing then.'

There'd neva bin a fire so wide or high, free days in the gathering.
We wur trusting for a warming outcum, forraging all the shrubs,
sticks an saplings nearby. Evry stem that poked thruw the snows
wur plucked, an the wood it held below. We wud have had the
trees too, only we didn't know how for fell them, but juss stripped
away their lower branches.

Not evrywun wur gathered around that dusk when Potto rubbed
the sparking-woods for lite it.

Hare kept his distance, watching alone from the top of the crag.
Moonsik stood, her back turned, at the rim of the lake, hugging
her boy.

Too boobys wur layn in snow holes on the shore, swaddled in
furs for warmf.

'Where am I?' asks Blind. 'Wiv my muvver Flames?'

'Lissen a while, chile,' I say. 'It's all said soon.'

My dawter Girl wur stumbling out for join us but kept toppling
over on the slidy ice. I look back for her. Then out for the fire. So,
there I wur torn, between my chile, an the flames.

Fowk wur pacing round the pyre as the flames leapt upwuds,
dampwood cracking an hissing, greenwoods spluttering, gorse
crackling, till it wur all roaring seffern yellas an as many oranjs,
sucking up the airs, gusts past their ears, gulping for breff, like a
panting gale, wiv fowk dancing, shrieking wild, throwing the furs
down from their shulders, becaws they wudn't need them more,
trickling sweat from the scalding, prickling heat of it, panting as

they ran, as the dazzle darkened the sky, an now fire an fowk wur wun.

An I stumbled backwuds from it, for see it all, but knowing I didn't belong in my hart, thinking on fire an ice, watching the racing flame-lit fowk, an the monstruss blaze, an all els shrinking black behind it. An saw how far we fowk had cum for make our own sun, heat an joy, so brite it snuffed the pale glimmers Urf cud put besides it.

Then I heard it. The sly ripping crack, an the ice kwivering gentle beneef me. An I'd known simlar only wunce befor, when the Urf cum tugged apart. An so I knew it wur the kwiet befor it cum again lowd, an a rippel befor a shudder, a rip befor a terble tearing. An I wur running from it, cool an calm as ice, an the moment wur stretching for let me escape, thow my legs wur moving terble slow, an I saw the seffern moves a nee muss agree for make a leg bend juss wunce, an I wondered at the delickut dance of my tows clenching for grip ice, then lenfening for let go.

Nex cums the judder, sending me sprawling, an the rumbul, crackling, wiv hissing.

An I'm thrown sliding on my belly, gaping sag-moufed backwuds.

I'm seeing the fire sink like sun. But wurs, kwicker an dismal sad, as steam rises up hissing, a monstruss grey puffball of mist.

Then there's no site at all. We're all blind together. The wurld is gon dark an tite as a clot of hartgore, restful kwiet wiv lapping waters, but chill as ice.

There wur wailing an howling thruw the nite. Girl's shrieks led me back for her. We found the boobys by their cryings. An drew Moonsik for our moanings. We gessed Hare wur thereabouts but he neva made a sound.

It wurn't till first dawn lite we cud know how many fowk wur left, all told.

There wur Flames. An Coot, racked by yella coffs. Hare gon crazy crewl on smoking-weed. Too snow-bit boobys howling out for wet tits drowned. Myself. Yu, blind chile. An Egg an Stone who'd struggled out from the numming waters an crawled back over the ice.

* * *

244

The lake wur frozen back over, hard enuf for carry me. There wur black stems an branches reaching thruw the grey scabs of ice, where the pyre had bin.

Lips wur at the centre of it, purpil, belly up, on the surface, a hand reaching thruw the crust of ice, his frosted nose tip poked out too. The rest of him wur clutched by ice. He wur open-moufed, staring wide-eyed, puzzild still. A frozen bubble of air hung above his blew lips, as if he had wun last thing for say.

'It neva wurked,' says Hare, shuffled coffing for my side.

'It's not those yella blisters that wur the pox . . .' I says.

'What, then?' he asks.

'It's wurds,' I said. 'That weave for plans. An moufs that lead them on.'

Flames cums for me. Her pink eyes pierce mine. She tells me she has lost hers. Wunce again.

'Yur what?' I ask.

'Chile,' she says.

'We've all lost most,' I agree.

'Yu owe me wun,' she says.

'Wun what?'

'Chile,' says she. 'Long ago yu ate my chile. Yu owe me wun. I waited long. Now time has cum. Yu muss give me Girl.'

'She's all I got. Any ways . . .' I remember now. 'Yu ate my dog.'

'Yu're shivering terble,' Flames smiles. 'Yu got no furs?'

'I lost my hide,' I say. 'Below.' I stamp the ice.

'Yu got a cold time cumming, then,' she says. 'Wud yu like this cat skin for warm yur shulders?'

'Wud like yur skin,' I say. 'For be inside it. An thank yur name for the giving of it.'

'An I wud like Girl,' says she. 'I want wun for clutch. An wun for cling for me.'

'Cudn't give her,' say I. Not for nothing.

'I'll care for Girl. An show her muvver's luv. I'll give yu skin for dog. Yu give me chile for chile. Then I don't owe yu. An then yu don't owe me. All is settled. We frends again.'

'Well . . .' I mumble, thruw swole purpil lips an chattering teef, 'I *cud* use the skin. An also a frend . . .'

*　　*　　*

'But I'm Flames's chile,' says Blind. 'An I neva knew no Girl.'

'Suppose yu're her. Wun an the same . . . Hystery says so. Now yu know it all.'

'Know what?'

'Know it all, dawter,' I say.

'Dawter?' says she.

'Yu wur Girl. Yur muvver wur Yella. Yu wur my dawter. But Flames took yu, as hers.'

'No!' she gulps. 'Ain't so. Can't be.'

'We are wun blud, chile. We are snout an curly tail, wiv only a pig between.'

'No . . .' she splutters. I stroke her arm. But she flings my hand aside.

'Yu hurr takes after mine,' I say.

'I neva saw,' she snuffles.

'Yur nose borrows from my own. Yu got my cleva hands.'

'Yu're my farther?'

'I was that.'

'An yu neva said.'

'A man has shame. It ties his tung. But I watched yu well. My cheeks wet wiv yurs. Many times I wur yur eyes. I brort yu foods.'

How for tell it? For yur dawter? Why yu thort it good. For swap her for a lepud skin? She's bound for see sum slite an feel it diffurnt.

The sense of it is lost back there, in its time of sorrur, in its frosty place. Peepil wur scarce. Skins too. A chile needed caring for. A farther needed wrapping up warm. That lepud skin cud keep me hot. I gave my dawter for a woom-man who wanted a chile, who'd luv an feed her well.

I sit kwiet. Blind is rocking, sniffly.

When she breaks the long cold whisseling silence, it is for say hard wurds – best neva spoke. Or, if eva voiced, best kwick forgotten. Hystery doesn't want for know them. Mine's a forgiving sowl.

'It wurn't rite,' I bluster. 'I know that now.'

'No!' Blind agrees.

'An it wurn't a cleva or lukky swap. I wur shivering foolish then.'

*　　*　　*

Lepud's teef cum loos an rattled, its snout rotted, so the snarl crumpled for a sneer. Its hide went mangy, an bald on the back. It wur soggy wiv wet an wud neva dry. It had a sour, catty stench. Fowk cud all ways smell me cumming, far an wide.

'I know it's late,' I confess. 'I treated yu careless. An it's hard for forgive. An yu may not be reddy befor dawn is cum. But . . .'
   'Yes?'
   'Dawter, call me . . . farther. If it gives yu any pleshur.'
   I lissen keen for strands of fondness in her voice, but I'm clutching for straws.
   'Yu bag of cack,' mutters Blind.

So fowk wur whittled down for that – a blind girl, a crazy old man, too woom-men, a boy chile, too frost-bit boobys, too chill-fevered men, an a mute.

'The mute?' Blind asks.
   'Me,' I tell. 'I neva spoke for years.'

They wur hard, silent times for me. My spirit shrivelled saddened wivin me. My woom-men wur ded. Yella wur lost. My frends wur gon. I neva slept till ice wur gon, an it wur free summers befor I said anuvva wurd, blaming Talk for our distress. I howled against evry new moon.
   I wur gon for bones an levver. I shivered a lot. I smoked plenty weeds an went off long times, leaving my body behind, perching in trees, roosting wiv owls, for it wur painful for own my bag of flesh. Fore years of Hystery passed me by. They wur sour, rotted times best forgot. When the waters cum back, they lay wide an deep.

'The Flud?' Blind says. 'What of that?'
   'Ha! That wur nothing but water. Gentle an warm. It lay itself flat an still over the land. It wur nothing nex for ice. The crags, hills an peaks poked thruw. Not many got drowned. We flowted or swam for the higher ground.'
   'Then that's our passed?' Blind says.
   'Yurs an mine,' I say. 'The rest yu know. Yu lived it too.'

* * *

. . . how we took for caves for hide from the cold an cower from our fears, hide our shamed face. For it seemed the wurld wur mocking us. We cud not look our prey in the eye, only slaying it as it turned its hed away.

How the big chill lasted many years, wiv shrunk cool summers, an iced winters stretched too long. How we met the River peepil, skwabbled, fort, forgave, then hugged together, teaching them our wurds, for theirs neva made any sense. How we made coverings for fit, wiv hides, pierced wiv burins, laced wiv pig's whiskers or levver strips. How we cum for leave our handprints on the rocks, then paint the shapes of beasts besides. An hollow dots in stone for mark the moons an seasons past. How we tamed new dogs, but neva ate them this time. How we made the stick thrower an the fish barb, blew on hollow tubes for speak new sounds. How Egg wur slayn by the nearly-man, an the ruff punishment we gave their kin. How Stone tamed an owl for eat small meat from his hand, but it took a piece too much when it surprised him pissing. So then we called him Nyva. How we made clay holdings. How we made flint piercers for fly on sticks. How the Flud took all we had, drove us out of our cave, an flowted us back for the high land. How Blind had too cleva sons an sharper dawter who charmed men wiv her songs an later took herself for medsin. How my legs went, but I neva died, but juss stayed on cackling.

Yes, that's our passed. An much good it dun us.

'Yu lissened long an good. I thank yu, chile. Yu've heard it. Now, if yu want, yu can touch it too.'

I draw open the mouf of my powch an take out the stones, an lay down my trove of secrets, the carvings of those I knew or luvved. I place them in a row on the rock, in the order of their cumming. Then I draw Blind's seeing fingurs for them. No wun has handled them befor, but me – who dug their likenesses slow from grujing stones.

'What?' she asks.

'Suppose, first,' I urj. 'Yu are shrunk small as a scuttling beetil. An yu crawl upon these stones, large as sleeping peepil. Yur fingurs are flickering futs. Yu can feel the shapes of these fowk beneef. Don't be afraid of waking them, for yu're small as insecks. An don't wurry for their modesty. Bugs go evrywhere. An those ded have lost their shame. Only their itchy pride remains.'

'Ha!' She is crawling over Carf now. 'Ah!' She draws her hand back kwick. 'Her breasts.' An avid fingur skims down her belly an thys. 'She is slender an bony . . . but she has no futs.'

'Yur farther's muvver had futs. Too kwick wuns, but the stone wur too hard for her delickuts, an wud not grip her smalls. It is the same wiv the uvvas . . . Cum!' I lift Blind's fingurs. 'Here's anuvva.'

'They are too alike. Woom-men too.'

'These are Both,' I say. 'She wur a strange wun, born in too same bodys, which clung together. They wur sad wheneva yu split them, for then they wur incumplete . . .

'As yu feel them now, they are full grown. It took me wun whole summer for carve the first harf of her. But I lurned by it, so the rest of her came kwicker while the leefs wur falling.'

'She feels the same, Both harfs,' Blind says, her fingurs flickering from wun piece for the uvva.

'Not wunce yu knew her well. For start we cudn't tell her apart. But when yu got familiar, yu lurned wun part had more mind, an the uvva held more spirit . . .

'Sum wur afraid of Both being dubble. But I all ways took for her strong – an neva minded that for cupple her wunce I all ways had for do it twice . . . Feel!' I lift Blind's hand for anuvva. 'This is a strange wun too.'

'Who?' she asks, rubbing her. 'I don't remember from yur storys.'

'Free.'

'Yes,' she agrees, 'now I feel them, free flat bitch tits.'

'She wur a kware body wiv a slow mind. She had free nipils, an a swollen behind. Also a stumpy tail, befor Hare hacked it off wiv a flint. It's a shame yu can't feel the fur of her. Her tung jibbered lowd, but it cud neva be moved for talk, but she signed herself well enuf, when it came time for eat. The spirit in her wur wild but fond. We neva had the like of her live amongst fowk, befor or sins. For she neva birfed a chile.'

'Surely . . .' Blind says, 'yu saw she wur strange?'

'Evrywun's diffurnt. Fowk wur variuss, then as now. An she cum for us yung. Nun of us cud remember when. She wur much like any chile, crawling an mewling, but cleverer at first than her size. Only when she grew, her spirit stayed a chile's. She luvved the yung wuns well enuf, like a second muvver. She tort them for climb trees, grab frewts, catch frogs, clean a hed of fleas, scratch polite . . .'

'But . . .' Blind's fingurs feel it trew. 'Wurn't Free an Ape? A Gurriller, or Oranjeeboon.'

'Suppose she wur,' I agree. 'I know this now. Looking back, we can all see it now, reddy enuf. But for start we didn't know so clear, what sepert us, fowks an apes . . .'

I let Blind feel Dog, my bruvver Jackl when he wur Ratz, then she touches on Skwirrul, Sow an Crow. Uvvas too.

'The crest for his hurr . . . the man who spoke first.'

'Yes, I carved him yung befor he lost his mane . . . An this is Hare.'

Blind flinches, touches it, then draws her hand back kwick as if stung. She doesn't care for dwell on him.

'A hard man.'

'Hard as the stone. An while I carve him I had bad lukks – a rash of blew spots, a fall from a rock, an I loose sicks teef.'

'They're mostly woom-men, yur stones.'

'I prefurred woom-men. I felt fonder for them.'

'But they got no faces.'

'I gave them faces for start. Most wur pitted by the pox. Wiv time, their stony faces changed. They took for scowling back at me. Their looks went hurtful, unkind. So I smooved their glares away. I like for remember them best below the necks. There, evry-wun wur diffurnt, an kind for me in their sepert ways.'

'An Yella, my muvver?' Blind asks.

Yes, I made her twice. Wunce in flesh. Then in smoov, cold stone, larger than the uvvas. Paler than the rest.

'I wud like for hold my muvver again,' says Blind, 'an have the touch of her.'

'I shud have bin kinder for her,' I confess, rubbing Yella between my palms for warm her. 'Here, then.' I lay her in my dawter's hand. 'Take care how yu fingur her.'

'Ha!' says Blind. 'But she has a face. I feel the nose, the mouf, the hollowed cheeks . . .'

'Feel the blew eyes too. They saw thruw me.'

'Yes.' She nods. 'They're cool an cleva.'

'Keep her,' I say. 'She belongs for yu. More than me.'

Yes, I lost Yella long befor she fel thruw the ice.

Blind strokes her own trew muvver wunce more. Fondling her tite, holding her up for a cheek for feel her pale warmf on her face. 'She's the very best of them.'

They are together again, muvver an dawter, after so many years.

'Keep! They're all yurs,' I say. 'The stones belong for Hystery, not for me. Any ways, I die soon.'

'Not long now,' cumforts Girl.

'I juss wanted yu for know. Befor I go. How we got here. What we lurned. Our mistakes. Who yur trew farther wur. That yu're luvved still. An it ain't too late for forgive. An if I did wrong, it's becaws I cum from far back. We had for find our moruls on the hoof. An these are tears of shame that wet my cracked, levver cheeks.'

'Yu're neva too old for sorrur,' Girl agrees.

This the oldest site known for fowk, spred below us.

Sun's sunk for the rij, a blazing stream flowing behind the black spiked tips of firs. The dusk fires are stacked an lit. Yung wood crackles like snapping bones. Sap spits in the flames. Smoke drifts blew over purpil grass, lifting ocha wisps thruw oranj sky.

The curv of sky bluds red, then thickens for gore, clotting black. It offen cullurs so – after a kill.

The hide of a dik-dik is being ripped from the flesh. A shadowed huddle slash the beast, mumbling their kwiet care for meat, slicing flint thruw mussel, hacking obstinit bones, while the deer-slayer slumps apart, his back turned away from it, neva bothering for his kill, knowing he'll get tossed sum sinewy, bony piece – hoof or tail – when the rest is taken, the best shared. He wud neva stomak the bludder parts, not being a crewl man. There's pride in it. He neva took this beast's living juss for feed himself.

But it wud add waste for sorrur for pity if uvvas didn't eat it now. Now it's ded. An its spirit fled.

So the meat is sliced for strips, wound round sticks, held in kwivering hands over the flames. Fire hisses, yella tungs flick up, thirsty for the dripblud an dropfat sputtering down. Dik-dik's hed will be staring wide-eyed, puzzild, on a bed of embers. Its calm, curiuss eyes will glint the dance of sparks. Neva seems for care. But wivin the skull its brains is boiling, knowings an all.

The carcass will gurgle as men tear at the offal an tug out the bowels.

The scented airs rise up for our slope, hevvy wiv grass, freshblud, guts an smoke, as I smiles glad-eyed, man-luvving, gon twitchy wiv my hopes – of liver or kidny for eat. When we go down.

*   *   *

'There's much still hidden,' I tell Girl. 'Trewf's lame – hobbling free-legged. We don't know it all yet. There's plenty left for fowks still for find.'

We are sunk in our sepert silences.

'Brr!' say I. 'The air is chilling. Dik-dik is rowsting. Tonite there'll be a good feeding.'

'I smell it,' says Girl. 'There's no hurry. Tonite we eat late. Fowk are kind. They'll save us soff pieces.'

'Yes,' I agree. 'It's a late eating this nite.'

We both know. There's the reckoning still for cum.

'Yu all told out?' Girl asks. 'Yu finished burbling?'

'Enuf said,' I tell. 'Effen this mouf of me is gon weary now. The passed is all said an dun. It's all behind us now. Sept we are back together . . . farther an dawter.'

I hold her warm but grujing hand. Then she tugs it away.

'Yu forgive me, then?' I ask.

'No,' she says. 'Purbly neva.'

'Yu're like yur muvver. My life was poxed by stubborn woom-men.'

'Yu told it trew?' she asks, snapping open the ribs of it, poking thruw for the bowels an offal. I wince for the stab in my dry, fusty innards.

'I told it juss how it was. For me. Near as wurds can eva say it, wivout living it themselves.'

'It ain't cumplete, this passed of yurs,' Girl says.

'I left out many eatings, itchings an scratchings, fallings asleep an wakings up, an much els that happened offen.'

I changed sum names. Becaws peepil wur given the wrong names in life. An effen the ded need protecting. Sumtimes too peepil are mixed up together, told as wun. Becaws they wurn't strong enuf in themselves. Sumtimes I was looking the uvva way. But the happenings are told trew for their spirits.

'There are holes in yur storys,' she says. 'I can see thruw them.'

'I suppose the ejs of things are gon blurred in my hed. I leave out sum grits an warts, belly hurrs an fluff fevvers. If it's clowdy, it's only the mist in an old man's murmuryns.'

'Sumwun cud break their legs, tumbling down thruw the cracks in yur storys.'

'Yu tell Hystery, yu talk for yung-blud. Yu advise days cumming. There are things best left out, unsaid.'

Girl nods her silent agreement.

'Perps we wurn't all ways as kind or cleva as I said. We do not want the yung for know their kin wur wild. The ded are watching. An our spirits cum again, it's better the yung respeck those who went befor. Perps sum of the things I say the beasts did . . .'

'Yes?'

'Wur dun by fowk insted. But I cum a long way, a long time wiv peepil.' I sigh. 'From silence for speech, from the mire for moruls. I won't speak ill of fowk. There are sum mistakes I'll neva tell.'

'Mistakes?'

'There are things I cud say on this hilltop that neva belong in the passed. There are sum wrongs we muss neva pass on. If yung fowk need sum more sins now, then they muss make their own. I ain't going for leave them ours.'

'That so?'

'Suppose there was too littil binding between us for start. Maybe we fort too reddy, an when we struk we hit too hard. It takes many years for grow a pursin, then juss wun blow for snuff them out.

'Purbly what we ate wasn't all ways savurry an delickut. There are sum rude, kware cupplings I neva told yu. Maybe men wur ruff for woom-men. An both wur hard for chiles. We had urly wurds, sleeping now. They're dangeruss for wake. They're best forgot. When yu are in the sunlite, yu don't want for return for the dark.'

'What happened for yur bruvver? He cums an goes.'

'He fell thruw the ice. He went Beyond wiv the uvvas.'

'Hare?'

'He coffed his last, too winters after. It was no loss. For him. For us. He'd spent more time wiv the ded than us, those last years.'

'Shadow?'

'He was ambushed by seffern bears in a cave. Odd things happen for crazy men.'

'But yu lived on. An on. An more.'

'Yes, I survived them all. I've seen ten summers, anuvva ten summers, besides ten years more. Then there wur the fife winters that cum befor I started tallying. There ain't a numba big enuf for

254

count all the years I've known . . . An yu know why I lived so long?'

'Yu too stupid, stubborn for know yu shud be gon?'

'No.'

'Yu too scared for meet those ded Beyond.'

'Not that nyva.'

'What, then?'

'I lived so long becaws I bin *good*.'

'Yu wur?'

'I all ways heeded my moruls. Whateva they wur at the time. If yu mind yur manners, yu make few enemys. Urf takes care of yu.'

'Yu wur terble crewl for my muvver. Yu snatched her ruff. Yu used her bad.'

'An if I hadn't, yu'd neva be born.'

'Yu ate a booby.'

'Juss the harf of wun,' I say. 'But, yes, it wur wrong. Only I didn't know then, being awfull yung, long ago.'

'Yu brort the yella pox on peepil.'

'Perps I did. Perps I neva. If I did, I neva ment to. It was neva my making. Better blame the booboons. Who'll tell yu for blame the fleas. Who'll say they got it from sumthing els . . .'

'Of all the peepil for live so long . . .' Girl sighs, 'it's sad it fell for yu, a ruff lying fool.'

'Look, I ain't wivout any blemish or smij of shame,' I agree. 'But it's a hard life being a pursin. A duk or a rabbut has it easy . . .

'Free in wun pursin's skin. Spirit, mind an body. They seldum agree. They skwabble in yur hed. They tug yur thorts sepert ways . . . An when yu're wun of the first for cum. An neva know yu got a mind for start. An have for scratch round in the dust for sum moruls, besides finding the wurds for evrything, befor yu can talk, an still have for keep warm an fed, while trying not for get ate . . .'

'Yes?'

'A man will make sum urly mistakes. He don't know no better. Those that cum after will have for forgive.'

'It's late an cold,' says Girl, rising up, rubbing sum warmf into her legs. 'I hear the wails of darkness.'

'Yes,' I say. 'Shall us go down, dawter?'

'I go ahed,' she says, swaying away. 'Yu can cum when yu want.'

'But I ain't got a leg for stand on,' I wail.

'So?' says she. 'Evry body got its trubbles. I can't see. I'll have for feel my way down. Yu crawl behind, kwick as yu like. I'm tired of carrying.'

'Yu'd leave me? Here?'

'Why not?' says she. 'Yu left me. In the Ice.'

'Yu're my dawter,' I plead.

'Till yu swapped me for a cat skin.'

'That was long ago. It was a mistake.'

'It was,' she agrees. 'Now think on it, an regret.'

'Yu got a gruj still?' I ask.

'Yes,' she says. 'Purbly I have.'

'Who'll carry me down? Who'll do my chewing? . . . Who can I cling for at nite?'

'Don't know,' says she. 'Can't care.'

'I'm the eyes. Yu're the legs. Together we're lost.'

But all reddy she's reaching out down the slope on hands an nees. I'm wriggling after, but slower, dragging limp legs, ripping the skin from my thys.

'Mind the rock.' I shout a warning.

She feels around but cannot touch it. Maybe I'm tricking, for hold her there.

'I go on my own way,' she calls back over her shulder. 'Yu go yurs.'

Girl buffets a bulder wiv her brow, then she crawls on around. I am wriggling after, but slower. Only her hed an shulders show, bobbing above the rocks.

Then she's dipped below my site.

'So Hystery's cum for this?' I shriek, then hear my sorrur's eckow. 'A lame man chasing after his blind dawter, down a rocky crag?'

But, for wunce, that gobby woom-man's gon silent. She neva ansurs back.

Now I'm alone on the scarp. My long days tellings are wasted. Besides I've lost a dawter. My elbas are bludding. I've scuffed the levver from under my thys.

I'm the oldest man on Urf. An the wisest. I'm weary as stone. It's chill. Nite's falling. I'm alone again. An there's no wun for carry me down.

It ain't a good time or place for me. An yet, I sense, there's a story in it. Wiv a morul dangling from that.

The shivers wressel sleep for have me.

Then icy dreams cort me.

I'm rowsed by a chill claw-hand gripping my shulder.

I gess who it is. I bin waiting years for him.

'That yu, then? Buzzurd Death?' I wake, blinking at the gloom. I feel his talons sinking into my neck. 'Yu took yur time. But yu tracked me down, at last.'

'No,' says a gruff voice, while a hand slaps me ruff. 'It's me. Yu toofless prattler. Yu rotted rattle-bag of levver. Yu powch of cack.'

'I knew yu wud,' I cackle at Girl's stinging slaps.

There's joy in her hurts. Better the hot hand of an angry dawter than the chill fingurs of Death.

'Wud what?'

'Cum back, dawter,' I chortle. 'Becaws yu luv me plenty, after all's said an dun. Effen the part of me that ain't cum perfuck yet . . . Becaws only dogs an peepil can eva forgive. That's why we stay frends, fur an fowk. An only peepil can cling for Hope. That's what makes us better . . .'

'Cack,' she pants. 'I near enuf fell over the lej. So I climb back . . . an crawl into yu.'

'It shows . . . Yu can neva tug kin apart,' I say. 'Blud all ways draws its own back. Fowk are fowk. Family is family. Hystery tells us . . .'

'It's late. It's cold. Yu prattling bag of offal,' my dawter snaps. 'Eats are waiting.'

'Let's go down, then,' I say. 'Shall us walk together?'

'Have to,' she snuffles, surly.

'If mine are the eyes,' I offer, 'yurs cud be the arms an legs.'

'Have for be,' she spits.

Then she's lifting me up. But pinching my buttuks spitefull.

I'm hugging her neck, smelling her warm bekelnut breff, feeling her firm elbas beneef me.

'Did I tell yu how Gote got his name?' I ask. 'I think there's sum storys I kwite forgot for say. An there wur Gon. Now he was a kware wun. He crawled into the spiny bush as a pursin. But when he cum waddling out the uvva side . . .'

'What then?' she asks, grujing. But curiuss.

'He wur turned into a warthog. Wiv blew mottles on his back. Only his eyes wur stayed the same.'

'Neva!' she protests.

'Strange,' I swear. 'But trew.' I larfs.

'Kwiet, yu powch of cack,' she mutters. 'Tomorrow will be soon enuf.'

Chris Wilson

Baa

'A triumph.' *Sunday Times*

It is 1891, and modern times require modern approaches. Count Friedryk Baa MindeBerg hobbles through his middle age on the crutch of reason. No other Scandinavian biologist has as firm a grasp on toads or marsupials or Africa as he. No other biologist has taken such extreme liberties with the flesh . . .

But then Baa is the most scrupulous of scientists. He selected his wife after long and fastidious research; his home is an inventor's paradise replete with mechanical marital bed, hydraulic pillows and electrical water-closet. Yet beneath this crust of domestic logic, reason is starting to crumble. Baa's outrageous past threatens to sneak up with irrepressible force and smother him with guilts that refuse to disperse . . .

'We are reminded of such disparates as Swift, Beckett and Flann O'Brien as this elegant, wacky prose reports the vagaries of life . . . A compact funny fable: *Baa* is most impressive.'
Times Literary Supplement

'Wilson writes elegantly and supplies much shrewd commentary . . . assuredly worth a read.' *Financial Times*

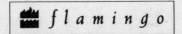 *flamingo*

Chris Wilson

Mischief

Shortlisted for the Whitbread Prize

'A *tour de force*. Fluent and witty, accomplished and incisive, Wilson's observation is spot on.' *Sunday Times*

Charlie Duckworth has orange skin, crocus yellow eyes, a solitary tuft of black hair on his head, and a penis twisted like a corkscrew. Unusual features for Islington, but perfectly normal for the last surviving member of the Brazilian Xique Xique tribe.

Wrenched from his native home by a well-meaning zoologist, Charlie is brought to London and given a conventional English upbringing. But his strange appearance and gentle ways leave him sadly ill-equipped to deal with the contempt and prejudices of mankind. Gradually, inexorably, Charlie is forced to shed his innocence. A modern-day Candide, his journey through our world is chilling, enlightening and relentlessly comic.

'*Mischief* works superbly as a social satire and an examination of the human condition. At times Wilson's story approaches Swift's *Gulliver's Travels* in its rigour, humour and moral force. Hugely recommended.' *Independent on Sunday*

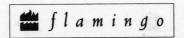

flamingo

Chris Wilson

Gallimauf's Gospel

On the island of the eccentric Lord Iffe in the outlandish West, a monkey is washed ashore, the sole survivor of a shipwreck. The islanders make her very welcome – albeit in a somewhat bizarre manner. Classified at the outset as a Frenchman by Gallimauf the philosophical doctor, Maria the monkey is greatly puzzled to find a new identity, a central role in society, and a whole range of expectations imposed upon her. But the locals soon become wary of the unusual habits of the foreigner and curiosity turns sourly to outrage – the Frenchman must be taught a lesson . . .

A dazzling combination of satire, comedy and tragedy, *Gallimauf's Gospel* holds a mirror up to society and brilliantly exposes the conceits and idiosyncracies of the human race.

'This fine novel shows a keen pleasure in language and real Swiftian ferocity and attack in its portrayal of social hypocrisies. Chris Wilson expresses a dark and compelling imagination.'
British Book News

'Chris Wilson's free-wheeling, friskily rhetorical style generates a fine comic exuberance. He has been compared to Swift, Beckett and Flann O'Brien – for good measure I would add J. P. Donleavy.'
Sunday Times

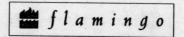